Photo by Five Petals Photography

Abigail Owen is an award-winning author who writes romantasy and paranormal romance. She is obsessed with big worlds, fast plots, couples that spark, a dash of snark and oodles of HEAs! Other titles include: wife, mother, Star Wars geek, ex–competitive skydiver, AuDHD, spreadsheet lover, Jeopardy! fanatic, organizational guru, true classic movie buff, linguaphile, wishful world traveller and chocoholic. Abigail currently resides in Austin, Texas, with her own swoon-worthy hero, their (mostly) angelic teenagers, and two adorable fur babies.

abigailowen.com

FICTION

ALSO BY ABIGAIL OWEN

THE CRUCIBLE

The Games Gods Play

DOMINIONS

The Liar's Crown
The Stolen Throne
The Shadows Rule All

INFERNO RISING

The Rogue King
The Blood King
The Warrior King
The Cursed King

FIRE'S EDGE

The Mate
The Boss
The Rookie
The Enforcer
The Protector
The Traitor

BRIMSTONE INC.

The Demigod Complex
Shift Out of Luck
A Ghost of a Chance
Bait N' Witch
Try As I Smite
Hit by the Cupid Stick
An Accident Waiting to Dragon

THE
WARRIOR
KING

INFERNO
RISING

ABIGAIL OWEN

First published in the USA by Entangled Publishing, LLC.
First Australian edition published 2024
by HQ Fiction
an imprint of HQBooks (ABN 47 001 180 918), a subsidiary of
HarperCollins Publishers Australia Pty Limited (ABN 36 009 913 517).

HarperCollins acknowledges the Traditional Custodians of the lands upon which
we live and work, and pays respect to Elders past and present.

Edited by Heather Howland
Cover art and design by LJ Anderson, Mayhem Cover Creations and Bree Archer
Stock art by Photo2008/GettyImages, draco77/GettyImages, getgg/Depositphotos,
and PHOTOGraphicss/GettyImages
Interior design by Britt Marczak

A catalogue record for this book is available from the National Library of Australia
www.librariesaustralia.nla.gov.au

Printed and bound in Australia by McPherson's Printing Group

MIX
Paper | Supporting
responsible forestry
FSC
www.fsc.org   FSC® C001695

The Warrior King is a high-heat fantasy romance—and not just from the dragon fire. As such, the story contains elements that might not be suitable for all readers, including war, classism, battle, blood and gore, violence, death, gang violence, murder, injury, hospitalization, perilous situations, graphic language, alcohol use, loss of family, grief, and sex on the page—on *a lot* of pages. Readers who may be sensitive to these elements, please take note and get ready to enter a spicy new world of dragon shifters!

My amazing team at Entangled.
You make all the difference in the world!

THE DRAGON CLANS

GOLD
King: Brand Astarot
Location: North Europe
Based in: Store Skagastølstind, Norway

BLUE
King: Ladon Ormarr
Location: Western Europe
Based in: Ben Nevis, Scotland

BLACK
King: Gorgon Ejderha
Location: Western Asia/Northern Africa
Based in: Mount Ararat, Turkey

GREEN
King: Fraener Luu
Location: Eastern/Southern Asia
Based in: Yulong Xueshan, China

WHITE
King: Volos Ajdaho
Location: Eastern Europe/Northern Asia
Based in: Kamen, Russia

RED
King: Pytheios Chandali
Location: Central Asia
Based in: Everest, Nepal/China

PROLOGUE

Samael Veles considered himself to be a solid judge of character, but he still wasn't a hundred percent confident about what his king had gotten them into. Supporting the uprising against the High King of dragon shifters was a dangerous gambit.

Suicidal, even.

But his king, Gorgon Ejderha, had been leader of the Black Clan for longer than any king of the other five dragon shifter clans— white, blue, green, red, or gold. He hadn't remained in power that long by acting stupidly or rashly. Which was why Samael hadn't argued with the orders that put him where he was now—standing in the throne room of Gold Clan's mountain, backing the man who'd come to claim that throne.

Brand Astarot had mated a phoenix. A fucking *phoenix*.

Phoenixes were a prize sought by every creature. Particularly dragon shifters, whose right to rule as High King over all the clans was dictated by who mated a phoenix.

Kasia Amon's appearance, after no phoenix had been seen in over five hundred years, had rocked the dragon shifter world and given Samael's own king hope where none had existed before.

A plague had infected the dragon shifter kingdoms since the last phoenix had died, and that sickness had a name.

Pytheios. The Rotting King of the Red Dragon Clan.

With no phoenix, Pytheios had named himself the de facto

High King. He'd put kings loyal to him on every other throne, Gorgon holding his seat through sheer luck and masterful political maneuvering. With Pytheios in power, the world had grown darker every day—fewer mates found for their people, more dragons going rogue, and more of their clans falling into poverty.

Except a second phoenix had been revealed. Skylar Amon, Kasia's sister, was now mated to Ladon Ormarr, the King of the Blue Clan.

One phoenix was something to celebrated, if she was real. But two... Impossible for a creature so rare, only one had ever been known to be born each generation. They could be lies, a show, a trick to turn the tide of the uprising against Pytheios.

But Gorgon supported this alliance, and Samael, Captain of the King's Guard, was here as Gorgon's representative, backing Brand's play.

He just wasn't happy about it.

The old men sitting on the dais, the Curia Regis council for the previous—and recently slain—gold king, didn't seem too impressed by Brand's claim to the throne so far.

Samael checked the corners, checked the doors. Getting into this mountain had been too easy. They should have been stopped. At the very least, Brock Hagan should be here. As the son of the previous king, he would be the man with the most legitimate counterclaim to the throne.

Suddenly, Brand's body wavered as though they were all witnessing a mirage in the middle of a castle, a sign the man was shifting.

Samael planted his feet while trying to appear at ease, waiting for what came next. There wasn't space here for a gold dragon in full form, but they'd already discussed this demonstration, so he made no move to give the gold rogue room.

Brand brought forward his wings only. The men on the dais went slack jawed, and even Samael had to admit to being impressed by Brand's display of control.

Brand stared down the old men and spoke. "*I state this for all the gold dragons within range to hear..."*

Dragon shifters communicated telepathically when in dragon form. Brand was doing that now, communicating to every shifter near him.

"My name is Braneck Astarot Dagrun. Son and only living heir of King Fafnir. Slayer of the false king Uther. And the man whose mark you bear on your hands. I am the rightful King of the Gold Clan of dragon shifters, and I will take my throne." Brand pointed to the empty gilded chair on a raised dais behind where the men of the Curia Regis sat.

Interesting that he didn't list his phoenix mate as a credential for that claim. Why not? Because he wanted the throne on his own merit? Or because she wasn't truly a phoenix?

Samael's mind spun with dark possibilities.

Do your duty.

He had orders—support and protect the new gold king. Samael did a quick sweep of the room, listening outside the doors for the running of feet, soldiers to come to the aid of the viceroys still seated on the dais.

Quickly, Brand introduced all representatives of his allies in the room—including Samael as Gorgon's man. The Blue and Black Clans stood together, and the Gold Clan would stand with them. *"They are here as proof of the support I bring with me,"* Brand said. *"I can take my throne by force, but I would rather save my people from the bloodshed. Swear allegiance to me now and you'll live."*

The previous king's viceroys paled with each word Brand uttered. Two of the men sitting before Brand covered the marks that could be seen on the fleshy part between their thumbs and forefingers. The king's marks. Magical marks that showed a dragon shifter's loyalty to the king of their clan—now Brand's family insignia, though some of the gold dragons still bore the now-dead king's mark.

Finished with his claim, Brand lifted his head. He listened for answers from the people who'd heard his telepathic message, and the room sat in silence for a long time, tension piling on tension until it reached screaming pitch. Until one corner of Brand's mouth lifted in a smile that would make the most hardened warrior wary.

"My people have spoken," Brand murmured. "Bow to your king."

One by one, each of the men stood and knelt. All except the oldest. Brand gave a single nod to one of the men on his left, who took that man into custody and led him out of the room quietly. Not for execution, but imprisonment.

A damn miracle that this had happened without a single death.

A movement in the back corner of the room caught Samael's attention, and everything inside him stilled, readying for a fight. He didn't move yet, waiting to confirm the threat.

Except nothing stood in the room over there. Another check showed an ornate mirror hanging several feet above the floor. He must've seen the movement of someone in the room, and no one here was a threat. Not anymore.

Not that he relaxed.

"Brock will not sit by for this without a fight," another of the viceroys warned.

Truth. The son of the previous ruler *should* be defending his father's throne. All reports showed he'd gone into hiding, leaving his people unguarded. Coward.

Samael did another sweep, using all his senses, not really listening as Brand addressed the comment and then had the Curia Regis ushered out of the room. Taking a throne shouldn't be this easy. Holding it would no doubt be more difficult. They couldn't let down their guard. Not yet.

As soon as the door closed behind the departing viceroys, Kasia threw her arms around Brand's neck. "You did it," she whispered.

Brand scowled, as if he didn't like that. "It's not over yet," he murmured before claiming her lips in a kiss so reverent, Samael glanced away, feeling the need to give them privacy.

The way the new dragon king watched his mate, with possession and something more in his golden gaze—adoration, love, desire, protectiveness... Phoenix or not, their mating was real. Fated. Samael couldn't deny that, not after being around this couple for five minutes.

A movement over by the mirror snagged his attention again. He looked harder, and another flash drew his gaze...*inside* the mirror.

What in the seven hells?

The reflection was moving, glowing almost, with...flames? Except the brightness didn't flicker through the throne room.

Slowly, Samael slunk nearer for a better angle. The second he got a full look, his body went quiet. Then his dragon rumbled in his head, a long purr of a sound. The reflection in the mirror was that of a woman, tall and willowy with strawberry-blond curls wild around her face lifted by the flames that danced over her body. Only a very few fire creatures had that kind of power. Was she a dragon shifter? Her manner of dress, though—almost medieval in appearance—brought him to ghost. But ghosts didn't light on fire.

Whoever—or whatever—she was, she seemed to be watching the proceedings with interest.

Samael turned his head, searching for where she would have to be standing in the room for that mirror to pick her up, except no one was there. He whipped his head back—she hadn't moved. She was definitely there.

Am I seeing ghosts now?

Brand and Kasia parted. "I need to talk to Ladon," Brand said. "Now."

Together, they led the remaining men in the room away, but Samael lingered, moving toward the mirrored image. She'd smiled watching Brand and Kasia together.

Why did she care? What was going on here?

With a final step, Samael moved directly in front of the mirror, directly into her line of sight, staring her down.

The woman froze. Except she thawed as quickly as she'd turned to ice, her glacial eyes turning darker blue as her gaze skated over him. The way she took him in, with an almost childlike innocence—it was as though she didn't know he was standing there watching her check him out. What did she see, anyway? A hardened soldier who'd achieved more than anyone had ever expected he could?

Her aura of soul-stirring susceptibility reached through the glass and wrapped around him. A conflagration of emotions exploded inside his chest—dark need, harsh possessiveness, and the strangest sense of knowing. The flood of it left him almost dizzy.

Her own gaze flickered. Awareness flared in her eyes—he saw it. He was sure he saw it. Only that awareness was quickly replaced by a cold fear as her gaze connected with his. The woman held still, not even daring to breathe.

"Who are you?" he demanded. The words came out harsher than he wanted, his dragon pushing to be released.

With a gasp, she stumbled backward, and the image suddenly changed. He found himself staring at his own reflection, his black eyes stunned.

A glance down revealed the same shimmering mirage-like waves that had surrounded Brand earlier. Except this was involuntary. Instead of booted feet, Samael stood on talons, black scales rippling up his legs.

"Fuck." He shook off the shift, regaining control over his dragon, who'd pushed closer to the surface than ever before.

Samael *never* lost control.

Mine, the beast inside growled.

Samael balked, turning his back on the damn mirror. She couldn't be his. He had no idea who she was...what she was. She could be a spy for Pytheios, for all he knew.

No. Better to forget this happened. If he saw her again, he'd get the truth from her. Now and always, his duty lay with his king.

CHAPTER ONE

Today, Meira Amon would mate a dragon shifter.

Not for the first time in her life, she wondered if fear could kill a person. Her heart was beating so hard it hurt. Not that she would back down. Her heart had to settle down eventually, right?

Phoenixes, after all, were able to choose their own mates, rather than rely on the fates, and that's exactly what she'd done. She'd chosen.

Gorgon's shock when he discovered not one or two but *four* phoenix sisters in existence had been the sharpest emotion the man had given off in the very short time she'd known him. Her and her sisters' existences had been a miracle that some dragon shifters might not believe to be real, but the king, at least, believed them and had accepted her offer to mate.

Her offer.

She'd partially expected the fates to give her a sign that she was doing the right thing mating King Gorgon—a dream, a gust of wind with creepy timing, a bolt of lightning, even. No such luck. Love and loyalty had driven her. She might not be her sisters— never having come close to Skylar's form of rash bravery, or Kasia's version of steady courage, or Angelika's bright confidence—but Meira was starting to find her own kind of resolve.

Including, any minute now, walking through the massive double doors that led to the throne room in Ben Nevis, the mountain stronghold of the Blue Clan, to bind herself to a good man, but one she didn't love.

Oh gods. I'm really doing this.

They'd taken a few months to plan the ceremony. Neither Kasia nor Skylar had had a mating ceremony, simply skipping to the physical part of binding their lives to their mates through fire and sex. Gorgon had insisted that all dragon shifters needed to see that at least one of the phoenixes had done things the proper way, which was why they'd risked waiting as arrangements had been situated to the smallest detail.

Not quiet months, unfortunately, with constant attacks from the Green and White Clans. The Red Clan, meanwhile, had remained unnervingly silent, more concerning than direct attacks.

What was Pytheios up to?

Meira had a hard time hating anything or anyone, but her hate for that man threatened to consume her, the emotion a physical flaying of her heart. Every single day.

Hate for the man who'd murdered her father and grandparents before she was born. Who'd sent her mother into hiding, pregnant and alone, until he tracked her down and killed her, too. More horrors that she'd learned recently could be laid at his feet. All in pathological pursuit of a crown and power.

Meira would do anything to help stop him.

Offering to mate a dragon shifter king fell under the heading of "anything." The tie that would bind the Black, Blue, and Gold Clans together.

If it turns the tide of the war as the legends claim, it will be worth it.

She'd made her decisions, ones that set her future in stone. A future that only needed her to open the door before her and step through.

If only her legs would stop shaking.

Needing to bleed off the tension buzzing through her, Meira fluffed out the skirt of her midnight-black mating gown, the color of her new clan. The sparkling jewels in all the colors of the dragon shifter clans—black, white, blue, green, gold, and red—sewn into the delicate material flashed and glittered with the movement.

Angelika, the only one of her sisters whose existence had still not been revealed to any but the three allied kings, was already inside with the wolf shifters their mother had sent her to for protection. She would continue to pretend to be one of them, hiding her existence from all but a handful who knew the truth.

She had been pissed as hell not to be included in the ceremony, storming into Meira's room the day she found out, luckily when only Kasia and Skylar had been around to witness.

"I'm supposed to be part of this day," Angelika had grumbled.

Meira had taken her by the shoulders. "You are."

That had earned her a wrinkled nose. "Yeah. Sitting at the back of the room with the rest of the rabble."

"Wolf shifters aren't rabble."

They'd stared at each other a second before both snorting. "To us, maybe," Angelika had said. "But as far as most dragon shifters are concerned…" She'd shrugged.

Meira had said nothing, because there was nothing to say. Angelika wasn't wrong. Dragon shifters called the wolves mutts behind their backs, sometimes to their faces. But they were men to be trusted as far as the sisters were concerned. As long as the wolves were keeping Angelika's existence secret, she had to pretend to be mated to one, which meant she wouldn't stand at the front of the great hall with Meira today.

But at least Angelika was there.

Kasia and Skylar moved to stand in front of her, their overbright smiles hiding their doubts.

Their emotions pelted her anyway.

Of the powers she'd inherited when their mother had died, being an empath was one she could've done without. It was what had driven her to bury herself in technology rather than interact with people. Computers and code were consistent, predictable. People were less so, even for an empath like her.

Right now, her sisters' concerns wrapped around Meira like

a thick blanket, stifling and suffocating.

Telling them she was okay wouldn't make it go away—she knew, because she'd tried. Instead, she just blocked the emotions.

"You look so beautiful." Kasia took her hands, giving them a squeeze.

Dressed in a silken gold gown the color of her own clan, her dark-red hair pinned up, Kasia was equally stunning. So was Skylar, beside her in a matching gown of blue, black hair also intricately coiffed, though she'd chafed under that decision. The sisters had inherited their drastically different coloring from the combination of their phoenix grandmother and mother, white dragon shifter father, and red dragon shifter grandfather. Her sisters' glacial white-blue eyes reflected her own worry and anticipation.

"Better than any fairy-tale princess," Kasia teased.

Meira managed a chuckle at that. Of the four, Meira had been the one who'd preferred the earlier eras they'd lived through. As the modern age had dawned, she'd fallen in love with fabled tales of knights and princesses that reminded her of those times. A reminder of chivalry and gallantry and a different way of life. "That's clearly what I was going for."

Skylar snorted but otherwise kept her derisive thoughts to herself. They were all well aware Meira had had little choice in today's events, swept along by tradition and the need for all three clans to put on a show for the rest of the dragon shifter world.

"Ready for the last touches?" Kasia asked.

At her nod, Skylar picked up a small gold chest, ornately decorated—a traditional token for Meira's soon-to-be mate—and placed it in her hands. Then Kasia lifted the sheer black veil with matching jewels decorating the edges, settling it over Meira's face, clouding her vision and giving everything around her a darker cast.

She glanced in the mirror off to the side. Only instead of herself in that reflection, for a heartbeat she honestly expected to see…him.

A memory she should do her best to forget.

That day when someone had seen through her magical ability

to turn mirrors into portals had shaken her to the core. No, not just someone…Samael Veles. Ever since then, when she looked into mirrors, a small part of her expected to see him standing there, demanding, hard, and suspicious.

Except she didn't. Instead, she saw him in person all around the mountain or at Gorgon's side. The only person in this place whose emotions were locked down so tightly, she had no idea what he felt, or what he thought of her and of this mating.

She jerked her gaze from the mirror and put a stop to all those thoughts, facing her sisters' expectant expressions instead.

"I wish Mama could be here." She smiled, trying to take the sting of her longing out of her words for herself but also for her sisters.

"She is," Kasia whispered. "In spirit."

Kasia and Skylar stepped closer and put their foreheads to hers through the veil, like they'd done since they were children, a show of solidarity.

Meira closed her eyes. Spirit wasn't going to help them win this war, or help her take this step.

. . .

*R*aw. The only word that could describe Samael Veles on this day.

Meira Amon's mating day.

Like a fresh kill ground up in the butcher's shop. Like a gaping wound left by the slash of dragon claws followed by a blaze of dragon fire disintegrating his flesh from the inside out.

He'd looked into a mirror and seen a woman. That was it. He'd seen her for a handful of seconds before he'd scared her away. At the time, he'd hardly been able to reconcile what he'd seen. A woman in a mirror like a damn ghost.

She was no ghost, it turned out, but she'd been haunting him all the same.

Raising a steady hand—his hands never shook, no matter

the provocation—he knocked on the heavy wooden door to the small chamber situated just off the front of the throne room. This chamber was usually reserved for the king and his Curia Regis of advisers. Today, however, three men stood inside waiting.

Samael offered a brief acknowledgment to Brand and Ladon, their allied kings. Then he turned his attention to his own leader, Gorgon. More than a king to Samael. His mentor, his friend, and after all this time without a family of his own, a father figure.

"All is ready," Samael said.

At those words, he struggled to quell the beast inside him, his dragon thrashing against what was about to happen. Even now, the smoky scent of his own fire wound around him, stronger, the beast close to the surface. Months of his dragon raging, lambasting him from the inside. The rage had grown bad enough that Samael didn't dare loose the animal side of him anywhere near Ben Nevis while Meira Amon remained safely ensconced there with her sisters. Not until her mating was complete.

He'd seen her for a moment in a mirror, and the next time she'd shown up in his life, she'd offered to mate his king. Samael knew his reaction to her, to this, was extreme. Unreasonable, even. And only growing worse the longer he'd been near her.

He knew what it meant. This kind of immediate possessive response could only indicate one thing. But Meira wasn't human, fated for only one mate. She was phoenix, and she got to choose. He had a choice, too, one he'd already made—to stay out of it.

The animal half of him, though, was all instinct and fighting this mating hard, but the man knew where his duties lay.

Though duty could only carry him so far. What in the seven hells would he do when his new queen came to live in Ararat, the mountain fortress of the Black Clan, making it her new home?

Nothing. That's what you'll fucking do.

This would go away. The gods and fates would have heard his many prayers and would take this…this endless ache of wanting… from him once this day was over. Once Gorgon claimed his new mate and the fates deemed each worthy of the other.

Then it would be over. Done with.

Samael could go back to doing what he'd been forged by the gods to do. He might not have been born to it, with not a drop of royalty in his bloodline, as lowborn as they came. Regardless, he'd damn well earned his place as Captain of the King's Guard. None could match his fighting skills, nor his intuition for danger. Nor his loyalty, dammit.

Gorgon turned to the other two kings. "I will see you out there."

Samael moved to follow Brand and Ladon out into the throne room, but Gorgon cleared his throat, so he stopped. As soon as the door swung shut behind the other two with a loud *thunk*, his king took him by the shoulders, his gaze deadly serious.

The fathomless eyes of a black dragon shifter peered at him from a face that was all angles. Older than Samael by close to eight hundred years, Gorgon's black hair was peppered with gray. How the man had yet to show more signs of the brutal aging an unmated dragon dealt with after he passed a thousand was a damn miracle.

"I need you to swear an oath to me, Samael."

He'd never seen Gorgon like this before, almost nervous, except the king was never nervous, not even when Pytheios deigned to visit in person. Dragon shifters wouldn't follow that kind of weakness, and Gorgon had been king longer than any other currently on a throne. Longer even than the rotting king himself.

Shoulders back, Samael returned his king's gaze with a steady one of his own. "I've already sworn you my fealty and my life. What more do you need?"

"Two things."

"Anything, my king."

"First, I have appointed you my Viceroy of War."

Samael jerked, shock a physical jolt of sensation. A position on the king's council? A political position that was typically reserved for someone of higher-ranked bloodlines. "No—"

"You are my captain and my best fighter. I trust you and lean on your guidance. I have faith in you over every other dragon within the clan."

Samael leaned his fists on a nearby table and shook his head. "The clan won't accept me in that position, and you know it."

Not with his muddy, lowborn bloodlines.

Gorgon held up a hand. "It's done. I've already informed Adish."

The king's beta, who was in Ararat representing the king to his people while Gorgon was here securing the clan a phoenix mate.

Samael clamped his lips around more words of protest. His king had clearly made up his mind. The clan would be pissed and resentful, and no doubt would protest. Hell, they'd barely tolerated his position as captain of the guard, but they'd have to deal with that later. For now, he nodded. "And the other thing?"

"The other thing…" Gorgon paused and almost seemed to gather himself. "If today goes wrong, swear to me you'll give Meira the same oath of fealty that you gave me. Protect her from the backlash. Our people will not be pleased, but she will be their queen. With or without me."

Rejection punched through Samael. "My king, no—"

Gorgon gripped him tighter, fingers digging into his flesh. "Swear it to me, Samael. She is a phoenix, even if her sister Kasia ends up being the only one who inherits the fullness of those powers. Our clan needs her."

Black dragons might be the quiet, contemplative shifters of all the clans, but they were proud, and danger didn't make them so much as blink. They shouldn't *need* anyone. "No clan has ever been led by only a queen."

With a huff of a laugh, Gorgon dropped his hands. "Maybe that's what's been wrong with us all this time." His expression hardened. "Do you swear?"

For this man? Anything. "I swear."

But Samael was confident that he wouldn't have to uphold that oath. If anyone was deserving of a phoenix for a mate, this king was.

Gorgon's shoulders dropped fractionally, but even that much

said enough. Shock reared up as the king pulled Samael into an embrace, almost as he would a son, and just as abruptly released him. "Go. Protect your king and queen on their mating day. All will be as the fates decree."

Samael executed a stiff bow, one he reserved only for those times when he wanted his king to know the honor coursing through his veins like wildfire at the responsibilities accorded him.

Following the king out of the chamber, Samael shut the door behind him and swiftly made his way down the side of the throne room, passing behind massive mirrors that stood every twenty feet around the circumference. Though he barely glanced out over the crowd gathered to witness the mating ceremony, he took in every detail, every scent, each covert glance in his direction, even the taste of the room.

No threats as far as he could ascertain, though with the stench of wolf shifters blending with the natural smoky scents of dragon shifters, it could be hard to tell if a threat was nearby. Thanks to those "guests," necessary or not, he'd need to be extra vigilant.

Passing through a smaller door at the back, he entered the vestibule outside the throne room, and his dragon rumbled and settled inside him in almost a reflexive way.

Meira stood with her sisters, achingly beautiful in her midnight-black mating gown, which shimmered, almost like an optical illusion, with a rainbow of colors that reminded him of dragon scales in the sunlight.

She'd worn black for her mating day. His colors.

Not your *colors, asshole. Her new clan's colors.*

Her bouncy curls were hidden from view, and he could just discern her face behind a sheer black veil. A minor break with tradition. Most veils were not sheer, hiding a mate's face from the man pledging himself to her until the ceremony concluded with him removing the veil. Why had Meira chosen to show her face?

So that Gorgon would be sure he was mating the right woman. Samael had no idea how he knew that to be true, but he was sure of it.

That kind of thoughtfulness seemed so...misplaced...in the dragon shifter world. He hated the idea of watching her harden through the years, or worse, be broken by the cruelness of their world.

"Are you sure?" Kasia asked her.

The same question had plagued Samael for months. The logical side of him knew exactly why she was taking this step, appreciated her bravery, even. And Gorgon was a good man who would care for her. But the way she seemed to float through life with a baffling kind of unresisting nature, like a leaf blown haphazardly by the wind, had him grinding his teeth with frustration any time he came near her. He'd swear she didn't really want this.

Meira nodded at her sister, her natural grace and long neck making the mundane action regal. Her vibrant reddish-gold curls at odds with her quiet nature, and those ever-changing eyes fascinated him. Her hands were slim and graceful with long, tapered fingers. The growing obsession to see their paleness against his bronzed skin gnawed at him. She was taller than her sisters, willowy, and would fit just under his chin if he held her.

And she smelled of jasmine and smoke. His personal weakness.

His dragon prodded him to go to her, but Samael gritted his teeth against the urge, like razors scraping the inside of his skin, and shut down that instinctive response. Instead, he stood to post at the side of the doors.

No one would harm the two people he was now sworn to protect to his dying breath. Not on his watch.

On an unseen signal, the doors opened just enough for Kasia and Skylar to enter ahead of Meira.

Facing the door, she glanced neither to her right nor her left, keeping her gaze straight ahead, eyes blank, and suddenly she appeared almost small, as alone and afraid as the last memory he held of his young sister, only ten years of age the day she died.

"My queen." The words passed his lips before he had the conscious thought to speak.

Gods, she was beautiful...and terrified. Holding herself

together by a thread, he'd bet. The tidal wave of need to wrap himself around her and shield her from anything that could put that look in her eyes was impossible to deny and still unwanted. She was not his.

Samael had to stop himself from doubling over to keep his dragon inside.

If you can't have her, you can still help her.

CHAPTER TWO

"My queen."

With a gasp she couldn't quite contain, Meira turned to face Samael, who was standing to the side of the door. A man she should not be so painfully aware of when she was about to mate another.

How had she not felt him there?

Too locked in her own fears, and his emotional walls were impenetrable, that's how. Now, in his eyes she found compassion. She swallowed, and suddenly a jolt of desperate protectiveness hit her. As though those walls of his had wavered, just for an instant.

Meira tightened her grip around the small gold chest she held. But she couldn't force her gaze away from the man before her. Samael was acting as security today, not part of the ceremony. As captain, perhaps he found it more effective to project a stomach churn–inducing kind of intimidation.

Forceful.

She'd thought so the first day she'd seen him in that damn reflection. Almost painfully handsome with a strong jaw covered by dark scruff. She could see why such a man would earn a high position. The Captain of the King's Guard, and it fit. The man had hardened warrior stamped all over him—from the wide military stance to a body honed for battle and a hard light in those eyes, as black as night, that never stopped checking the corners of the room. But she suspected there was more to him, walled away from the rest of the world.

Getting behind that wall shouldn't be her concern. Nor a curiosity. She'd made promises. Her life was on a specific path. She couldn't let herself want...something else. Gorgon deserved more. He deserved all of her.

"My queen," Samael repeated.

Meira blinked at him through the haze of fear coating her own delicate emotions in a thin veneer.

"Meira," Samael said, softer now.

A small frisson of surprise threaded through the fear hanging over her, like a sliver of sunlight breaking through dark clouds. He'd never used her first name before.

Would she be feeling the same disquiet if he were standing at the end of the aisle—

Meira cut that insidious thought off like chopping the head off a snake.

Samael seemed to press closer, though he didn't move, ebony gaze entirely fixated on her. "You can do this."

Shock held her immobile. How did he know she'd been trying her damnedest not to run? Was it that obvious she was terrified? Conflicted?

Meira swallowed hard and jerked her gaze forward. *I can do this.*

She should probably thank him for the support, acknowledge his helping her over a moment of fear and doubts, but the words just wouldn't come. She focused instead on what she had to do.

I can do this, she repeated to herself.

With a whisper of will, she ignited her own fire. Like walking or breathing, her body just seemed to know how, and had done since the moment her mother took her last breath. As though the fuel was in her blood and all she needed was the spark of a thought to set off the firestorm. The flames started inside her and pressed through her veins and her flesh to manifest outside her in red-gold flickering glory and dance across her skin as though rejoicing their release.

She risked one last glance at Samael, who had remained close, a pillar of strength she suddenly needed there, to draw that steadiness into herself for what she was about to do.

Steeling her spine, she waved at the two women waiting to open the door for her. With a flourish, they pushed the remarkably silent doors forward, revealing the massive chamber beyond.

A hush of feet sounded as those gathered to witness and celebrate with the new mates stood and turned to observe her lonely trek over the age-worn, uneven stone floor to the dais where her future mate waited.

For her mating day, they had set up ornate golden mirrors around the circumference of the throne room. She used the magic that came from her fire, tapping into it like a well, manipulating the mirrors. Through those reflections, she allowed the Gold and Black Clans to witness this ceremony from their own mountains, rather than leaving those hard-won havens unguarded and at risk of attack. They and their allies couldn't afford to lose even one of their strongholds.

I could jump through one of those mirrors and disappear.

After all, she was the one controlling the magic.

She could simply change the location in the nearest one and be gone before anyone could stop her.

The gargoyles would take me back.

Maybe. Notoriously closed off from the world, the protectors her dying mother had sent her to tended to not like visitors coming and going.

Not that she was seriously considering returning to them. She'd made a promise.

With a will she didn't know she possessed until this moment, Meira pulled her shoulders back and forced her feet to move, taking one step, then another. Away from the man at her back and toward the king at the end of the aisle who was meant to be her future.

Standing at the back of the dais, Maul, their massive hellhound, watched the room, eyes glowing red, ever their protector since they'd found him as a puppy. As Brand and Ladon stepped forward to lead her sisters to their places at either side of the steps to the dais on which the throne sat, they cleared the way to Meira's own future mate.

Strong and tall, with wisdom in his eyes, Gorgon bore himself with a regal authority that, after ages on the throne, was probably as natural as blinking. He didn't need to be dressed in the formal onyx suit—detailed with intricate embroidery in shimmering threads, again of all the colors of the dragon clans, matching the design of the jewels in her gown—to project an air of utter control and power.

Despite the fact that he should scare the hell out of her, over the last few months, he'd been nothing but kind. She'd come to genuinely like this man—a fact that she saw as a good start.

If Meira was honest with herself, Samael intimidated her more. Something about the way he held himself—leashed violence. Leashed emotions, more like. Then there was the way he looked at her. Only twice since she'd been here had she caught that particular look, gaze full of an emotion she couldn't pin down—or maybe didn't want to identify, because she suspected it too closely mirrored ones of her own that she'd cut off and buried deep. Even so, those emotions in his gaze had reached out and twisted around her. Binding. Compelling.

Stop it.

Gorgon must've seen her expression through her sheer veil, lips pinched with nerves and gaze perhaps a bit twitchy, because his eyes crinkled at the corners in a smile meant for her alone. He smiled easily. She'd come to like that about him. However, he held his ground, a strong dragon shifter king who waited for his prize to come to him.

Maul cocked his head, giving a doggie whine she took to mean a sort of support for her. However, he didn't show her any images with his telepathic means of communication, merely stood quietly.

As she took those final steps to Gorgon's side, he took her by the hands. Quickly she remembered to douse the fire on her skin there. Kasia had said Brand could touch her fire before they'd mated, but, then again, they'd mated successfully. Better not to risk it in front of all these people.

Gorgon rarely exhibited any emotion around her, not that Meira could sense, anyway, almost as though his emotions didn't run deep enough, or were held so tightly in check none leaked out. Different from the wall his captain put up, though.

Even now, she could only make out the faint traces of power that lingered around him. And something else. An astute kind of judgment, maybe? Patience? She still wasn't sure. All she knew was—regardless of today's bout of nerves—around Gorgon, she personally felt calm. As though she could lay her troubles at his feet.

"You wore my color," he murmured.

Meira managed to smile and nod. No sacrificial, virginal lamb all in white. "My color now."

A blip of satisfaction reached her as he squeezed her hands in appreciation. "Are you still sure?" A question he'd asked her several times over these months of preparation.

Meira shored up her own mental blocks against the emotions swirling throughout the room, including her own, and smiled back, trying her best to make it appear confident. He *would* care for her, be gentle with her—that at least she knew. "I'm sure."

He searched her gaze, she wasn't sure for what, then with a nod, turned them both to face the sacra, the obsidian urn that featured in the start of an hour of various rituals, rites, and oaths.

After presenting her mate the chest of gifts, which he would open later, she and Gorgon each burned sacrifices of their old lives to the gods—a lock of hair, vials of blood, old letters from loved ones. Meira said a symbolic good-bye to her family, making eye contact with Angelika at the back of the room with the wolf shifters even as she kissed the foreheads of the two sisters allowed to stand up with her. Ladon and Brand led their mates away, no longer part of the ceremony as Meira joined her new family.

Finally, after other traditions were observed, Gorgon gently lifted the veil over her head and kissed her. Again, she doused her flames over that swath of skin. A pleasant kiss, tender, if not exciting.

At her back, a blast of darkness, like a bomb had been set off in the room and the shock waves struck only her, made Meira gasp.

As though a wall had collapsed under the onslaught, Samael's emotions pummeled her like a hurricane that had beaten down on a tiny island where her family had lived for a short time when she was a child, whipping at her, threatening to peel away every layer of protection to expose her, raw and vulnerable, to the elements.

Confusion, rejection, need, desperation, despair, possessiveness…but also determination and resignation.

A combination that didn't make a lick of sense.

She dared to flick him a single swift glance to the side to find neither his expression nor the set of his body showed an iota of what was going on inside him. Totally blank. Before she could shut out the emotions screaming at her, just as fast as his wall had crumbled, he shored it back up, bricking himself off from her so completely that all she felt now was the echo of her own reaction.

Holy hellfires. How could he stand the cauldron of raw, biting emotion that boiled within him under the surface where none could see?

Except her. Now. In this moment when she'd pledged herself to another man.

In desperation, Meira focused on Gorgon. On his steady presence and his more muted emotions, hardly a whisper reaching out to her. Satisfaction and a kind sort of liking for her.

Interpreting her gasp as meant for him, Gorgon smiled. Shakily, she managed to smile back. She didn't dare glance again at the man at the back of the room.

Your mate. Focus on your future with this good man.

What came next? Another dragon might choose this point in the ceremony to consummate their vows, both through sex and by pushing his fire into his mate, creating a made dragon for all to see, doing the deed right there in front of all and the gods to witness. Gorgon had chosen, instead, to take her to his private suite for that part. Thank heavens.

Meira hid a shadow of her fears for the next part behind a serene mask. At least, she hoped she appeared serene. Not the sex, but the possible results. When mating humans, the woman risked burning in the male dragon's fire. However, when mating a phoenix, the dragon shifter was the one in danger if she didn't choose him with all her heart.

Theirs was a political alignment. Hearts were secondary. She had chosen this path, this man, and she intended to put everything she had into that choice.

Gorgon must've caught her thoughts in her expression, because he leaned forward to whisper in her ear. "Time to find out if I survive you, little firebird."

A snort of a laugh sounded in the back of the hall, no doubt one of the wolf shifters, who had better hearing than dragons, though not by much.

Meira anchored her own chaotic emotions to his steadiness. She was horribly aware of the expectations of the people watching, but she could project outward confidence when she wanted. Put on that mask, even if she found it exhausting. As a queen, she suspected she'd have to get used to wearing that mask often.

She managed to chuckle at the ironic tone in Gorgon's voice. "Nervous?" She cocked her head playfully but answered in an equally low voice. "I didn't expect that of you, my king."

Gorgon's gaze glittered as though he were pleased with her response. "I've been a king for almost a millennium and *you* are the only thing that has ever scared me."

Feeling emboldened by his gentle teasing, Meira patted his hand. "Don't worry. Maul will protect you."

A few chuckles arose now from the dragon shifters seated closest.

"Not you?"

"I'll probably be busy cowering." She wasn't kidding, but he laughed like she was.

"Then I guess I'll have to do the protecting." He pulled her hand through the crook of his arm to escort her. "Are you ready?"

Was she ready for cheers and knowing looks to follow them down the aisle as Gorgon led Meira to the chamber where they would complete the final binding act? Not really, but she pasted what she hoped was bridal pleasure onto her face. Very deliberately, she kept her gaze away from Samael.

While she and Gorgon took this final step, everyone else in attendance would gather in the training arena, which had been transformed into a glittering ballroom where a massive feast would be provided. Once they mated, Meira and Gorgon would change into second outfits, again matching, and join the revelries as a fully mated couple.

They took one step, then a fizzing sound, like a TV set on a station of snow, cut her off, filling the chamber, louder and louder until many of the shifters around her covered their more sensitive ears.

Then, as quickly as it started, the sound ceased, leaving the gaping hole of silence in its wake. In the same instant, tiny flames appeared in the reflection of every mirror in the room, a single flame in each. In *her* mirrors. The ones she controlled. Deep red in color, the flames flickered and danced, glowing red embers jumping out of the mirrors and drifting to the ground to bounce across the stone flooring.

Behind her, Maul growled, the sound so menacing the hairs on her arms stood up.

"This is your High King." The words rang out clearly, as though the speaker were standing in the room before them.

Why does his voice sound like it's in stereo?

The thought passed through her mind just as her gaze skittered to Samael, still standing at the massive double doors on the other side of the room. Emotions pummeled her from every corner—even Gorgon's grim concern pressed into her, chaos in her head. All except Samael. A point of calm inside the room. Calm she reached for, clung to. An oasis.

Then he pointed to the mirrors and, looking back at her, made a slashing motion across his throat.

Of course, Pytheios was using her magic. With a gasp, Meira doused her flames, and the reflections from within the gold and black strongholds disappeared, leaving only the silvery refractive surfaces of the mirrors…but the flames remained.

All around the room, hushed whispers spread like wildfire, along with a stinging fear she couldn't entirely block. She caught a few of the comments. Most wondering how Pytheios was doing this at all.

"He has a witch," the whispers said.

"No witch is that powerful," came some of the replies.

"Our queen killed his witch," others within the Blue Clan insisted.

Suspicion filled the gazes of many turning toward Skylar, who had come back from the Red Clan's stronghold of Everest, after being kidnapped, reporting that she had killed Pytheios's witch, Rhiamon, in the process of escaping with Maul and another prisoner.

For her part, Skylar, up on her feet the second a threat appeared, ignored the looks, concentrating entirely on the orb, Ladon at her back, equally focused.

"Rumors have abounded of an old magic returned to us," Pytheios continued.

Meira swallowed and looked to her new mate. "Is that what Pytheios sounds like?" she asked softly. She'd only ever heard the roar of the dragon the night her mother died, never having seen him in human form.

Lips a grim slash, Gorgon held himself as stiff as a steel rod. "That's him."

"Rumors that a phoenix has been discovered by some miracle after these many centuries are true."

Every eye in the room turned away from the mirrors to assess the three women standing at the head of the room.

"Behold," that odious voice thundered. "Tisiphone Hanyu."

Hanyu? Their mother's maiden name?

The flames grew in size, and an image formed at the center of each. The image of an old man, body stooped and withered with age, skin hanging from his features in a grotesque mockery of what should be a human face. Pytheios. Beside the man who'd claimed to be High King when he had no phoenix stood a gloriously lovely woman with white hair and ice-blue eyes so familiar Meira had to swallow back a guttural sound of reaction. Because this woman could easily be mistaken for one of her sisters. Especially Angelika.

As she watched in horror, Pytheios lifted the heavy fall of the woman's hair from the back of her neck and blew a stream of red-tipped fire across her nape. Immediately, a fire-branded design glowed from her skin in bright-red swirls—delicate feathers forming over her arms. Then the flame ignited around her, forming sparkling wings behind her.

The sign of a phoenix.

Shock sliced through Meira, holding every part of her immobile as though an electric current had passed through, holding her bones in rigid formation.

That sign was supposed to be indisputable. How was this possible?

...

Samael started across the room toward Meira and Gorgon before Pytheios even got to the worst part, the need to protect driving his steps.

Instinct told him that no way would the red king pull a stunt like this unless the revelation would go nuclear, implode the new kings sitting on the gold and blue thrones along with the old king sitting on the black throne. Pytheios would see Gorgon's actions, allying with Brand and Ladon, as those of a traitor. No better way to destroy the power of a leader than by attacking the hearts of those who gave them that power by following.

Pytheios was making every dragon shifter question the validity
of the women they believed to be phoenixes, women mated to
their kings.

Half an ear tuned to what the eerie orb was saying, Samael
made it to Meira's side in time to see her face drain of color,
leaving her as pale as a vampire on a diet. Her hands shook visibly,
clenching and unclenching at her sides in an unconscious gesture.

Deliberately, he addressed Gorgon, otherwise he'd give in to
his dragon's insistence and take the woman who was his new queen
in his arms, fold her into his wings and let nothing and no one near
her. "My king, we need to get both of you to your chamber. Now."

Maul, standing practically at Meira's back, pulled his lips back
in a silent snarl that had Samael eyeing the hellhound closely. He
hadn't much experience with the beasts, but all rumors said to
steer clear. But damned if that mutt was getting in the way of
what Samael had to do.

"I've got this," he said.

To Maul's credit, the dog stopped snarling, cocking his head
to study Samael, muscles rippling under his fur.

"What?" Meira visibly forced herself to drag her gaze from
the mirrors to him, as though his words to Gorgon had taken a
minute to seep into her head. "Shouldn't we discuss this with my
sisters and the other kings? Address our people?"

Did she not hear the growing buzz of doubt and even anger
in the voices filling the room? As though a swarm of wasps had
been disturbed by a swift kick to their nest.

Samael shot her an impatient look, though careful still to keep
his features neutral. "You need to solidify this mating."

She was shaking, reaction setting in. "But...I need to figure
out if I have another sister. We have to get her away from him. We
can't just let her—"

"With what clans behind you?"

He wanted to shake some sense into her. That tender heart
would only lead to trouble if she followed it so blindly.

Meira slow blinked at him, then slid her gaze around the room, landing finally on the man she had pledged her life to not minutes before. As she did, those ice-blue eyes of hers darkened to a color almost navy. Every emotion showed in those mercurial eyes, the color changing like seasons in the mountains with each thought.

Fisting his hands at his sides to keep from reaching out to... what? Comfort her? Convince her? Not his job. Samael forced his gaze to his king.

Gorgon already held one of her hands. With a small tug, he pulled her attention to him. "Samael is right. My clan trusts me. They'll trust you more if you are my queen in every way."

Maul let loose a low rumble of warning.

Rather than answer, Meira laid a tentative hand on the hound's bristly, furred shoulder. She didn't say anything, but the giant dog settled, his glowing eyes appearing to dim. Then she glanced over Gorgon's shoulder to where Kasia and Skylar stood talking with their own mates. Almost as though they felt her gaze, both women turned their heads. Skylar even started forward a step but stopped when Meira shook her head.

"My place is with you," she said to Gorgon, though the words came out unsteady.

"Stay with the queen," Gorgon instructed Samael.

Jerking his chin at Ladon and Brand, Gorgon stepped into the small chamber to the side, closing the door behind the allied kings.

"What's he doing?" she asked. "I thought time was—"

Touching her was out, but somehow his feet stepped him closer to her just the same. *To keep her safe, that's all*, he tried to reason. "He's assuring his allies of what he's doing before you disappear."

Could a woman of her tall grace manage to appear any smaller? "Oh," she murmured.

A few seconds later, Brand and Ladon appeared, moving to their mates' sides. Several seconds after, Gorgon emerged and walked directly to Meira. "Let's go."

She turned to her sisters again. "I have to go." Meira mouthed the words. "I love you."

After receiving reluctant nods, she turned to face Gorgon and

Samael, though she paused and cast a quick look into the crowd. No doubt at Angelika. Did her eyes darken more?

Samael didn't give a shit. The buzz of voices was growing louder with each passing second. How was he going to keep his king and queen safe if the room erupted?

Meira suddenly inhaled a sharp breath and seemed to steady. "We'll never get out of this room easily." She unconsciously echoed his own concern.

He glanced at the now-passive mirrors. "I have an idea," he said.

Without waiting to see if they followed, he hurried to the nearest mirror and waved at it, looking to Meira expectantly.

After a small pause, she stepped forward. With a mere thought, flames feathered over her entire body, reminding Samael of coal burning on low. Her flames were still red and gold, normal everyday fire. In theory, if she was like her sisters, as soon as the mating bond snapped into place, those flames would turn black, the color of her new family.

She touched a tentative hand to the mirror and almost seemed relieved when it changed. "Go ahead."

Both Samael and Gorgon stepped over the gilded frame of the mirror and through the reflective surface. The sensation of being dragged against, a force flattening his face and pressing against him, surrounded him and flowed with him. He'd expected it to be cold, or silent and blinding, the way teleporting when Skylar used her version of that power to send them far distances had been. But this was more immediate. Like stepping through water, or something thicker.

One second, he was in the throne room with the dissonance of voices. The next instant, they stood in the human-size hall just down from Gorgon's suite. Though they had to climb down from the small table the receiving mirror sat over, the voices from the throne room shut off as Meira followed and doused her flames, leaving them in blessed silence.

"Don't let anyone near the door until you have new orders,"

Gorgon commanded.

Samael pretended not to notice the way Meira had paused and stared at him closely for a heartbeat, tugging against the king's hold before following Gorgon. Then the king led his mate inside, the lock clunking as he engaged it across the thick wood door.

Samael spun, standing to post, his back to the stone wall. Closing his eyes, he rammed the back of his head against the rock. Once. Twice.

"She's doing what she must," he muttered to himself. "Now do your duty, soldier."

Shoving every emotion as deep as he could, as far away from himself as he could, he straightened, senses tuned to the tunnels rather than anywhere in the suite, and prayed to every god he'd ever heard of—even the minor ones he only sort of remembered from childhood—that he didn't have to hear the mating.

Before, his new queen stirred his dragon, something no other woman had ever managed to do. But now, knowing what was going on behind that door, his dragon was going berserk—roaring inside his head, beating against Samael's insides. Teeth gritted, only loyalty and sheer will, developed by being the toughest son of a bitch in his clan, held Samael still.

Until Meira's scream split the silence.

CHAPTER THREE

No. Gods, don't let this happen.

Meira tried to get closer to Gorgon, tried to take it back, to pull her fire back into herself. Bile stung her throat, blending with the vomit-inducing stench of burning flesh. The king stared back with shocked, awful, horror-filled eyes as her flames consumed him. He fell to his knees, and she could see him fighting the flames, his own black fire flaring out like sunspots only to be devoured by the red gold of her own fire in an instant.

One kiss was all it had taken.

They hadn't even gotten to the undressing part, let alone the sex part. She'd turned on her flames and he'd kissed her lightly, so sweet. Except then he jerked back, a silent howl of pain contorting his features.

Already his bronze skin had turned charred before cooling to gray. Other parts continued to burn, glowing bright embers, and parts of him were sifting to ash. Like her mother in that field all alone.

"No, no, no," Meira cried, hardly aware of the words pouring from her mouth.

She fell to her knees beside him, reaching in past the flames, which didn't hurt her, to take his hand, already ashy against hers. "I'm so sorry. I'm here. Look at me."

His eyes, already solid gray, shifted in his face as if searching. Could he see her? "I won't let you die alone."

Speaking words she wasn't even aware of, words that tried to pass what little comfort she could to a kind man who didn't deserve such an end, Meira gathered him in her arms, her own heat enveloping her even as his legs disappeared from beneath him. The terrible shuddering racking his body rattled the teeth in her head. Gods above, had death by fire been this horrible for her mother?

Gorgon suddenly gripped her hand tighter, though all that remained of his own were frail bones, then his mouth opened and the gaping hole of what she had to assume was pain, except something was going on with his face. As though the bones were shifting beneath the ash, changing shapes.

No longer his face at all.

The layer of ash fell away, revealing fresh new skin and a completely different face—younger, a softer chin, and red-brown eyes, the hallmark of a red dragon shifter.

One emotion above the fear of death buffeted her.

Deception.

Meira yelped and dropped the body of the man she'd thought was her doomed mate, scrambling back on the floor away from the stranger until her back hit the foot of the bed.

A thunderous *thud* rattled the door. Samael.

The new face didn't stay fresh for long. The fire claimed and charred the new skin just as the old had been, only by this time most of his body had already disintegrated.

Another slam against the door, this one causing a crack to appear in the thick wood. "Let me in!" Samael shouted, his voice muffled.

Meira forced herself to her feet and stumbled around the impostor. That was what some corner of her scrambled mind told her he had to be, the only thing that made sense. Her hands were shaking so hard, it took three tries for her to manage to unlock the door. She jumped back in time to get out of the way as Samael slammed it open. The door hit the wall behind with such force it embedded in the rock, small fragments of wood and stone falling to the floor, the gritty sound loud in the sudden silence as the man on the floor finished disintegrating and the fire disappeared all at the same time.

Samael ran to the heap of burned flesh and knelt beside it. He ran his fingers through the dust and ash then made a fist, seeming to grasp for control.

He won't hurt me.

Meira shouldn't be sure of that. He was Gorgon's captain and would believe what his eyes were telling him. That she'd killed his king, the man he was sworn to protect.

"What have you done?" Samael asked in a low voice.

Hands to her mouth, Meira could only shake her head in horror. Was he asking her? Or asking his king?

Samael turned his head to spear her with a dark gaze full of rage, his fire sparking, like looking into an abyss that was reaching out for her. "What. Have. You. Done?"

No mistaking those growled words were directed her way. "It's—" She had to stop and swallow around a throat so dry it felt coated in dust. Coated in a nameless man's ashes. "It's not—"

Samael bolted to his feet, crossing the room in two long strides, backing Meira up against the rock wall of the cavern the suite was carved from. "Don't you dare say it's not your fault."

She should be terrified. This man had every right to kill her here and now. She'd heard many of Ladon's men speak in hushed tones of respect about Samael's skills when it came to killing. A rational person would be cowering and begging for her life.

But part of her refused to be that woman. Not in front of him.

Samael's emotions, released from their bonds, swirled and eddied around her like a riptide—anger, grief, blame. And one other, above all others. Protectiveness.

For her? Or his clan?

That same part that refused to cower also found the strength to step forward, stopping him with a shaking hand in the center of his chest. Most likely he allowed it thanks to shock that she even tried.

"That's *not* Gorgon," she said, the words clearer than she expected given how her throat was closing up.

Thick brows pulled down over eyes still licked with obsidian flames. "The fuck you say." He pointed a finger at the pile where the body had been. "Only two people came into this room—"

She gave her head a frantic shake. "I thought it was him until his face turned into another man's. A man with red-brown eyes."

Deliberately, she left out the bit about sensing the man's deception.

Samael took a step back, hands going to his hips as he directed his gaze between her and what had once been a man. He almost seemed to be waging a war within himself. No wonder, as he had no reason to believe her. No proof, beyond her word.

Given Pytheios's display, what if he decided she was false? A liar and pretender.

Suddenly, Samael's arms rippled, turning to shining, jet-black scales before returning to human skin, his dragon obviously close to the surface. Was he deciding whether or not to kill her now or turn her over to his people to do the job for him?

"Gods be damned," he spat. Then raised his head. The fire doused in his eyes, leaving them smoky for a heartbeat. An eerie calm settled over him, stealing through her, exactly how she imagined him in battle. Meira held her breath, waiting for the final blow to come.

Samael grabbed her by the arm and turned toward the bathroom.

"What are you doing?" she asked, though she didn't dare struggle against his hold.

"Move," he commanded.

Fear had Meira digging in her heels. "I shouldn't—"

Frustration rippled across his features. "We have to get you out of here," he said in distinct, almost insulting clips. "We use your mirror trick to get away, obviously. The question is where to go?"

Meira stilled in his grasp. "If we run, everyone will assume I'm guilty."

"They'll assume you're guilty either way."

Couldn't he see? "At first, maybe, but *you* believed me."

He stepped closer, lowering his head until his warm breath fanned across her face, the sand and smoke scent of him replacing the smell of melted flesh in her nostrils. Close enough to step into him and let him take the weight of her troubles. Close enough to kiss—

"I haven't decided if I believe you or not," he said.

"Oh." She dropped her gaze to her feet. Disappointment played hopscotch in the region of her heart and made Meira want to wince, but she kept her inexplicable feelings to herself.

She raised her eyes only to find Samael staring intently at her, a small frown between his brows as though he were trying to figure her out.

His next words to her came out almost gentle, for him. "We'll figure it out."

Not a threat. More a reassurance.

Samael straightened suddenly and stepped back, his thoughts concealed behind blanked-out features, emotions fading like disappearing ink, as he walled them off yet again. "If that wasn't the real Gorgon, then hopefully my king, and your mate, is still alive. We find him, we fix all this."

He turned away, but Meira still didn't follow him into the bathroom.

Pytheios had dropped a big stinking bomb of doubt in their midst. She couldn't leave her sisters and new brothers-by-blood to deal with that on their own. The fake Gorgon's death and her disappearing would only escalate the speculation, turn disbelievers within the clans against them.

"Bleeding heart," came a muttered imprecation from the bathroom.

She lifted her head. "What?"

"I can practically read the bubble over your head," Samael said.

"The best way to help your sisters is to find Gorgon. Besides, they'll be able to point out the pile of ash they think is him as proof that you are what you claim. Only a phoenix can kill a dragon that way."

"What if they think the pile of ash is me?" It would kill her sisters to believe that. They'd already lost their mother. She couldn't put them through that pain. Not again.

Samael opened his mouth as though to answer, but paused, head cocked, the gathering tension running through his body practically vibrating the air around them like a tuning fork. "They won't think it's you…because there will be witnesses."

"Witnesses?"

Again, he grabbed her by the arm, only this time his grip was such that she knew she wouldn't be able to break free. If anything, he'd leave a mark from his grasp alone, though she knew he didn't mean to harm her, even in a small way.

He hustled her to the bathroom and pointed at the mirror. "They're coming. Now. Do your thing."

Meira processed the urgency in his voice and swiftly came to the horrible conclusion that he was right. Maybe finding Gorgon was the best course of action. Even if it hurt her sisters.

Either way, they were out of time. She needed to make a choice.

Still not sure it was the right one, Meira reached for a peace she was far from feeling, then closed her eyes, shutting out her concerns about her sisters, the dead remains of whoever he was in the room beyond, and Samael beside her, not to mention whatever the dragon shifter captain was hearing that she still wasn't yet. She scrounged for a calm she'd been practicing all her life to find in the midst of fear.

Because she was *always* afraid.

"Please don't touch me," she begged, eyes still closed. "I don't want you to end up like him."

Samael released her as though she'd just declared he was holding a poison-dart frog, which would have been amusing in other circumstances. With a flick of her will, flames ignited across her skin. She opened her eyes and silently told the mirror in front of her to show a different scene than the reflection of their faces in the bathroom.

"That's not far enough away," Samael snapped. He wasn't even looking at the mirror, so she wasn't sure how he knew that. His face was turned toward the door.

"I need to change clothes," she explained.

"They'll know to look for you in your room."

"Good thing we aren't going to my room."

He blinked, almost as though surprised she'd popped back like that. She was a little surprised herself, actually. A creak of leather, like a new saddle, had her glancing down. Sure enough, Samael's hands had formed into fists pressing against the well-worn, medieval leather gauntlets he always wore on both hands. In the same instant, Meira finally picked up the low rumble of voices, an echo down the hallways. Whoever was coming didn't know yet that they needed to be concerned.

"Hey!" a voice shouted. They probably noticed the door crashed in. The sound of feet breaking into a run against the stone flooring threw her heart into a faster cadence to match.

Closer and closer.

"Up you get." Samael went to take her by the waist, to lift her onto the countertop most likely, but he paused, remembering the flames, and waved at her to move herself. Scrambling a bit on the slick stone surface, she climbed up. As soon as Meira stepped through, she dropped to the floor inside, turned and pressed her hand against the mirror, allowing him to step through.

A shout sounded and several of Samael's men burst into the bathroom, their faces a comical reflection of shock as they saw her and their captain in another room before she turned off the fire and shut down the link. As though nothing had happened, only two faces gazed back at them in the mirror on the other side, Samael's dead calm while hers appeared slightly wild-eyed, not helped by her hair, which had started to stand out from her head with static electricity.

Get moving. It was almost as though she could hear her

mother's voice prodding her along like she had when Meira had been a child.

This time she listened.

Meira ran through Ladon and Skylar's suite to their bedroom. In one of the large armoires, she found what she was looking for—Ladon's clothes. Grabbing a pair of tactical pants and a black T-shirt, which would work better for where they were going, she tossed them at Samael. "Um…I hope they fit."

Samael was roughly the same height, but slightly leaner than Ladon. She didn't bother to wait and see if he took her suggestion to change.

She moved to the next armoire and pulled out one of Skylar's preferred outfits of skintight but breathable material in black, matching sports bra, and a short-sleeved workout shirt overtop. Skylar was curvier and shorter, but these stretched and hopefully should fit. Except maybe the sports bra.

Meira's dress was pooled around her feet before she thought about her company. Pausing, she tossed a glance over her shoulder to make sure Samael wasn't watching and stilled at the sight of a broad, bare back, ripples of muscle, and taut, burnished skin.

Her brain short-circuited.

Around gargoyles and wolf shifters and dragon shifters, she'd seen her fair share of muscled men. Shifters were fighters, these men predators, and naturally fit. On top of that, Samael was a warrior. While dragon shifters claimed an accelerated healing that helped, he should've been marred with scars or other evidence of the battles he'd fought. Ladon himself boasted a scar down one side of his face.

But Samael's skin was clear of blemish. Perfect. Except for the family crest emblazoned on the back of his neck, same as every dragon shifter bore.

She tipped her head, studying him as he left his gauntlets on, struggling to tug the shirt over them.

Samael turned his head and caught her staring. He straightened slowly, the play of muscles across his back with the movement nothing short of fascinating. All leashed power, ready to spring. What would it be like—

I just watched a man die a horrible death and Gorgon is missing. What in all the hells is wrong with me?

He said nothing, simply staring back, and Meira's chest went instantly tight, like her ribs clamped down on her lungs.

It took the mere flick of his gaze down her body, leaving a trail of sensation in his wake, for her to remember.

With a gasp, and no doubt a full-body blush, if the heat sweeping her skin like wildfire was any indication, Meira forced herself to turn away. Keeping her back to him, she quickly changed. She also helped herself to socks and a pair of Skylar's boots, which were surprisingly comfortable and supple.

In addition, she grabbed a handful of throwing knives, slipping them in various pockets she knew Skylar kept hidden in her clothing. Knives had been one of the few things Meira had been capable at when it came to the fighting skills their mother had insisted they learn. She was crap with any kind of firearm or stick weapon. Not too bad with a bow, but not great, either.

Next, she grabbed a carrier, more a hydration pack, smaller than a backpack. Removing the bladder, she stuffed a long-sleeved shirt in it along with underwear, socks, and her veil.

"Feeling sentimental?"

She turned to find Samael watching her in that close way of his, though he still stayed on the other side of the room, like a wild animal wary of a human in his territory.

Meira shook her head. "These jewels are worth quite a bit of money. I'd rather not have to sell them, but if we need to, it gives us options."

Samael's brows shot up. "Good thinking," he said slowly.

Underestimated tended to be where she thrived. If no one had high expectations, then at least they'd always be pleasantly surprised.

"One second." Her vision went red as she reignited her fire and turned to the massive mirror leaned against the bedroom wall. A memory floated through her head of her and Skylar in here one day.

"I'm surprised you'd want such a big mirror, Sky," she'd said to her sister. *"You were never vain like that."*

Skylar had lit up with a secret smile. *"It's not for looking pretty, Mir. It's for...other things."*

"Forget I asked."

Now, she changed the image to the rooms she'd been staying in. Specifically, to her own dresser with a mirror above it.

Samael started to reach for her. "What are you—"

She reached a hand through and grabbed the tablet device she'd left within thankfully easy reach. Pulling it through, she shut off the reflection. "I need this." She waved it at him and then stuffed it in the pack as well. "You ready?"

"We need to decide where to go first."

"I think..." If she was queen, she really needed to work on speaking up more forcefully. "I mean, I have that covered."

Meira took a deep breath, gathering the small amount of courage she had left. Last time she'd left her sisters, she'd made the heart-wrenching mistake of believing she'd never see them again. Barely over a year later, and she'd seen that error corrected. She'd see them again this time, too.

Believing that was the only way she could make herself go.

"You planning to just stand there?"

Samael's voice shook her out of the memory, and Meira focused her mind. The image she called forth from the other side showed a stone floor, walls, and ceiling, but different from the caverns of Ben Nevis. This stone appeared man-made, like a castle. Inside the room, across from the mirror they would step through, an ornate four-poster bed covered in what she now knew to be pale-yellow silk took up most of the space, along with a matching carved armoire to one side and chest at the foot. The decor harkened back to another age. An age of castles, knights, and fair maidens. Fairy tales. Again.

Pulling the fire back from her hand so it wouldn't touch him, she took Samael's arm by the sleeve and guided him through the reflection. As soon as they were across, she doused the fire and the mirror returned to normal. The one they'd come through on this side was a bit dingy with age, especially around the edges.

She didn't bother to get out her tablet, though her hands were itching to. Where she'd brought them, it wouldn't work, anyway.

Samael looked around, the tense cast to his shoulders, the way his gaze darted about, showed him ready to defend them both if he had to.

Meira moved her hand to grasp his forearm, the muscles jumping under her touch. She almost let go as an electric charge passed from his skin into hers. If she lifted her hands, would her palms be imprinted with Samael? Slowly, as though reluctant to do so, he brought his gaze round to hers.

The rush of his emotions blindsided her—pure need, a wanting so deep every part of her lit up with tingling, blinding awareness. A searing heat rushed inside her, pulsing in an answering rhythm.

She jerked her hand back, stuffing both behind her back like a child caught doing something she shouldn't. This man was her only hope to find her mate and fix this. What was wrong with her?

"Where are we?" Samael asked, his voice dropping to a low rumble that skated over her skin like a caress.

Meira licked suddenly dry lips, trying her best to contain everything inside her. "Somewhere safe."

CHAPTER FOUR

"Where?" Samael snapped.

At the same time, he resisted the urge to rub at where her touch had landed, the imprint of her fingers still warm from her fire, soft against his skin, like he'd imagined they'd be since the moment he'd seen her in the mirrors at the Gold Clan's mountain in Norway.

"I…can't tell you where," she said. "I made a promise."

He breathed through his mouth, reaching for control like he'd never had to before, trying not to take in her scent as his dragon urged him to claim. One more distraction he didn't need. What he needed was to make sure they were secure.

Gods above, seeing her in that room with Gorgon—or some impostor—turned to ash, his first instinct hadn't been to go to his king, but to take her away from the danger. She'd stared at him with wide, trusting eyes, watching him like he could fix this.

But he couldn't. This was too big, even for him.

Now she'd dragged him somewhere, and that protective instinct that kicked in around her was screaming at him to secure the area. Only he couldn't do that if he didn't know what he was securing.

"Can't tell me?" He glowered at her upturned face.

Clear eyes gazed back. When this woman made a promise to someone else, she stuck to it, even to her detriment. He knew that much about her. Didn't she know he was here to protect her? How was he supposed to do that if he didn't know where they were?

"The hell with that." Samael stalked to the wide, open window set into one wall. A window with no glass, letting in the biting chill, winter still grasping onto life here despite being early spring, assuming they were still in the Northern Hemisphere. With a quick scan, he took in the scenery.

Seven hells weren't enough.

His first impression of the room wasn't wrong—they *were* in a castle. Except not one like he'd ever seen. Ancient, obviously, based on the architecture and the wear on the stones. One surrounded by jagged peaks still covered in snow. The structure itself blended into the topography, almost like camouflage, but, looking in either direction, as far as he could tell it made up practically an entire side of the mountain.

The design to the structure was an unusual blend of several cultures—English castles, but with Russian styling in the spires, bulwarks that could give the Great Wall of China a lesson or two in Chinese architecture, other more impenetrable parts, which reminded him of Spanish and African fortresses, flying buttresses of the French Gothic style. A marvel. Truly.

Where on the earth were they?

What mountains could hide such a place? Meira wouldn't have dared take them to the Himalayas—too close to Pytheios. The peaks in view weren't steep enough or high enough for the Alps. So where?

The room Meira had brought them to apparently stood high in a turret with a sheer drop not only down the side of the edifice but continuing over a cliff to a deep ravine below.

Samael gauged the distance. If he had to jump, he might have time to shift before he hit bottom.

A change in the air around him told Samael Meira had come closer. Turning slightly, he found her behind him, gazing out the window with an expression of wary concern. Why? She'd said they were safe here.

"It's almost night," Meira said.

He followed her gaze to a sky full of purples slowly fading to dark blues then to black as darkness made her slow, conquering slide across the heavens.

"It won't be long now," she murmured more to herself. "He'll have already sensed us."

Tension took hold of Samael, tightening his muscles in preparation and centuries of training honed to a finely tuned weapon. "He who?"

What next? Was he going to have to slay a monster? Take on a ghost?

Suddenly an odd sort of clacking sounded from outside. Like something was tapping on the rock face of the castle.

Samael put an arm out, scooting Meira back, away from the opening.

Meira tried to speak. "It's—"

"Quiet," he warned. Whatever was scaling those rocks was coming right at her window.

"But—"

He shot her a sharp look that silenced her before jerking his head back around, ready to defend her from what came through it.

A tiny bleat sounded a heartbeat before a goat leaped in through the open window.

"Vincent!" Meira cried and rushed around Samael, who stood there gaping as she wrapped her arms around a shaggy white goat with a beard.

"What is that?" Samael demanded.

He didn't miss the amused smile she hid or how she lowered her lashes over laughing eyes. "This is Vincent Van Goat," she said without even a snigger. "He's mine."

He had no fucking clue what to say to that.

"I found him as a baby. Wolves had killed his mother, and I had to bottle raise him. He couldn't come with me because this is his home." She paused. "Though maybe now—"

"I don't care about the damn goat."

Vincent, as though determined to change Samael's opinion,

pranced over to him and butted his hand for a pat, his deep-brown eyes soft as though pleading to be loved just a little bit.

Samael clenched his jaw, but almost against his will, he found his hand uncurling to pet the darn thing. "You're a snack to my kind," he warned.

"You wouldn't," Meira gasped.

His gaze flashed to her. "Of course I wouldn't—"

At her soft chuckle, he cut off. She was teasing. Meira opened her mouth to say something else but froze as a shadow passed across the window, and then she winced. Samael stiffened, but she hurried to her feet and put a hand on his forearm. Again. This touching-him business needed to stop, or he'd be compelled to return the favor. A betrayal of the man they should be focused on finding.

He went to shake her hand off only to find she wasn't restraining him but imploring. "Whatever happens next, do not attack, do not fight. Please?"

Attack? The goat wasn't what was coming earlier? Years of training and instinct had him tensing, ready to fight. "You need to tell me what the fuck is going on."

Her reticence was turning into a hazard he wasn't sure he could afford. Her need to protect others with her silence or her help, no matter the cost to her, could also cost him.

She gave him a little shake he'd lay odds she never would have dared before today. "Promise me," she insisted.

Vincent heaved a sigh.

Samael gazed into Meira's eyes, which were already starting to darken around the edges, making the whiter centers appear to glow slightly. Her hand did not tremble. Neither did her voice.

She was not afraid.

Samael frowned as realization penetrated his frustration. She was protecting someone. Before he could ask, a large creature burst into the room through the window and grabbed Meira by the shoulders, hefting her off the ground as it flew her across the room.

Samael lurched forward, but he only got a few steps before

Meira shook her head at him and he pulled up sharply, despite his dragon going wild inside him. Instinct had taken over, and it took him a full, painful minute to calm the rage. Hands still in hard fists, he finally managed to focus enough to get a closer look at the creature—the back of a winged man, one made of gray stone.

Literally stone. Gargoyle.

He'd heard of them, of course, but he'd never seen one in the flesh, so to speak. Why did Meira bring them to a creature notoriously shy and reportedly of a nasty disposition?

The creature set down, folding his wings behind him with the sound like a stone and pestle, rock grinding on smoother rock.

Vincent gave a happy little bleat and started to prance over, but one look from the creature and he stopped, cocking his head like a dog.

"You brought a stranger to my house?" In the same way dragons sounded of smoke and fire when riled, the gargoyle's voice sounded like gravel and sand.

Meira grasped the creature's wrists, less to pry his grip away and more to beseech the thing. At least Samael hoped that was the case. "I'm so sorry, but I had no choice. He's my bodyguard, Carrick. I *need* him."

The word "need" forming on her lips, when talking of him, sent a fire through Samael's veins. Inappropriate, for too many reasons to count. He shoved it back down deep, his dragon growling low. A sound Samael couldn't hold on to as it came up his own throat.

The creature didn't move, and Samael couldn't see his face. "Something happened?" it asked Meira, ignoring him.

Meira nodded, then her lips twisted. "Do you…mind changing forms?"

Was she afraid of this Carrick in this form? Samael took a step forward, but the gargoyle turned his head to the side, almost owl-like in the movement, eyeing him sideways. Samael stopped, holding up both hands in a gesture of temporary surrender.

The gargoyle had yet to be violent—its grabbing Meira that way clearly a means to protect her from a potential threat. She trusted it, though with her soft heart, maybe trusting her instincts wasn't his best move. Still, Samael wouldn't provoke him.

With his first decent view of the creature from the front, he could see why Meira was nervous. Grotesque didn't cover it. Carrick appeared to be made from the carvings of many different beasts—the mane of a lion, head of a water buffalo, brow of a gorilla, tusks of a wild boar, legs and tail of a wolf, ears of a bat, and body of a bear. The strangest part was his eyes. Human eyes surrounded by delicate, purple-bruised skin that faded underneath the cracked rock that surrounded those eyes.

Like a being possessed.

Carrick left his head turned so he could watch Samael and Meira at the same time. "Does anyone else know where you are?"

"No one saw us leave to come to *this* place," Meira assured him.

"Then you don't need a bodyguard."

Try to make me leave and see what happens. Samael deliberately remained loose, nonthreatening in appearance, hands hanging at his side, feet set wide, but he was ready to go if Carrick made a move.

"He's... It's important," Meira insisted. "We have to find Gorgon. He's been taken. We won't stay long but needed to hole up for a day or two and figure out a plan."

The gargoyle remained silent.

"Please, Carrick," Meira whispered, begged.

His back still facing Samael, though head turned to keep an eye on him, Carrick released her and appeared to shift. Unlike dragons, or wolf shifters, or any other type of shifter Samael was familiar with, who all completed the act in silence—except maybe werewolves, who were a different breed altogether—a gargoyle sounded like rock being gouged out of a mountain by force. More than that, the process appeared painful.

With what Samael could see of his face contorted, Carrick jerked his body in violent movements, and again that grinding sound filled the room as his wings absorbed back into his body and his face changed to that of a man, though his features remained both broad and sharply angled. Skin turned from solid rock to something more human, though it still had a gray undertone to it.

Like other shifters, clothes formed over his body during the transition. Medieval garb of trousers, belted tunic, fur-lined cloak, boots, and gloves. He could've passed for human royalty in the fifth or sixth century dressed like that.

Clothes like the dress Meira had been wearing that day he saw her reflection. This was where she'd been hiding.

"We must take this in front of the chimera," Carrick said. "I owe your mother my life, and I'll use it to protect you, *solnyshka*." He sent an indifferent glance Samael's way. "He does not fall under the same protections."

"I don't need you to protect me," Samael snarled.

Sunshine. The gargoyle had called Meira sunshine. It fit, from her bright hair, to her eyes, to her name, which meant "one who illuminates." But the term of endearment was too casual, too easily cast from the tongue. Was there more here? Had Meira fallen in love with the protectors her mother had clearly sent her to?

Carrick ignored him, instead reaching out to run his fingertips down the side of Meira's face. An intimate gesture that had Samael gritting his teeth to keep from ripping the fucker's hand off. A violent response that he should ignore, except...

He'd learned long ago to rely on his instincts. The trouble was, what his instincts, and the dragon inside him, were telling him was...complicated. Potentially deadly at worst. At the best, catastrophic. So he ignored it like he'd been doing since the day she offered herself as a mate for Gorgon.

Focus. They had to fix the problem staring them in the face first.

"You are unharmed?" the gargoyle asked Meira softly.

Her eyes faded to light blue, allowing more of the white in. Clearly whatever threat she was worried about earlier had passed. She smiled softly at their reluctant host, and a burn of jealousy scored through Samael. Until she happened to glance over the gargoyle's shoulder directly at him and blinked.

"Other than losing the man I'm supposed to mate, I am well," she said.

Carrick stepped back and gave an oddly formal little bow. "Come with me." He shot Samael a look swimming with distrust. "Both of you."

The gargoyle stomped out of the room, his thick boots sounding as though they were still made of stone.

"Goat," Carrick called back into the room. "Come."

Vincent trotted out after him, short tail wagging away.

"I guess he's Carrick's goat now," Meira murmured.

Side by side, she and Samael followed the animal out into the hall.

"This is where your mother sent you?" Samael asked quietly.

"Yes."

Rumors were right for once. In the midst of her own death, Serefina Amon had split her four daughters up and teleported them to the corners of the earth, each to a different protector. He knew Kasia had ended up in Alaska with Maul as protection. Angelika was still pretending to be part of the wolf shifter pack she'd been sent to in the Pyrenees Mountains between France and Spain, though they now stayed with Ladon's clan. And Skylar had gone to somewhere in the Andes Mountains with a band of rogue dragon shifters, of all things, though she remained reticent when it came to the details of who or where.

Meira's reticence made Skylar look like an open book with audio and even a visual aid. She'd merely contended that wherever she had gone, she'd been safe.

"Do you trust him?" Samael mumbled under his breath.

She shot him an annoyed scowl, brow furrowing, and adorable with it. "That's a silly question."

"Is it?"

"Carrick is a friend, and I trust him." She walked a few more steps, then muttered, more to herself, "Seems obvious to me."

Samael held back a snort of laughter. Now where had that

come from? Normally, she wouldn't say boo to him. Maybe she was showing him the real her, a side he'd guessed only her sisters saw. Suddenly, in the most unexpected circumstances, she had him wanting to laugh, shake her, and cuddle her at the same time.

Wrong. Wrong. All wrong. Terrible idea. Their mission was the king, her mate in vow if not in deed. Samael needed to focus on that, and that alone.

His dragon violently disagreed.

He ignored the beast inside him, trying to think through all the angles. Adish, Gorgon's beta and next in line for the throne, would get a hold of the clan, bring them in line. After he secured them a safe place to stay—here or otherwise—his next step should be contacting Adish as soon as possible and filling him in.

Carrick led them through a wending series of endless hallways, each decorated in a way that, similar to the gargoyle's clothing, hearkened back to medieval times, and even earlier. Like with the outside and all the different styles of architecture, the inside's decor was that of a blend of various ancient human cultures. He even spotted a few Greek columns.

A place out of time. Or of time. A reflection of the ever-changing world.

"Is this for real?" Samael said, though quietly.

"You haven't even seen the best part," Meira tossed at him, lips tipped in a secretive smirk.

"What's the best part?" Now she had him distracted with inconsequential details. Did he want to know?

"You'll have to wait and see."

Probably they wouldn't have time. He tucked the odd sense of disappointment away, because the sparkle of delight in her eyes had him more curious than he should be given the circumstances and surroundings. How did she do that?

You don't do curious, he reminded himself.

The sounds of a large group gathering—the low murmurs of men, the more melodic tones of women, and the higher-pitched squeals of children, granted all with that gravelly texture—had

Samael tensing long before they entered a room that reminded him of the great hall in his own mountain of Ararat in Turkey. Ben Nevis also had a similar room, used as a sort of social common room, though more for the upper classes.

A massive fireplace and hearth took pride of place at each end, incorporated into vaulted ceilings, the structures of which extended to the floors. Murals graced each section formed by the buttresses, but the paint had not faded with time like most found in human castles or fortresses these days. These were pristine and brightly colored, edged in glittering golds and silvers and coppers, the telltale sparkle of jewels decorating various spots.

The room reminded him of Russian Orthodox churches. Breathtaking.

Groupings of chairs and a few long tables formed smaller seating and meeting areas throughout the larger space. All the furniture matched the theme—heavy, wood, and ornately carved. Kings and queens, czars, emperors, maharajas, and other human royalty centuries before would have had to swallow down envy if they'd ever found this place.

The space was filled with many more gargoyles than Samael had expected. One hundred at least. Every single one of which snapped their heads around to stare at him and Meira. Mostly him. The low rumble of voices that had sounded down the hallways ceased immediately, leaving a gaping silence in its wake.

Samael went still. All except his gaze, which he cast around the room, searching for any sign of threat. *And I thought dragons could be intense.*

"Stay here," Carrick commanded.

The gargoyle stomped away, Vincent Van Goat following on his heels, to a corner at the opposite end of the room, followed by at least half of the adults, both women and men. They formed around him in concentric circles, then one by one, stilled and shifted to their stone forms, faces contorting and bodies changing to a multitude of grotesque shapes.

The accompanying scraping sound might be Samael's second

most hated sound in the world after the memory of his sister's screams.

Beside him, Meira gave a little shudder.

He raised his eyebrows at her, and she grimaced. "That sound reminds me of chalk."

"The screech of nails..." He totally got it.

"No. Chalk on a chalkboard."

"Isn't the expression nails on a chalkboard?" Now why had he indulged this conversation?

"Thank you, Webster." She blinked, as if she'd startled herself with that response.

"Webster?" Again, that urge to chuckle struck him the wrong way.

"The dictionary guy," she explained with an apologetic wince. "Sorry. I didn't mean to be rude."

She thought that was rude? Dragon shifters were going to tear her apart if she didn't toughen up. His dragon's instinct was to fly her away from all of it to keep her safe. But he couldn't.

"The sound of actual chalk on a chalkboard was always worse to me." Her explanation cut into his silent worries. "Like spiders."

"Spiders?" What did those have to do with chalk?

She scrunched up her face. "Same sensation. Makes my skin crawl."

"I see." Samael battled the sudden and highly ridiculous urge to squash every spider in the world, his grip on the possessive, protective side she brought out in him slipping, his dragon pushing him even more. All while the gargoyles huddled in their silent, stone forms, deciding his fate. Strange didn't begin to cover this.

Meira side-eyed him. "I think you actually do."

Despite himself, Samael gave in and laughed at the suspicion coming from her. "Is that a bad thing?"

"Mimi!" a tiny girl called out as she ran across the room toward Meira, stealing her attention from him before she could reply.

All the rest of the gargoyle children, many more than Samael would've guessed existed in the entire world, took up the cry, rushing the woman he was supposed to protect.

They all circled her, tugging at her clothes and talking, but with words Samael couldn't understand. Most dragon shifters spoke a majority of the most regularly used human languages. They'd been on the earth long enough, and, because female mates were found primarily among human women, other languages and cultures were integrated with dragons' own regularly. He'd never encountered this one before. It had a vaguely Russian buzz to it, but also drawn-out sounds using intonation to form words, more like Chinese dialects.

Though Meira didn't speak, she leaned over, holding out her hands. The children surged forward to touch her skin, making sounds that he interpreted as oohs and ahhs.

More vulnerable souls. She seemed to draw them to her…like the damn goat.

She glanced up at him, and Samael had to quiet a grunt of reaction at the lightness of her eyes, the closest he'd seen the color to matching her three sisters'. Like starlight, glowing white.

She's happy here. Among the children.

"Why?" he asked.

She flicked him a glance that turned more serious, as though collecting back into herself. "Why what?"

Good question. "Why do they touch you?" he opted to go with.

She didn't stand up, allowing the children to continue their exploration of her arms. "I think it has to do with how my skin is softer than theirs. I'm…different…is all."

She waved at a tiny girl who appeared too shy to reach out and dropped to one knee to get closer to the mite, who tentatively touched one of Meira's fingers.

"When we first lived in the Americas, most of the people there hadn't seen Kasia's, or Angelika's, or my color hair before," Meira said. "Angelika especially drew a similar response, though maybe more reserved, everywhere we went. At least until Mother used her ability to make people think we'd always been part of their community." She gave a small shrug. "I learned early that normal in my own life might be extraordinary for someone else."

For creatures who had a regular influx of other cultures, dragon shifters could learn a thing or two from this woman. She didn't draw away from him or the children, but even so, he could feel her closing off even more. He didn't like it. "Have you shown them your fire?"

The question pulled a full-on grin from her, and a pair of dimples flashed at him. Practically knocked him on his ass. So, this was what winning one of her real smiles was like. It could become addictive.

"Oh yes," she said. "They weren't much impressed. As far as I can tell, the only thing gargoyles are afraid of is ice."

"Make sense," he speculated aloud. "After all, ice splits rock apart. Glaciers have been known to flatten mountains, or even shear them in half."

Meira cocked her head, studying him with an expression that hinted at her being oddly impressed. "Exactly."

He grunted to cover another reluctant chuckle, still put off at the absurdity of the situation—the gargoyles, the woman, and the conversation. "Why do you sound surprised that I figured that out?"

She turned her gaze back to the children. "I thought you were a warrior."

"What's that supposed to mean?"

"You know…" Then she bit her lip, obviously regretting the words.

What did she think he was? A dumb brute? A killing machine with no mind of his own?

"On behalf of myself and all the warriors under *my* command, I must say I'm deeply offended." He should be, at least. He was fucking proud of who he was and the position he'd earned. Only he wasn't offended. Probably because he could tell she didn't mean to hurt his feelings.

Her cheeks turned rose red, and not from the heat put off by those massive fireplaces. "I apologize," she said stiffly, not looking at him. Drawing inside herself again.

He told himself to give her space, take a firm step back. He wasn't the one who should be coaxing her out of her shell.

Instead, Samael found himself squatting down before he knew what he was about. He pulled back his sleeves to reveal his own skin, darker beside hers, made more so by the whorls of black hair over his arms. With a push from his dragon, which was always lurking close to the surface around her, he turned the skin to scales so black they would've sucked any light into the void had they not also been glasslike, reminding most who saw him in dragon form of obsidian.

He held his arms out to the children, who transferred their oohs and ahhs to him, touching the diamond-hard scales that, to the touch, were also surprisingly supple, more like a snake's underbelly, but impenetrable. A living armor. To him, the roughness of the children's own tentative touches was like being rubbed down with a dried-out loofah.

"You did that earlier," Meira commented.

He glanced up to find her gaze on him, surprisingly unguarded fascination in her eyes, and his body quickened in response. "What? Shift only part of me?"

She nodded. "Isn't that a rare skill?"

Samael gave a noncommittal grunt. The truth was, she was correct. In theory a skill reserved for royalty, though he knew of royals who couldn't, but it had always been one of his talents. Only the scales. No other parts, except the day he'd seen her in that mirror and his feet had changed to talons. That had been out of his control, though. Not like Brand Astarot, who could shift any part of himself he wanted to any size. *That* was impressive. "Why do you think warriors are dumb brutes?"

She gasped, seemingly horrified. "I would *never* use words like that."

No. She wouldn't. It would hurt her to hurt someone else's feelings that way.

"But you were thinking them. Don't worry about my feelings.

I'm just curious."

He turned his head to find her watching him with worry in her eyes that disappeared as she once again tried to turn off an inner light that apparently she didn't like to share. Or maybe that was just with him.

He didn't think she was going to answer, but then she sighed. "I spent my entire life running from your kind because apparently you can't discern for yourselves when a leader is as rotten as a bad apple riddled with worms. You keep taking bites anyway."

Which begged the question, why had she left the safety of the gargoyles? Why had she offered herself to Gorgon? Especially when she could probably have hidden here indefinitely.

Carrick returned to human form, which seemed to be some kind of signal for the goat. After a pat from the gargoyle, he danced to a window, hopped up on the ledge, then seemed to drop out of sight. No doubt the thing was nimbly scaling the rocks that made up the castle walls.

Carrick, apparently unworried about his pet, crossed the room to them, speaking to the children in that foreign tongue and scattering them as he waved his arms to shoo them away. Though they seemed to giggle as they ran to their mothers. Hard to tell.

Samael rose to his feet and almost offered a hand to Meira to help her up, clenching his hands to stop himself. Touching was out.

"We have discussed it," the gargoyle said. "You may stay." He focused on Samael. "Our existence and location must remain a secret from the outside world."

"You have my word," Samael said.

Carrick stalked closer, human face contorting as if the monster was trying to get out. "Do *not* break our trust."

CHAPTER FIVE

Pytheios stood in the doorway to the recently abandoned room. One built for a specific purpose.

Roughly carved from a natural cavern, it contained only a rock slab the height of a table and size of a long, single bed. Like a pedestal for a vampire's coffin, or a platform for ritual sacrifice. The latter was closer to the truth. Against one wall dangled chains and shackles of varying sizes, all made from dragon steel.

This place had been his secret in a never-used part of his mountain. Everest, with its massive size in combination with the many millennia that dragon shifters had made their homes within its caverned walls, was now a twisting maze of tunnels, rooms, and chambers. No one, not even Pytheios, knew all of it. Which was why it had been easy to find a place for Rhiamon to wield her powerful magic.

Here they'd spent countless days together as she'd siphoned the energy, the life force, from supernatural creatures into Pytheios and herself, a necessary evil in order to prolong their own lives, granting them more time to find immortality.

They'd been close. He'd tasted that power for the briefest moment.

Now, he glared at the spot where that bitch of a phoenix, Skylar Amon, had attacked. Even still the room reeked of magic, which had a remarkably similar scent to ozone, sweat, and smoke. The smoke would be from the phoenix and the hellhound Rhiamon had been draining. Pytheios, locked in the spell and weakened, hadn't gotten the chance to light his own fire.

"*My king.*" The voice of one of his guard reached him telepathically. Likely one flying patrol tonight.

Needing to conserve energy, Pytheios shifted the smallest part of himself he could, a single finger turning scaled with a claw at the end. "*Yes?*"

"*King Volos of the White Clan is on approach. However, we were not informed of his arrival. He is asking permission to speak with you.*"

Satisfaction settled in Pytheios's gut. He wasn't surprised that Volos had come, merely at how long it had taken him to get here given the incentive. "*Let him in. Tell Jakkobah to greet our guest. I will join them when I can.*"

"*At once, sir.*"

The telepathic connection shut off, but Pytheios did not leave to meet Volos as he arrived. The white king could wait.

Pytheios had a more immediate problem. If he didn't get another boost of energy soon, he wouldn't make it through the next two weeks, let alone through the war. A big influx, too. Smaller creatures like kitsune would no longer suffice. In his state, a hellhound might not even be enough. Not that they held one captive to suck dry anyway. The dogs were damn difficult to capture.

The question was, did he risk Rhiamon's currently unsteady grasp on reality to ask this favor? If he did, what creature would they siphon and where?

Which was why he was here, staring at an empty room.

Looking at the space now, no one could detect the horror the phoenix had wrought in this small, unassuming space. Skylar had murdered his witch and sent him far away when he was so low on energy it had taken interacting with pathetic humans to get in touch with his people and slowly find his way home. All while that Amon cunt had escaped under the noses of his people.

Layers of humiliation and fury lashing at his insides he wasn't soon to forget.

That one act, and the results, were exactly why he needed to eradicate the world of their kind.

No dragon—the most powerful and ancient of all shifters—should be dependent upon another creature. Their kind should not rely on outside influences to determine their leaders or provide supernatural bullshit luck. Dragons were glorious and perfect without intervention.

But his people couldn't see past their own mortality. He'd been blind himself once, only seeing the need to mate a phoenix to secure his claim to the throne of the Red Clan and the title of High King. Belief in his destiny had centered his world.

It had taken Serefina choosing another, choosing Zilant Amon as a mate, for Pytheios to see the true danger of submitting to the supposed power of the firebird lore.

Now he had four to contend with, dammit. Her daughters.

No matter. If he could take their powers—all four of the sisters—and kill them afterward, then *he* would be everything his people needed. High King forever, able to lead all dragon shifters into a new and glorious era.

One that would last forever.

First, he had to capture each of those bitches. All four of them, though he only knew the whereabouts of three. That had been his earlier mistake, going after one at a time. The mated ones posed a greater complication. Little in this world was more dangerous than a male dragon protecting his mate. The best plan would be to take all four at once and drain them quickly.

Hopefully the trap he'd laid, and the bait he'd set out, would lure them to him. Could Rhiamon keep him alive that long?

He'd brought her back from beyond the grave, but altered—more powerful, angrier, and uncontrolled. Bitter that he'd killed their useless son, sacrificing Merikh to bring her back, using a dark magic that required a life for a life.

Pytheios didn't dare bring his witch to this room. She wasn't stable. Any child could see that just looking at her. Seeing the scene of her death might tip her mind into the void.

With careful movements, every action an effort in the state of decay he'd reached, Pytheios locked the door and made his way to the supersonic elevator he'd had installed in the last century, then down to the lower levels. Jakkobah would have known to escort Volos—and Volos alone—to his private study. Pytheios's own private chambers were off-limits.

Avoiding the halls most traveled, Pytheios didn't bother to knock or have either of the guards announce him. Though he nodded at one to open the door for him.

Inside only Jakkobah and Volos waited.

For a man who dressed in custom-made suits, styled simple and straight with a standing collar but with intricately detailed embroidery and luxurious materials, Jakkobah had chosen to decorate his spaces in a more minimalist fashion with clean lines and sparse furniture.

Volos rose from a straight-backed wooden chair.

Tall and hefty-shouldered in human form, more akin to gold dragon shifters despite being white, Volos had broad features and wide-set eyes. Swarthy skin appeared even darker against his shock of white hair, worn short and slicked back, and his white-blue eyes practically glowed. The King of the White Clan had remained unmated all these years. Pytheios had seen to that. Both Volos and Gorgon—a way to keep kings in line. Age was starting to show its slow march across Volos's face.

The time had come for a younger king for the White Clan. Placing Brock Hagan there, a gold dragon, would cause ripples, but he had little concern that the White Clan would obey. Brock was of royal blood—he should have been the gold king if it hadn't been for Brand Astarot and his damn phoenix. The man hid a cruel streak that Pytheios had every intention of leveraging to his own purposes. Once they defeated the rebel kings, maybe he'd give him both the Gold and White Clans as a reward.

He'd sent Brock on a mission. If he came back from that

unharmed, then they'd take the first step with the White Clan.

Volos bowed, breaking into Pytheios's thoughts. "High King."

Keeping his hands steepled before him, Pytheios did not offer to shake. Physical contact hurt too much in his current state. "My old friend. What brings you here?"

He knew. He wanted to hear Volos say it.

"Tisiphone."

Allowing a small smile to stretch his lips uncomfortably, Pytheios nodded. "Of course. A miraculous find, isn't she?"

"Is she?" Volos asked, pale eyes narrowed with a blatant display of suspicion. "A *find*, I mean?"

Pytheios gazed back through his one still-good eye, the other giving him only a milky image behind cataracts. "You question me?"

To give him credit for still possessing some brains, Volos paled slightly, but he didn't back down. Rare for the white king, the puppet Pytheios had been sure to put on the throne in place of Zilant Amon after he'd killed him. Volos had been so grateful that not once in five centuries had he questioned Pytheios like this.

Behind Volos, Jakkobah raised his eyebrows in what appeared to be mild surprise, but that was quite a statement from the man people nicknamed the Stoat—thanks to both his weasel-like appearance and other attributes, including being known for his lack of emotional responses.

Pytheios couldn't have this. He already had three traitor kings to deal with. Until he solidified his position of power by draining those phoenixes dry, he couldn't have the two remaining allied kings turning on him like rabid dogs.

How fortuitous that he'd already planned for this eventuality.

"Is the woman claiming to be a phoenix my niece?" Volos questioned in a voice with a slight tremble.

"Yes."

Volos took a step back, shock twisting his expression.

"You expected me to lie to you?" Pytheios queried in a deceptively mild voice.

Volos shook his head, gaze skating around the room as if searching for a new reality to find purchase on.

You won't find it. Pytheios settled inwardly. Ready to get on with what happened next. *I am the solid foundation. Fix your gaze on me.*

The white king swallowed. "If she is my niece, then her name isn't Hanyu, and how can she be a phoenix?"

A question, rather than an accusation. Poor Volos. The man never had developed a spine. "Why don't you ask her yourself?"

Pytheios waved at Jakkobah who, hands clasped behind his back, strode from the room.

"Shall we sit as we wait?" Pytheios lowered himself into the cushioned, wing-backed chair set by the fireplace. Though dragons didn't need much extra heat, this was Everest, and March was still damn cold. His old bones ached with the chill that the low ebb of his own fire couldn't hold at bay.

"I'll stand, if I may." Volos faced the exit Jakkobah had departed through.

Pytheios waved a careless hand. Standing or sitting wouldn't change who walked through that door, or who held the power in this situation.

Ten minutes later—Volos visibly tenser with each passing second, his overwide shoulders practically twitching from the strain—Jakkobah entered with two women, not one.

Rhiamon, paler than she used to be, her white curls wilder, and her eyes more darkly shadowed, as though the magic lurked under the surface, no longer under her full control. Before, when she used her powers, her eyes would turn solid black with silver pupils and the black would appear to leech into the skin surrounding, like poison in her veins. Now it constantly marred her pale skin. Or perhaps death had filled her with such power, she could no longer disguise it behind human eyes.

Volos's eyes widened, and Pytheios swore he picked up the pungent scent of fear in the air as Rhiamon entered, but immediately the white king dismissed her as the second woman appeared.

"Gods above." The words jerked from Volos. "It *is* you. Though you look...different."

Doubt again. The time had definitely come to find a new king for the White Clan.

"Uncle." Tisiphone crossed the room to kiss her relative on the cheek.

For his part, Volos searched her face with a disbelieving gaze, like maybe if he stared long enough the woman would change to someone else. No doubt the man had been hoping for someone else. "What have you done to yourself? I hardly recognize you."

Tall and slender, like most white dragon shifters, Tisiphone glided across to where Pytheios sat. She didn't dare touch him, but she slid her arm across the back of his chair in a clear show of solidarity. "I have found a way to better myself, Uncle."

"Better yourself?" Volos was sounding shell-shocked now. He dropped into the wood chair he'd occupied earlier.

Tisiphone gave her uncle a superior smirk. "As a female-born dragon shifter, you know my only prospect was to mate for political convenience and resign myself to never providing my mate with children. Possibly have to watch him use a human surrogate to bear us sons. Other options were never a consideration. Until now." She curled her lip in a sneer. "Now you want to take away the only choice that makes sense?"

"Choice?" Volos's deep-set eyes practically disappeared as his thick brows lowered. "When it's all lies?"

"It's not lies. Pytheios's witch has made me into something new. Something...better." Satisfaction coated each word.

"Better?" Volos's repetition was growing old quickly.

"A phoenix," Tisiphone breathed, and glanced down at her arms as though the glowing sign might appear at her will.

Volos spared a glance at Rhiamon, appeared to contain a shudder, then moved his gaze to Pytheios. "A phoenix cannot be made."

Tisiphone slid a questioning gaze to Pytheios, who waved

for her to go ahead with her sharing. "We won't need the real phoenixes after Pytheios has drained them of their powers."

As they had discussed, Tisiphone did not mention his plan to mate her, making her a permanent fixture as "the phoenix" at his side as far as the rest of the dragon shifter world was concerned. With no other phoenix to contradict his claim, because he'd kill them, and holding all that power himself, no one would be the wiser.

The plan was perfect.

But Rhiamon couldn't know that piece on the board, or she might not act out her part for him if she believed he'd mate another. Not after the promises he'd made. Promises he'd released himself from the instant she'd died.

"What do you get for this deception?" Volos asked, voice thready.

"The High King has promised his witch can make me fertile when we succeed in shutting down this rebellion. When she does, I shall give my *mate* the offspring he deserves."

In the corner of the room where she'd slowly moved, Rhiamon's shoulders twitched. He'd have to talk to Tisiphone about calling her "his witch." They needed Rhiamon to play nice for now.

Volos dropped his gaze. "That's...a generous offer." He was quiet a long beat, then pulled back his shoulders. "I should have trusted that you had a master plan, my king."

Yes. But that wouldn't be a problem anymore.

He bowed his head in acceptance of the apology, the movement slow mostly because of the effort to lift it again.

"I wish you had come to me sooner," Volos said next. Pandering evident in the sort of flailing urgency in his voice. "I would have offered my niece to you without hesitation."

"I'm glad to hear it."

Volos approached Pytheios and bowed. "I will return to my mountain and take this secret to my grave. I shall be proud to know my kin is part of your plan."

"I don't think so."

Volos paused midbow and lifted his gaze. "Pardon?"

Pytheios shifted his gaze to Rhiamon, who had already been chanting quietly in her corner. Even reborn, she knew his wishes without a word. Now she lifted her gaze—silver irises floating eerily in a sea of black death.

Satisfaction tore through his veins.

Before her demise, it took almost an hour for her to work up to the moment she could pull a soul from a body, and another hour of concentrated, exhaustive effort to place that soul into Pytheios. That effort had been why they'd needed their special, private room for the act. That and the screaming.

But she was already there, ready to pull a soul from a body. Within minutes. It appeared death *had* only made her stronger.

As soon as she fixed her gaze on Volos, the white king froze as still as the dead in their tombs. Men he would soon join. The only movement in his body came from the pupils of his eyes, which dilated, consuming the white irises. Slowly, Rhiamon crossed the room, lips moving as soundless words tumbled out, her gaze focused entirely on her prey. When she reached his side, she laid a hand on his shoulder. With tiny jerks, like watching a stop-motion film, Volos straightened from his bow and faced her.

Rhiamon put her lips to his, and the white king's mouth opened wide in a silent scream. A shadow of his face appeared to lift away from his body, a spectral form drawing into her mouth, as she pulled his ghost, his soul, from his corporeal form into her own. The process took less than a minute. Then Volos's eyes clouded over, his skin turning a deathly gray, before he collapsed to the floor without so much as a twitch of life left within him.

Rhiamon turned to Pytheios, then paused, glancing over his shoulder at Tisiphone, her eyes narrowing.

"Rhiamon," Pytheios rumbled, wanting her focus on him.

She continued to home in on the false phoenix with venom in her gaze.

"My king," Tisiphone whimpered behind him. He ignored her.

"*Rhiamon*," Pytheios growled now, letting cold demand freeze the word.

He needed this, needed the power, the added time. A soul as old as Volos's wouldn't help for long, but a dragon shifter, no matter the age, especially one as powerful as a king, would tide him over. Hopefully long enough.

Rhiamon's gaze snapped to him, and Pytheios had to contend with the sudden, unusual sensation of fear clutching at his heart, its fingers icy and grasping. He wasn't sure of her intent until she leaned over him in his chair, placing her weight on her hands on the arms, then paused. "For you...my love."

She placed her lips to his, then released the essence she held inside her, filling him with it.

CHAPTER SIX

Meira lay on her side, knees pulled up close, tucked awkwardly so that she could study her tablet. She'd set up a program that was scanning and analyzing a host of ancient texts she'd downloaded while at Ben Nevis, searching for answers to so many questions. Just one way she was trying to help. If she could find proof of who she and her sisters were, or more information about her kind, proof that there could be more than one, or even proof of the legends surrounding mating them, maybe it would convince more dragons to follow them.

She'd been going over the results any time she could get away from the ceremony plans and her sisters. With no electricity here, she'd have to ration her time until she could get somewhere to charge the device, so she couldn't read long.

A shiver chased itself up the curve of her spine and spiraled out from there. Thanks to the location and the open window—and despite the fireplace and her own inner heat—she was rarely warm in this place—her only complaint when it came to living with gargoyles. Actually, that wasn't true. She'd desperately missed her sisters.

Samael, meanwhile, stood at the window, broad back facing her. A watchful sentinel in the black of the moonless night. Her protector.

Not because he wants to be, she reminded herself. Because

the only emotion filtering through to her from the man was that of reluctance.

"You should sleep," Meira said quietly, the words floating in the air between them.

Other than turning his head slightly in her direction, he gave no other indication that he heard.

Typical macho shifter. "This is the best shot you're going to have at getting decent rest," she pointed out. "Carrick and all the others are out there. Nothing is getting in this place tonight."

Samael did turn to face her at that, only to lean his hips back against the windowsill, arms crossed, stretching Ladon's T-shirt and distracting her. A solid wall of man doubt. If anything, that holding back in his emotions strengthened as he gazed at her.

Irritation itched at her like chigger bites. After avoiding him all this time because of those emotions that he held in check, she shouldn't be annoyed that he held them back so hard. If anything, she should be grateful. So why wasn't she?

"*We* got in here," he pointed out.

Meira turned off her tablet and propped her head up on one hand to address him more upright. "Only because I have permission. Gargoyles hold a special magic that makes the place they guard impenetrable. When Carrick agreed to watch over me should the time come, he and my mother made a blood oath on my name. Otherwise, I would never have found this place again once I left."

Face in shadow, she could see enough by starlight to watch Samael's jaw work as he chewed over that information. "That's handy," he said. "How does one get a gargoyle to swear a blood oath like that?"

Good question.

Meira shrugged, the silk of her duvet rustling with the movement. Her turn to strap down strong feelings. A necessity when she thought of her mother. "We didn't even know Mama knew any gargoyles, and Carrick gives me a different answer every time I ask."

Samael ran a hand around the back of his neck. The first outward indication of stress she'd ever seen from the man. "I suppose it's not an option that gargoyles would want to be widely known?"

"I came to the same conclusion. Like the mob."

A pulse of amusement coming from Samael lit her up. Only not at her expense...more like he thought her cute. "I'm almost afraid to ask," he said. "But the mob?"

"You know. Secretive. It's all about who you know. But don't break that trust. I mean, where is Jimmy Hoffa, anyway?" Meira shifted in the bed and tried not to blink at how easy it was to talk to him. While she'd never call herself shy, she wasn't exactly a talker, either. Except, maybe, with her sisters.

Samael lowered his head. Was he smiling? Hard to tell in the darkness. "Makes sense."

A small part of her tension eased. Not everyone found her factoids interesting.

"Do I need to order you to come?" she asked. Then winced. That had way too many connotations that she hadn't meant.

"To bed," she tacked on. No. That was worse. Heat flared in her cheeks. "To sleep. Order you to come sleep."

His head snapped up. "You are not my queen yet. I only respond to orders from my king."

She frowned. Not, for once, because she'd apparently angered him, but because of his words. "You've called me your queen before," she pointed out. "And if I'm not, then why are you here?"

He said nothing, a wall of nothing.

"If I'm *not* your queen, and you are protecting me, in the eyes of your clan, that makes you a—"

"Traitor. Yes, I am well aware."

Oh gods. She'd done that to him. Any fool could see how important his role in his clan was to Samael. He lived to be the warrior he was. Now she'd stolen that from him. Guilt heaped on the piles she'd already collected today. "I'm sorry—"

"Don't." He levered off the windowsill and stalked around

the bed in that strangely silent way all black dragon shifters had.

Surprise skittered through her as he lay down on top of the duvet rather than getting between the sheets. Still, at least he'd decided to finally rest. Exhaustion dragged at her like grasping fingers pulling her into a grave. He had to be the same.

Samael folded his hands behind his head and stared at the canopy overhead, eyes glittering in the firelight. Gods, the man smelled incredible. Like smoke and sand—reminding her of heat.

Quit noticing.

Her body should definitely not be on high alert. His warmth, his size weighing down the mattress and rolling her slightly toward him. Rejection slapped at her, coming from both of them.

Sharing a bed had *not* been her idea.

Carrick was the one who had insisted they remain in the same room, though his reasoning had been to keep the two people they now guarded together for his own people's sake. However, Samael had agreed. Okay, not so much agreed as growled that he wasn't letting Meira out of his sight. Meira had tried to dismiss the warmth those words sent blooming through her as embarrassment.

Pushing aside the echo of that memory, she tried to remain focused on the practical, which was sharing a bed if they both wanted to get sleep this night.

Meira wiggled onto her side to face him more fully, wrestling with the sheets and covers to get comfortable and recapture a modicum of her warmth. "Is there anyone we should contact among your people?"

"No." He didn't turn his head.

No one? She found that difficult to believe. Perhaps he'd misheard the question. "I mean family, or friends maybe, who might be worried about you?"

"My family is dead." No emotion.

Given what he'd just said, she knew without a shadow of a doubt that he was holding back everything associated with that history. The continued wall of nothing but reluctance was like an invisible barrier between them.

Knowing exactly how badly losing family hurt, Meira couldn't help reaching across the space between them to put a hand on his arm above the leather gauntlets that never came off. "How old were you?"

He tensed beneath her touch. She hadn't missed that he always did, at least the few times she'd dared to make physical contact. But he didn't shake her off. "I had just reached my hundred and fiftieth year."

She did quick mental math. Given the rate at which dragon shifters aged, that would've put him around nineteen in human years, both physically and developmentally.

"They died in dragon fire."

She sucked in a gasp at the words. How could that be?

She wanted to ask a hundred questions but got the impression Samael would only share what he wanted. The fact that he offered up any information without her prompting she took as a positive sign. If they were going to figure all this out, find Gorgon and fix the rift, they needed to be able to work together.

When he didn't offer more, she cleared her throat. "I never knew my father, but I know what it's like to lose both parents." Meira had to stop and swallow down a grief still fresh. She forced images of her mother to leave her mind, focusing, instead, on Samael's pain. "I'm sorry you had to go through that."

He turned his head and searched her face. Still no emotions. Nothing to help her. Meira got the distinct impression that he was debating with himself. Perhaps the stiff way he held his mouth.

Her breath caught in her throat when he covered her hand with his own and squeezed. "It will get easier for you," he said. "The memories. For a long time, you won't want to think of your mother at all. Then one day when you do, it won't hurt so much. Eventually, you'll be able to think of her and smile."

This from a man who never smiled. At least not that he let her see. The unexpected offer of comfort unfurled inside her, wrapped around her. Gods above, she wanted to kiss him. Lean forward and steal that unexpected understanding from his lips.

Lips Meira could only describe as sensual, saving his face from harshness.

And more. All different sorts of kisses. A soft brush of her lips as a thank-you. A kiss that lingered, taking its time to weave a spell around them. Something hot and openmouthed that let her taste him and generated enough heat to scorch every part of her. She was already on fire.

Except she shouldn't be wanting this. Any of it.

More guilt. She'd suffocate under the heaps if she wasn't careful.

Meira slid her hand out from beneath his, the cold air of the room rushing against her palm making her shiver after the heat of his touch and her thoughts. "So...back to what I was asking. What about someone who could help us? Is there anyone like that we could get in touch with?"

Though his expression didn't change, she got the distinct impression he was scowling on the inside before he turned his head to stare up at the canopy again. "I need to let my beta know what's happening. He's in charge now. He'll decide what to do. Otherwise, I don't want to bring anyone else into this mess."

The man had a protective streak a fathom wide, it appeared. Which made her less special in his eyes, his watching over her coming from who he was, not who she was to him.

And I'm not disappointed that I'm not special. Even she didn't believe herself, the twinge plucking at her heart evidence enough.

"So, *do* you have any friends?" Curiosity prompted her to ask. Gods, why couldn't she shut up around him? This conversation was already a thousand words more than she usually shared with people.

Samael heaved a sigh with an edge to it and turned his head to face her again. "Do you always have this many questions?"

She offered him a prim look, lips pursed. "My lawyers say I don't have to answer that."

Samael gazed at her blankly, then turned his face back up.

"Was that you trying to be funny?"

"Did it work?" She bit her lip, waiting for his answer. Most people didn't get her sense of humor.

"That depends."

"On what?" she prompted when he didn't continue.

"Your intent. Were you genuinely trying to make me laugh? Or were you trying to change the subject?"

What if she was trying to flirt? Clearly failing miserably at it. Pathetic. Not to mention she was promised to another man who may or may not be dead. A fact that kept slipping her mind despite finding the king being the only reason she and Samael were together at this point.

"I guess I'm nervous." Now why had she gone and admitted that?

Rather than turn his head again, Samael shifted to his side to face her, his smoke and sand scent swirling around her, soothing her when she should've been bracing for whatever he was about to ask. His hand lay on the mattress beside hers. Not touching. What would he do if she hooked her little finger around his, as though he was her anchor?

Maybe he'd been right to want to avoid sharing the bed. This was too close, too intimate. Too damn confusing.

"Are you afraid of me?" he asked.

She should lie and say yes. Any person with an ounce of common sense would be wary of him. His danger evident in the simple way he moved—a prowling, rolling gait—screamed perilous predator.

Meira slowly shook her head. "No."

Nervous of giving her unfortunate thoughts away? Yes. Of the lash of his volatile emotions? The answer would have been yes before they'd come here. Now...

"You should be," he said, voice going rougher, harsher.

She gazed into a face devoid of emotion and yet sensed his urgency just the same. "Why would you say that?"

"You don't know me. Not truly. I'm as dangerous as they come."

Meira shook her head. "If you wanted to harm me, you would already have done it."

"I could be a spy. Getting you on your own, or getting you to reveal where you've been hiding, may have been my agenda all along. What if I have signaled others to come attack and now am waiting for them to arrive?"

Was that why he'd been watching out the window? She thought through his words and actions this entire day. No.

"You wouldn't." In truth, she'd been watching him closely for months. Watching everyone around her closely, as she always had done, even in childhood. Samael in particular, though. A morbid sort of fascination for a man whose emotions, if let loose, could flay her to the bone.

The leather of his gauntlets creaked, which told her he was making fists. A tell she had noticed a while ago. He didn't like having her trust? Why?

"What if *I* killed Gorgon?" he threw at her next.

Given their interactions, the loyalty Samael showed his king, Meira couldn't help the tiny laugh that punched from her at that. "You would never."

"No?"

He wanted her to doubt him for some unknown reason. "Why would you?"

"Why—" The word cut off as he gave a small growl that had her body coming fully online, only with awareness rather than fear, blood rushing to fill her veins with a fizzing sort of heat. What a sound...

"You've got to be kidding me," he snapped.

Before she could answer, he moved on top of her, faster than a lightning strike. He had her by the wrists, pinning her with his weight, mouth hovering over hers.

In the semidark, the flames in his eyes ignited, silver-tipped black, casting a strangely gray sort of light over them. Frozen above her, Samael seemed to drink her in, gaze moving to her lips, then down farther to her breasts, which pressed against him with each sharp intake of breath. That gaze feathered over her like a physical caress, skating across her skin, pressing, lingering...

"Why would I kill my king?" he demanded in a voice full of fire and smoky need. "Maybe I want to press my luck and see if the fates might have finally been kind and granted me a mate. A *phoenix*, no less."

A metaphorical devil—the ghosts of Skylars past, perhaps—prompted Meira to a bravery that usually escaped her, an act of sheer stupidity. "Why don't you try to claim me?"

Samael stopped breathing above her, and time hung trapped in the stars outside her window for a heartbeat. "Dammit, Meira."

In an instant, emotions reached for her, wrapped around her—anger and passion all mixed up and confusing. And compelling.

He lowered his head, and, with a burst of anticipation, she waited, breathless, for his kiss. Everything she'd imagined when she hadn't been able to stop herself, his lips demanding and hot and perfect as he plundered her own. Curiosity gave way to temporary insanity as her body took over from her mind. Meira was a jumble of impressions—heat infusing her skin, blood pulsing through her body, and intensity, heady and strong. The hard demand of his lips and yet how soft they were against hers, the flavor of him, subtle and dark against her tongue, and how with each press, each sweep of his mouth against hers, she craved...more.

"Ambrosia," he pulled back to whisper against her lips. "You taste like ambrosia."

Then he was kissing her again, laying claim to everything she was with the mere touch of his lips—frantic, desperate, and demanding. Emotions, vivid and unrecognizable, rose up inside her—from her, from him—and Meira whimpered with the force of them.

At the sound, Samael jerked back to gaze down at her, harsh breathing mingling with her own.

They stared at each other in the light cast by the fire

consuming his eyes and that coming from the fireplace. Then he flung himself off her to drop beside her on the bed. Once more, his anger and desire pelted her, except now a small, stupid part of her wanted it.

"See? I could have claimed you if I wanted, and you wouldn't have stopped me," he pointed out in that low growl of a voice, his dragon so near to the surface she expected Samael to shimmer with the transition any second.

A small part of her flinched inside. Was that how he saw her? Someone who didn't fight back? Who just endured whatever hardships life hurled at her and waited to be rescued?

That image stuck inside her, like a rock in her shoe. She didn't like it.

"Or died in my fire," Meira pointed out, stung by his words, his sudden rejection that left her colder than the stone gargoyles outside.

Samael shut his eyes, hiding the flames still dancing there and casting them both into more shadow. "One more dark mark against you as far as my clan is concerned."

Meira reached for her power, needing to shut down her emotions this time. Not his, because he'd already walled them back up. Cold. Remote.

Vincent chose that moment to leap in through her window, his hooves clacking on the stone flooring. With a happy sound, he jumped up between her and Samael and lay down, like a puppy. Gargoyles spent the long, cold nights in their stone form on the parapets of the castle, and Vincent preferred sleeping somewhere warmer. No doubt he'd missed her the last few months.

"Are you kidding me?" Samael muttered, only to get a cold nose in the armpit for the effort.

Meira, meanwhile, absently patted the goat's long, wiry fur. She had no idea what had just happened before Vincent showed up, but she did know Samael did nothing without a reason. "Why are you trying to scare me?"

He eyed her over the goat's head. "Because your trust is too easily given. You aren't scared enough."

Another laugh punched from her, this one, though, edged in disbelief.

Despite a kiss that had reached into her soul and touched the essence of who she was, this man didn't know her at all.

She rolled away from him, her back up against Vincent's warm, fuzzy body, and closed her eyes. "You're wrong," she said quietly. "I'm always afraid."

CHAPTER SEVEN

Samael stood before the massive, gilded mirror, currently reflecting his and Meira's forms in her bedroom in the gargoyle castle. "Are you certain of this?"

In the reflection, he slid his gaze to the woman standing beside him. The woman who had snored softly in his bed all night. Technically her bed. The woman whose scents of smoke and jasmine lingered on his skin still, leaving him aching and empty.

He'd woken to find her using his chest as a pillow, her bright curls spread across him in soft waves. He couldn't let himself think about the sweet blush that had stained her cheeks when he'd shifted positions and woken her. Or the way the innocent trust in her eyes darkened to embarrassment, not the wariness he'd expected, as she'd backed away. The ache would only get worse and his dragon louder.

Seven hells, that conversation last night. That kiss. The unexpectedness of it all. Of the way he'd opened up, even a little. But so had she. Of comfort given and taken. But also the frustration with her determination to look at the world—at him—through that innocent prism. Her trust might just get them both killed.

Speaking of which, how Meira had talked him into this latest plan, he wasn't entirely sure. She'd spent the entire morning on that tablet of hers, pulling up schematics and possible places the real Gorgon might have been taken, he discovered, using coded analytics to determine the most likely places and the highest probability of success to get him out of each.

Then she'd walked him through all of it systematically. The woman truly was an enigma, all logical calculations with her computers, a side of her he was only just now getting to see, but then she led with her heart in every other way. And he'd agreed to her suggested plan. As though he, like the rest of the world, just couldn't say no to her, and she happily wandered through life with that power in her pocket.

She met his gaze, and something flickered in those ever-changing eyes that he didn't catch. "With only one exception, no one has ever seen me in the mirrors when I didn't want them to."

He knew exactly the exception she was talking about. Him.

I'm the only one to have seen her?

Fuck. One more nail in his coffin, because the longer he spent with this woman, the more a certain knowledge settled deep within his core, bone-deep, soul true. Inside him, his dragon slashed his tail back and forth, impatient for Samael to act on what he knew.

But now was not the time. There might never be a time.

"That wasn't a slip on your part?" he asked, desperate for any alternate explanation.

"I don't think so."

"And you're sure about this?" he asked again, waving a hand at the mirror.

"I can't make any guarantees," she said slowly.

They had already spent a decent portion of the morning debating what their next steps should be. This was the best they could come up with.

They needed help.

"Right. Let's get it over with." Just in case, he dropped into a defensive stance, ready to unleash hell if needed. "Go ahead."

Meira dropped her gaze to Vincent, who was standing between them. "Go find Carrick," she told the goat.

Samael snorted. "Like he'd understand—"

Vincent trotted out the door.

Meira shot the black dragon shifter a shrug, then focused on what they were about to do. In an instant her fire flared over her body, the residual heat radiating out to him. The image staring back at them changed instantly to that of a different room. An empty room. In rapid succession moving quickly from space to space, Meira searched for her sisters throughout Ben Nevis. It didn't take long until she found Skylar, but that particular sister was surrounded. She stood in the main training area located in the hangar of the mountain with all her and Ladon's warriors, running through a series of physical exercises. Maul, lying in the back corner of the room, popped his head up.

"That's a good sign," Meira mumbled, more to herself than to him.

Yes, it was. "Skylar hasn't been ostracized by the Blue Clan yet."

Even through the wash of flame over her face, he still caught Meira's sideways glance in the mirror, though she didn't comment. They couldn't talk to Skylar with a crowd of witnesses, so Meira continued to change the locations she searched.

"Kasia is not here," Meira finally acknowledged, disappointment weighing the words. "She must've gone back to Store Skagastølstind with Brand. I'm searching for Angelika now."

Again, the picture changed. Flashing, flashing, flashing. Like strobes. "There. Got her."

Samael wasn't sure what Meira had seen in the reflection at that speed. Perhaps she could sense her sister's presence, because it took another few flashes before the image settled. It showed a smaller bedroom suite, the kind he recognized because he had grown up in a similar setup. Cramped, with fewer amenities and furnishings, meant for the common folk. He and his family had been happy in a suite like that. Right up to the end.

Only this place appeared as though bats have been living in it for decades—dirty and decrepit. He was fairly certain smells didn't come through the mirrors, but Samael swore the musty scent of bat guano permeated regardless.

An unremembered, unused section of the mountain, perhaps? This was where they had put the wolves? How were those shifters, with their overdeveloped sense of smell, standing to stay there?

"Where's your sister?"

Before she could answer, Maul suddenly appeared in the bedroom on the other side of the mirror. Samael was well aware of how the hellhound teleported. If he could see it, or knew what was on the other side, he could get there in short hops.

"Wait." Samael frowned. "He was just in the training room."

Maul's head whipped in the direction of the mirror Meira was using. With happy dog sound, he disappeared only to appear just as suddenly in the room with them.

"Oh my gods, Maul," Meira exclaimed, losing her hold on the mirror to whirl around and face the hellhound. "You can't be here."

The massive black dog that reeked of smoke and decay ignored her, instead bounding over, practically knocking Samael out of the way in his eagerness to get to Meira. With a chuckle, she wrapped her arms around the big dog.

"I thought this place was warded?" Samael asked.

Glowing red eyes turned his way, but he couldn't tell if Maul was glaring at him or just looking in the direction of his voice.

"I guess not from hellhounds." Her voice sounded from Maul's opposite side.

Meira peeped at him from under the hound's neck—the thing was as big as a Clydesdale. Bigger, probably. "Just for a moment," she seemed to be pleading with him. "He worries about us."

A hellhound protector. Gargoyles. Wolf shifters. Even rogue dragons. Serefina Amon, the girls' mother, must have been something.

"Carrick is going to lose his shit," Samael reminded her. He didn't also point out that they didn't have time for another of her strays.

"Right. Okay." Meira's hands dug deeper into the dog's spiky fur for a moment before she stepped away.

"Now Maul," she said, in a voice that he could tell she was

trying to make firm, and adorably failing. "You can't be here."

The dog woofed, more of that smoke and rotting scent filling the air. Then Meira shook her head. Maul communicated in telepathic images. What was he showing her?

"I have Samael," she said, with a nod in his direction. "He'll keep me safe."

Her faith set his protective instincts on high for all of two seconds before Maul looked directly at him. Then he showed him a series of images—first of Meira smiling and sweet, and then the tiniest scratch on skin drawing a single drop of blood, and then of Samael lying dead with a big dog bite in his chest.

Samael got the message. "I promise," he said. "Not even a scratch."

After a long, piercing stare, Maul turned his head to nudge Meira. She chuckled and then hugged him again. "I'll be safe, but I'll feel a lot better if I know you're watching over my sisters while I'm gone."

Another soft woof stirred her curls. Then Meira drew away and reignited. A second later, the mirror was showing the training room where Skylar was still working at Ladon's side. Giving her one last nuzzle, the hellhound disappeared, only to show up back in Ben Nevis.

Meira took a deep breath and glanced his way, giving him an apologetic little shrug. "He must like you."

After the image of his death by hellhound bite, Samael wasn't so sure. "What makes you say that?"

"He wouldn't have left me if he didn't."

Oh. The responsibility of her life, her safety, that already rested on his shoulders suddenly lightened in the strangest way. As though Maul's faith in him only confirmed who he was supposed to be to this woman. Protecting her was not his duty. It was his right.

"Angelika?" Her soft voice broke into his thoughts. She seemed to be asking permission to resume what they'd been doing.

He nodded. What else was he supposed to do?

Immediately the mirror image changed, back to that shabby

room. Two people were now inside. Immediately, Samael recognized the bright swath of Angelika's white hair—no doubt inherited from their white dragon shifter father. Amazing how each of the sisters was so starkly different from the others. He also was familiar with the tall, military-looking fellow who dogged Angelika's footsteps everywhere she went. Familiar in a way that one warrior sized up another, even if no immediate threat existed.

The man's name was Jedd, if Samael remembered correctly. "Can he see us—"

Meira opened her mouth to speak but paused and closed it silently. No doubt she had also picked up on her sister's distress. Angelika, her back to Jedd, pinched her eyes shut as if reaching for peace.

"I asked you a question," Jedd said. He put a hand on her arm and turned her to face him. "Will you mate me?"

"Holy shit," Meira exclaimed, then slapped both hands over her mouth.

Samael jerked his gaze from her to the two in the other room, but neither acted as though they'd heard. He wasn't sure if he was more stunned about that or by the fact that Meira had used a swear word.

Angelika shook her head. "I can't." The two simple words were laden with emotion. Guilt or regret, Samael couldn't tell which, since he didn't know her beyond her name.

A muscle at the corner of the wolf shifter's jaw twitched in a steady rhythm. "Because of some warped sense of belonging to those arrogant, asshole fire breathers?"

"To them?" Angelika shook her head, gaze earnest, her usual sunny smile missing. "No. To my sisters? Yes. To my family's legacy? Yes. To my murdered mother and father? Even more, yes."

"But you can't—"

She put a hand out, stopping him, white-blue eyes suddenly sparkling with the kind of optimism he was starting to associate with Meira, though hers was different, more serious. "I can't offer much, but I know I can make a difference. The gods blessed my mother with four daughters for a reason."

Jedd grasped her by the shoulders, dark eyes intent and pathetically hopeful. "You can do that as effectively at my side. You feel something for me. I know you do."

There was no mistaking the sadness in Angelika's gaze as she lifted her hands to frame his face. "You have become one of the most important people in my life. My best friend."

"Then why not—"

"Because that's *all* I feel for you. Friendship." Her words were quiet but firm.

Jedd's hope visibly died a quick, agonizing death. The wolf shifter's eyes darkened with pain even as his expression contorted with anger, turning ugly. "This isn't about me. It's about that dragon shifter. The white captive."

A jolt of shock ricocheted through Samael. Only one man inside Ben Nevis fit that description. Airk Azdajah. The man who'd come back with Skylar from Everest after she'd escaped. Who'd been caged and held by Pytheios most of his life.

An aura hung about the man, a knife's edge of danger. Granted, he'd been the son of Meira's father's beta, which meant royalty did run through his veins. In fact, other than the phoenix women themselves, he should be the one on the White Clan's throne by right. That said, Samael didn't think Airk could ever shift, not after so long without. His animal would go mad, was probably already there. No dragon shifter would follow a man who couldn't lead them in the sky.

Angelika smiled, kindness and sadness both mingling there, seeming undaunted. "I don't know what part he has to play yet."

Jedd paced the room. "I've seen the way you watch him. Like you're studying him. I guess it makes sense in a warped way. Another phoenix mated to another dragon shifter, and four out of six clans with one of the Amon sisters at the helm if you put him on the throne. No way will the other two clans stand against you after that."

Angelika dropped her hands to her sides, though Samael could see in her expression that she was still hoping Jedd would come to understand. "It's not about our family ruling all the clans, Jedd. It's about taking out the man who destroyed things in the first place."

Jed whirled on her, urgency in the taut line of his shoulders. "That's not fate. It's politics and strategy."

She shook her head.

The wolf shifter studied Angelika's face, and what he saw there must've convinced him. His head dropped forward, a sign of total defeat. If he'd been in his wolf form, he might've dropped to his belly, nosing at her ankles.

Then he pulled his lips back, baring his teeth in a wolfy way. "If you think I'm going to stand by and watch you make the biggest mistake of both our lives, then you aren't the woman I thought you were."

Jedd prowled from the room, though he closed the door behind him with a quiet click at odds with the anger vibrating around him.

At the sound, Angelika sighed, then slowly lowered herself to sit on the chest at the footboard of the bed. "That could have gone better," she murmured to herself.

"Angelika," Meira called softly.

Her sister stilled, obviously listening.

"In the mirror, baby sister."

Angelika's head snapped around, and she gasped as she looked directly at them. She jumped to her feet and rushed to the mirror, flattening her hands on the surface. From their side it appeared as though they were talking to her through a sheet of glass, her skin smashing up against it.

"Let me through," Angelica practically begged, pushing at the reflective surface.

Meira shook her head. "I can't."

"Where are you?"

"You know where."

Samael lifted his eyebrows. So, she *had* told her sisters where she'd been hiding. Just not Gorgon, her intended mate. What kind of trust did that show? Though, now he knew why. She was protecting the gargoyles. This phoenix apparently couldn't resist the urge to protect any and everyone around her.

"What do you need?" Angelika asked. The sisters showed no questioning or hesitation with each other. Though, surviving for centuries with only them and their mother, he wasn't all that surprised.

"Get Skylar and Ladon and bring them back here. I wish Kasia could be here, too, but that would draw too much attention. Meet in thirty minutes."

Serafina Amon had trained her daughters well. Angelika didn't quibble or question. She merely hurried out of the room even as Meira shut off her own fire then turned to face him. "That's my backup. Now for yours."

This next part was trickier. As part of her analytical walk-through of options, she had convinced him that rather than just his beta being informed, the only way to get his people on their side was to appeal to the entire Black Clan. Two people searching for the king could only get so far.

But if they were going to address everyone, they couldn't do it from here. Not when they had made a promise to the gargoyles. Especially not after Maul had breached that edict.

"Let's go."

Meira's fire crackled beside him, casting a pleasant glow around the cool castle room. Different from his black fire, which both illuminated a space even as it stole the light directly around it. Would her fire change once she was fully mated to a black dragon?

Again, the mirror in front of them changed, showing a new reflection this time. Samael studied the image, which was warped and curved, as though he was peering through a prism or maybe a crystal ball. The curving made it difficult to see exactly what lay beyond. Blobs of white and green and blue. A house, maybe?

"This might be a tight squeeze," she warned. "I'd go through one of the bathroom mirrors, but I'm not sure what we'll find there, so I'm trying something else. I'll go first."

"Wait." Without thinking, Samael shot out a hand and grabbed her arm.

Just as fast he yanked his hand away as realization struck that he was touching her fire. Then he paused, lifting that same hand to hold it in front of his face, watching in silent fascination as the flames he'd taken away with him danced across his skin with no impact. No burning. Then, the tip of one licking red flame turned black, then another, and another, until the fire had become his own.

Samael lowered his hand slowly, his focus moving to the woman standing in front of him, watching in wide-eyed silence.

Her mouth parted, and he startled as it hit him that she knew, too. Or at least suspected.

Meira Amon was his fated mate.

In the worst possible moment, all he wanted to do was ask her if he was right.

"That wasn't the smartest move," she murmured.

"I'm well aware." In more ways than one. More ways than she probably realized herself, which was either a blessing or a curse.

Through sheer will, he tipped his head at the image still displayed in the mirror. "Where are you taking us?"

When they'd discussed this earlier, she'd only said far away. Somewhere in the colonies not close to any dragon settlements. Somewhere safe.

She turned her head to stare at it, too, emotions playing across her features in swift array. He didn't catch them all, but the one that was unmistakable was an anguish-laden dread.

"Home," she said softly. And stepped into the mirror.

A dread of his own dropped boulders into Samael's stomach, trying to drag him down as he watched helplessly from his side. Meira's form twisted and warped until she appeared to drop out of the other side, but she was tiny from his perspective. From what he could tell, she got to her feet, dusted herself off, then her hand appeared through the center of the image on his side.

"Watch out for the last drop." Her voice sounded as though she was speaking through water, muffled and slurred. "It's a doozy."

She'd doused the flames on that part of her body despite what just happened. He grasped her hand, soft but still warm from her fire against his, and had to fight his mind and the crazy idea looming larger by the second. His dragon side wanted to curl around her. This time, instead of the sensation of walking through water and a doorway, his field of vision shrank and narrowed, like walking through a circular tunnel. Good thing he didn't suffer from claustrophobia.

"Jump," her muffled voice commanded.

Into what? All he could see was a smaller bent image of her in a field, blue sky behind her, and blackness around the edges. Nothing.

"Trust me," she called.

Samael jumped.

The world hurtled toward him, the same way the earth did when he tucked his wings in tight and dropped straight down, rushing up at him with each passing millisecond. His feet hit solid ground and his body hit Meira, tumbling them both to the ground. Samael didn't have time to flip so that he took the brunt of the impact, but he did manage to get a hand under her head.

The world solidified to the right size half a second later, and he found himself nose to nose with her, gazing into eyes slowly turning whiter.

My mate.

Immediately, his body stirred to the feel of her under him, her soft hair against his hand, her scent filling his lungs.

But gods above, she smelled amazing. "You smell…"

He cut himself off before he could say the wrong thing. Like how she smelled of heaven and ambrosia.

Wariness gazed back at him. "I do?" She wrinkled her nose as he left the sentence hanging.

"Not bad, just…" He stared at her dumbly, even as a voice in the back of his head told him to get up. Get off her. "My mother used to grow vines of jasmine in our cave using a system of trellises and aiming the mirrored lighting at the plants, filling our home with the scent when they bloomed."

Meira tipped her head, her silky hair winding more around the fingers still cradling the back of her skull. She searched his face and almost seemed to relax beneath him, wariness peeling away, leaving curiosity. "Why?"

Didn't the woman have *any* self-preservation instincts? She shouldn't be lying beneath a dragon. One quickly becoming aroused, his hard length pressing into her belly.

I should stand up. Move away.

He didn't, and she watched him with that gaze that was a combination of curious and assessing and waited for an answer.

Samael shrugged. "She'd said it reminded her of the family and life she'd willingly left behind."

"I can't imagine being a human dragon mate," she murmured. "To have to leave behind everything you know. Everything you thought you were."

"For love the fates have bound together since the time of your birth." He couldn't help the way his gaze dropped to her lips.

He knew how she tasted now, and the taste was becoming a craving. A fire in his belly.

Again, she wrinkled her nose. "I've always wondered if those stories are made up to influence those same human women into believing they have no choice."

"I believe the bursting-into-fire thing makes them believe that," he said drily.

"So, you'd have no trouble taking a reluctant mate?"

Was she trying to relay some sort of subtle message? Or was she really lying here beneath him debating this? With Meira, he suspected the latter.

He toyed with the soft strands of her hair, letting the tresses slide through his fingers. "I don't think it's like that. I think a dragon shifter's need to protect his fated mate, at all costs, would keep him from hurting her in any way. It would make him not only want to make her happy… It would be a…compulsion."

That's what he'd seen with his own parents. His grandparents, too. Every mated pair in his clan, come to think of it.

It's what he felt for her.

Meira smiled slowly, though her eyes reflected a sadness that ran as deep and dark as an underground river. She lifted a hand and whispered her fingertips over his jaw, that damn curiosity in her eyes growing, but at the same time, clear to him that she wasn't really aware of her actions, just following a compulsion. "I hope that's true. I never got to see it with my own parents."

The sudden impulse to chase that sadness from Meira's eyes about blindsided him, and he did his best to take every emotion he was feeling and shove it into a box in his mind.

Now's not the time, jackass.

Forcing himself to unwind her hair from his fist, he pushed to his feet and offered her a hand, helping her up.

"Where are we again?" She'd said home, but whose? He looked around them at the new location. "And what the hell did we come through?"

Turning, he discovered a silver orb set atop a pedestal. Some sort of seeing-eye object? Perhaps a magical ward?

"We came through lawn art." Meira's voice held a not-so-secret laugh.

"Lawn art," Samael echoed slowly.

A choked sound had him jerking around to find her holding back laughter, a hand covering her mouth. At his raised brows, she lowered her hand to reveal a full grin, and the dimples that had him clenching against the urge to tumble her back under him.

"Lawn art is something humans do in parts of the world. Decorations in their yard. Only I think Mother put it there on purpose—"

The twinkle in her eyes doused like a candle snuffed out by a sudden gust of wind, her smile a falling star, fading away to nothing.

"Oh gods," she whimpered. "Mama."

Then she turned away and, almost like a wraith walking a graveyard, pushed through a gate in the metal fencing that appeared to be constructed of some kind of ineffective chain mail, and moved through the tall, spring-green grasses beyond.

Keeping his mouth shut as well as his distance, Samael followed until they reached a spot near a charred tree, the blackened bark reaching into the blue sky in spikes. The ground here was equally green, but beneath, he could see the evidence of fire. He could also detect the distinctive scent on the air, though faint now.

In the middle of that healing scorched earth, a bloom of flowers lay hidden among the taller grasses. Many different kinds. A burst of color, vibrant and glorious.

Meira dropped to her knees, still silent. She sat that way long enough that Samael debated reminding her that she'd given her sister only thirty minutes to meet. Then she reached out and used her hands to dig beneath the flowers, her actions growing more frantic.

"She's not here," she said in a voice so low he knew she wasn't talking to him.

He didn't have to ask who. Meira had said home, and now he knew what that meant. Her home...with her mother. Their last home. Underlying the smoky scent of fire was a sweeter scent. Kasia smelled of chocolate. Skylar of cinnamon. Meira of jasmine. But here, that layer of ambrosia smelled of honey.

A phoenix had died here.

"She's not here," Meira repeated, louder, distress tightening the words.

Samael dropped to a squat beside her. "What do you mean?"

"There should be...more of her. Ashes." She raised her head, her expression one of such hopelessness, even as her eyes implored him to fix this. "He *took* her."

Seven hells. What purpose could Pytheios possibly have with Serefina Amon's ashes, other than a need to disturb her final rest or hurt her daughters?

Meira was holding herself so carefully still, he worried she might shatter if a strong breeze touched her. The hell with others waiting for them. Unable to stop himself, he pulled her against him, cradling her head. "We'll find where he has put her. I swear it."

After a beat, she leaned into him, muscles relaxing. Comfort given and received in a hushed silence. Only the earth made noise—a soft wind stirring the grass to rustle around them, the sweet chirping of birds in a nearby tree. The sunlight wasn't as intense as it could be where he came from, but his dark hair warmed on his scalp as they sat together.

She stirred against him and pulled back, then laid a hand against his cheek, and Samael's heart derailed like a train blown off the tracks. "You're a good man, Samael Veles."

"We need to work on your sense of self-preservation."

She moved to place her fingers over his lips, stopping his knee-jerk denial. "You *are* a good man," she insisted in a stronger voice. "But don't make promises you can't keep. We may never find her."

With that, she pulled from his grasp and stood—fragile and yet incredibly strong at the same time. Like the flowers over where her mother had passed to the next life.

"Angelika and Skylar will worry if we're late." She walked away, back through the gate. Now that he wasn't looking at it from through the curvature of the lawn ornament orb, he could see clearly a small wooden structure with dirty windows, missing tiles on the roof, and the back screen door off the hinges.

At the back door, she paused and flipped open a small piece of wood in the doorframe. Frowning, Samael watched as she pulled out her tablet and connected it to the socket exposed underneath. Quickly, fingers flying over the screen, she set to work.

"What are you doing?" he asked.

Meira didn't lift her head or stop what she was doing. "Checking the security system."

The security? His brows lowered farther. "That's not like any system I've ever seen."

Her lips tipped in a soft smile even as she continued to peck at the tablet in her hands, concentration focused, utterly in her element. Confident, unhesitating, and utterly in charge. As though he was getting a glimpse of the real Meira. "I installed this custom setup myself. We were pretending to be poor waitresses. We couldn't have a state-of-the-art system visible—both for the humans and for any supernatural creature that came snooping."

"How custom?"

She shrugged. "A fully integrated alarm system with video and infrared cameras, motion sensors, footstep detectors, and, instead of a command center, a hidden panel in each room to allow us to monitor and arm the house as needed. Outdoor sensors with a half-mile range. A protective blast film applied to the windows. Keyless biometric authentication both for entry and the system. That kind of thing."

The way she rattled off the list had him staring.

She glanced up, eyebrows raised. "What?"

"What else do you do with these...skills?"

"Nothing too crazy. Doctored our paperwork to hide our aging. Moved our money around in different accounts." Her lips twitched. "Mother told me to stay out of anything dragon related, in case they traced it back to me, but I had...monitors on your tech."

He crossed his arms. "Uh-huh. What's the shadiest thing you've ever done?"

She thought for a minute, brows knit. Then brightened. "I might have sent Pytheios to Antarctica on a wild goose chase for us."

She paused, her attention pulled back to her device, watching closely as a series of videos danced across the screen. "Oh dear," she sighed. Then hit another series of keystrokes. "I'm shutting it down now. We won't need it again."

So saying, the door sudden clicked, the bolt sliding back. Then her screen went blank. She folded it into its casing and tucked it away in the leg pocket she stored it in. Then let herself into the house.

"This was your home?" he asked as he followed her inside. Then jerked to a halt at the sight that greeted him.

The door led into a small galley kitchen with yellowing linoleum countertops and faded wallpaper sporting what must have once been bright-blue flowers. The place had obviously been ransacked. Broken dishes strewn throughout. Every cabinet and drawer gaping wide-open.

Meira sighed. "Yes. The last one, at least. We lived here a few decades. After pretending to go through school—again." She made a face. "We all worked as waitresses at a diner not far from here."

The irony in her voice when it came to schooling wasn't missed. Repeating basic human schooling must've been torture. He didn't see her handling boredom happily. Quietly, maybe, but definitely not happily.

"This way," she said.

Indoors, the house was stuffy and warm, with a lack of moving air in an unlived-in, abandoned way. They passed through a small living space with couches that buckled in the center sitting on thick brown carpeting, all also ripped to shreds. Knives, he guessed. Not dragon claws, or the roof would've been ripped off.

A small squawk of sound reached his ears. Some kind of rodent in the walls, at a guess. Samael ignored it. They walked down a hallway past a series of smaller bedrooms. Each one he passed sported a single twin-size bed and basic dresser and desk. Nothing more. Once again, these rooms appeared as though a large predator had slammed through, ransacking the place. No doubt in search of any clue as to where the phoenix might have gone.

What would they have thought when they found multiple beds? That more than one phoenix existed at all was nothing short of miraculous, leaving an unending list of unanswered questions when it came to their legend and lore.

Samael paused at one bedroom with what appeared to be computer parts, though no computer. "Was this your room?" he called after Meira's retreating form.

"Yes," she answered over her shoulder, not stopping.

"Don't you want to pack up some clothes or go through drawers for keepsakes?"

Meira paused in a doorway several down. "No. He already took anything of value."

"He?"

"Pytheios. The video showed him going through the house." She shrugged, but he got the impression that she was holding herself together by sheer will. "We weren't allowed keepsakes, anyway."

Nothing? Not a single thing to remember her life by? Remember her mother by? "And I thought I had a rough childhood," Samael mumbled to himself.

Another tiny sound from one of the rooms down the hall, and Samael held in a sigh because now he recognized it. At the same time, a glint of glass catching sunlight streaming through the window snagged his attention, and he stepped inside to inspect it more closely. Caught in the thick carpeting, the same ugly brown as the rest of the house, was a silver ring with a small, polished gem of orange amber.

Not wanting to upset Meira more, Samael slipped it in one of the pockets of his borrowed pants. He'd give it to her another time.

Still following her lead, they made their way to a slightly larger room. Their mother's room, no doubt. Meira had stopped before a tall free-standing mirror.

"Here. By me." She pointed and he took up his position.

"Are you ready—" She paused and cocked her head, listening.

Samael had already caught the small sound again, much closer now, and grimaced.

"What was that?" she asked.

"Nothing."

"I know you heard that."

"We don't have time."

That only got him a narrow-eyed scowl.

Samael sighed. "Under the bed."

Meira dropped to her hands and knees, colorful hair spreading out on the brown carpet as she looked underneath.

"Oh, baby," she cooed. Then slowly reached out, carefully and gently lifting something out from under the mattress.

A tiny, scruffy, skin-and-bones kitten. Difficult to tell its color under mud-matted fur. "You were just going to leave her here?"

Samael gritted his teeth against both her judgment and the guilt that she seemed to so easily elicit in him. "Cats are resilient."

She held up the scrawny body and he—hardened dragon shifter warrior that he was—flinched inwardly. "Obviously not," she said, still accusing.

Dragons might have protective instincts, but they had nothing on this woman. She collected strays wherever she went, it appeared. "What are we going to do with it while we track down Pytheios?"

That stubborn chin popped in the air. "Find it a home."

Samael ran a hand over his face. Why was he not surprised? "At least put it on the floor out of sight while we do this thing."

She pursed her lips but moved to stand beside him and settled the mite at their feet. For its part, the kitten stayed right where she set it. Out of fear or the recognition of a savior, Samael wasn't sure.

At least I'm not the only one who does her bidding so easily.

Standing up, Meira looked at him. "Okay. Ready now?"

This was a horrible idea, but Samael honestly couldn't see any other way. Meira was right. Secrets were Pytheios's weapon. The only way to combat secrets and rumors was with the truth, even if it meant screaming into the storm.

"Are you sure you can do this?" he asked.

Appearing in every mirror in Ararat, a mountain she'd yet to set foot in, to deliver their message would stretch anyone with this rare ability, it seemed to Samael. Young dragons didn't attempt to blow fire for the first year or two after they learned to shift. Meira had only been a phoenix for two years. Not even. And most of those were spent cooped up with gargoyles.

"We should stick to the plan. My calculations showed a high probability of success if we have more help."

"That's not what I meant." He was talking about her powers, and she knew that.

Meira grimaced. "I've never tried something this big. We might have to do it in phases."

That wouldn't be as effective as Pytheios's display. Still, it would prove she had power to those starting to doubt. What kind of power was a different story. Likely she'd be called a witch by the naysayers of the clan. Or, as Samael privately thought of them, the bitchers and complainers who apparently had nothing better to do in life than drag others down and see everything in a negative light. Humans weren't the only breed with skeptics.

"No turning back now." Meira closed her eyes, and the flames he was becoming intimately familiar with flowed from her skin in rivers of gold and red until she stood ablaze before the mirror.

CHAPTER EIGHT

I can't do this.

The plan was to reach every mirror in Ararat to address as many of the Black Clan dragons as she could in one shot. Pytheios's floating flame trick at her mating ceremony had given her the idea.

But this was... After the first ten or so, with each mirror she reached, a shard of pain split through her mind, as though the mirrors were splitting her with each new reflection. Like she had to donate a part of her soul to gain that reflection. Was this what Kasia had gone through with her own migraines with each vision before she'd mated?

"Meira?" Samael's voice came at her from a hundred different directions.

She slapped her hands over her ears, closing her eyes, even as she tried not to lose the connections she'd already made.

"Talk to me, Meira. What's happening?" Urgency underlined the dark tones of his voice and hovered around her own emotions. As well as command, the captain of a king's guard showing through.

"It's...too much," she said.

"Stop."

Vaguely she was conscious of the squeak of the kitten as he swung in front of her, trying to force her to open her eyes and look at him, hands on her arms, steadying and compelling at the same time.

"Stop, Mir." If she hadn't been fixated on the pain and the power, she might've paid more attention to his use of her childhood nickname her sisters sometimes still used and the slight tinge of panic brushing against her emotions.

Samael didn't panic. She knew him well enough to know that for certain.

"No," she mumbled. "I *can* do this."

Silence greeted that. Had he heard?

"What do you need?" he finally asked in a voice gone dragon.

Her mind managed to break away from the pain enough to latch on to that question. What did she need? More of herself? No, that didn't make sense given how she'd done this on a smaller scale. She wasn't splitting her soul to teleport the way she did, no matter what this felt like.

So, what was she doing?

"Fire." She wasn't sure if she said the word aloud. Didn't matter. She needed more fire. More power. Maybe if she could get to her sisters—

Suddenly the searing agony in her mind eased under an unexpected onslaught of heat. Perhaps merely thinking of her fire had stoked the inferno inside her? The hundreds of connection points grew less painful with each passing moment until she was able to drop her hands and open her eyes.

Oh. My. Heavens.

The fire wasn't coming from her, but from Samael. He stood before her, ablaze in flames of pure black sparking silver at the tips.

Living, dancing, beautiful death.

Eyes consumed by the inferno, he focused solely on her in a way that turned her insides liquid, melting her, feeding her his fire, turning her own red-gold flames blacker with each passing second, as if his power consumed hers.

A gasp threatened to escape her, but Samael covered her mouth with his hand. "Let's not risk my fire getting inside you."

In other words, let's not risk an accidental mating, if such a thing was possible without the sex.

A shard of hurt, not from the use of her powers, embedded in her chest. Why? Because he didn't want to mate her? Why would he? She belonged to his king. No matter what she'd thought she'd seen in his eyes earlier.

Even so, she couldn't rid herself of the sensation it left inside her. Emptiness. Like the time they'd had to abandon their home and her mother made her leave her favorite toy behind.

Abandoned.

"Is it working?"

His question jerked her back to the task at hand. *Gods, what am I doing?* She forced her concentration to her powers alone and the task she'd set herself to complete. "I think so."

All those connections sliced and pulled at her. A glance over his shoulder showed her tiny images across the mirror, like a thousand picture-in-picture screens. Concentrating, Meira used the power coursing through her, making her fingertips tingle. The points of connection came easier now, as though she simply had to sift through the mountain to find each one and add it to her display.

"I've got them all," she said when she could feel no more within the mountain.

Even through the flames she could see his eyebrows go up. "*All* of them?"

"Yes, but let's not test how long we can do this." She waved at him to step to her side.

The kitten weaved around his feet but remained close. Once he stood beside her, she took a deep breath and made it so those on the other end of the connections could see. Gods knew what the clan would think about Samael feeding her his fire like this, but they'd have to risk it.

Now for the worst part. Public speaking.

"Dragon shifters of the Black Clan," Samael boomed beside her.

In the tiny reflections, those who already hadn't turned to look did so now, expressions reflecting a hundred different reactions—

mistrust, hate, curiosity, horror, hope. No sense of emotions bombarded her though, not through the reflection. At least she didn't have that extra chaos to contend with.

Meira held on to the hope.

"You know me. I am Samael Veles. You have heard from Pytheios, the false High King," Samael continued. "Now it's our *queen's* turn."

Shouts rose from the mirror. "She is not our queen," they said, or various versions of the same.

Meira held on to the solid determination radiating from the man at her side and put on that mask of confidence she'd known she'd have to wear the day she offered to mate a king. She tipped up her chin the way she'd seen Kasia and Skylar do a thousand times. "Your king still lives."

"Liar!" came the louder response from the collective.

She hid a flinch. "The man who died in my fire was a red dragon bewitched to look like Gorgon. We are searching for our king now."

Those who fell among the angrier of the clan continued to shout, but others quieted, listening. She said the words Sam had told her to use.

"Gorgon's most loyal protector stands at my side. Gorgon is my mate in words, and when I find him, we will be mated in deed."

She tried not to pay attention to the doubts wanting to take the strength of conviction away from that declaration. Or the sudden fracture of denial coming from the man at her side.

"Pytheios claims to have a phoenix, and he may have. That does not mean my sisters and I are not also phoenixes. I want only peace for both my phoenix family and for my new dragon family. Will you help me?"

He'd warned her not to beg, not to ask, but to command. But the question slipped from her lips naturally.

Deciding not to take them back, she let the words drop into what had become a void of silence and blank faces.

Beside her Samael stood unnervingly still, shoulders held back, all warrior. "I will stand by our queen as King Gorgon would want," he said. "He would want you to do so as well."

They gave it another few moments to sink in.

"If you have any information, or wish to help us in this search," Meira said, "please get in touch with the Blue or Gold Clans. My sisters will know how to reach us at all times."

Defeat stared at her from a thousand reflections, clawing at her. This wasn't working. She still wasn't getting through to most of them. The hostility reflected at her, despite the mirrors blocking her empathic powers, faces bearing scowls or narrow-eyed suspicion or outright hatred, told her so.

Meira swallowed and stepped forward, though Samael held on to her hand. Forget not begging. It might be beneath dragons, but it wasn't beneath her. "Please. Gorgon has been honorable and nothing but a friend. For his sake, please help me."

A blast of sound boomed overhead, the reverberations of it hitting her like a physical punch, and the house shook with the impact. Something massive had struck, knocking the ceiling fan to the floor, the popcorn ceiling shaking loose and cascading over them in a fall of white.

In the same instant, Samael tackled her to the floor, covering her with his body. He grunted as the ceiling fan broke free and landed on his back before falling into the mirror and shattering the glass.

Meira lost her connections, her fire extinguished by a fear that stole her breath and her mind. Pytheios.

"He's come for me." The child who'd always lived in terror, never fully gone even as she'd grown into a woman, whimpered. With grasping hands, she practically tried to burrow into Samael's chest.

"It's not Pytheios."

Panic tossed reason out the window as she scrambled against him, shaking so hard her teeth rattled in her head. "He's going to kill you and try to mate me and—"

Samael shook her by the arms. "It's not Pytheios."

"What?"

"By the scent, I'd say gold dragon. Waiting for you or one of your sisters to show would be my guess."

Samael's total calm reached to an answering part deep inside her, like a balm, a rock on the rapids she could cling to. With a deep, shuddering breath, she lifted her head, focusing on his eyes, his gaze intent and steady. "We need to get out of here," she said.

"I agree—"

The house howled and splintered as the creature outside ripped the roof off faster than a Kansas twister.

Samael was on his feet, the floating mirage of his shift eddying around his form before the roof had even cracked. Instinct kicked in, and Meira lit her fire and jumped to her feet.

"Let's go!" She grabbed him by the hand before he could finish his shift and dragged him away. She jerked to a stop as he lunged for the kitten, scooping it into one big hand. Then, without question, he ran after her into her mother's bathroom and through the mirror hanging on the back of the door. They emerged in a cavern that reminded her of Ben Nevis.

A hangar of sorts, with a gaping hole open to blue skies and mountain peaks beyond. Only no dragon-steel door to shut out the world and protect them.

The roar that followed them had Meira spinning back to what they'd come through, a glass partition separating the hangar from another room—no doubt a control room of sorts. Abandoned and dark. With a yelp as a golden eye peered at her through the reflection, Meira shut off her powers, the fire leaching from her skin in an instant.

The fear didn't disappear with the flames, though, even as she gaped at the glass and the room beyond. She grabbed for Samael, only to have him shove the kitten in her hands and back away.

"Stay there," he warned, backing away into the center of what appeared to be a massive foyer. His body continued to shimmer and waver with signs of an oncoming shift.

"What are you doing?" she called, though she remained where

she against the wall, with no place else to go.

"My dragon is already close to the surface with you," Samael called back. He glittered with obsidian scales, his body warping and stretching to accommodate his larger size. "That was...too much—"

He threw his head back on a primal roar that made the glass beside her ripple. Holding still, as though he were a T. rex and wouldn't see her if she did, Meira waited out the rest of his shift. An incredible process as human features broadened and lengthened, vicious spikes emerged along his back, and a tail whipped out behind him. Finally, wings unfurled thirty-five feet on either side of him.

Black dragons were sleeker than blue or gold dragons, everything about them built for stealth—wings attaching differently, spikes lying flat differently. Even their scales were smaller and layered so that they could seal up, cutting wind resistance.

Samael, in full dragon form, was the most brutally magnificent creature she'd ever beheld.

The dragon fell to his forefeet in total silence and craned his neck to size her up from a single massive eye on one side of his head.

Meira watched him closely. In theory, this was still Samael. Her mind knew he wouldn't hurt her. The reality was a different experience. "You're not going to use me as a human toothpick or anything, right?"

She wasn't entirely sure the question was teasing, either.

She didn't have time to process shock as he plucked her from the spot she stood with claws she was fully aware could rend her into tiny pieces. He gently placed her on the ground, then curled around her in a circle, going so far as to drape a single wing overhead while his snout ended up directly in front of her. Warmth cocooned her from every direction.

He's protecting me.

Slowly, Meira reached out and ran a hand over one of the scales, fascinated by the glasslike appearance. Obsidian, yet strangely softer.

He growled at her touch, though the sound was more of a purr.

"I'm safe," she said quietly.

At least, she hoped she was. She still wasn't sure exactly where she'd brought them.

• • •

I t took a while—the protectiveness his dragon side held toward Meira meant it didn't want to cede control to the weaker human side—but Samael managed to wrest it back. That was the closest he'd ever come to losing himself to the animal. Even his first shift had gone smoother.

Meira watched in silence until he finished his shift. Then her eyebrows rose slowly. "I was worried I was about to be a snack earlier."

"I would never hurt you." The words left his mouth before he thought about them.

"I know."

"How do you know that?" He could have killed her.

"Call it instinct." She glanced away, pulling into herself and away from him.

Instinct. Right. Did she know what she was admitting? That instinct drove her to a faith in him that was beyond reason. Couldn't she see the danger of trusting that or, worse, what that might mean?

Samael lifted one hand then dropped it back to his side before she saw. Now wasn't the time or place to discuss it. "Where did you bring us?"

"I don't know." Her expression turned so rueful, if his own protective instincts weren't screaming at him, he'd have laughed.

Instead, he glanced around, dread sinking through his bones. This was a dragon mountain, no doubt about it.

The natural caverns had been hollowed out more. Though slightly smaller, the space was like the training area in Ben Nevis and Ararat with its tall ceilings and flat floor, obviously created for the purpose of easy landings, an entrance large enough for a 747 to fly through. Or one extra-large dragon. At least one hallway no doubt led deeper into the mountain, though several doors were placed along the walls.

"Do you have a guess at least?" he asked.

"I would love to hear this myself," a familiar male voice sounded from behind him.

Pissed his focus on Meira had allowed anyone to come close without his knowledge, Samael swung around with a snarl that he cut off midsound as soon as he saw the owner of the voice. "Rune?"

"What the hell are you doing here, Veles?"

"Rune?" Meira asked, breaking into what was already heading toward an awkward reunion as she glanced back and forth between them. "Rune Abaddon?"

Now how the fuck did she know that name?

Dark eyes not unlike his own slid to the woman at Samael's side, glittering with a hard sort of curiosity, and Samael had to stop himself from stepping between them. "You know me?" Rune asked.

"My name is Meira Amon."

The black dragon shifter who'd been labeled a traitor for years narrowed his eyes and said nothing.

"You helped my sister Skylar." Meira started forward, but Samael stepped in front of her. Only to get smacked on the shoulder for the effort. "Stop that. He's not going to hurt me. My mother trusted him."

The fact that she dared to hit him, even just that tiny tap, made him pause, but it was her words that pulled him up sharply. "Trusted *him*?"

Meira's eyes narrowed, turning icy white. "Why the disbelief?" she asked, voice uncharacteristically cool.

"Because I know this man better than you do." Once a reliable member of his clan, a respected warrior, Rune had gone rogue and had been stealing mates for a decade, at least.

"Obviously not anymore," Rune said drily.

Rather than question him, though, Meira shot Rune a glance filling quickly with doubts. "How do you know him?" she asked Samael slowly.

A show of faith. In him. Despite her mother's trust and her sister's situation, whatever that had been.

"Rune was captain of the guard when I first joined. Before he left to become an enforcer, upholding the laws of the clans in the Americas colonies."

"He was a scrawny rookie with more brains than brawn last time I saw him," Rune commented, his calculating gaze turning wryly amused.

Samael cursed his luck. Of all the dragon shifters in the world, she brought them to this one.

Meira's white-blue eyes darkened, her brows drawing down in a slight frown as she gave the man an unimpressed stare that would give his old mentor a run for his surly money. "Clearly you don't know him now, either," she pointed out, about as irritated as Samael had ever heard her get.

Then her eyes flared wide and she flicked a quick glance at Samael, and he had to tamp down on a ridiculous grin because he could easily read her thoughts. Where had that outspoken side of her come from? The woman he'd been around the last three months would never have spoken back to Rune that way.

For him.

His phoenix was changing, finding her own voice, almost before his very eyes.

Meanwhile, Rune, whom he remembered as being an emotionless bastard, shifted on his feet. Only slightly, but Samael caught it and struggled between shock at her defense of him and another arrow of ill-timed amusement at Rune's discomfort.

Given how hard Rune had pushed Samael those few years they'd worked together, their relationship had been contentious to say the least. An odd combination of respect and dread on Samael's part. Seeing his old mentor put on the back foot by Meira was worth all the mishaps that had brought them here.

"Why do you have a kitten?" Rune asked, almost idly.

Samael ignored the red herring and skipped to the bad part. "Rune steals mates."

Meira shook her head, cuddling the tiny cat closer to her breast, as though worried the black dragon shifter would rip it away from her and kick the thing out. "There I know you're wrong. He protects them. Skylar told me."

Samael swung his gaze to the man, watching with narrowed eyes. Rune gave a lazy shrug, basically saying they could believe it or not. He didn't care.

"Why are you here?" Rune drawled, clearly having run out of patience with the conversation.

Meira visibly paused at the question, then turned to Samael as though he'd been the one to ask it. "I guess I was thinking of safe places my mother sent us. Maul's no longer in Alaska, and the wolves are with Angelika in Ben Nevis. But my uncle is…"

Realization parted her lips in a silent gasp before she jerked her gaze to Rune. "Is my uncle here? Can I see him?"

The traitor who apparently might not be a traitor glanced between them, then shook his head. "Why me?" he said, more to himself. Then turned and walked away. "Follow me."

Hell. They had no choice.

Meira raised her eyebrows in question to Samael, who waved her ahead. They followed Rune down a long, dark corridor. Everywhere around him was the sound of water, a constant *drip, drip, drip*, like the snow and ice on the towering peaks outside seeped inside the mountains to melt and weep through the walls.

Apparently here they used old-fashioned torches set into sconces to light the main corridors. They passed several corridors that weren't lit, the scents of darkness, decay and fallen rock telling Samael that those sections hadn't been used in a long time and were no longer safe, prone to cave-ins.

Which was Samael's first clue as to which mountain they'd landed in.

No one, not even Gorgon, had known where the mate stealer hid himself and the women he took. Though, to be honest, the king had been focused on problems closer to home. Maybe they should have been giving the colonies a little more attention. If they had, perhaps the answer to Rune Abaddon's location would've been more obvious.

The Andes.

Clearly, the man had taken over the old, abandoned enforcer base deep in the Andes Mountains in Argentina, one of several that had been located on the South American continent at one time. Thanks to a treaty with other shifters in this region of the world, the previous High King Hanyu—Meira's grandfather, in fact—had agreed to abandon South America and leave it for the indigenous supernaturals in exchange for their help identifying dragon mates in the region and sending them to the clans.

Pytheios apparently hadn't seen any reason to break that treaty. Or had been too busy keeping his crown. Either way, it had been smart of Rune to hide here. Samael wondered how he'd located the place but didn't ask.

After several twists and turns, Rune led them past a large room full of monitors, one similar to a room in Ararat, used for monitoring the mountain security along with any indications of dragon shifters in the region.

They didn't stop there, though. Instead they continued on to a dragon-steel door, which stood slightly open.

Samael grabbed Meira by the wrist, pulling her slightly behind him. "No way in the seven hells am I letting her walk into dungeons."

Rune turned slowly, eyebrow raised. "These aren't dungeons."

"Meira?"

She jerked against Samael's grasp as an older man appeared in the doorway. Tall and lanky, he wore his stark white hair cut short in a flat-top, military style. White eyes gazed out from a wizened face. A gaze that zeroed in on the woman at Samael's side.

"Uncle Tyrek?" No mistaking the curious hope in her voice.

The man walked forward and took Meira's face in his hands. A growl slipped from Samael's lips, which earned him a sideways glance of warning, only to then be ignored. Not exactly what he was used to. As captain of the king's guard, people tended to get the fuck out of his way.

"Skylar looked like your phoenix grandmother, with her black hair, but I see your father and your grandfather in you," the man said to Meira.

She smiled softly and flipped a curl. "I'm the mutt."

Samael had to swallow another growl at the derogatory word. He didn't like anyone disparaging Meira. Not even Meira.

"The red dragon genes come through a bit," she said. "Mama always said I was Dad but with the mix of all our bloodlines. Kasia's a true redhead with our grandfather's blood in her veins. Angelika is all Dad, white dragon with white hair. But I'm a mix."

"Holy shit," Rune muttered to himself. "Four of you?"

"Maybe," Meira answered vaguely. And Samael found himself choking back an unexpected laugh.

Rune's jaw clenched. Tyrek didn't appear surprised in the least.

Comparing Meira to the man who was supposedly Zilant Amon's brother, Samael had to admit to the resemblance. Meira was a softer version, her high cheekbones less angular, jaw not as sharp, but the same winged eyebrows, same catlike shape to her eyes.

Speaking of her sisters, however, reminded him. This wasn't a family reunion.

Samael cleared his throat. "Angelika and Skylar will be frantic."

Meira gasped. "Oh heavens." She turned to her uncle. "Is there someone who might take this little girl?" She held out the kitten, who'd stayed still and quiet this entire time. "And I need a mirror. One positioned so that it will not hint as to where I am."

No doubt to protect Tyrek and the people shielding him—traitors or not—more than herself. More strays to take in like the cat her uncle was eyeing with concern. Terrific.

Without a quibble, Tyrek looked to Rune. The two men silently debated, possibly shifting a small part of their bodies so they could telepathically discuss. Then Rune grunted, took the kitten, and handed it to one of his men. "Take it to the common room." He shot a look at Samael and Meira. "This way."

He led them back through the twisting maze of the mountain home and down another endless corridor until it dead-ended. He reached for the last door on the left. "No one uses this suite," he said. "There's a mirror in the bathroom."

Meira paused beside her uncle. "You might want to listen in on this."

Tyrek raised his eyebrows at Rune, who gave them both a flat-lipped glare. "I'd like to be in on it, too."

Samael stepped between her and Rune. "Fine. But you don't come near her and stay the fuck out of line of sight."

"Dragons," Meira grumbled behind him, then gently pushed him out of her way. "If my uncle trusts this man, and Skylar trusts him, then so do I, and my other sisters should, too."

Knowing Skylar, given how long they'd been kept waiting, she might be burning down Ararat by now, trying to find Meira.

Before any of the men in the room could protest or question, Meira stepped before the mirror and did her thing.

"I'm here," she called out even as the image was changing.

"Fuck me, that's a handy trick," Rune said under his breath.

Samael shot him a cautionary glare.

Immediately, Angelika's and Skylar's faces appeared in the reflection. "About damn time," Skylar snapped, her white-blue eyes practically shooting sparks.

"Sorry." Meira compulsively reached for the mirror as though she could touch her sister, then stopped and slowly lowered her hand. "We ran into...complications."

"What kind of complications?" Skylar demanded.

"A gold dragon was waiting for us at our old home."

Silence greeted that.

"You went home?" Angelika asked quietly.

Meira nodded. "Someone ransacked the place, and now it's missing the roof."

"Did you recognize the dragon, Samael?" a male voice called a second before Ladon stepped into view.

Samael glanced at the woman beside him. He hadn't had a chance to tell her this yet. "Hard to be sure in dragon form, but I'm pretty sure the dragon was Brock Hagan."

Meira whipped her head around, and he sent her an apologetic glance. They hadn't exactly had time to discuss.

"Fuck." Ladon groaned and ran a hand over his jaw.

Samael's thoughts exactly. "Please inform Brand."

The blue king gave a single nod. Brock was a direct threat to the gold throne, the son of the previous king, Uther, whom Brand had killed. They'd been pretty damn sure Brock was dead, too, killed in a fight for Ben Nevis.

If they were wrong, they had a big problem. Especially if Pytheios was involved. Given where Brock had shown up, a place only the rotting king had known about, that was a pretty damn good bet.

Meira continued to glare his direction, and Samael grimaced. "Sorry. We landed here and then dealt with this asshole—" He hooked a thumb at Rune.

"Is someone else there with you?" Skylar demanded.

"We ended up in a safe place with our uncle," Meira acknowledged. "I thought he and the man he hides with should hear this. They're here with us, though, listening."

After a silent beat, Skylar flashed a grin. "Give the old man a hug from me."

"My hearing is still as sharp as ever," Tyrek answered for himself, voice desert dry.

Skylar's grin widened. "And if the men who I think you're with are there, tell the red and black dragons they still owe me."

Rune's flat expression didn't change a hair, though he was likely the black dragon who owed her. Samael had no idea whom the red dragon Skylar referenced might be.

"I'm pretty sure helping me is about to cancel that out," Meira said slowly. "And we don't have much time. I've used my powers too much today already delivering our message to the black clan."

Every person on both sides of the mirror snapped to attention.

Samael stepped closer, studying her, taking in the slight tremble to her hands. Dammit. Why hadn't she told him she was weakening?

Quickly, Meira filled them all in on what had transpired the last two days. Then Skylar did the same, Angelika smartly remaining quiet.

The situation was worse than Samael expected. His clan had gone radio silent, those in direct attendance at the mating already having left Ben Nevis, presumably for Ararat.

Brand's tenuous hold on the Gold Clan was showing, thanks to his not growing up in the clan and spending most of his life rogue. His numbers were dwindling daily, either languishing in his already overflowing dungeons or having left, likely to join other clans. Or perhaps join Brock, if any knew he still lived.

Ladon wasn't in as bad shape, having been chosen by the people he'd grown up with to overthrow the previous king. His clan already trusted him implicitly.

Pytheios's propaganda stunt at the mating ceremony had inflicted the damage the High King had intended.

Which reminded Samael that he needed to get in direct contact with his beta after this. The contact with the clan hadn't been enough. That much was clear.

"Even people in the colonies got that message," Rune informed them.

"What are your thoughts?" Samael asked. His gaze told his old captain that he'd better answer wisely.

Rune shrugged. "I'd say it's pretty obvious my men and I don't trust the current regime."

So a rogue—a man who swore no allegiance to a clan and therefore would typically be hunted down and killed—was on their side. Great.

"Who is this other phoenix?" Skylar said. "That's what I want to know."

Rune turned his stare on Tyrek.

Meira's uncle didn't acknowledge him. He did, however, take a step forward. "I'm afraid I can't help answer that."

"Did you know all our names?" Meira asked. An obvious question, but one Samael hadn't thought of.

"No." Tyrek swallowed. "When your mother got in touch years ago to set me up as a safe haven for Skylar in the event of Serefina meeting a violent death, she only told me about Skylar. She implied more children, but not how many or any other names. I eventually heard about you. Whispers, mostly."

What was Pytheios's play here? Samael couldn't see it yet.

Everyone absorbed that information in silence.

"If this woman *is* a phoenix, she may not be our sister, but she's our kind," Meira said. "We have to help her. We can't leave her with that monster."

Skylar glanced off to the side, likely at Angelika or Ladon. "Agreed."

"First, we must find my king," Samael said, already hating the idea forming in his head, one that had a lot to do with strategy Meira had already gotten him to agree to. "If you're going inside Everest on a rescue mission for this woman, you need all the clans behind you that you can get."

Every protective instinct bucked against the suggestion, reactions so complicated he couldn't untangle them. His job was to keep her safe, dammit. But this was Meira. He might not like the way her need to help those around her led her straight to trouble, but he was beginning to understand that the beauty of her soul was her heart. She had to protect the world. He had to protect her. Not even a choice.

He looked at Meira, who regarded him with an emotion he couldn't quite pin down. Something uncomfortably close to gratitude. Not the emotion he wanted from her, but maybe the one he'd have to settle for.

"What's the plan?" She put the question to Samael, not turning her gaze away.

"Like you said. If Gorgon is alive, the most likely place is—"

"Everest," she supplied.

He nodded.

"Damn," Skylar said. "I seriously didn't want to go back there any time soon."

"I think this time it's my turn," Meira said.

Samael scowled at the words, but his dragon rumbled a different concern, not at the specific words, but the way she slurred them.

"No," Skylar snapped.

"Mama trained me, too, Sky," Meira said with a frown of concentration. She was also starting to sway on her feet. "I can get in and out easier. Move from room to room faster. You know I'm right."

"Meira?" Samael held a hand out to steady her, and the image in the mirror started to flicker. "That's it. I'm calling it," he said. "Shut it down."

She blinked at him with eyes turning heavier by the second. "We'll call again later," she said, not turning her gaze away from his. Then the flames shut off, the mirror cutting off whatever protest Skylar was about to make.

She'd listened to him. Not even a question. Samael had to keep himself from scooping her up and running off with her. "What next?" he asked.

"Sleep," she murmured, visibly drooping. "Definitely sleep."

CHAPTER NINE

Meira blinked herself awake to a pitch-black room. No window. No source of light. Nothing.

The all-too-familiar sensation of having no idea where she was kicked her heart rate up. Meira jackknifed to sitting and frantically felt around her to figure out her situation. A bed. She was in a bed with sheets, pillows, and a soft blanket. That couldn't be bad, right?

A soft click sounded an instant before a light turned on to her right. Meira blinked then forced her eyes to focus on the man sitting on the floor in the corner of what appeared to be a cave bedroom.

"Sam?"

As soon as the name left her lips, protectiveness gathered around her like another blanket. His protectiveness toward her, she realized. Like he'd taken the walls he put around himself and built them up around her instead. He got up and sat on the bed beside her, dark eyes searching. "It's me. You're safe."

She blew out a low breath as her body relaxed into the knowledge that he was here. Watching over her.

He supported me. Without question. About going to Everest to rescue that other phoenix. He hadn't been happy, more resigned. But also...accepting. She'd felt it, even as she'd been focused on keeping her powers running. "Sorry."

"For what?"

"Not giving you more warning that I was running out of juice—"

He shook his head at her. A gentle remonstration for him. She'd expected flat-lipped irritation. "You don't have to be brave and do everything yourself all the time, you know."

Meira wrinkled her nose. "I'm not brave. My sisters are, but I have to fake it."

Samael leaned closer. "I'll tell you a secret."

She waited, casting her gaze over his harsh features, trying to make sense of the emotions surrounding her.

"We all have to fake being brave," he said.

Meira gave an indelicate snort. "Some more than others."

Rather than laugh at her, though his lips twitched, Samael reached out and tweaked a curl. "I think you're brave."

"*You* think I'm reckless."

He shrugged. "Maybe if more people were your kind of reckless, the world would be a...kinder...place."

Whoa. Where was this coming from?

He grinned, his face lighting up and stealing the air from her lungs. "Even if it gives me a daily heart attack."

Meira chuckled, relaxing into the way his emotions cosseted her. No longer screaming, though a tension rode the edges. Worry. Fear. Something else.

"Would it help to know that I won't leave you?"

Until this was all over, he must've meant. Except her heart took off at the thought of him watching over her always.

She gazed into his dark eyes—not fathomless or cold, but warm, reaching inside her.

Except Samael didn't get to be that person for her. She'd made promises. Plans that affected many more than herself. And Samael was loyal to his king.

"Meira?" he asked, voice turning low and rumbly.

Oh gods. Had her longing reflected in her eyes? Had she given away her secret wishes, dreams she'd held close, tucked into dark spaces inside her where they couldn't make her ache for things? Impossible things.

She cleared her throat. "What time is it?"

He gave her a narrow-eyed, searching look, then sat back, pulling his emotions back inside himself, leaving her cold. "Evening. Back to using up all your...juice. In case it happens again, how does that work? I didn't even know it was a possibility."

She plucked at the blanket. A patchwork quilt, she could now see in the dim light. "It's a bit like dragon fire. I mean, I think of my power like a tank that I use up, so I knew I didn't have an unlimited supply. Unfortunately, it turns out my powers cutting out on me is a lot like the way alcohol affects me. I skip the getting-drunk feeling and go straight from nicely buzzed to puking. I honestly didn't know I was that drained until I started swaying."

"Good to know." He shook his head again. "Remind me to keep you away from alcohol."

She smiled and he stilled, suddenly intent, and a ribbon of desire threaded through a hole in the wall. Meira did her best to mute the emotions. Her own well-guarded frustration surging to meet his didn't help.

"How are you feeling now?" he asked. Apparently, they were going to act like nothing was going on between them.

"Better. Still tired. Hungry."

He nodded slowly. "Hopefully it won't take you long to recharge?"

She flopped back against her pillows. "We'll both have to find that out the hard way. I've never used it so fast or so long before." Or teleported quite so far, come to think on it. There was a big difference between jumping from western Russia to England versus western Russia to the U.S. followed by South America right after.

"Meira."

His voice shook her out of her head, and she pushed back up to sitting only to frown at the expression in his eyes. "Yes, Samael?"

He paused a beat. "You called me Sam earlier."

"I hope you weren't offended—"

He shook his head. "I don't mind when you say it."

Oh. Dang. There went her heart again, wishing impossible wishes.

He sobered. "I need to tell you something." A new emotion hit her, though she could tell he was trying to claw it back inside him only to have it slip from his fingers. Like he was trying to find the right way, the right direction. Like he was lost.

Apprehension had her gathering the blanket to her chin. "I really hate it when people start out a conversation that way. It only means bad things."

"Sorry." He stared at her, seeming to search for words. Then jumped to his feet. In the months she'd known him, Samael Veles had only once shown his emotions outwardly, always in perfect control. Solid. Unshakable.

Until this moment.

"Sam?" His intensity built, like a presence in the room with them, pressing into her. "Talk to me. You're starting to scare me."

"Shit."

He came back to kneel at the bedside, taking one of her hands in both of his, face as serious as the first time he'd seen her in that mirror, and somehow with that physical connection, her nerves settled, despite the swirl of emotions coming from behind that wall of his, contained chaos surging over the top.

"I think we have a big problem," he said.

No more problems. Didn't they have enough? "Bigger than Gorgon being missing and Pytheios having another phoenix?"

His jaw twitched as though he'd clenched and unclenched his teeth. "I—" He gave his head a shake. "Fuck."

Meira waited, trying not to let his tension feed her own.

"I...think we're mates." He dropped the bald statement like a live grenade between them.

Meira's mind short-circuited, his words clanging around in her head like bats in a belfry, drowning out everything else and temporarily erasing all her words. He'd actually said it. Voiced the question in her own mind.

Gods, it explained a lot—his pain and the need focused on her any time she came near. His stark rejection the day of her mating ceremony. The way he'd stayed away from her until he couldn't. The same way she'd avoided him. How he seemed to understand her, get her. How he saw her in mirrors when no one else could—other than Maul, apparently.

Sam leaned in closer, eyeing her, worry setting his jaw hard. "Meira?"

Words still weren't coming, her mind a total disaster.

"Mir?" He waved a hand in front of her face.

She focused on his eyes, so close to hers and full of emotions she couldn't identify, not while her own drowned out what she could receive from him. He'd said those words with no intonation. None. Like it didn't matter. His face, however, told a different story. What did he feel about it?

"Meira?" he begged now, rubbing her hand between his. "Say something. Please."

Only she couldn't.

"Talk to me." He resorted to teasing her with her own phrase. One her mother had spoken to her often as a child when emotions would overwhelm her.

"I...don't believe in fated mates." Ah, there were the words she was searching for.

A small muscle twitched at the side of his mouth, and that invisible wall slammed up between them, impenetrable and telling her exactly how much she'd hurt him with those words. "Why not?" he demanded.

"Because I can't." The idea had never made sense to her. Seeming almost...cruel. "This world is too big for there to only be one perfect match. When I was younger, I wrote an algorithm to predict the chances of finding that one person in all the world." She grimaced. "The odds were terrible. And look at my sisters. What are the chances Kasia and Skylar would both find their mates here and now, among kings? Isn't it more likely that we end up with the mate who is perfect in that time and place?"

Sam's hands clamped down on hers. "Don't be so sure."

"Of course I don't know for sure." This was not going well.

"What about the dragons who die unmated, their bodies riddled with disease, as opposed to those who find a mate and live twice as long?"

"I assume the mating bond is what affects the life span, fated or not. Most creatures deal with disease in old age." Couldn't he see beyond tradition and what all dragon shifters had been told?

Sam jerked his head in what had to be a rejection of her arguments. "What are the odds that the red dragon pretending to be Gorgon would die in your fire, if not for fated mates?"

"Bewitched or not, I didn't choose him. I *chose* Gorgon."

Sam flinched at that. Not visibly, but she felt it in a twitch of his hands, and that wall holding back his feelings rippled. "You don't know that," he said. "These are all just guesses."

"That may be true, but I have to believe it."

"Why?"

Because all the choices I've made are wrong if it's not true. And what about the people I'm trying to fight? The ones I need to help?

Sam grunted when she didn't answer. "And the dragons who've had to watch the devastation of a woman burning in their fire when they choose the wrong mate?"

Meira looked away. Mostly because she'd always hated the idea of those poor women. Also, because her reasoning around that was difficult to swallow, let alone put into words. What if mating was simply a matter of faith? Of a belief strong enough, or a choice solid enough, to stand the test of flame?

"Kasia fell in love with Brand and chose him. Skylar chose Ladon for specific reasons. Choice is the key."

"For a phoenix."

She didn't have enough evidence to refute him. "Why do you think we're..." She trailed off, not wanting to voice the word. It gave too much power to the seductive idea. An idea that aligned too closely with secret wishes she should never have allowed to remain within her, no matter the dark corners she'd stuffed them into. Now those wishes were turning dangerous.

Instead of answering, he reached out and traced her lips with his fingertip, leaving a trail of tingling nerves in his wake. "Don't you feel it?"

My own response to your emotions. It's not real. "Pheromones. A biological response." Except her voice came out all husky.

Sam's lips quirked in a tilted smile more frustrated than amused. "So, you *do* feel it."

Dammit.

She must've given away her emotions by a flicker in her expression, because his smile turned predatory. "I *need* to protect you."

"You're meant to. It's your job."

He shook his head, trailing that finger over her skin, tracing her jaw. "No. This isn't duty. It's a compulsion. I have to make sure you are safe...and happy."

He frowned over the last word.

Meira frowned, too. "Not adding more complication to my life would make me happy. I'm bound to your king."

Sam closed his eyes. "I know. I've stayed away—not let myself believe—because of that, because of loyalty to Gorgon, who is almost a father to me, and because I don't deserve you." He snapped his eyes open, black flames consuming the orbs, scales framing the sockets, his dragon closer to the surface than she'd ever seen. The burn of his desire reached for her in the night.

An answering heat ignited inside her, flowing through her veins and coalescing in her belly. A reaction she desperately tried to ignore. This couldn't be happening. She'd made her choices. "Why now? What changed?"

"I couldn't ignore the signs anymore." His voice had dropped to a deep growl, the sound rumbling over her skin, stoking the fire. Was she glowing yet? "And..."

Meira held her breath. And what? She should be stopping him.

"And this." He slid a hand up under the fall of her hair and claimed her lips with the softest of kisses.

· · ·

Meira whimpered against him, the response uncontrollable. Undeniable.

And a tiny balm to the panic rioting inside him. He'd told her they were mates, and all she could do was deny it. Even the pain that had privately taken him to his knees the day she'd promised herself to his king didn't come close to this.

The small sound she made set him off. With a groan that welled up from deep inside his chest, he pressed into her. Claimed her with mouth, body, hands. Kisses that he used to try to reach into her, through her, speaking to her soul. He coaxed and demanded at the same time, asking for her submission. Asking her to admit the truth of what he'd said. Because while her mind could deny, could make other plans, could know that this thing had no future, mates or not, her body and her heart couldn't say no to him.

Samael lost himself in her.

With a shuddering breath, she opened to him, skating her tongue over his, twining with his, the first time she'd taken the initiative between them. He recognized how big a moment that was for her.

Fuck.

He hauled her across his lap so she sat straddling him. Meira was so far gone, she followed where he led, wrapping her arms around his neck. He smoothed a hand up her back, pressing her into his hardness, and she shuddered and let loose another whimper.

At the sound, Samael jerked his mouth away and they stared at each other, both panting, the tips of her breasts pushing into him.

He let out a sharp breath and put his forehead to hers. "I'm sorry."

Meira stiffened.

Almost in a convulsive spasm, he tightened his arms around

her. "No. Whatever you're thinking, no. I just...didn't mean to go that far."

Though she relaxed against him, closing her eyes, he could still feel her pulling away. Feel her mentally reaching for what was right, just as he'd been doing for months. The right thing. Helping her family, helping take down Pytheios, her promises to Gorgon. *His* promises to Gorgon.

Fuck.

"Don't do that, either." He released her to take her face in his hands and Meira opened her eyes to stare at his, the flicker of the flames he knew reflected there illuminating her face.

"I'm not doing anything," she said.

"You're pulling away from me."

She started under his hands, eyes going wide.

He pressed a quick, soft kiss to her lips. "Don't deny us."

Meira pursed her lips in the way she did when she was thinking hard. "I hardly know you. This is..." Her hand fluttered then landed on his chest. "Lust combined with a fraught situation."

His dragon snarled in his head. How could she deny this connection? What about every other indication? Seeing her in the mirror. His dragon's instinct to claim. His need to make her happy. None of those things happened with just anyone. Not for dragon shifters, at least. Realization lined his heart with a thick layer of lead. He couldn't force her to see. She had to get there on her own.

The dragon inside him wound tighter and strained outward, already not liking where Samael's thoughts were headed. He willed himself to loosen his hold, dropping his hands to his sides, though he couldn't make himself lift Meira off his lap. If he touched her again, he'd be lost.

Quietly she climbed off and stepped back.

"If you truly believe in the fates, then you should have faith that things will work out as they should," she said, her husky voice scraping over raw nerves.

Even Samael had difficulty putting *that* much faith in the

universe. He knew deep in the marrow of his bones that he was right, even though circumstance had laid waste to plenty of mates who'd made the wrong choice. Perhaps that was what scared him most.

However, if he was anything, he was a fighter. Now that he'd found her, had allowed himself to admit what she was to him, no way was he letting her go without trying.

"You're right." Samael lifted his head, and she stepped back again, eyes wide. No doubt she was seeing his dragon. "But sometimes the fates need a little help."

Meira stilled. "What do you mean by that?"

Samael did smile then. "I mean I'm just going to have to prove it to you."

Her lips clamped tight, and an emotion flashed in her eyes that looked painfully like fear. At the same time, though, her eyes remained more white than blue, and his enhanced hearing picked up the increased flutter of her heartbeat.

She wanted this...even if she didn't want to want it.

Good. That was something. A start.

Meira's eyes narrowed suddenly, and he could see her sister Skylar in the expression. Stubbornness was apparently a trait all the Amon women shared. "Let's concentrate on all the other problems that need our focus."

His mate might be the most mild-mannered of the four sisters, but damned if she might not be the toughest nut to crack. If anxiousness wasn't clawing at his insides at the thought of losing her now that he'd found her, Samael might have enjoyed the challenge she'd set in front of him. "I'm an excellent multitasker."

That earned him a glare this side of adorable.

A knock at the door to the suite where they'd put them interrupted anything she might've responded with.

Shooting him a look that clearly said *this conversation is over*, Meira went to the door and opened it to find Rune standing there, expression his usual brand of dark. "Kasia Astarot would like a word."

Meira blinked and glanced over her shoulder to Samael then back. "She's here?"

Rune shook his head. "No. She's teleconferenced in."

"How did she find me?"

Rune watched Samael closely, expression dripping in suspicion, eyes narrowed but not yet ablaze. "I'd love to know that myself."

CHAPTER TEN

"Kasia?" Meira called out to her sister even as they hurried down the narrow corridor after Rune.

She followed him into a room not unlike one she'd seen in Ben Nevis, though more rudimentary, with wires snaking out the door. It sported a solid wall of screens and monitors with a long console filled with various computers underneath. Older ones, and an odd mix—a Genesis midtower, a Compaq Elite, even a Medion all-in-one. Top of the line, ten years ago. Hopefully they'd at least upgraded their operating systems and software. The room was also crowded—Rune, Tyrek, and one more. A man with Mediterranean coloring and striking blue eyes. A blue dragon shifter. Rune had mentioned his men.

She paused and glanced to Samael. He stepped up beside her, legs planted wide, arms crossed, expression as dark as his eyes. "We weren't expecting an audience."

She had to bite back a laugh as the other man exchanged a look with Rune then backed up slightly. Not giving ground per se, more like a token show of acknowledgment that Samael would rip his arms off and beat him with them if he so much as glanced at her wrong.

The urge to laugh disappeared under the realization that cozy warmth wrapped around her because of it. All that talk of mates. Not to mention that kiss.

Hell's bells.

"This is Aidan Paytah," Rune said. "He was part of the Huracán team of enforcers until he found his mate, Sera. You'll meet her in a bit."

Meira glanced at Samael, but he was still in intimidation mode and not emoting.

"Why are they with you?" she asked.

"Because before they mated, Sera had three different brands interlaced on her neck."

That pulled Samael out of his glower. "Holy shit."

"Indeed." The glance Rune flicked him seemed significant, though Meira wasn't sure how.

"I can see that that's unusual," Samael said slowly, not taking his gaze from the blue dragon shifter. "But why would it require him to go rogue and join you here?"

Meira dropped her own gaze to the man's hand. Sure enough, on the back of his hand between his forefinger and thumb, where Ladon's mark should have shown, was only a patch of blank skin.

"Because." Aidan spoke up for the first time, calm and resolute. "One of the marks on her neck belonged to Pytheios, and the Alliance was not going to allow me to be part of the process. They wanted to find the High King his mate, be the ones to save his life."

"Fuck." Samael spat the word, but he also eased up. She had no idea what tipped her off to that fact—the set of his shoulders, perhaps, because his emotions remained steady—but she knew he'd accepted that answer.

"Why is he here, though?" Meira leaned closer to Samael to ask.

"Good question," he said. "Why are you here?"

"I have a family to hide. But any king who stands against Pytheios is all right with me." Aidan held up his hand. "With or without the mark."

Meira glanced up at Samael, who gave a small shrug. She had no doubts they were of the same opinion. Regardless of what sent Aidan rogue, which sounded legitimate at first glance, here stood a man of honor.

Besides. He could do nothing to Kasia and Brand through a screen.

"You may stay," Samael said.

Aidan's lips tipped sideways. "Thanks."

Rune hit a button, and the wall came to life.

"Kasia?" Meira called.

"I—ear—ira—" Kasia's voice cut up. Meanwhile the screen stayed black.

Rune grimaced, leaning over to fiddle. "This happens sometimes. We're patched into the closest city, but weather and the distance and mountains cause issues."

Meira tapped him on the shoulder. "May I?" she offered, hesitantly. Not wanting to step on his toes.

Raised eyebrows greeted the question. Then he waved at the console. "Be my guest."

He hardly finished talking before she pulled one of the chairs up in front of a keyboard, typing away, immediately looser because she could finally tune out all the people and messy emotions in the room and just focus. Fingers flying across the keys, she brought up a series of diagnostics and then started adjusting.

"Can you hear me?" Kasia's voice sounded more clearly, but the screen remained black.

"Just a sec," Meira said, distractedly.

"O-kay." Her sister drew the word out. Not that Meira really noticed.

Then the screen lit up with a clear image. Kasia's lovely face, red hair a halo, larger than life, peered out at her from four middle screens paired together. Her sister was in a similarly set-up room in the Gold Clan's stronghold of Store Skagastølstind.

Meira stood and scooted back. "Hey, Kas. How did you find me?"

Even virtually, Kasia must've picked up on the tension that crept into every man in the room as she cast her gaze around. She locked in on Rune. "I expected to speak privately with my sister..."

"My name is Rune Abaddon. This is my installation." He held

up his hand, which showed no mark between thumb and forefinger. "But I owe no king my allegiance. Meira remains here as our guest, but her presence is a danger to us, especially after what we've been through. You speak with her with us in the room, or not at all."

"The fuck you say." Suddenly Brand stepped into the picture behind his mate, gold eyes blazing, face set in a scowl that made Meira step back only to bump into Samael, who steadied her with a hand at her back that then curled around her waist. She sucked in as awareness filled her with the weight of longing. But she didn't step away.

Kasia ignored her glowering mate, holding up a hand. "We appreciate your help."

Rune glanced between the king and queen, then gave a brusque nod.

Kasia's gaze moved to Meira. "I had a vision. That's how I found you. Are you all right?"

"We were attacked at our old home in Kansas. Brock Hagan."

"I saw. He's a bigger threat than we realized. Something to do with Ararat next."

"A vision?" Rune stepped forward. "Skylar never mentioned having visions."

Kasia paused then smiled, her eyes twinkling. "Rune... So, you're the one, huh? You and your men have even more of my thanks and trust for keeping Skylar safe. I'm sure Skylar would say the same. She's spoken of you often."

Rune lifted a single eyebrow. "Hiding her from my kind didn't last long."

Kasia laughed. "It never does when Skylar is involved," Meira murmured.

That earned them a minuscule smile from the black dragon shifter.

"Did you see anything else?" Meira asked. No way had Kasia sought her out simply to check on her health. The risk would be too great.

"I didn't see more than that, but your message got through to the Black Clan. They've sent their own message in return through me. Gorgon's beta is dead. Do not approach Ararat until they have determined a new king."

At her back, Samael stiffened, the creak of leather telling her he'd fisted his hands at his sides.

"Fuck that," Rune snarled. "The next king after the beta should be the Viceroy of War."

Of course, that's how dragons would set it up. Meira inwardly rolled her eyes. Bloodthirsty lot. "I'm surprised there's not a fight to the death involved," she murmured.

Rune swung around to pin her with a serious stare. "Often there is, despite the system in place."

Samael had yet to speak, a hole of silence behind her, the chink in his walls letting through only a pulsing sort of tension.

"How did Adish die?" Rune directed the question to Kasia and Brand.

"We were not informed," Brand said.

Why wasn't Samael speaking up? The pressure emanating from him was filling the room, suffocating her. Meira turned to him slowly to find a man who reminded her of Carrick and the other gargoyles, made of stone. If she touched him, part of him might chip away, so she didn't dare reach out. "Sam." She said his name quietly.

He seemed to have to drag his gaze down to hers, staring without seeing for a second before his midnight eyes focused.

Meira didn't have to say anything. Perhaps he could see the questions in her eyes, and the message that they were in this together.

Sam reached out, almost convulsively, like he wanted to wrap one of her curls around his finger but dropped his hand before he touched her. "Someone is systematically taking out the leadership of the Black Clan."

"You can't know that," Rune said behind her.

Sam didn't take his gaze from her. "Adish is far from old, already mated, and healthy as a god. Disease did not take him.

He is well respected, well-liked, and an impressive fighter, despite remaining out of recent skirmishes, in order to lead at Ararat. That's why he was named beta."

And left behind at the mountain while Gorgon was trying to secure himself a mate and allies. A leader the clan respected. Only traitors would kill such a man.

"Hrag is Viceroy of War," Rune said. "He must be behind this."

Samael shook his head, dropping his gaze to watch Meira closely, and she couldn't look away. "Hrag stepped down," he said. "He has not found his mate, and the aging process has taken hold of his mind."

"Who was named Viceroy of War in his place?" Rune asked, impatience giving the words a crack.

Sam lifted a hand and wrapped that curl around his finger, almost as though tethering her to him for what he was about to say. The skin on his neck shifted to scales of obsidian briefly before rippling back to human, the way she'd once seen an octopus change colors in an instant to blend with its environment as it flowed across the ocean floor.

Then he lifted his head to gaze over her shoulder at the other black dragon shifter in the room. "I was."

. . .

"Bullshit," Rune snapped.

Heavy silence fell over the room, like the doldrums on a ship he'd once sailed on in the Mediterranean, when nothing moved. Not a whisper of wind, and the water didn't even dare lap at the sides of the ship. As still as the world ever got.

That was the room now.

Sam shifted his gaze to Meira, searching her expression. Was she angry that he didn't warn her? Not that she really ever got angry. But did she believe him?

"I will only ask you this once."

At his side, Meira visibly jumped at the venom in Rune's voice, and Sam tightened his grip on her hair compulsively. At a small sound from her, he eased up.

Rune's words were edged with a poison that made no sense. Why was *he* angry?

"I am not the traitor in this room or to my clan," Sam pointed out.

Meira winced, though the way she was positioned in front of him, only he could see it. She gave him a small shake of her head, and he got the message. Probably not a good idea to antagonize the people giving them shelter.

The silence from Rune wasn't still anymore. Instead it pressed into him like a physical presence, strain expanding against his skin, and Sam used his hold on her locks to tug Meira closer to him, even as he drew his shoulders back.

"I believe you," Rune finally said.

Meira took a breath, but Sam didn't move. "I don't give a fuck what you believe."

Rune barked a sound that might have been a laugh. "You haven't changed, Veles."

"I could say the same about you, Abaddon."

The tension in the other man snapped, turning to full-bodied anger.

"You come here," Rune snarled softly. "With her, bringing danger down on me and my people."

Sam felt the way Meira had to stop herself from flinching, no doubt blaming herself.

"Don't you dare try to blame her," Sam said, a dangerous edge to his soft voice. "Because of our kind, she's been on the run all her life. We *owe* her. All dragon shifters owe her and her sisters our allegiance."

Samael didn't wait for Rune to respond, dropping his gaze to the woman he'd tied to himself, the silk of her hair wrapped around his finger.

As though she were his...

Meira had yet to say a word, though her eyes had done plenty of talking for her. Clear, pure white. As though she trusted everything he was. No one, other than maybe Gorgon, had done that for him before.

A more suspicious woman would've wondered if he'd taken out the king in order to claim her. She was smart enough to put things together the same way Rune had and ask herself if he wasn't behind these deaths and the overthrow of the leadership of the Black Clan. The question had to be asked. The way Pytheios got to people, and given Sam's history... No lowborn commoner in the history of the clan had every been named to the king's Curia Regis, his private council. Especially not to the position that put that man in direct line to the throne.

"He informed me the day you...the day of the ceremony," he told her.

"*I have faith in you over every other dragon within the clan.*" The memory of Gorgon's words echoed through his mind now.

He'd earned his king's confidence and friendship with years of loyalty and service and had always tried to be a true friend when the king had turned to him as a sort of sounding board. An occurrence that had happened more and more over time.

"You trust me?" he asked Meira softly.

She nodded without hesitation, and something unfurled in his gut—something warm and soft and, hell, mushy. All because she trusted him. Then, the next moment, he wished he hadn't, because she smiled, dimples flashing, and every molecule of air remaining in him vanished with a whoosh.

"You thought I'd doubt you?" A silly question, if the small shake she gave her head was any indication.

"I'm not used to anyone except Gorgon trusting me like that." A confession that cost him, given who was listening. Showing any weakness in front of other dragons was an idiotic thing to do, but Meira was...Meira.

"Your men," she said, a hint of a question in the word.

He cocked his head, not keeping up with whatever turn her mind had made.

She waved a hand. "They follow you into battle. That must take trust."

True. But would he find that solidarity still there when he saw them next? He'd need to find out eventually but couldn't say he was certain. Too many smoking guns pointed his direction.

And that would only worsen if he claimed his mate. Which he wouldn't do. Not yet. Maybe not ever.

Fuck.

The only way to put any of this right was to find Gorgon and...what? Beg the king for permission to mate the biggest prize their kind could imagine? Treasure to be taken and claimed and hoarded. A political lightning bolt that could both electrify their kind or burn a hole through them.

No answers presented themselves to him yet, beyond knowing that she was his. A fact that caused a shit ton of problems and didn't solve a damn thing.

"We won't figure this out today." Rune's voice pulled Samael out of the spell Meira had cast over him, and he lifted his head to find his old captain watching him with narrowed eyes.

"I agree." He unwound the lock of hair from his finger, forcing himself to step back from the woman who was supposed to be his queen and not anything else. "Meira must gather her strength to send me to Ararat alone."

"What?" Meira squeaked the word, then shook her head hard, her curls tumbling about her face. "No. No way. Not unless I go, too."

He put a hand to her face, and she stilled under his touch. Did she even realize she did that? "I'm not one of your strays who needs protecting. That's my job. If we lose you, we lose everything."

She glared at him, eyes swirling a darker blue, swallowing the white with her inner turmoil. "If I lose you..."

She cut herself off, eyes going wide, then shook her head and took a step back, away from his touch, her expression turning suddenly uncharacteristically cool as she guarded her heart, hiding herself from him, and, seven hells, he wanted to chase that look away.

She crossed her arms, the defensive move a jab to the gut, but he forced himself to remain still and calm.

"I can't do this without a black dragon shifter at my side to guide me and stand up for me." She canted her head slightly to the left, as though acknowledging Rune's presence in the room, but didn't take her gaze from Samael. "*You* are Gorgon's most trusted adviser. It has to be you. I... I..." She dropped her arms, pulling herself up to her full height. "I *order* you not to go without me."

She did just not say that. Albeit with a waver in her voice, but still. Samael crossed his arms, mimicking his unclaimed mate's stubborn scowl.

Tyrek stepped beside them, in view but not between them. The white dragon clearly had enough sense not to try that. "Why don't we pause, take the time Meira needs to rest anyway, and discuss options?"

"Get some rest," Kasia reminded them all that she and Brand remained distant witnesses to the room. "Gather your strength. Let's regroup in your morning time. What time zone are you?"

"U.S. Pacific," Aidan answered when no one else did.

Kasia reached for a button on her side of the console. "Eight a.m. Pacific, then. We'll call you."

The screen went black. Meira didn't even turn to say good-bye to her sister, holding her ground and her glare at him.

"You need to eat," Samael said. All he could think of to say.

She rolled her eyes, then turned to Rune, her expression shifting to a polite but distant smile. "According to my captain of the guard, I must be fed now."

Ouch. She really was upset, relegating him to staff, essentially. And that was not at all what he'd said, or even implied.

Despite the two-ton weight that had settled over his shoulders the second he'd learned of his beta's death, knowing exactly what that meant for him, Sam had to bite back a smile. Meira might be unaware, but she was changing. Growing bolder. As if she'd given herself permission to speak her mind and take a stand. Still sweet, but that core of steel always had to have been there. Though he suspected she didn't realize that herself.

"Would that be possible?" she asked, her expression softening for Rune. Because Meira would hate taking her frustrations out on an innocent bystander.

Rune's eyebrows went up, and he glanced at Sam, who shrugged.

"Of course," Rune said after a moment. "It's close to dinnertime, and I think Sera's cooking tonight."

"She is," Aidan confirmed.

"At least it'll be edible, then." Tyrek offered her an arm and walked her out of the room. Meira went without another glance in Sam's direction.

Sensing her need for space, even if he wanted to crowd her, make her admit they were meant to be, Samael waited for the others to file out before following.

Except Rune stood outside the door, clearly lying in wait for him. "We need to talk."

No shit.

Watching the distance grow between him and Meira as she walked down the hallway, away into the darkness untouched by torchlight beyond, felt almost like a vision, like the fates warning him of things to come.

That, in the end, he would lose her.

Every trace of amusement vanished, leaving him vibrating with dread and no outlet for it, like a live electric wire flapping in the fucking wind.

"If you're thinking what I think you're thinking, then you are well and truly fucked."

Samael jerked his head around to find Rune watching Meira's progress down the hall. "I'm well aware of my fuckedness."

Rune blew out a sharp breath and turned to face him. "And Gorgon? After all he did for you?"

Samael closed down at the question. But Rune, maybe more like him than he cared to admit, didn't give up. "He made you Viceroy of War because he trusted you."

"I know that," Samael growled. "I also know his last request was that I protect her. I'm doing everything I can."

Rune eyed him in silence for a long moment. "Yeah. I guess you are."

A hell of an admission from his hard-ass captain.

"But you need to ask yourself… Is your priority her or the clan?"

"Is that what you asked yourself when you went rogue?"

Samael waited for Rune to lash out at that, aware he was being an asshole. Except the other man merely shrugged one shoulder. "I told Gorgon what I was planning before I did it."

Shock stopped Samael's feet midstride. "You…what?"

For once, the dour expression lifted. "Didn't expect that, did you?"

No.

"I couldn't tell my team. I wasn't going to drag them down the same path. But Gorgon understood. In fact, he's the one who reminded me about this place."

Samael shoved his hands in his pockets as he mulled over that piece of information. "The king sanctioned you going rogue."

"He couldn't openly do that. But…yeah. Gorgon was a good man."

"*Is* a good man. And I'm going to find him." But what the hell would that mean for him and Meira, because he couldn't turn his back on his mate, either?

Rune gave a sharp nod. "I believe you." He glanced down the hall the others had disappeared down. "But if you can't see the conflict of interest, I sure can."

Not see it? It's all he could think about, seeing no path to get them all where they were supposed to be. Where his bones told him he needed to be.

"Are you sure she's your mate?" Rune asked.

"Have you mated yet?" Samael asked, rather than answer the question directed at him.

A muscle ticked at the side of his old mentor's jaw. That was new.

"No," said the man who'd been labeled a mate stealer but apparently was something else entirely.

Interesting. Samael didn't push. They hadn't exactly been close before, the relationship more that of asshole, know-it-all older brother. Rune had once told him that to make him the best fighter he could be, the scariest motherfucker on the planet, meant soft feelings like friendship were a waste of time.

Granted, his training technique had worked. Samael had risen quickly through the ranks, taking over as captain when Rune left for the colonies.

"This will be hard to explain, since you haven't experienced it." How did you tell a cold bastard like Rune Abaddon that, even now, with her walking farther away from him, his lungs were constricting, making it harder to breathe? "It's primal. A knowing that settles deep."

"Primal," Rune sneered over the word. "Like we're only as good or bad as our animal? Uncontrollable?"

"You control your dragon. So do I. But do you remember the first time you shifted, that edge to it that you might slip? That something bigger, more powerful than you might take control and never give it back?"

Rune snorted. "If finding a mate is like that, then no thanks."

Again, the edge to Rune's voice told Samael more was going on with the other black dragon. Something deeper than what he was letting Sam see on the surface.

"I took one look at her, and my center shifted. So did what was important to me." Humans must have felt similarly when they discovered that the sun was the center of the solar system, not the earth.

Rune clicked his tongue and shook his shoulders as though twitching a cape off. "For now, I'll just be grateful that the fates didn't land me with a phoenix who is meant for my king, who may or may not be dead."

A laugh punched from Samael. "Fuck you."

Rune grinned, or his version of it, one side of his mouth

drawing up. "You're not my type." Without saying more, together they started down the hallway. "Does she know?" Rune asked.

Samael stuffed his hands in his pockets. "She doesn't want to believe in fated mates."

"Maybe you need to make her believe," Rune murmured.

Samael had to keep from slamming a fist into the man's face. He'd never force Meira to do anything. "You definitely don't understand mates. Feel free to stay out of it."

Rune didn't so much as blink, then gave an easy shrug. "Good luck to you, then."

CHAPTER ELEVEN

Meira kept quiet as Tyrek led her to what appeared to be a kitchen, stewing over what had just happened. It had been unfair of her to throw the eating thing back in Sam's face... and call him her captain. He'd just been trying to take care of her. To be honest, that had been more about the shock, because she'd realized suddenly that losing him would cut her to the quick. More than that, actually, but she was terrified of examining those feelings more deeply, because if he was right...if they were mates...

"Here we are," Tyrek said as they entered a larger space.

More or less a mess hall. A tall-ceilinged cavern, the space broken up by several large stalactites and stalagmites that had grown into each other, forming columns. The hum of what must be a generator used for electric power throughout the mountain hadn't been as obvious in the tunnels, though a constant whir of sound and was louder here.

Harsh fluorescent lights cast a wavering purple hue over multiple wood picnic tables that reminded her of the one in their backyard in Kansas. They'd eaten out there when the weather was nice. She didn't even remember walking by it today. The thing was probably starting to turn gray and splintered by now.

To one side, along a wall with pipes and wires hanging down, was a rudimentary kitchen setup with a long counter formed by a series of tall tables with laminate tops, an old fridge with chipped, yellow paint, and an oven/stove combo in an ugly green that was supposed to be avocado, but reminded her of baby poo. The thing would've fit right in at that Kansas house, too.

Home, sweet home. Sort of.

Thankfully, only a woman and kid were in the room. Good. Meira was starting to flag under the onslaught of each new person she had to deal with, had to create a relationship with or convince to believe her.

Aidan crossed the room to the petite blonde who was cooking. Based on the way she lit up, and the kiss he dropped on her lips, lifted for his touch, this had to be his mate. Sera, she thought was the name he'd mentioned.

A gangly boy ran at Aidan only to pull up short and shadow box with him, both man and boy laughing. They had a son? She got the impression their mating had been more...recent.

"Let's get you fed," Tyrek said.

Following her uncle's lead and trying not to notice how Samael hadn't shown up yet, Meira crossed the room.

"Welcome to our hideaway," Sera said with a kind smile. The first Meira had received in a while if she was honest. "This is our son, Blake."

"How do you do?" The boy, who couldn't be more than nine or ten in both human and dragon years, held out a hand, a tiny man with an old soul.

Meira shook with all seriousness. "Lovely to meet you."

"Do you want to see me shift?" Suddenly he was an eager little boy, his grin showing gaping holes where teeth should've been.

"You can shift already? I didn't know that was possible at this age." She glanced to his parents, and Sera rolled her eyes.

"Blake is my son from when I was human. When I shifted the first time, he did, too. It took a very long time for him to learn how to shift back."

"Wow." More questions piled up in her mind.

"Aidan says you're a phoenix and on the run, too?" Sera asked, interrupting the litany of questions that wanted to pour from her.

Meira cast a wide-eyed look at Aidan. He'd said all that in the two seconds he'd taken to kiss his mate before their son had distracted him? Or was their connection that strong?

Sera turned back to the stove top. Her chin-length hair didn't cover the marking that stood out starkly against the pale skin at the nape of her neck. Meira didn't need to check Aidan's neck to know that was his mark. His mate.

More questions piled up. Like how long had it taken for the mark to show? And did it hurt when it appeared? Did it do anything for them beyond show them as a bonded pair? What about the other ways mates connected? Most likely they could communicate telepathically, like many mates could, which was probably how Sera knew what she did already. What else?

Even now, Aidan and Sera watched each other with a knowing, as though their souls settled around each other, and with an intensity that bordered on uncomfortable. Like Meira's sisters and their mates.

"Can I help with anything?" Meira offered. At home, they'd always split the chores, with whoever was working at the café that evening taking a night off from dinner duty.

Sera shook her head, shooting a smile over her shoulder. "It's basically done. We had dinner earlier, so this only needed to be reheated."

Which meant more dragon shifters lived here. How many? Probably better if Rune didn't tell them. Knowing nothing was better if they were captured. Torture scenes from movies popped into her head. Scenes based on human experiences. Imagine what dragons could do.

A shudder tumbled through her, clenching her stomach.

With a few twists, Sera turned off the propane flames on the stove top. "If you don't mind, we'll serve from the stove?"

"Of course." Meira had no wish to cause anyone extra work.

Taking her cue from Tyrek and Aidan, she took a plate from the counter and piled it high with heavenly smelling chicken alfredo.

A small movement at the entrance caught her attention, and Meira's gaze stole across the room to where Samael entered, talking quietly with Rune. At least they weren't snarling at each other like before.

I think you're my mate. The memory of Samael's words echoed softly in her mind, and suddenly Meira was tempted to close her eyes and see if she could sense that knowing.

But no. Her life, her loyalty, had to remain with her sisters, and their only goal was to take out Pytheios. As long as Gorgon was still alive, her promise to him held. Life had left her with terrible choices.

Frustration welled up inside her like oil spewing from the earth, coating everything in poisonous liquid gold.

Driven by a sudden urge to step away from the harsh boundaries set for her before she was even born, Meira defiantly snatched up a glass of wine, ignoring how Samael lifted an eyebrow at the alcohol given what she'd told him about her tolerance levels. Spying a seat across from her uncle at the end of one table, tucked into a private corner, almost, she took it.

Tyrek lifted his head as she set her plate down and smiled, which she suspected he didn't do often. The way the skin pulled across his aging face made the expression appear strained. More like a grimace. They sat together in silence, both simply taking each other in.

Her uncle reminded her of old black-and-white movies about war, or footage of the human Second World War. Sadness lingered in his eyes, behind a keen intelligence, like clouds obscuring the sun from shining, leaving him colored a murky gray.

Were traces of her father in that face anywhere?

"Tell me about him," she said quietly.

Tyrek must have followed her thoughts, because rather than frown his confusion, he leaned back and the sadness deepened, casting him farther into shadow. At least to her eyes. "Zilant was born to be king," he started slowly.

He spoke in such a low tone, Meira scooted forward. Their

mother had shared small details, but she'd rarely talked of her love, the pain too sharp no matter the passage of time.

"I don't mean because of the bloodline we come from," Tyrek continued. "Amons had ruled the White Clan for generations, and he was the firstborn. I mean he always knew the right thing to do. I've never met a man, then or since, with a stronger sense of protectiveness over the people he loved." He slid a glance toward Samael. "Though I'd say your bodyguard shares that trait." He shifted his gaze back to her. "You too. You get that from your father."

Meira's heart squeezed in tight with the knowledge that she carried some of her father in her.

Tyrek's gaze shifted as though he was watching a reel of memories in his mind's eye. Memories she wished she could watch with him.

"He loved your mother from the instant he laid eyes on her, long before they mated, and wrote her love letters every day they were apart. Their connection was so strong, so powerful, it filled a room with an electric charge." Tyrek grimaced. "Almost painful to be around, actually."

Meira sighed at that, softly, an ache creeping over her at never having seen her parents together. "Do you look like him?"

Her mother hadn't even had a photograph of him to share, the technology coming centuries after his death, and dragon shifters didn't do painted portraits. Something about not needing to capture their youth in image as it lasted a thousand years or more.

Tyrek shook his head then shrugged. "In some ways. Most said we looked alike in our faces, all sharp angles. I was more muscled, but he was taller. I have more cream in my coloring as a dragon, where Zilant was brilliant white. Blinding, practically, and he used that to his advantage. We both wore our hair long then." His lips twitched at a forgotten detail remembered. "He was missing part of the pinkie finger on his left hand. Lost it in a fight with a bully when we were kids, before he ever learned to shift."

Mama hadn't told them that. Why that small detail made her

father more real, she didn't know. Meira sat quietly, waiting for more. For anything.

"He laughed a lot." Tyrek shook his head. "Especially after meeting your mother. For one who took the throne at a young age, and with all the responsibilities he bore, he never let the weight of leadership change who he was. He found amusement in any kind of absurdities—a turn of phrase, a silly story, foibles of life."

Wonder lit Meira up from the inside, like fairy lights she'd once seen over a summer's eve pond in a forest. Part of her loved that her father had innate happiness in his life that way. "Did Mama laugh, too?"

Tyrek sobered. "Before she lost him, yes. They made each other laugh, often with just a glance."

To have that and lose it. *Oh Mama.* Unconsciously her gaze drifted to Sam. *Oh gods.*

Tyrek sat forward, covering her hand with his. "I rarely saw Serefina after Zilant died. I thought her dead for almost a hundred years, until she managed to track me down to arrange Skylar's safety in the event of her own death. How she found me, I'll never know. After that, she'd show up about once a year to confirm my location." He grimaced. "I moved a lot. She loved you girls. A mother that fierce, that dedicated, especially after losing her mate…" He shook his head, respect gleaming in serious eyes. "She loved you."

Meira patted the hand covering hers, his bones sharp and distinct through the thinning skin. "I know."

She couldn't say more. The tightness in her throat wouldn't let her.

A sudden warmth, like snuggling into a comforting blanket, enveloped her, and she didn't need to look around to see who'd approached.

"Everything okay?" Samael asked in a low voice.

"Fine," she said.

Samael's eyes narrowed, turning assessing, but with such a protective edge to it, her irritation with him just sort of fizzled out.

Or maybe the walls she was desperately trying to keep erected around her heart were starting to crumble. Which could only lead to disaster.

"We were talking about my parents," she found herself explaining.

A glance at Tyrek showed her uncle to be watching with no expression, though his curiosity buzzed against her. Samael tucked himself awkwardly onto the picnic bench beside her, opposite her uncle, and put his hands on the table, his pinkie finger close to where her own hand rested, but with an inch of space between them. Like an acknowledgment that he wanted to touch her but knew he couldn't.

If they had been alone, would his approach have been different? Would he have dared? Would she have let him?

Trying not to focus on his hand beside hers—larger, skin a darker shade, stronger—and how she wanted to tuck hers into his, Meira forced her gaze to Tyrek. "If we're able to overthrow Pytheios, will you come out of hiding? Come to stay with me or one of my sisters?"

"That's the plan?" Rune called across the room, voice full of skeptical doubt. "Take out the High King?"

Meira straightened, meeting the black dragon shifter's stare. "He is *not* the true High King." Her words echoed off the tall ceilings. "My father was. When Pytheios is gone, a new king will rise."

Though only the gods and fates knew which one. Kasia had tried to see, but she claimed that part of the future was murky, like a veil covered it.

The entire room went silent, every dragon shifter in the room focused on her.

Aidan, his arm hooked around Sera, turned piercing blue eyes their way. Then he leaned down to Blake. "Why don't you go play, buddy?"

At a nod from his mother, Blake groaned and trudged out the door, muttering, "I don't get to be around for anything good."

"Who *is* the true High King?" Rune shot back as soon as the child was out of dragon ear shot. "More than one phoenix mated to more than one king begs the question, don't you agree?"

Meira's mind took a step back from the emotions clotting the air and assessed the man in front of her. As a rogue and a traitor, did he care who led? Something in the set of his jaw, the way he watched her, the single beat of emotion that tapped at her empathic shield, told her this mattered to him, but not because of multiple phoenixes.

Find out what he wants.

The thought came from that same empathic power. Calm stole through her with eerie ease and Meira let it. Because the truth of those words was so crystal clear to her. She slowly, deliberately, lowered those shields that held out others' emotions, and braced herself for the impact.

Only instead of a tsunami hitting her, threatening to drown her, the emotions came at her softly.

Am I doing this?

Harsh emotions swirled around each person, and yet they weren't overwhelming her, more like lighting each person in the room up so she could read them like her computer code. Worry and a deep love from Tyrek. Curiosity and hope from Aidan and his family. She didn't dare look to Sam, moving on. Suspicion and also...hope...from Rune. Now, that was interesting.

Meira focused on the black dragon shifter and the surety of her first thought. What did he want? "How about we take down the one who's not and figure out who is after?"

Her heart tumbled around inside her at being so bold, except she wasn't nervous or edgy or any of those other things, like before. She wasn't putting on a mask right now. *This* was how she could contribute, and that gave her...authority.

Sam's hand inched over, brushing against hers in a barely there touch. A show of solidarity. He couldn't touch her. Not really. Not here. And she shouldn't want him to, but dang if that small spark of physical connection didn't zing through her, bolstering her confidence even more.

"I don't know you," she said to Rune. "And you don't know me. But my mother trusted you." She glanced at Tyrek and back to him. "My uncle trusts you. My sister trusts you."

Sam straightened beside her. "Based on what I've seen, I think we could be stronger together than apart. Don't you?"

Exactly what she'd been thinking. She inched her hand into his and squeezed. The warmth of his emotions hit her right in the solar plexus, spreading deliciously outward from there. All coming from Sam. Realization sneaked inside her with it. She wasn't scared of his emotions. Not anymore.

What was going on inside her? What was driving this sudden change? The empathy? Had opening herself up flipped some kind of switch?

Regardless, some piece of her, unknown to her until this moment, was sure that they were the same in that way. Both of them felt like outsiders. Both buried their emotions deep down and did what had to be done. They were...the same. Or two parts of a whole. Like a lock and a key.

Meanwhile, Rune crossed his arms, considering both of them. "I'm not coming back into the fold only to find another dictator rising up in Pytheios's place. I've been pretty fucking alone cutting off the heads of hydras with nothing to show for it except more heads." He held up his hand, missing the mark of his king, his bitterness a stark sizzle around him.

"Until now," Aidan said quietly.

Meira locked gazes with Rune, needing him to hear her. "You think my sisters or I want another monster to lead?"

When he said nothing, she spread her hands wide. "You've met Skylar."

Beside her Samael gave a small snort that might've been a laugh but only served to remind her how she was still holding his hand. Slowly, she inched away, hers turning colder at the loss, the wood of the table rougher against her skin.

"What are you suggesting?" Rune asked with narrowed eyes.

That tiny spark of hope inside him pulsed.

Meira rose from the table. Extra confidence was helpful, but she was facing down a powerful shifter. "I suggest we start trusting each other."

Silence. But she could feel a subtle shift in him, as though he was considering all the pros and cons.

She raised her eyebrows at Rune.

After a second he dropped his defensive stance, hands falling to his sides, resolution rising to the top of the emotions filtering through to her. "It means you fill us in on what's happening with the clans." Rune was dead serious.

"Don't you know?" Samael asked.

Rune shook his head, frustration beating at her. "The Alliance is the main group that gets any direct communication from the clans. Obviously, I don't talk to them, but our team of enforcers do, and they still aren't sure what information to trust."

"That would be frustrating." She gave voice to the emotion rolling off him even stronger now.

Rune gave a jerking shrug.

Samael regarded them in silence. Seeing what?

Finally, he glanced her way and gave a small tilt to his head, as though seeking her permission. He was asking if they'd share everything. Including Angelika. Trust couldn't be forced, but the truth was a good way to earn it. Again, that sensation of being in sync with someone, both foreign and oddly familiar, the way she was with her sisters sometimes, struck her hard.

You are his queen, she reminded herself. *He needs your permission.*

She nodded.

"We will tell you of the clans—all of it—on one condition," Samael said.

Rune crossed his arms. "That would be?"

"That you give us your side of the events here. Because I sense this group isn't the only one involved."

Rune and Aidan both had once been part of that enforcer

team—men dedicated to protecting the interests of the clans and kings within the colonies, appointed directly by the kings. They looked at each other, communicating in that way people only could if they'd been through years and battles together.

Relief was the last thing she expected to feel from the man, but that's what hit her hardest. With a sigh of satisfaction, Meira shored her empathic shields back up. Reading all those emotions might be easier now—not a tidal wave, but it wasn't restful, either.

"Fair enough," Rune said finally. "Who wants to start?"

. . .

Samael's internal clock told him they were well into the middle of the night. They'd hunkered down in that massive kitchen and talked. For hours. At least three different times, he'd tried to send Meira to bed. She should be resting, recovering her powers and her strength. But she'd blown off the suggestion with a scowl that reminded him of a feisty kitten.

A fact that only added to the tension building inside him all night. Tension that needed to be bled off either by releasing his dragon and taking to the skies or claiming his mate...

Now, as they were finally dispersing and heading to their beds, he leaned over where she still sat beside him, body humming at her nearness, her heat, her light. She'd been understanding, dealing with Rune, and suddenly so self-assured it had made his heart soar to witness the transformation. No flames like a phoenix, but certainly the soul of one. As well as clear vision, as though she could see to the heart of what Rune needed. Information and trust. Way more understanding than Samael would have thought to be. Seemed that the soft touch she had, that big heart, could reach people. Maybe he'd been wrong about her strays after all.

She'd make a wonderful queen. But then...she wouldn't be his. *Unless we don't find Gorgon, because then* I'm *the king.*

Bile burned up his throat at the disloyal thought. Everything that made him was being torn to shreds, pulled in two competing directions, and he didn't know what the fuck to do about it.

"Do me a favor." The words came out gruffer than he intended as he tried to throttle his tangled emotions back. "Stay with your uncle in his chambers tonight."

Meira frowned up at him. "You're going to do something ill-advised, aren't you?"

"Just do it." He needed the space. From her. From everything. Especially from her. Time to think.

Hurt flashed in her eyes a beat before that stubborn chin tipped up. "Please don't order me around." She gave him that miffed-kitten stare he was starting to think might be a superpower. "Talk to me."

Giving in, Samael leaned closer to put his mouth to her ear and whisper so that the others, with their enhanced senses, wouldn't catch all the words. "I've offered to be one of the scouts tonight, in return for keeping us safe."

She shook her head, her curls brushing his face, her jasmine and smoke scent rising up around him, curling into him, making his body clench. "I don't think that's a good idea," she said.

"It's either that or mate you," he growled, at the end of his endurance, his dragon leaning into him with those words.

The more danger they found themselves in, the more he needed to make her his. A compulsion that beat at him from the inside, thanks to the animal side of him. He wasn't kidding about the mating. The more they'd talked with Rune and the others, the more tension had crept and coiled inside him, the more he needed to claim and protect and...

Fuck.

Without another word, he shoved away from her and stalked out of the room.

Leaving Meira in her uncle's capable hands, trusting him above all the others—many more others than Samael had anticipated—in this place to watch over her, Samael prowled down a tunnel Rune had pointed him to. The back entrance to the mountain base.

Despite the ongoing situation with the Alliance, and how

many were after him, not to mention the fact that more people knew about his location these days, Rune had determined that a fortress was better than being caught in the open. He and his people had dug in like ticks. Though Samael had yet to see more than the four in the room, Rune apparently had plans in place on the likely event of an attack.

Hopefully one involving escape. A large number of those protected by the stone walls were unmated women. Human still, though they showed dragon sign. Mates Rune had found and protected from a system Samael had no idea had broken down horribly.

Rune's decision to go rogue hadn't been a whim or a sudden turn to evil. He hadn't been joking when he'd said that mates, or more precisely the mating system, had driven his own traitorous actions.

Mates disappearing or dying in greater numbers. It seemed Pytheios had his greedy hands in everything, including controlling the Mating Council. That body of already mated dragons was supposed to welcome and care for newly found mates. They were supposed to help those women understand who they were, ease into the culture, find their fated mate out of all the male dragons waiting, many desperately. Only that's not what had been happening, apparently. The system was rigged, mates going to those more loyal to the High King, or more instrumental in his plans.

Had Gorgon known?

Had the king fucking known? Was that why he'd secretly sanctioned Rune's actions?

Samael's dragon was pushing hard to get into the sky. He needed release, having been pent up too long and given the situation with their own mate, who was driving him to madness.

After skirting several sections that had collapsed, with human-size portions cleared, Samael reached the area Rune had assured him was clear to the outside. The second he hit the part of the tunnel large enough to accommodate a full-size dragon, Samael unleashed the beast inside him, willing the shift to happen.

Starting with his skin that turned black and shiny with scales, overtaking even his clothes as everything human about him pivoted around the anchor of his soul, absorbing that form to mold and change into the dragon. Broad shoulders grew broader, his spine realigning and his form pitching forward to all fours. Wicked spikes of razor-sharp bone protruded from his spine and around the crest of his skull. At the same time, wings formed on either side of his shoulder blades, the membrane attached at his armpit, a variation for black dragons, allowing them to fly near silent.

Rune, also on patrol now, had been more than happy to have another stealthy motherfucker out there flying patrol and keeping them all safe. Now that trust had been reestablished.

Pushing off, Samael didn't even wince at the screech of his talons on rock as he gouged deep gashes into the floor of the tunnel. No doubt the dragons who'd come before him had done the same over time. The bigger concern was how his dragon wanted to go back. To Meira. Turning their headlong plummet down the tunnel into an internal wrestling match.

Until they burst away from the mountain into the moonless, starlit sky.

Only then did the dragon side of him ease up. The world here smelled different than their home in Ararat, or Argi Dahg, as it had once been called. There the smells were sharper, sweeter, and, thanks to being a dormant compound volcano, sometimes the sulfur scent would give the impression of rotting eggs.

Here, the air was crisper, thinner, like the mountains themselves that spiked into the sky all around him, a solid four thousand feet higher than his home. Samael stayed low to the ground, skirting the treeless boulders and jagged peaks as he flew the border in ever-widening concentric circles.

Rune would be out here somewhere as well, just as silent, just as deadly if anyone or anything were to attack. Samael didn't bother to reach out to his old clan mate.

He needed the silence.

The blink of lights on the far horizon, the city of Mendoza, Argentina, over a hundred miles away apparently, meant he'd hit the edge of the dragons' territory. Tipping slightly, he shrank the circles to return to the mountain.

As he flew, Samael focused outward, away from himself. He tuned his senses, reaching with them. Below a vicuña dropped to its knees under an outcropping of rock to find rest for the night. To the west, and at a lower elevation, a royal condor dived off a rock, its heavy body dropping, most likely having sighted carrion in the open spaces below. Lower and farther out still, winds gently stirred the leaves of the trees, and a pine cone dropped from its branch to the forest floor. However, no threat came near that he could detect.

A wail of sirens, coming from inside the mountain, pierced the calm like a needle popping a balloon.

Samael bobbled in the air as his dragon's first instinct was to protect his mate, jerking them around to return as quickly as possible. The human side, the trained warrior in him, had to course correct, staying where he was, senses tuned to any possible hint of danger from outside.

"What the fuck is that?" He directed the telepathic thought to Rune, whom he hadn't seen but knew was out here.

"Fire," came the grim response. *"That's the alarm for dragon fire big enough to hit our sensors."*

He didn't need to explain more. Samael already knew. Rune was an enforcer, whether or not he still acted as one. As the policing arm of the clans in the colonies, one of the enforcers' main duties was to put out dragon-caused fires. Dragon fire burned hotter, longer, spread faster, and was yet another way for humans to discover supernatural creatures existed in the world. No doubt Rune tracked them for different reasons. He wouldn't want unknown dragons anywhere near his base.

Dragon fire on his sensors had to mean dragons were close.

Urgency held Samael taut as a drawn bow, ready for what came next, but he held his course. "*I assume we remain at our posts.*"

"*They'll contact us if the threat is in the immediate area or if we have to send out a team.*"

"*To investigate or put out?*"

Rune was silent long enough that Samael assumed he wouldn't answer. The guy never had been big on explaining. The fact that Rune had trained him might explain why Meira was always telling him to use more words.

"*A small band of dragon shifters, unaware of us as far as I know, have moved into the area,*" Rune came back.

But the tone in his voice didn't sound angry. More focused. An enforcer never stopped enforcing, it seemed. After everything Samael had been told tonight—about Rune leaving his team and risking his own death to protect mates who weren't even his—he believed that was true. But not the only truth. "*You still protect the shifters in your region, from the Alliance now, whether they are aware or not. Am I right?*"

Silence did greet that statement.

"*Yeah. I'm right.*"

"*You always were a smug asshole,*" Rune growled. "*Keep your senses tuned. The fire could be a diversion.*"

"*No shit.*" As if Samael would make a rookie mistake like that. Through this entire conversation, he'd been sweeping the area, attuned to any possible threat. He didn't bother to point out that he outranked Rune these days.

Especially if they didn't find Gorgon.

King Samael Veles. What the seven hells?

Though, if they didn't find Gorgon, king or not, there was a high chance he wouldn't be accepted back into the fold of the clan. The truth of that moved like a wrecking ball through him. His entire identity was wrapped up in who he was, the rank he'd fought with everything he had to rise to. To return to being...nobody.

The earth suddenly hushed, the sirens going silent, but so did every creature in the area.

"*Something's wrong.*" He shot the thought to Rune.

"I know. Hold."

Samael knew his duty. They were the first line of defense against an attack from the outside. *"Any communications?"*

"Radio silence. I trust my men."

Except Meira was in there. A phoenix. Unmated, technically. *His* mate. Good men had made bad decisions with less enticement, and Rune's men were all rogues. He had to suck in a roar of challenge to any creature who dared, like stoppering a bottle.

A sudden blast sent shock waves through the air.

Samael wasn't waiting anymore. That explosion came from inside the mountain. Pulling his wings in close, he dived at the ground below, aiming for that back entrance he'd come out of, already turning over what he'd do once he was inside. That fucking tunnel would take forever to navigate down, especially once he was forced to shift and walk through the collapsed parts. The large hangar would've been closed off by the heavy dragon-steel door Rune assured him was there the second the alarms sounded.

He had no other way in.

Another boom and green flames erupted from the hidden gateway, a bright flash of light in the darkness. Green. One of Rune's men? Or a different dragon shifter?

The explosion blasted out from the back side of the mountain, throwing dirt, boulders, and grasses now aflame outward a kilometer, the debris field taking out a swath of land. The ominous rumbling of collapsing rock sounded a few moments later, and another blast, this one of dust and dirt, shot from the maw of the tunnel entrance.

The tunnel must've collapsed fully.

Fuck.

Desperation had him diving at such a rate, he'd probably have trouble pulling out of it, but no way was he slowing up. Not with Meira in there. He'd damn well dig her out.

The image of her body, crushed and bloody, only drove him harder, panic poison in his blood and in his mind.

Suddenly, a black dragon dropped from above, aligning with

him in the dive. Rune. *"That was my man, Jiǎ, closing the tunnel. Follow me."*

Except Rune tilted his wings away from the mountain.

Samael didn't follow. *"I'm not going anywhere without Meira."*

"You have to. Jiǎ will have also closed the main entrance. He's taking everyone out the secret way we've been digging since holing up in there."

Meeting them there would only lead whoever Rune's people were protecting them from right to them. Still, nothing pinged on Samael's own personal radar around the outside of the mountain itself. Not a sign of another single paranormal creature, let alone dragon shifters.

With reluctance, Samael followed Rune as he flew off in another direction. Deliberately, Rune gained height. As silent as they flew, at altitude and on a moonless night, they were invisible.

"Where are we going?"

"I'm not sure yet."

Samael flared his wings, slamming his body to a stop. *"The hell you say."*

"Meira's taking them somewhere."

Every cell in Samael's body wanted to tackle his old mentor and beat him until he revealed every detail of what was happening. He couldn't. He couldn't even ignite his fire in warning. The glow would give away their own position to anyone tracking them. *"Tell me there's a fucking plan."*

"Yeah. Get my people out safely. That's the fucking plan."

Samael bit back a growl of frustration. After this was over, and Meira was safe, he and Rune were going to have a reckoning.

Rune turned and continued the journey, and Samael had no choice but to follow since no one else was communicating with him. Every instinct told him to find his mate. He had to cut the thought off or he'd turn and go back to the mountain and take it apart rock by rock until he got to her.

Except she might not be there.

That's when he heard it. The hushed whoosh of dragon wings.

At least five. A thousand feet below them. "*Rune.*"

"*I know.*"

Without another thought, they both held their wings steady, gliding silently on the currents of air. Remaining as still as possible, Samael slowly lowered his head to scan below them, tuning in to the sound of the dragons below.

"*I make five,*" Rune said.

"*Six. A dark-green fucker is bringing up the tail.*" Like a black dragon, at night that color was harder to spot. "*Not ours?*" Samael asked.

"*I'll give you one guess.*"

"*They're searching for us.*" Otherwise, they'd be at the mountain.

"*Agreed.*"

A flash of dark gold, nearer to bronze in color, caught his eye, and Samael stared harder at the dragon in the lead.

"*Shit. I think that's Brock Hagan.*"

"*The son of the previous gold king? You sure?*"

"*No. But he came after us in Kansas, too.*"

"*No way could he get here from the U.S. that fast. It would take too long to fly that distance.*"

"*I know. But I'm pretty damn sure that's him.*"

"*Fuck me.*"

Exactly. "*What's the play?*" He might not like it, but Rune knew this region and Samael did not. They had three options—lead the attackers away, giving Meira and the people she was with more time to get away. Let them go past, unaware of their presence above, and head in a new direction. Or attack.

He and his dragon were not on the same page as to which plan they should go with, the dragon wanting blood on his tongue.

Rune decided for them. "*They have no idea where we are. We should head back to the mountain. We'll get in through the new passage, see if there's anyone left.*"

Given that Meira was operating on fumes, she might not be able to get everyone where she wanted. The plan was solid, and maybe the only one the animal side of him would accept over blood and carnage. The draw of getting to his mate was enough.

As one, Samael and Rune tipped their wings ever so slightly, making a wide, sweeping turn with the agony of slowness because the move was more silent. They wouldn't take a direct route back to the mountain, instead taking their time and laying false trails for the fuckers below and any others that might be out there.

This was going to be a long night.

CHAPTER TWELVE

The wail of a siren had Meira jackknifing in the bed to put her hands over her ears. Before she could call out for her uncle, an unfamiliar voice came over a loudspeaker, one of the men who ran this mountain.

"We have a dragon fire. Large. Situated fifty miles west near the town. Holding to determine cause."

Only the alarms kept going.

She went to throw back the covers only to have a thick arm wrap around her waist from behind, yanking her painfully against a hard wall of chest with a knife to her throat.

"Scream and I slit you from ear to ear and drink your phoenix blood," came a low-voiced threat. Almost a whisper, probably so Tyrek wouldn't hear.

Only, instead of a fear-crazed whimper—the response that would have been normal for her not that long ago—Meira stuffed her fear into a box and shoved that box behind a wall, thinking of Sam and how he turned coldly purposeful both the day the fake Gorgon died in her fire and when Brock came for her in her home.

Somehow that worked, her mind clicking on like the whir of a booting computer. This person had come *for* her. He knew she was a phoenix. Which meant he also knew what she was worth. No way would he kill her.

A scream burst from her, making her throat raw.

"You bitch—"

Something or someone yanked her assailant from her, the knife slicing through the first few layers of skin on the side of her throat before falling to the ground with a clatter of metal on stone. Meira turned with a gasp, hand to her neck to test the deepness of the cut, to see Tyrek, partially shifted and grappling with a man dressed all in black. With a roar of threat that shook the furniture around her, her uncle speared the barbed end of his tail through the man's gut, hoisting him into the air.

The skewered man gurgled before going limp and silent. With a flick, Tyrek tossed him to the ground, his tail absorbing back into his human form in a misty haze. There then gone.

"The others will have heard you," he said. "I doubt he's the only one. Let's go—"

With the crunching of bones and a grunt of agony, a hand burst through Tyrek's chest, his beating heart clutched in a partially shifted talon. "You're not the only one who can do damage in human form, old man," a voice like a hiss snarled from behind him.

Shock protected her from what she was seeing, separating her from the moment so it almost seemed to be happening to someone else. Her mind trying to make sense of it. She'd only just found him. He couldn't already be gone—

It hit her on a wave of nausea, and she pitched forward, hands on her knees, breathing hard. Her heart tore apart to shreds. Dragon talons would be less devastating. Then her empathic shields failed her in the face of her own devastation, the rage and hatred of Tyrek's murderer beating at her, leaving her insides bruised and bloodied.

No. No. No. No! The words screamed in her head.

Then, suddenly, a wave of...resolution. From Tyrek. His white-blue gaze turning milky, her uncle had enough life in his body to mouth one word to her. "Run."

Somehow, cutting through the explosion of emotions rioting in her, all those years of her mother's training kicked in.

Her uncle slumped forward, and Meira jumped from the foot

of the bed at the mirror on the dresser across the room, igniting her flames. She jumped through the reflective surface headfirst, tumbling off the console that sat in front of the wall of screens in the room where she'd talked to Kasia, the only other place with a reflective surface inside this mountain that she could think of on short notice.

A taloned hand followed her through the massive black monitor, and she shut off her fire with a yelp, even as she scrambled back on the floor. The second the reflection changed to normal, the hand reaching through was severed, dropping to the floor between her feet and twitching there as it returned to human shape.

"What the fuck?"

Meira tipped her head back to find Aidan looming over her, blue eyes a blaze of light in his dark face.

"Meira?" Sera, standing beside him, shook out of a stupor and squatted down. "What happened?"

She sucked in a shuddering breath. "Tyrek is…" *Oh my gods.* Her heart clenched so hard she couldn't breathe. "Dead. He's dead." *He's dead* hit a loop in her head until Sera took her by the shoulders and squeezed.

Meira sucked oxygen sharply in through her nose. "They're inside the mountain." Whoever the hell "they" were. "They've come for me."

Rather than ask questions, Aidan immediately turned to a console, one with a microphone. He hit a button. "Level one attack." That's all he said.

"Oh God, Blake," Sera choked, her gaze shooting to her mate.

"We'll get him," Aidan assured her, mouth grim. Then he keyed in a few strokes and every monitor in the room started going black, each giving a pop as the computer attached shut itself down. Aidan grabbed Meira by the wrist and yanked her to her feet. "We have to run. Now."

Run? The word held no meaning. Shock was starting to creep back in on her, Tyrek's face swimming in front of her eyes. Where was Samael? Only she couldn't think about him or she'd start to hyperventilate. What would he do right now?

No. What should I do right now?

That resolution from only moments ago, her own this time rather than Tyrek's, filled her up and she yanked against Aidan's hold. "Wait. I can help. Where will everyone gather?"

Aidan's brows snapped low in a glower of impatience, but Sera put a hand on his arm and answered. "A new chamber we can access through a few different means, each with a keypad set to our handprints."

"Is there a mirror in there? Anything reflective?"

Aidan cocked his head and glanced over her shoulder at the hand still on the floor. "No, but there's a natural pond in the cavern. It's like glass."

"That'll work." It had once when she'd rescued Skylar, at least. "Bring one of the bigger screens with us."

"Why?"

She shook her head. "No time. We'll get Blake first."

At the mention of his son's name, Aidan went into a mode she could only describe as unemotionally set, so like Sam. "Do it," he said, and yanked a monitor off the wall as though plucking the head off a daisy.

Immediately Meira lit her fire. "Describe where he'd be," she said.

Sera, surprisingly calm, as though they'd practiced for a moment like this, or had already lived through other moments like this, did so quickly. "Our bedroom, not far from Tyrek's. He knows to stay put in an emergency and hide."

"Is this it?" She brought the image up on the screen.

"No. One more down."

In an instant she had it. "Go through."

Without question, they stepped inside, and she followed.

"Blake," Sera yelled.

"Mama!" Immediately the patter of small feet sounded before Blake appeared in the bedroom from wherever he'd been hiding. Sera caught him up to her.

"Let's go," Meira said, not sure how long she was going to hold out. Luckily, she had enough to get them into the chamber safely.

Walking through the screen into the pond was like being submerged in a pool sideways and immediately being immersed in pitch-blackness. Luckily the cavern pond was shallow and all she had to do was maneuver to her knees, Sera, Aidan, and Blake right there with her. Blake must've gotten water up his nose, his coughs echoing off the rock and water.

Feeling their way carefully, they stumbled out of the water, no doubt disturbing the glassy surface, which meant she'd have to wait for it to settle to use it again. Which was why she'd asked Aidan to bring the screen.

Meira lit her fire again, giving them enough light to see by. Immediately Sera reached for her, but stopped when Meira stepped back, not wanting to risk anything.

"Thank you," she said, holding up both hands.

Aidan also gave her a nod of thanks.

"Of course." Now for the others.

Soaked and shivering with the natural coolness of the cavern against her wet skin and clothes, Meira ignored the discomfort. Her fire would dry and warm her quickly. A glance around the room showed they were the first to get there. "Prop that against the wall. I need more light."

Without question, Aidan did as she asked, and Sera blew fire over old-fashioned torches, adding to the flickering glow in the room.

Please don't let me run out of juice too soon.

Igniting her own flames, washing the room in a red-gold hue, Meira turned the screen into her own searching device and started hunting through every room she could find a reflective surface in throughout the mountain, starting with the bedrooms she'd walked by to get to Tyrek's rooms.

In short order, she pulled two women—unclaimed mates, she assumed—through and into the chamber with them. Then a boom rocked the mountain, and for a second she thought the whole thing was coming down on top of itself. The cavern held, dust and rock shaking loose to drop down over them. She kept looking, finding three more women before the first short single beep sounded and a door that blended into the cavern wall itself opened.

A green dragon stepped inside—a stocky man with burnished skin, black hair, and green eyes the color of jade in sunlight, which had tipped her off. One of Rune's men? Aidan's reaction, moving to help instead of attack, told her yes.

The green shifter had five more with him, including another man sporting a nasty gash across his forehead. Already healing. "I collapsed the back-tunnel exit," the green dragon said, mouth a grim slash.

Sam was still outside—

No. Don't think like that. He can handle himself. And if she let herself start worrying, she wouldn't stop. "Who are we missing?" she asked.

"Who the fuck is she?" the green dragon demanded, looking to Aidan.

Old Meira would've gone quiet and let them work it out.

Not anymore.

"Someone who can help," she said.

"Long story, Jiǎ," Aidan said. "But she *can* help."

Rather than waste time arguing, the man named Jiǎ stepped beside her. "How?"

Immediately, Meira showed him. That's all it took. With painstaking slowness, given the urgency, lives on the line, quiet all around her as she worked with the dragon shifters on either side helping her search, they gathered their people. Some made their own way, others Meira pulled into the room, until they got everyone else inside the chamber.

Another massive boom, this one closer, was swiftly followed by the unmistakable rumble of falling rock shaking the room, sending more age-old dust falling on their heads.

"Jiǎ?" Aidan asked.

The green shifter shook his head. "Not us. That has to be them, trying to get out." His grim smile set a cold rock in the center of her chest. "I might have melted the gears for the hangar door. They're stuck in here now."

Aidan grimaced. "According to Rune, nothing is happening outside. I have no idea how they are getting in."

"How do *we* get out?" Meira asked.

Everyone else looked to Jiă. The clear leader in Rune's absence.

Meira bit her lip at the distrust spinning off the man in her direction. But if this was Rune's second... She stepped forward and put a hand on his arm without thinking it through until he tensed under her touch. "I'm a phoenix. They're here for me. Let me out and wait long enough. They'll be gone and you can get out."

Of course, she'd likely be walking into her own death. But better one life than many. She'd already lost her uncle. Putting these good people at risk was unacceptable. She may not want to die, but knowing others did because of her would break her.

Jiă jerked his head back, disbelief slapping out at her. "You'd do that?"

"This is all because of me."

The muscles under her hand relaxed, even though his face didn't change. "We don't sacrifice our own."

Meira blew out a silent breath of relief. Was it selfish of her to have wanted someone to not let her sacrifice her life? Unfortunately, unless they came up with a better plan, she'd have no choice.

"We've made a new tunnel that leads out a different side of the mountain," he said. "It's on the other side of this chamber."

But...leaving the mountain was a risk, especially with the still-human women. So was staying. The men inside the mountain might have others out there. They could wait them out, starve them out. Meira struggled through the options. "I can get a few to safety, but not all of us before I need to rest."

"Where?" Aidan demanded.

Skylar was going to kill her, but she'd done the same sending Airk to Ladon's mountain. And Angelika's wolves were there now. Precedent had been set. Though, given these dragon shifters' current situation as rogues, they might not like it, either. "Ben Nevis."

. . .

They'd been walking for a long fucking time down a tunnel hardly big enough for a human woman, which as a dragon shifter meant stooping over and frequently whacking his head into overhanging chunks of granite. Easier to do given that the only light came from both their eyes. Black flames weren't exactly bright.

"Dammit, Rune. Warn me." Samael rubbed at the raw lump forming on his head.

"Sorry," Rune tossed back.

No, he wasn't.

"Hold up." At least Rune gave him a warning before coming to a dead stop. The telltale click of buttons sounded a heartbeat before a beep, then the cavern wall appeared to swing wide. A hidden door.

"Move and I fry your ass," a now-familiar voice growled.

Aidan.

"Asses, rookie," Rune corrected. "And you don't want to do that."

Samael didn't wait to hear the next part, shouldering past both men into a large, dank chamber to find it lit by torches around the part of the circumference that wasn't taken up by an underground cave lake.

Beside an oddly propped computer monitor, the black surface of which was shattered, the splinters of glass reflecting the firelight and water, Sera sat with Meira's head in her lap.

The relief at finding her disappeared at the sight of her still form. Too still. Samael was by his mate's side, gathering her to him, one hand tangled in her hair to support her head, before he processed making the decision to move.

"What happened?" he demanded.

Sera flinched, and behind him Aidan let loose a soft but definite warning growl. Sera shot her mate a glare. "I can growl for myself, thank you very much."

"Sorry, baby girl. Instinct."

She huffed and turned back to Samael. "She's fine. A blast from whoever is attacking us shook some rocks loose. A bigger one hit the screen. A little one managed to hit her."

She grimaced and lifted a lock of hair away from Meira's forehead to show a knot already turning purple there. About the same spot as his, though his was probably healing by now. "I haven't mastered the dragon speed thing yet to try to shield her," Sera said ruefully.

"I see." Samael held her closer, the warmth of her breath against his arm the only thing keeping him sane at that moment.

The shifters in the room seemed to understand that he'd need a minute. He needed longer than that. They weren't safe yet. Still holding Meira, he lifted his head. "I thought you were getting out of here."

Aidan's mouth flattened, and he nodded at the screen. "*That* was our way out."

Well, hell.

Having not yet met everyone, Samael couldn't have said who was missing from the room. "Where was she sending you?"

"Ben Nevis."

He jerked and Meira murmured an incomprehensible protest, so he eased his hold on her. "Holy shit." How the hell had she convinced them to do that?

"Are you fucking kidding me?" Rune snarled.

Beside him, Sera winced. Even Samael knew not to screw with him when he sounded like that.

Aidan stood his ground. "Ben Nevis."

"You fucking sent the mates we've been keeping out of the hands of the kings to a king?"

Suddenly, Meira's hand fisted, curling into Samael's shirt.

"Safest place," she slurred. "Promise."

The words came out as hardly a sound. He watched her face, her eyes still shut.

Rune stepped forward, violence in every line of his body.

A snarl ripped from Samael's throat and Rune stilled, hands fisted, gaze locked.

Meira twitched in his arms. "S'okay," she mumbled.

Samael growled again, even though Rune hadn't made a move. "They'll be safe with King Ladon. I swear it," he managed to grate.

Rune pinned him with a stare full of black death, eyes alight with flame. "If they're not, yours is the head I take first."

He'd take those odds. Ladon wouldn't abuse his position. Samael was sure of that. "I won't even run," he said to Rune. "In the meantime, back away from Meira and let's talk about getting the rest of us out."

. . .

Meira's senses returned to her one at a time. Eyelids weighted with sandbags, the steady rise and fall beneath her head reached her first.

Am I on a boat?

No. Only her head was moving in that way. A now-familiar scent wrapped around her. Desert and fire.

Samael.

She sucked in a sharp breath as memories bombarded her all at once.

"You're okay. You're safe. Mostly." His voice rumbled against her cheek. "You seem to be a target for danger. *Rocks* tried to take you out this time."

Rocks?

Meira forced one eye to open and gave herself a minute to adjust to the fact that she was still in the hidden cavern, the damp of it leaving a film on her skin and probably frizzing her curls. Except things had changed since her last memory.

Samael was here. With her.

The relief that clenched and released inside her reflected the same emotions coming off him. Like waves beating against a shore before retreating, the force of it was more violent than she was prepared to deal with. She sucked in another sharp breath, disguising a sob, and jerked upright, leaning one hand against his belly to prop herself up, and stilled. Samael watched her with fathomless black eyes. But his emotions...subtly shifted.

Why did she suddenly feel as though the sun had burst back into her life? In this dark cave up against a creature hewn from night, she shouldn't. But she was fire and joy and happiness all over. "You're here?"

His lips tilted slightly. "I'm here."

"You were outside—" Meira swallowed, her hand fisting in his shirt, twisting it up and contorting it. Samael stayed perfectly still, watching. Waiting.

For what?

"You left me," she whispered, knowing that wasn't fair in a fuzzy way.

His flinch twitched against her palm. "I'm sorry."

It wasn't his fault. She had a horrible feeling it was hers. More memories floated to the top of a mind struggling with everything she'd gone through and still blurry with exhaustion.

She wanted only one thing. To give in.

So she did.

Meira collapsed against him, wrapping an arm around his neck and burying her face in his chest, breathing in his strength. "My uncle is dead," she choked.

She'd hardly known him, and yet that loss wanted to tumble her into darkness. Into going back to the gargoyles and hiding in peace. But she couldn't do that, because people needed her.

Hard arms pulled her closer, settled her against him, and lashed her there as though he'd never let her go again. "I know. I'm sorry for that, too."

"Sam...I only just found him. I had questions." She gulped,

trying hard not to let the tears pressing against her eyes fall. "We didn't have enough time."

His arms convulsed against her, almost as though clutching her to him. "I know you're hurting and tired, Mir. But we can't stay here."

Of all the things she expected him to say, it wasn't that. Slowly Meira lifted away, only now more came into focus beyond Samael.

Dragon shifters, all those she had yet to save, sat or stood around the room, watching them with serious eyes. Curious eyes.

Eyes reflecting a myriad of questions.

She couldn't give them answers.

"I'm too exhausted to do more right now," she said finally. At the same time, she pulled fully out of Samael's embrace, moving to shaky knees and trying not to let regret at the loss of contact chase her back to him.

"We know," Sam said.

"My being here brought this down on them, killed my..." She couldn't say it. Meira closed her eyes and gathered calm around her like a worn and tattered shirt, drawing it from the man beside her.

Then she frowned. "How'd you get here?"

"Rune brought me to a secret passage."

"You're unharmed."

He tucked one of her curls back from her eyes. "We met no resistance. Just a few clueless assholes who flew on by below us." His mouth tightened, and she knew he was holding back.

"What?"

His eyebrows went up, then he sighed. "I should be annoyed that you read me so well."

She didn't follow the red herring. "What aren't you telling me?"

Sam blew out a short breath. "*Brock* was leading the men I saw."

Shock skittered through her. That was too fast. And how had he even known where to look?

"He's tracking us somehow," she whispered.

"I know."

She lifted her gaze to his, knowing settling inside her. "We need to leave. Without the others."

Sam's eyes crinkled around the corners, even as the black depths remained serious. "I had a feeling you'd say that. I have a plan."

CHAPTER THIRTEEN

As plans went, Samael had to admit his fell in the stupid bucket. However, using Meira and himself as bait before disappearing themselves was the only option he could come up with that he knew his mate would agree to. Despite her worth in their world, she didn't assign much value to herself personally, more concerned about others.

He'd make sure she stayed safe.

"You want to *what*?" Rune snapped as soon as Samael explained the idea.

"There are already two mated phoenixes with plenty of power out there," Meira said, expression earnest. "I'm a complication more than a help. Expendable, when it comes down to it. Definitely not worth your lives." Almost word for word how Samael had imagined this conversation going.

"Sisters who would be devastated to lose you," Sera said.

Meira winced, but the resolve in her eyes didn't waver. "I brought this down on you—"

"We did this to ourselves," Jiǎ muttered from his corner, earning a warning glance from Rune.

"With a little help from the regime of kings and clans," Rune added. Arms crossed, the man was black dragon still, though from previous experience Samael knew a mass of angry energy lurked beneath that stoic surface. Much of it aimed at the woman now blithely agreeing to sacrifice herself for them.

"If you didn't trust Meira before," Samael didn't hesitate to point out, "you should now. She's putting her life on the line. For you." He left *asshole* unsaid, but it hung in the air regardless.

Rune's gaze slid to Meira and, Samael would've sworn, softened slightly. Then the other man drew himself up. "Do you know why I was happy to take the role of enforcer?" Rune asked, almost casually.

Which had Samael pausing to look closer. "I assumed because Gorgon asked you, as one of our clan's greatest fighters." To be an enforcer was considered an honor.

"He was going to send you, actually. I asked to go instead."

Truth. Samael had no doubt. "Why?"

"Because I didn't like how things with the clans were being handled, and I couldn't stand by and watch my king, my *friend*, do nothing but insulate our clan and allow each small change, each subtle new shift in policy, each suspicious disappearance or death, happen. I didn't know things would eventually get this bad"—he waved a hand around the room—"or I would've stayed and made sure we fought. The matings are one of many systems that have broken down since that red fuck took power. But to watch Gorgon, a man who'd been a giant, reduced to...something lesser—" Rune shook his head. "So, I came here."

With each word, Samael's muscles bunched and shifted, the burn of resentment rising up inside him like a tide of acid. "*Gorgon* kept our clan safer from Pytheios than any other king managed to do."

"Through appeasement."

Samael jerked his head, but not with as much conviction.

Rune must've seen it, his lips stretching in a proximation of a smile, but with no amusement in his eyes. "I heard a quote once that said an appeaser is one who feeds a crocodile, hoping it will eat him last."

"Winston Churchill," Meira supplied.

Samael would've laughed if he wasn't in full rejection mode.

He drew his lips back, baring his teeth. "Rune—"

"What?" his old mentor demanded. "Are you angry? You should be. I'm goddamn furious."

The loyalty in Samael refused to budge. "Better what Gorgon chose to do than end up dead, leaving Pytheios to put a puppet on the throne like Thanatos or Uther. The Blue and Gold Clans suffered more than we did. I've seen it with my own eyes. Ben Nevis has become a sad ghost of its former glory, their numbers reduced, their wealth disappeared."

"I don't doubt it."

"That could have been the Black Clan. You weren't there. I was. Every fucking day. I witnessed the decisions Gorgon was forced to make."

"I *know* the decisions he had to make," Rune growled. "And I wouldn't have been able to keep my mouth shut. So I helped him the best way I knew how and came here, until the effects rippled their way to those I was—"

Rune bit off the rest of what he was going to say, and silence dropped over the room.

Meira's hand snuck into Samael's, cold and small in his, her trust, whether she realized it or not, total. And humbling. Something about that touch got to him, opened him up and ripped out his heart. Had his life been that wrong? Everything he'd been protecting been the wrong way? The weight of the implications hit Samael hard enough that he bowed his head, staring blankly at a spot on the uneven stone floor of the cavern.

Had keeping his clan safe been the wrong move? Isolation meant that black dragons hadn't suffered, or that was how the thinking had gone. Had their people been impacted anyway? In the colonies. In lives lost that could have been prevented. In mates they didn't even know were gone.

Rune stepped into him. "If you're going to take the throne—"

Samael jerked his head up. "I can't—"

Rune cut him off with a pointed look at Meira. Based on the way her eyes tightened, Meira caught it, and she understood the implication but said nothing.

"If you do," Rune insisted, "I suggest you be ready to fight. That's what we need now. A warrior. It's what we always needed."

Samael shook his head. "Gorgon is alive. We'll find him, and he's a fighter now. He was waiting for the right time, the right allies, and he's found that in Brand and Ladon."

Rune settled back, the passion dying from him as though stripped away, replaced by a bitter disappointment. In Samael? Or in Gorgon? Or all of it? "I pray you're right."

"We'll figure it out together." Meira's voice dropped quiet as rain into the void, soothing and yet, at the same time, filling Samael with an odd sort of pride. He squeezed her hand.

Rune gave a sharp nod. "Together or not at all."

"Then let's get on the same side," she said. A challenge to everyone in the room, though put so mildly, it sounded almost like an entreaty.

"If we're on the same side, then we can't abandon you," Aidan said. Each man in the room straightened, turning to face her fully. Even the green shifter in the back.

Except Samael knew Meira. She wasn't going to allow them to protect her at the cost of their own lives. Not if she could save them. To a big heart like hers, the needs of the many outweighed the needs of the few. Always.

He knew he was right the second she sighed, the sound determined. "As the only queen in this room," she said slowly, "I believe I outrank you all."

Gods, she was incredible. "There's a way we can all get away, but the timing has to be right."

· · ·

"*This is only going to work if we can get enough of a head start. Agreed?*"

Samael's voice when he was in dragon form dropped lower, more of the animal in the raspy, dark tones. After years fearing the creature he was, Meira half expected to be terrified right now, standing beside the massive black shadow of a beast. But she wasn't. Not even close.

They'd walked down the narrow tunnel leading out of the mountain, even Meira had needed to stoop to get through. How Sam, well over six feet, managed it, she didn't know, though a few soft grunts told her he hadn't been entirely successful.

Now they stood in unspeaking silence inside a wide caldera with a hole in the ceiling overhead, the moonless sky black above, stars scattered as though the gods had thrown diamonds up there. Only things that flew could get in and out of the room they stood in.

Only the two of them. The others waited for Samael's signal.

Meira nodded.

"If I'm going to fly silent, I need to lay my spikes flat. You won't have anything to hold on to, so I'm going to carry you."

Not her preferred way to try dragon flight for the first time, but she understood. She gave a thumbs-up.

"Even the smallest sound, before we're ready for whoever is after us to know where we are, could alert them to our presence."

She kept herself from rolling her eyes and gave a more exaggerated double thumbs-up.

"Right." It said a lot for Samael's tension levels that he didn't laugh. She almost expected him to.

Instead, he stood on all fours and flipped one large taloned claw under, opening the spikes of razor-sharp talons for her to be able to walk through and stand on his palm, before closing the talons upward around her, like a creepy birdcage.

With more qualms than she wanted to give voice to, or he'd talk her out of this—they'd all already tried to—she sat down in his palm and wrapped herself around the slimmest digit, the skin there more like leather, the scales starting farther up around the base of each talon.

"Ready?" he asked. Odd that the telepathic communication sounded so clear in her head. She almost expected to feel the

vibration of the noise through his body, but he was utterly still.

With no way to vocalize without risking giving away their position, she patted the digit she held on to.

"Hang on."

Samael extended his wings to either side, then gave a massive push, wind buffeting her and scattering small rocks across the surface of the ground. Good thing her clothes had dried from earlier. He rose, dipped, and then another downstroke, and up he went another twenty feet or so. Another dip. Another beat of silent wings until he cleared the mouth of the caldera. Still, he continued to lift them slowly from the ground, one stroke at a time until they hovered above the rocks. Even in early spring, the mountains were still blanketed in snow, the air cutting through her clothes and, since her own inner fire was spent for now, immediately freezing her to the bone.

Only she couldn't say anything. So Meira gritted her teeth to keep them from chattering and held on tighter.

With a move that reminded her of a roller coaster dropping to gather momentum, Samael changed their trajectory. Like a shot, they flung forward. At the same time, he raised his legs, lifting her up until she lay almost on her stomach with her back to his belly, still surrounded by her taloned cage.

To cut the wind, she realized. The way an airplane pulled its wheels inside.

Also, against his belly, the warmth of his inner fire kept her slightly less frozen, allowing her to unclench her muscles. Not that she relaxed.

Like flowing ink, black against the only slightly less blackness of the sky around them, he set a steady rhythm of soundless strokes of his wings. After the initial shock of speeding through the air over the ground under the canopy of dragon wings, Meira closed her eyes and let herself simply feel. Gods, this was glorious. Total freedom. As though nothing, not even gravity, could contain them. Kasia was nuts for fearing this. Meira wanted to climb up Samael's leg to stand on his back and fling her arms wide. If she fell off, she had every confidence he'd catch her before she hit the ground.

Silly and fanciful.

"They're behind us."

The gruff warning tumbled her out of the beautiful space where she was safe and free, and Meira instinctively grabbed onto him tighter and turned as much as she dared to glance behind them, but his tail, with the flat, mace-like barbs at the end pointing in the direction of the wind, blocked her view.

Behind them where? Too close? Not close enough?

This entire gambit depended on how they timed this. They needed to be followed, not so close that they didn't have time to get away. But close enough, drawing their attackers away so that Rune and all the others could get out through the main entrance to their mountain. According to Rune, their attackers had blown it wide-open.

"Here we go."

The wind tearing against her increased in violence as he put on a spurt of speed that made the mountainside blur beneath them. Or perhaps just made her eyes blur as tears naturally welled up to keep them from drying to dust or freezing to ice cubes in her head.

How much farther? Gods, she wanted to call out. Were they close?

"Almost there," Samael said, no strain to his voice, utter confidence. This was where he came alive. It was obvious in the almost casual way he used his body. He was meant to fly.

A roar split the night air. Way too close. Practically on top of them.

"Are we going to make it?" she dared to ask softly.

He said nothing, his quietness an answer all by itself.

Suddenly, an answering roar blasted, but from far away, almost like a faint echo of the first one.

"Rune," Samael said, voice grim.

The black dragon shifter—now in direct violation of her

orders—seemed determined to make himself into a martyr. Not if she had anything to say about it.

She opened her mouth to scream or call out to alert those following that they were on the phoenix's track, but Samael gave her a warning squeeze, cutting off her sound. *"They're far enough away, and we could use a few extra seconds."*

Meira clutched him harder.

"There." A flash of silver ahead. A pond Samael had spotted during his earlier patrol, a plan that had come about after her use of the pond in the cave earlier.

Their way out. Bait and escape.

The next few minutes happened in a rush as he dropped suddenly, arrowing at the ground. Boulders and jagged edges of the sheer mountains rushed up at her so fast she closed her eyes. He stopped hard, slamming his wings wide, and Meira grunted as her body was forced against the cage of his talons. Rocks tumbled away under the force of the wind his wings generated and Samael landed, careful to keep her upright in his one talon.

Then he released her. In an equally silent glide of movement, as he shrank and realigned, Samael returned to his human form. Then ignited, allowing his black fire to dance on his palm, reflecting in the water of the mountain lake he'd brought them to.

"Quickly," he said. "They're coming."

Without hesitation, Meira took his hand, letting his fire flow over her, seeping into her skin, igniting new flames inside her, which rushed over her in a torrent of red and gold quickly eaten up by the black of his own.

She couldn't take them back to the clans, certainly not all the way to the gargoyles, but they'd already discussed where to go. She pictured it now, the way Kasia had described it to her. Maul had once shown her a mental image of the place, and Meira held that in her mind as she willed the thankfully still pond to display it. A breathtaking image appeared in the reflection, oddly angled, like they lay on the ground and gazed up at the sky.

"It's going to be cold," she warned. "It may be spring, but

Alaska is too far north to realize that yet, and we're starting in freezing temperatures here. Dive head—"

A shadow passed overhead, and, without warning, Samael grabbed her around the waist and jumped into the pond feetfirst.

Plunged into icy darkness, water went up her nose, and she struggled to reorient. Because up was down on the back side of the water. The grip around her waist tightened, and suddenly she felt as though she were being dragged down deeper.

Was he going the wrong way?

Darkness crushed in on her, and panic ignited in her chest. What if they didn't make it to the surface? Without her fire, she'd never get them out of here.

Oh my gods, I've drowned us.

That same panic took over her muscles as flight instinct kicked in and she struggled against Samael's grip. He clamped down, grip bruising, and, in a vague corner of her fraught mind, she felt him kicking hard through the water.

They burst through the surface, and Meira spluttered even as her lungs tried to replace water she'd sucked in with much-needed oxygen.

"Cold...fuck," Samael spat as he released her. "If we don't get out of here quick, we'll turn hypothermic."

A dragon, with his own heat source, saying that—and his voice told her he wasn't joking—meant they needed to move. Now.

Muscles already turning heavy, her blood sluggish in her veins and making it difficult to force her limbs to function, Meira struck out for the shore, swimming as hard as she could make her limbs plow, skin already numb, aware that Samael matched her stroke for stroke. The shore seemed to hover out of reach, not coming any closer, for the longest time. The freezing air in her heaving lungs turned to razor blades with each inhalation. She kept pushing. Suddenly, her fingertips touched a slimy rock bottom, and she knew they'd made it. Meira swam a few feet more before she tottered to her feet on shaking legs that didn't want to work and stumbled the rest of the way out.

Onto snow-covered ground.

Her teeth set to chattering so hard, she was worried her brain might dislodge.

"Dammit, woman." Samael scooped her up in his arms, but even his warmth was obscured by the soaked clothing that was already turning crunchy in the night air. "Which way?"

"It's n-n-nearby." She managed to stutter the words. "Kasia said you can s-s-see it from the l-l-lake. A s-s-s-small c-c-cabin."

Vaguely she was aware of how Samael jerked around. Thank the gods for dragon sight, because it took him only a few seconds, then he took off at a dead run, his speed, even in human form, a marvel she was too frozen to appreciate. Meira grimaced against the wind his speed created against her shuddering, soggy form.

In seconds, he made it around the edge of the water and into a one-room cabin. The place her mother had sent her sister, along with Maul for protection, the night she'd died.

Samael set her on the floor, not standing, but on her backside, because her legs wouldn't support her anymore. He ran to the fireplace. "We're in luck. There's logs." Then he blew a stream of black-tipped flames over them, igniting them in seconds, the wood popping and hissing a protest at such extreme heat.

Meira knew she needed to get her clothes off, but she couldn't stop the rattling that was clenching her entire body or force her fingers to work themselves out of the fists they'd spasmed into.

"H-h-how'd I l-l-let you t-talk me into this-s-s?" she chattered.

"Me? I've learned to just go along with whatever you want these days." He turned and caught sight of her trouble with her clothes. "I've got you. Come here." Samael picked her up and stood her in front of the fireplace.

One arm around her waist to support her, he managed to strip her of her clothes. She was so damn cold, she didn't even think to be embarrassed about her state of undress or how much skin he was witnessing. She only needed to get warm. Then he grabbed a blanket from the single bed that stood pushed up against one wall of the one-room cabin, wrapped it around her, and sat her down facing the fire, as close as he dared.

Behind her, she vaguely recognized the sounds of him undressing. Then he scooted her off to the side. A tiny whimper of protest escaped her, as the distance away from the fire was significantly cooler.

"It'll be quick," he assured. Then Samael dragged the mattress off the bed and over to her so that it lay as close to the fire as possible.

He picked her up and set her on her feet. "Sorry, but we need to share body heat right now."

Before she could wonder what that meant, he unwrapped the blanket from her body, laid her down on the bed, and lay down with her, facing each other, her back to the fire. He covered them both in the blanket, tucking it in and around them tightly, before he wrapped his arms around her, resting his chin on the top of her head.

"You j-j-just wanted to get me n-n-naked," she teased through chattering teeth.

A pulse of amusement reached her a second before Samael huffed a laugh, his breath teasing her hair, which was already drying, no doubt in a disastrous pouf of chaotic curls. "Not like this."

"N-n-no?" Warmth was starting to steal through her, thawing first her chest and spreading out from there.

"No. Cold and wet were definitely not part of the fantasy." She could hear the smile in his voice.

Lovely warmth was curling through her muscles, relaxing each in turn. She inched closer, pressing her cheek to his chest and enjoying the sound of his voice in her ear. "Makes you wonder how mermaids get it on."

"Or water nymphs," he murmured.

"Or the kraken."

That made him snort, and Meira tucked her grin into his chest. Getting him to laugh was turning into a small obsession.

"There's only one kraken. I don't think he breeds," he pointed out.

"Who said anything about breeding? I'm talking about sex. I'm sure even the kraken gets lonely, too."

"I can't believe we're talking about this."

Only now that Meira's body was thawing, her mind was, too, and had glommed on to the question of kraken sex. "I mean, given his size, it could be difficult. He needs someone as big as he is."

"Seriously, why—"

"A cyclops maybe, though they're not the most attractive... Of course, the kraken isn't exactly a runway model. Definitely a face only a mother would love. And the tentacles..." She shuddered. "Everyone deserves love, though."

"I can't believe I'm asking, but who said sex and love are the same?"

"Oh heavens..." A giggle escaped her, then another. "Could you imagine the size of his penis?"

"Are we still talking about this?"

He sounded strained, which only sent her further down the rabbit hole of giggles. Meira buried her face in her hands, laughing against him. "Gives a whole new meaning to 'release the kraken,' don't you think?"

He tipped her chin up with one finger, inspecting her face in all seriousness. "Maybe you do have hypothermia and are delirious. Or in shock. We've had a lot thrown at us. Should I be worried?"

A statement that should've sobered her up, because it wasn't entirely inaccurate, but didn't. Instead, she only shook harder with laughter, picturing kraken sex and Samael's face at the same time.

"I'm really kraken up here." Then she smothered a hoot in his shoulder and just kept laughing.

"Gods, give me strength."

Which only served to keep the laughter going.

"Maybe I should give you something more serious to think about," he offered.

"I'm sure the kraken takes his love life seriously—"

"We need to contact your sisters."

That had the desired effect, and all traces of laughter disappeared. Meira lifted her head on a gasp only to find Samael smiling softly at her. "I thought that might do it," he said. Then he lifted a finger to trace her mouth. "Though I'm sad to see the smiles go."

"No," she whispered against his touch. "I was getting hysterical. I needed that."

"I like the sound of your laugh."

No one had ever told her that before. Though mostly only her sisters and mother had had a chance to hear it, probably. "Maybe someday I'll get to hear yours."

His eyes crinkled at the corners. "Not if it's about kraken sex."

Meira buttoned her lips against another wave of laughter. He must've seen how close he was to sending her back over the edge. "Come on."

He reached for her hands, but Meira pulled back, staring at his wrists. Samael had removed his leather gauntlets, and the skin underneath was...

Without thinking, she reached out and smoothed her fingers over the ridged, uneven skin that had been badly burned at some point in his life. So badly even shifter healing couldn't remove the scars. The only part of him marked by trauma. "What happened?" she asked quietly, still touching.

"Remember that fire that took my family?"

"You tried to get to them?" The ache of his pain wrapped around her, seeping into her bones. She knew that kind of grief. "I'm sorry."

What would he do if she kissed the scars?

"Me too." He pulled away from her touch before she could give in to the urge. Then he got them both up and wrapped her in the blanket—keeping his gaze strictly on hers, she noticed this time. She hadn't paid much attention earlier, too consumed by her physical condition.

Meira didn't do the same when he turned away to grab another blanket for himself. The studious part of her mind appreciated the perfection of his form—lean and muscled and well balanced. No one part of him overpowering the other parts or underdeveloped. Delicious bronzed skin covered in rough black hair only shouted his masculinity.

"Ready?" he asked.

She jerked her gaze to his. "I should probably get dressed."

"Your clothes are still soaked."

She went to an old-fashioned armoire standing at the foot of the bed and started digging through it. "Kas left in a hurry, so I bet she left clothes behind." She grimaced. "Nothing for you, though. You should probably put yours in front of the fire to dry faster."

Then she frowned, because the armoire was empty. "Nothing."

"No luck, huh?" he asked from behind her. "I'll put your clothes with mine."

She barely heard. The more she thawed, the more urgent what they needed to do next became. "Where are my pants?"

"What?"

"My pants. I saw a satellite setup as you ran me up to the house. I need my tablet."

Samael grabbed them from where he'd placed them by the fire and tossed them to her. Quickly she fished the folded device out of the leg pocket where she kept it. Good thing she'd slept in her clothing.

Unfortunately, the thing had been through two soakings. It wouldn't turn on. "Dang," she muttered. Then moved into the kitchen, fishing through containers.

Found it.

A bag of rice. She dumped her tablet right into it and then set it by the fire, but not too close.

"Rice?" Samael asked dubiously.

"Don't knock it. It's a hack that works. Let's hope it saves my tablet." Holding her blanket tight around her, she stood and looked around the room. "We should look around the place. If Kasia had a satellite hookup, she probably had tech."

Unfortunately, a search turned up nothing except a hidden wall panel that, when slid back, showed a bunch of exposed wires. Someone had been here.

What next?

Her sisters. They should touch base. No doubt Kasia and Skylar would both be awake. Skylar would be wigging out with the new arrivals, whom Meira had sent directly to her via the mirror in her bedroom. Which meant waiting for dry clothes was out. She'd have to do this wrapped in a blanket, unfortunately with Samael at her side, feeding her fire.

She'd barely been able to get them through to Kasia's cabin, even with his help. Hopefully this worked and they didn't have to wait for her to recover fully. That would not go down well with her sisters at all.

Meira moved back to the armoire and closed door to stand in front of the narrow, inlaid mirror, then turned to Samael and held out a hand. "Let's get this over with."

His gaze ran over her form wrapped in the blanket, and desire—heavy and real—touched her more in that one sweep than when she'd been pressed up against him, skin against skin, leaving her pricklingly aware.

"This should be interesting," he said. Then stepped closer. Rather than take her hand, he tugged the blanket up in a few spots, covering more skin. "There. That's more...respectable."

Meira clutched it tighter. Either that or drop the blanket and beg to go back to earlier when she lay pressed to his body and ruined the moment with jokes about kraken sex.

Thankfully unaware of her thoughts, Samael took her hand then lit his fire, the dancing black-tipped flames flowing over him to her, warming her better than any puny burning logs in a fireplace ever could. Meira took a second to close her eyes, absorbing the power he gave so freely. Steady resolve fed through the connection. Both previous times, they'd been in a rush. Right now, selfishly, she wanted to indulge in the way the heat touched every part of her, sank into her skin, and traveled through her veins.

The sudden need to know he was going to be okay, always, shook her to the core, setting up a trembling inside her. Because, somewhere along the way, this man with his loud emotions and his walls and his faith in a fate she couldn't see had become important to her.

Oh gods, she was going to lose him soon. Once they found Gorgon and got to Ararat, and she took up her new role as the queen and he was back to being her captain...

"Mir? You okay?"

She snapped her eyes open. "Mmm-hmm."

On that witty and succinct explanation, she reached for her own power, pulling up a new image in the reflection even as a draining sensation immediately sucked at her, exhaustion winding itself around her. She couldn't let herself want impossible things.

Luck was with them and Skylar was in her rooms with Ladon, sitting in front of the mirror with a chair drawn up, elbows on her knees, and expression drawn.

"Thank the gods," she burst out the second she saw Meira. "What the fuck has been going on?"

Before Meira could answer, Skylar jumped to her feet. "First, all these women show up in my bedroom." She leveled a glare at her side of the mirror. "While we were fucking, I might add. It's a good thing you sent the tiny dragon boy through last, or he would've got an eyeful."

Meira grimaced. Beside her, Samael choked. For his part, Ladon raised his gaze to the ceiling as though he might find peace up there.

"Sorry," Meira said. "They're—"

"They explained," Skylar cut her off. "It would've been nice to hear it from you, but you disappeared. I thought you were—" Skylar flung out an arm.

"I'm sorry," Meira said.

Skylar paused in her ranting and pacing to stand before them.

"I've been worried for *hours*. With the other news we got, your timing was damn ugly."

"News?" Meira prompted. More had happened beyond the people she'd sent for protection.

Skylar hesitated—never a good sign with her outspoken sister— and glanced at Ladon, who'd gone scarily serious, his mouth a flat slash.

"Gorgon is dead."

CHAPTER FOURTEEN

Those three words flayed Samael from the inside. His dragon loosed a terrible roar in his head, and he flinched.

His king was dead.

The man who'd given him a chance no other royal would have, let alone a king. In a time when Gorgon precariously held his clan together already, he had given a poor, lowborn, orphaned nobody a place of honor.

He can't be dead...

Samael tipped his hand. The brand, the mark of his clan, had disappeared as quietly as his king apparently had. Without his knowledge. That or he'd missed the loss in the rush of everything else going on. From all accounts, losing a brand was supposed to be painful, a burn. But what if his loyalty to his king had been tried and found wanting? Why hadn't the mark been replaced with the new king's mark? *His* mark, in theory. By technical right. Shouldn't that have happened immediately, or was he rogue now?

Meira squeezed his hand, and he realized he'd been squeezing hers hard with his other one. Damn. He loosened up.

"How do you know? What happened?" He didn't mean to sound accusing, but he didn't take it back, either.

Ladon crossed his arms. "A man named Amun has been in touch and told us the king's mark had disappeared. You know him?"

"My second in command, and the Viceroy of Defense. He's been running Ararat with Gorgon's beta while we've been in Ben Nevis these last months—"

"Gorgon's beta, who is also dead," Ladon pointed out.

"I know." Fuck. If anyone knew what came next, it was him. Because there was one easy solution standing right beside him. But his king—his *friend*—had just died. What kind of man did that make him that he was already thinking of filling his shoes? In every sense?

"Without Gorgon, your clan is falling apart, Samael. I'm getting reports of black dragons flying east and north to the Red, Green, and White Clans."

"By the gods," Samael snarled.

"I'm pretty sure the gods abandoned us eons ago," Ladon replied drily.

"We have to get me there," Meira said. "Let me try to unite—"

"No," Samael snapped, turning a glare on her, and her cringe ricocheted up his arm. But he wasn't going to soften that any. "Not you."

"But I'm the queen Gorgon chose for the clan."

"You go there now, and they tear you apart. You're just some woman who can hop through mirrors who they think killed their king. Even your role as a phoenix is disputable."

Something in Meira's expression changed. He couldn't say what, exactly, but suddenly an entire ocean separated them. A distance no dragon could cross. She turned away, facing her sister. "I know what to do, but first I have to rest. I won't make a move until I've talked to you first. Be in your chamber at two in the morning in two days."

Skylar tried to answer, but the sound of her voice cut off as Meira jerked her hand out of Samael's grasp and shut down her power, the mirror returning to normal.

As though nothing had happened, she moved to the bed and lay down facing the fire with her back to him.

"You are not going to Ararat," he snarled. "I forbid it."

"You can't stop me." The determination in her eyes was lined with a sadness that told him she was going to make this move with or without him.

Cold surety settled into him as he walled off everything else. "You may be the queen, but *I* am the new *king.*" Though his clan was as likely to rip into him as into her at this point. Meira's entire body went rigid, but she didn't turn his way. She wasn't getting this, dammit. "If I have to tie you down, I will. Don't test me."

"I'll burn the ropes," she said as quietly as before. He had a decent guess an eye roll went along with the words, though he couldn't see her face.

Frustration erupted from a place where his worst fear was realized and she ended up dead. Samael dropped to his knees on the edge of the mattress and, with a hand on her shoulder, forced her to roll over to face him. "Without Gorgon at your side, you're *dead.*"

She didn't even blink at the word. "I understand perfectly. I still have to try."

"Dammit, Meira. They won't listen to you or me—"

"But if you mate me, maybe they'll listen to *us.*"

Shock held Samael as still as a pond on a windless day. Gods save him from this woman. He thought he had a protective side, but she had a heart that overruled even her sense of self-preservation.

"That's not fair," he said, struggling around a voice that wanted to choke him. "You know what I believe. What I want."

"I know," she whispered.

"Are you fucking kidding me with this? I *just* found out Gorgon is dead."

Meira's eyes darkened with what he instinctively knew was her own sorrow for that fact. Then she crawled to her knees to face him. "I'm *sorry.* Truly. I know what he meant to you. Anyone could see your loyalty, but also your affection for him. I thought to mate him, but, more than that, I genuinely liked Gorgon. I think you know that. But even he would want us to do what's right here."

Seven hells. Did she not understand the position she was

putting him in? Gorgon had been a second father to him. At the same time, a dragon shifter waited for ages to find his mate, a day they lived, breathed, dreamed, and fought for. Stole for, too, apparently, based on Rune's stories.

Meira was *his*.

He had absolutely no doubt of that. But to ask him to simply forget that and take her in such a clinical manner? "How can you sit here and propose—"

She put her hand on his forearm, the physical connection cutting off his words. "We don't have time, Sam," she said quietly. "You know this."

That she used the nickname only she dared sent a few more arrows into his heart. Because, gods forgive him, he wanted her with the force of a thousand suns.

He shook his head.

"I wish we could take the time to mourn Gorgon together, to honor him first and figure things out later, but the clan is falling apart. If we lose them, the war is lost and that monster who killed my mother wins. Is that what you want?"

Sam dragged a hand over his face, because part of him reached for her with everything he had inside him. She could be his. Except the hole in him left by the death of his king might be too deep in this moment. This was too soon. Too hasty.

Meira held her blanket around her body with one hand and cupped his face with the other. "To be a king is a terrible honor. Gorgon knew that. I think…" She took a deep breath. "I think by placing you in the position he did, he believed you could be a man worthy."

"I'm as common as dirt."

"Not to the king, you weren't. I saw that. You *know* that." She moved her hand over his heart.

Sam closed his eyes, trying not to lean into her touch—or the dangerous, seductive answering thoughts swirling inside him.

"Your people need an anchor, Samael," she said, low and soft, her voice a seduction by itself. "Together, we can be that for them.

Together, we're both harder to deny. A king with a phoenix at his side, and a queen mated to a king from the clan, a leader chosen by the previous king. Together we're stronger."

Politically, she was talking about. But what about…

She searched his face, her expression almost willing him, compelling him, to buckle to this new possibility.

Only…

Another shake of his head, and he opened his eyes. "This isn't choosing *me*, Meira. Dammit."

A confusing mix of sorrow and surety swirled in eyes gone navy.

"Just because circumstance has put us here doesn't mean I don't want to be here," she said softly.

His control slipped a notch. "What are you saying?"

She tipped her head. "I'm saying that you're right. You've been right all along."

Was she saying what he thought she was? "Right about what?"

"We are mates."

His shock must've shown in his face, because her eyes widened, her face paled, and she jerked her suddenly trembling hand from his cheek. "Oh gods. You were testing me? You didn't mean it—"

He snatched that hand in both of his, flattening her palm against his chest so she could feel the tattoo of his heart against his ribs. "I meant it."

Through that connection, he felt the shudder that rippled through her body—her emotions like his, like an underground river, so deep and strong they had to bury them. "Why didn't you tell me sooner?"

She huffed a bitter-sounding laugh. "How could I? I've been fighting it with everything I have because I *promised*…" Her voice broke, and she shook her head. "We weren't possible when Gorgon was alive. A human woman is fated, but a phoenix gets to choose. That's what I was taught. I had made my choice, made a promise, one that potentially affects not only a clan, but all dragon shifters."

The pain in her voice was like dragging sharp blades over his own skin.

"Turning my back on you was killing me a little at a time. You spoke to me in that mirror, and that was it. I looked for you in every reflection I saw after that, until the day I proposed to Gorgon, and there you were..."

Samael could only shake his head in wonder. "I never would have guessed. Still waters run deep with you, Mir."

She gave a small shrug that about knocked him out, because she so obviously didn't expect his understanding, her dark-blue eyes full of worry. "The same as with you, Samael Veles."

She couldn't be playing on his emotions to ensure their mating? His dragon gave a small growl in his head that he even considered that to be her motivation.

"We should sleep," he forced himself to reason. "Rest and make decisions tomorrow."

Meira's chin wobbled, and he groaned a protest as he kept himself from pulling her into his arms. "You're not sure if you can believe that I've chosen you. Are you?"

He wouldn't lie to her. "This is happening too fast."

"I know."

"I won't use you to buy my clan's loyalty."

Her lips twitched. "I'm the one propositioning you." A blush bloomed in her cheeks, spreading down her neck. "I've been pulled in a thousand directions and torn to shreds trying to do what's right." She swallowed hard, a plea in her eyes. "What if what's right is also what we both want?"

How could he walk away from a world with her in his life? Even with everything that it brought.

"Sam." She whispered his name. Almost like a vow.

Then shock speared through his heart as she, with a boldness to rival her sisters', opened the blanket, arms wide, before dropping it, baring herself to him, her skin aglow in the firelight, beckoning, turning deliciously pink as her blush spread to every part of her skin. But she also refused to look away, chin tilted proudly.

Samael's dragon lunged for her, and he barely held back from doing the same. "Meira—" He clenched his eyes shut, but the image was burned into his mind's eye.

Earlier, when he'd undressed them both, it had been clinical, all about making sure they didn't die of exposure. But now... This. What she was offering...

"I want you," she murmured. "I always have."

He opened his eyes to find her watching him with eyes swirling with pure white consuming the blue, such open longing that his soul cried out for her. Unbidden, he released her hand and ran the backs of his fingers softly over her breast, tracing the shape.

She moved restively beneath his touch, and he continued to lightly trace the contour of that heavy breast, feathering under the bottom before traveling back up.

"This isn't a snap decision," she said. "We couldn't. Now we can, and I don't want to let the chance pass us by. Not again. We don't know how Brock is tracking us, but what if he finds us here? Takes me away? Or we make it to Ararat and we wait until you're established as the king, only they don't want me, too? There are so many things against us. I couldn't handle—" She broke off. "I can't lose you..."

She gasped as he brushed her nipple. Then swallowed and took his hand by the wrist, first raising it to kiss the puckered, scarred skin, an action that swelled his heart, before lowering that same hand until he cupped the soft, damp curls at the juncture of her thighs.

The gesture was bold, the real Meira emerging from the flames, tested by fire and forged into something amazing. His phoenix. He knew she meant everything she was saying. Her heart was there in her eyes for him to see. No more distance. No more denying.

"I want to be your mate, Samael Veles," she said, her gaze steady on his. "Forever. Yours."

On a groan, Samael leaned forward and captured her lips, his hand at the back of her head, winding in her curls and holding her to him. "Mine," he growled against her softness.

She smiled against him. "And you'll be mine."

A claim and a promise dropping from her lips like rain from heaven.

"Do we dare claim each other?"

After all her bravado, her insistence and logic, she still asked?

"I don't think we dare go against the fates," he said against her lips.

. . .

Could this be happening?

Meira was afraid to search for a true answer to that question, lest she wake to find this was all a dream.

Except Samael's emotions bound tightly around her—need and desire, yes, but also a profound understanding and connection. As though they were two parts of the same. Like a circuit and signal, both not working without the other. At the same time, his lips were real against hers—hot and urgent and demanding. Each press, each kiss, the stroke of his tongue against hers led her deeper into a haze of wanting. Needing his touch like shelter from a storm.

In his arms, the world became...perfect.

His hand, still cupping her mound, heated her, turning her molten in his arms. Then he moved one finger, brushing in just the right spot, and she widened her legs, wanting more.

Samael buried his face in the curve of her neck and inhaled deeply. "Jasmine," he whispered, and she smiled.

"In some cultures, jasmine is thought of as the scent of sex, a true aphrodisiac." Then she grimaced. Way to ruin the mood with facts.

Only Samael chuckled against her. Then left her gasping as he sucked on her earlobe. "I'm definitely aroused."

Then he pressed a hand to her back, moving her into his touch. Slowly he trailed those tantalizing fingers lower, teasing her with the barest of touches, stroking through her rapidly dampening folds until, finally, he slipped one finger inside her in an agonizing, slow slide that had Meira panting by the time he was done.

He paused there, and her breathing hitched as she waited for his next move. Using his thumb, he pressed into her clit, pressure and sensation stealing all her reason. At the same time, he ran his other hand up her thigh, over the curve of her hip, the dip of her waist, brushing the underside of her breast, and the barest flick over her nipple before moving higher to cup her neck.

Through the pulsing desire buffeting her from him came another emotion that set her own desire to screaming pitch. Pure alpha control.

"I'm going to love you slowly," he murmured, low and rough, his dragon hovering at the surface. "I want to memorize every part of your body. Learn what makes you catch your breath."

Meira closed her eyes and gave up all her control, willing to follow wherever her mate wanted to lead.

That thumb pressing steadily against her, moving in the slightest of circles, held most of her attention. "You're doing a good job so far," she choked.

His smile tickled against her neck. "I've been thinking about this since I saw you in that mirror."

She had, too, if she was honest. In dark corners of the nights when she shut down her own guilt by assuring herself that fantasies were only that.

Keeping that torturous hand in place as she knelt, legs spread wide for him, open to him, he claimed her lips, possessing her in such a way, with the softest kisses that reached into her soul, that her brain went fuzzy. She hardly noticed how he ran his other hand down her arm, then brought her own hand up to his mouth.

He released her lips so that he could press kisses to the pads of each of her fingers, and one in the center of her palm. He blew a stream of fire, caressing her skin with heat as he drew away, then placed that palm on his chest directly over his heart.

"Soon now, we'll share our fire and our bodies...and we'll

belong to each other."

The heat in her hand seeped into her skin and traveled her veins to her core. She was already wet, but he grinned as he felt her reaction to his words. "Tell me where you like to be touched."

Meira shook her head. "I don't—"

He pressed into her and derailed her brain.

"Tell me, Meira." Both humor and intensity gleamed at her from eyes turning to liquid black flame.

"I don't know. I've never—"

Shock reverberated out from him, followed swiftly by a primal kind of satisfaction that buzzed through her like fine wine. "Fuck. Woman, are you trying to kill me?" His voice came out strangled, and she chuckled, but that only made her rub against that steady hand, which made her gasp.

"You can't tell me what you want, huh? How about you tell me what feels good?"

He left her hand over his heart and trailed his fingers down the oversensitized skin of her arm.

"Why?" she managed to ask.

He leaned forward and planted a kiss on her lips. "Because the mind is as much a part of sex as the body," he growled against her mouth. "And I want you here with me, feeling every moment, every touch, to the fullest."

She blinked up at him, her body already on fire. "I don't see how—"

He dragged his hand over her, between her breasts to swirl a finger around her navel. "Do you like this?"

Her stomach muscles jumped beneath the featherlight touch. "Mmm-hmm."

"And this?" He brought that wandering hand up to cup her full breast, brushing over the nipple.

"Yes."

"What does it feel like?"

Meira licked her lips. "Tingling, and, um…warm."

"Warm where?"

She forced the gears in her mind to engage. "Where your other hand is..."

"Your clit."

She nodded.

"And what about this?" He rolled the tight bead of her nipple between his fingers, and she arched up into his touch.

"Oh, yes. Zapping and heat."

"And here?" He pressed into her clit then eased off and she chased the touch, her hip tipping forward.

"Different."

"Describe it."

"Like an urgent ache." Gods in hell, he was right. Getting her mind in on the action was only turning her on more. The way the skin tightened over his cheekbones, he was enjoying this as much as she.

"What about here?" He rolled her nipple again and this time swirled the finger embedded inside her.

Meira could only moan. Samael smiled, the flames in his eyes giving the expression a dark edge that sent excitement fizzing through her.

"What if I use my mouth?" He left her still kneeling but scooted back so he could lean down and swirl his tongue over her nipple, and Meira threaded her fingers through his hair, not to pull him away. More to hold on for the ride.

"Meira?" He pulled back only enough to blow on her nipple, sending shivers through her.

"It feels good."

"Want more?"

"Yes."

"Harder?"

Oh, hell yes. "Suck me."

The order felt both shy on her lips and full of power, liberating in the strangest way.

He smiled against her breast as he licked and sucked everywhere but the nipple. Meira clenched her hands in his hair harder. "Suck my nipple."

Immediately he obeyed, drawing her into his mouth, but he only teased as he flicked his tongue over the sensitive tip.

She pulled his hair. "Harder, dammit."

"My pleasure." And he sucked so hard she came up off the bed, her body pulsing to the rhythm of his mouth on her breast.

"Sam—" She moaned his name. "I don't think I can wait for slow."

He released her only to move to her other breast and suck as hard, and her climax hovered just out of reach, the ache building. "You can wait," he whispered.

Only desire came from him now, filling the room, winding around her own and driving them both. He moved up her body gradually, one hand and his mouth worshipping her, the other hand staying as her anchor and her torment, pressing, and enticing, and building. Meira clung to him, riding that hand, reveling in the solid planes and muscles of his body, hanging on for the sheer pleasure he built inside her.

"Did you know wolves bite here to mate?" He nipped at the curve where her neck and shoulder met, then soothed the small hurt with his tongue.

"Are you going to bite me?"

He must've caught the excited edge to her voice, because he bit down harder. Not breaking skin, but that edge of pain to the pleasure shot straight through her.

"No. I'm going to fill you with fire." He shuddered against her. Then rose up. He removed that pressing hand, slipping his finger out of her and taking that thumb from her clit, and Meira cried out with the loss.

A low growl vibrated against her, coming from his dragon. "I thought I could wait, take our time to explore each other, but you liked that too much, and—" He moved to kneel in front of her. Almost rough now, when he'd been so gentle and in control, he lifted her up to straddle him, pausing with his cock pressing at her slick entrance.

"I want you to claim me," she said when he paused.

Words she never thought she'd ever say became right on her tongue. The ache in her body spread at the sight, at the feel of him doing exactly what he wanted with her, to her, out of control and yet hers to command.

"Tell me if you need to stop."

Gripping her hips hard, he surged and lowered her at the same time, sinking into her, the stretch of him a burn inside her. At her small gasp of pain, he paused, then pushed forward, breaking through, not stopping until he was balls-deep. There he paused, letting her adjust, holding her body as she breathed.

Gradually the pain disappeared, and the pleasure spilled back in, swamping her. Meira reached out and ran her hands down the ridges of his stomach.

"You smell like smoke, and jasmine, and sex." His eyes glittered with fire and possession.

He lifted her by the hips, agonizingly slowly, only to pause again, breathing hard, before he guided her forcefully down his shaft, only to hold there, filling her, and Meira whimpered.

"Light on fire, Meira," he growled. "Now."

Her flames were already there, waiting at the surface, ready to be unleashed. Red and gold spread over her skin, only adding to the heat. Her fire traveled over Samael only to be consumed by his own power, turning black.

Her lover threw his head back and roared his claim to the gods and all who could hear, then pistoned his hips, moving her hips with his hands, fucking her hard and fast. Meira's body spiraled in an overload of sensation, slamming through nerve endings in time to his thrusts, and she gloried in the sight of him claiming her for his own, even as she did the same, clenching around his cock with each slide in her body, arms wrapped around his neck as she held on for the ride.

"Yes," he hissed.

Then he lifted her and flipped them so that she landed on her back. He fell with her, dropped forward to his elbows, his weight pinning her to the mattress, his chest grazing her nipples with every move of his hips. His eyes level with hers, smiling and yet almost terrifying, consumed by black flames.

"Now to make you mine," he declared.

"Please," she begged.

A sound that reminded her of an old-fashioned forge, fire being stoked inside him, rumbled all around her.

"Ready?" he asked.

"I'm yours."

With a groan, Samael sank into the kiss, even as his body pounded into hers. Then heat passed from him into her as he blew a stream of fire down her throat, filling and engulfing her from the inside out. That heat joined the inferno already raging inside her, traveling along nerve endings to the juncture of her thighs.

Samael pulled back and watched her carefully, though he didn't stop moving. He threaded his hands in her hair, but Meira wasn't worried. This was right. She'd chosen this man not just with her mind, but with her whole heart.

The fire didn't burn to kill; it burned to transform. To bond. To meld them together until they were one.

She smiled, and his muscles bunched under her hands, a breath of relief punching from him, followed by a long, purring growl.

He sped up, fucking her harder, faster, building the sensations, layering them inside her.

"Meira. Now."

His command shoved her right over the cliff into oblivion as sensation exploded outward from her core. Samael swelled inside her as he thundered a shout. A new heat joined the rest, from inside her, tumbling her into a second orgasm, the waves of it smashing her on the only solid thing in her world—the man inside her and over her and around her.

Her mate.

Gradually, they slowed, the waves of sensation turning softer, gentler, lapping at her. Meira was vaguely aware of Samael turning to his side and pulling her into his arms. His finger traced her face and wound through a lock of hair.

He didn't stop touching her as her body, replete and sated, drifted away for the gods knew how long, before returning to him. A soft brush over the nape of her neck and her eyes fluttered open. She found him watching her with a smile both tender and possessive that stirred an answering knowledge inside her.

He was hers. Forever. No matter what came next.

She sucked in and lifted her hand to his face. "You're content," she whispered. "I haven't felt that from you before."

His eyebrows shot straight up. "Felt?"

Meira bit her lip. Oh, shoot. She should have told him. "I… might be a bit of an empath."

Samael gazed back at her, his reaction a rash of emotions that he shuffled through faster than she could keep up. "Did you know we were mates?"

She shook her head. "Only that you wanted me, and that you hurt to be around me."

"I bet that was damn confusing."

"I should've known, though."

"Why?"

"Because I wanted you, too. I just couldn't let myself."

"An impossible situation," he muttered.

She said nothing. Mostly because he was right.

"So, you feel everything or—"

Meira shook her head. "It comes and goes. Some people more than others. With you, it tends to be what you feel strongest, but sometimes, if it's too strong, you shut it down, like bricking it behind an invisible wall."

"And I'm content right now." Not a question.

Meira grinned at him. "A little irritated, too, probably with me for not telling you until now. But yes. Content. Like I am."

Samael blew out a sharp breath that might've been a laugh. "Yes."

"Is it there yet?"

"What?" He didn't follow her change of topic.

"The brand?" Once the mating bond solidified, they'd be tied together for life. If one died, the other would follow to the grave. However, the process was unpredictable. It could happen immediately or take months, even years.

Some made the argument that love had to be present, but her own parents had loved each other. The depth of her mother's grief over half a millennium was proof enough, and yet, their bond had not yet formed before Pytheios had taken her mate's life.

That was the only reason Serefina had survived and Meira and her sisters had been born into the world at all.

"No," Samael said quietly.

Meira sighed. "Disappointed?" If she was honest, her heart had dropped a tiny bit with his answer.

Samael shook his head slowly as he traced an absentminded pattern of whorls over her shoulder, then lower, to the sensitive side of her breast, lower still to the dip of her waist and down her thigh, bent up and over his legs. "We're through the worst of it. Neither of us died in the fire."

That wandering finger came back up her thigh and over the curve of her backside.

Meira swallowed as he left a sparkling trail of heat in his wake. "I'm curious to see what design shows."

Human women showed their mate's family crest, but phoenixes blended the crest her mother carried with that of her mate to create a new design. Except her mother hadn't carried a crest.

His touch crept lower, closer to her most intimate parts, but not yet touching. "Maybe we should keep trying. Just in case," he murmured.

That ache they had assuaged once already bloomed between her legs at the words. "Already?"

"You told your sisters two days, right?" He slipped that errant finger between her legs, teasing her with it, parting her only to feather across her slick entrance.

"To rest," she pointed out with a smile. Not that she wanted him to stop.

Contentment remained, but now hot need swamped the feeling, drawing an answering need from her, heat searing her veins.

"You can rest all you need," he murmured.

She gasped as he slid that finger inside her.

"I'll do all the work."

CHAPTER FIFTEEN

Pytheios stood with Tisiphone's hand on his arm facing the door to his bedchamber. At their back, the bed had been prepared especially for this occasion, sheer crimson panels draped over the massive, ornately carved canopy. This bed had once belonged to a human monarch of some renown. Flower petals, also red, had been strewn across red silk sheets, filling the air with a sickly-sweet scent he could have done without, but they might help his mate stomach the stench of his rotting flesh.

"What are we waiting for?" the woman at his side asked, impatience—or perhaps nerves—rife in her voice.

Though he'd yet to see Tisiphone nervous. The female-born dragon shifter was cunning, a quiet watcher. While his methods of getting what he wanted were more overt, hers were sly. A whispered word of poison in an ear. Effective. Together they would be unstoppable.

"Witnesses," he said.

Though she didn't make a sound or move, the flutter of her pulse sped up, tapping through the thin skin of her wrist against his arm. "For the ceremony?"

"For everything."

He waited for her to protest, but none came. A glance revealed a coolly assured expression in her white-blue eyes. If anything, a tiny smile curled the corners of her mouth.

"This pleases you?" he demanded. "To have others watch me fuck you?"

She lifted a negligent shoulder. "To have them watch me become the mate of the High King? Indisputable proof. I don't mind an audience for that."

Satisfaction thrummed through him. Had this been Rhiamon, he doubted the response would have been the same. His brother's plan to create a phoenix from a female-born dragon shifter had been beyond brilliant. Not even Nathair, however, had thought to have Pytheios *mate* the Trojan horse they'd created.

Pytheios had reasoned through that one on his own. He'd declared her his phoenix—of course he would mate her. All dragon shifters would expect that. The question was, how would it work? A dragon shifter didn't have to be turned, already a creature of fire, but Tisiphone was something else now, something different thanks to Rhiamon. Still fire, but new.

Surprisingly, it had not taken long to find the right candidate. A female-born dragon, sterile and unable to provide children, didn't have much of a future to look forward to. To be offered a position as mate to the High King had been an incentive none would pass up. Still, he'd been lucky to find one who fit in so beautifully with his plans.

I have chosen well.

The chamber door opened to admit Jakkobah, his black-and-red suit appropriate for the occasion but somehow only making him appear sickly. Behind him, Pytheios's younger brother, Nathair, entered, his jet-black hair a mess and clothing rumpled. He'd traded in the Rubik's Cube he used to keep with him at all times, a tool to keep his mind and hands busy, for a similar toy, one more complicated, shaped like a star.

Pytheios scowled. "Where—"

Jakkobah held up a hand. "Rhiamon, and I quote, declines to watch you bind yourself falsely to this whore who has not earned your love or respect."

Fire stirred in his belly, and Pytheios let it burn. He would need it for the mating.

Tisiphone patted his hand carefully, as though she couldn't stand to touch his rotting skin. Not rotting for much longer. "Probably better she not be here anyway," she said.

She was right, of course. He should probably be glad Rhiamon hadn't burned Everest to the ground when she'd learned of his plan to mate another.

He glanced to Jakkobah. "And our other witness?"

Jakkobah gave a birdlike bob of his head. "Shall be here shortly, my king."

As though on cue, a knock sounded at the door. "Enter," Pytheios called.

First to enter was a large man who, despite being a gold dragon, could almost pass for a black dragon with his darker hair and eyes. "I almost had her," he snarled as he prowled into the room. "Why was I called back?"

"To witness my mating."

Brock pulled up sharply at that, his gaze cutting to Tisiphone. "I'm...honored to be included."

"And after that, your own position might be addressed..." He let the sentence dangle, enticing.

Satisfaction lit Brock's eyes a molten iron ore, and he dipped his head in an uncharacteristic approximation of a bow. "Then I am doubly honored."

Four armed guards appeared behind him, two hauling their almost incoherent charge, who appeared unable to keep his feet beneath him or his head, which hung limp from his shoulders, raised. One guard grabbed him by the hair and forced his head up.

"Who am I?" Pytheios demanded.

A dark-gray fire, like billowing smoke, lit the eyes of his prisoner. "A murdering, thieving bastard," the prisoner slurred.

Excellent. He needed this witness above all the others. "You are here to observe my mating with the one true phoenix, solidifying my claim as High King. When this is done, we will return you to your clan so that you can report to all what has transpired here before your eyes. Understand?"

The man before him forced his feet beneath him, grunting with the pain and effort of it, and slowly shook off the men supporting him. He swayed, but he faced down Pytheios on his own. "Get on with it, then," Gorgon spat. "I haven't got all fucking day."

· · ·

Firelight made Samael's mate glow, or was it her soul shining outward through her happiness?

They sat on a thick alpaca rug on the floor in front of the fireplace, his back propped against the couch and Meira between his legs, leaning against his chest.

Meira *was* happy—relaxed in a way he hadn't seen from her before. He'd gifted her that much, at least. He intended to give her so much more.

These two days, as his mate recuperated and renewed the fire within her, despite being on constant alert, had been like a moment stolen from time. Their own private world where only the two of them existed. No politics. No High King. No people to lead to a better life. No place where convincing the Black Clan to follow them still hovered on this side of impossible. Two days of laughing together, talking, exploring, discovering her past and sharing his own. No planning for the future beyond returning to Ararat to claim the throne, and, please the gods, unite his people.

Samael allowed his gaze to linger on the nape of Meira's neck. She'd piled her curls on top of her head, giving him a direct view of unmarked, unmarred skin there.

While she was his mate, the clan might not believe them until the brand appeared. However, they couldn't wait for that to happen. Not when it could take up to a year. Not with reports that more and more black dragons had disappeared, abandoning their home and their people.

Without consciously deciding to do so, he feathered a kiss across that bare patch of skin.

Against him, Meira shivered, then turned her head to eye him, concern pinching her lips. "Whatever you're feeling, don't hide it from me. Are you disappointed?"

Samael shook his head. "Not disappointed. Worried."

She frowned and scooted around in the circle of his arms to face him more fully. "Proof, right?"

Samael smiled and wrapped a lock of her vibrant hair around one finger, the tresses silky against his skin, and soothing in a strange way. "Reading my emotions again?"

She shook her head. "No. You and I are often on the same page, I think."

"That's nice."

She nodded slowly, tracing a pattern over the back of his hand with her finger. "I'm not used to it. Not even my sisters think the same way I do."

He tugged on her curl to draw her closer and placed a soft kiss on her lips. "A good thing for mates, don't you think?"

Sky-blue eyes sparkled at him. "I'd never thought of it like that."

Damn adorable. His cock stirred, but he forced it to settle, though it left him heavy and aching. "To answer your question… yes, proof."

"Hmm…" She flipped his free hand over and traced the lines. "But we can't wait."

"My thinking as well."

"Did you know humans believe they can see a person's future in the lines on his hand?"

He managed to keep up with her change in subject, starting to wonder if she did that when she needed time to process something. "Oh?" he asked mildly.

She nodded primly, obviously enjoying herself. "We lived with a band of Roma at one point. One of the women taught me the way."

"And what do the lines on my hand say?"

"Let's see…" She tipped her head to the side. "You have a long palm but shorter fingers."

"My fingers are not short." He tried to tug out of her hold, but she held on.

"It means you are of the fire element."

"I could've told you that."

She ignored him. "Fire means you are passionate and confident but can lack empathy."

"So now I have short fingers and am an asshole. I'm not sure I like this hand-reading thing."

"Palmistry, they call it." She brought his hand closer to her face, studying it. "Your mount of Mercury, here"—she pointed to the base of his pinkie finger—"is raised. You're strategic and resourceful."

"That's more like it."

"Your fate line"—she traced a finger over his palm, and Samael was damn tempted to end this session with something else guaranteed to engage her mind as well as her body—"is deep and straight. However, your sun line gets closer to it until they intersect. An external event will affect your fate in a way you can't change."

Samael shifted, suddenly no longer comfortable with this game.

"But your lifeline is strong, indicating a richness and passion in everything you do." She lifted her gaze to his. "Why do you think the clan won't believe in you?" She switched topics all over again. "Gorgon clearly did."

Samael knew Meira wouldn't care one way or another, but he didn't talk about his background. Not to anyone. Not even when he'd first joined the King's Guard and Rune had questioned his loyalty, his bravery, his abilities. Pretty much everything.

"I grew up lowborn...common," he said.

A small frown pleated her brows. "So?"

"Thanks to dragon shifters' long lives, specific bloodlines have been around for ages. My bloodline is relatively new. Not a drop of royal blood in me. Only royals sit on the throne. Getting to where I am already was about luck more than anything. That and a king's guilt."

"Guilt?"

He nodded slowly. "My father was part of a minor revolution against Pytheios. My father had yet to find his mate at the time. He was aging and desperate. He claimed Pytheios was doing something wrong with all the mates. Fewer and fewer common folk were finding theirs or being given the chance to attend a mating ceremony."

Meira pulled a face. "After what Rune had to say, I'm not sure he was wrong."

Samael had already wondered at that. Had his father been right, seen the early warning signs, all those ages ago? "That might be worse."

Meira tipped her head and waited for clarification, and, for once, Samael didn't mind talking about his past.

Maybe the lack of judgment in her eyes settled him, or knowing she was his mate now and forever. "Shortly after organizing a handful of peaceful protests, my father found my mother. Not through the process we have now. He found her in a human village at the base of Ararat. One whiff, and he knew."

Meira's eyes widened. "Wow. He scented her and knew? How?"

Samael lifted the curl still wrapped around his finger and inhaled. "He said her scent reminded him of everything that was lovely in the world. A very specific scent."

"What scent?"

"Guess." Samael grinned, then chuckled when her eyes narrowed playfully.

"Hmm…" She scrunched her face up something adorable, gaze moving around the room but not seeing as she thought it through. Then she gasped, and he knew she'd hit on the right answer.

"No," she breathed.

"Jasmine."

Meira's lips formed into an "O" of surprise, and Samael, laughing, kissed her until she was dreamy-eyed and warm against him.

"See?" he said against her lips. "You were *always* meant to be mine."

Tempting to do more, strip her bare before the fire and sink into her body. Except they weren't long from the meeting with Skylar and Ladon.

She gave her head a tiny shake, blinking away the haze and searching his eyes. "There's more to the story, though. Where does the guilt come in?"

Samael grimaced. "Gorgon regretted the way they died because he didn't listen to the protests my father had originally led."

"Oh?"

"My sister and I were conceived quickly, especially for dragons, but the men my father had led to protest, most of them didn't find mates in that time. Resentment grew. They despised him for finding his happiness and leaving the cause to flounder."

"Oh no." She put a hand to her mouth. "They killed him?"

Samael nodded. "They tried for all of us, only I wasn't there that night. I often snuck out to watch the King's Guard train. If I'd been there—"

Leather creaked, and Meira covered fists he hadn't even realized he'd made with her own hands. "You could've died, too."

"They shot my dad, I've been told. And my mother died with him. Then set fire to our home. My sister was still alive—" He broke off and swallowed.

Meira glanced at his scarred hands and knew without his saying that his sister had been whom he'd tried and failed to save. She took his face in her hands. "You don't have to."

"She was still young, too young for her first shift, unable to protect herself. She died in the flames. I tried to get to her, but it was too late. Sometimes, when I close my eyes, I can still see her charred body..." Samael trailed off and closed his eyes, trying to squeeze the memories out of his mind.

For once in his life, Samael put everything out there. Laid it before his new mate because he knew, with everything inside him, that all he would get back was acceptance and comfort. Not just because he was her mate, but because of her heart.

A heart that he'd considered a liability at first, but now realized was the most beautiful part of her. Their people would bow down before her *because* of her softness and her need to save everyone, not the opposite. They needed her combination of innocence and self-sacrifice.

The fates knew what they were doing, because he'd do everything he could to protect her from herself.

As her mate, he would make sure to put her needs first. Always.

Sweet lips pressed against his, cool and calming. A balm for his pain. Just as he'd known he could trust from her. "I couldn't watch my mother die. I closed my eyes, and she sent me away. I will regret that cowardice forever."

"You're not a coward," Samael scowled.

She smiled and smoothed away the frown with her fingertips. "I told you. I'm *always* afraid."

He shook his head, hating that she viewed herself that way. "Fear doesn't make you a coward, love. It makes you smart. Only a fool doesn't experience fear."

A twinkle brightened her eyes, chasing out the blue, and she gave him a cockeyed stare. "Are you calling Skylar a fool?"

Samael barked a laugh. "Let's just say I'm glad you're my mate. I don't think I could handle the rash sister."

"See?" She straightened and grinned. "A political answer. Proof you are ready to be king."

"Huh." He set her back slightly and got to his feet, then offered her a hand. "We shall see soon enough."

She tipped her head, smiling at him. "I know you'll make an amazing king, you know how?"

"How?"

"Because you love your clan, you're loyal, and you're a fighter, but you're also fair. Even if I didn't know you, I would follow a leader like that."

Samael grunted. The thing was, dragons followed leaders based on bloodlines. "I hope you're right. I want to be a king like that."

"You will be," she said with total confidence, grinning at him, that hidden dimple winking at him.

"What kind of queen do you want to be?" he asked, tracing her face with his finger, her skin soft against his.

"A kind one," she said.

He chuckled. "I should have guessed."

Meira shrugged. "I want to live in a world where people don't suffer, don't starve, don't have to fight. Numbers may tell us to give up hope of that—we are what we are, that kind of thinking."

"If I didn't know anything about you other than your tech side, I would have guessed that would be you."

She nodded. "I think my mother is who taught me that I can be both. I can use numbers and analytics to help me make decisions or figure out a best path. But when it comes to the world around us, I believe we only find peace with kindness."

Even in the change he'd seen her go through these last days, finding her footing and her confidence, she still hadn't lost that innocent kind of faith that things could be better if she tried hard enough. He'd do his damnedest to make sure she never lost that.

"I will be so proud to have you as my queen," he said, then kissed her. "And our children, when they come, couldn't ask for a more wonderful mother."

"Children," she whispered, eyes sparkling. "That sounds... lovely."

"Yes, it does." He pressed another kiss to her lips, loving how she lingered and clung. She hummed low in her throat, a sound of pure contentment.

If only they could stay here forever. Happy. Safe.

Samael reached into the pocket of his pants. "Before we go, there's something I'd like to do..." Would she take this the way he intended? Nervous wasn't a feeling he was used to. But some small corner of his heart still wondered if she'd chosen him because she really believed they were meant to be mates, or because she had to.

"What?" Meira watched him with curious anticipation.

Samael held out the ring he'd found on the floor of her room, the orange of the amber stone catching the firelight. Meira's lips opened in a silent gasp.

"I found this."

She lifted her gaze to his. "It was my mother's. We pooled our money and bought it for her as a gift when we had to leave where we'd been staying. A place Mama had liked more than most. A memento for her."

"Will you wear it now? As a symbol of our mating?"

Meira didn't smile but held out a hand that trembled slightly. Once the ring slid home, she lifted her hand to stare at it. "I'll never take it off."

...

"You'd better be joking," Skylar snapped, her expression about as shocked as Meira had ever seen from her unshakable sister.

Ladon's reaction wasn't much better. His crossed arms dropped to dangle at his sides, a thunderous glower descending.

"We are mated," Meira repeated.

With a shake of her head, Skylar set to pacing.

A small growl escaped Samael, but Meira put out a hand as he stepped forward, stopping him. "Please don't ruin this," she pleaded softly. "Just wish us happiness and luck and many blessings upon our union."

Skylar stopped in front of the mirror, seeming to take in Meira's expression and her need, then grimaced. "You are right, of course. I just…" She shook her head as though trying to access thoughts that weren't coming. "You caught me by surprise."

Ladon seemed to reset at his mate's words, recrossing his arms. "Congratulations," he said. "Was this for political advantage, or—"

"I believe we're fated," Samael said.

Meira honestly still wasn't sure that was a thing, not for phoenixes, but it didn't matter either way. She'd wanted him, had been an unraveling mess over the idea of losing him. He was hers now, and she was his. "Samael is next in line for the black throne, and now with a phoenix as a mate, we are hoping to reunite the clan. We will go to Ararat today."

She waited for another round of shock, but neither blinked at the news. Which meant Sam's rightful place had become common enough knowledge. That might help.

"No." Skylar slashed a hand through the air.

"This is *our* decision," Meira pressed, and Skylar startled.

Her sisters had a tendency to take her acquiescence for granted, because she'd always gone along with their plans. Not this time.

"Not a lot of information is coming out of Ararat." Ladon stepped in. "It's gone quiet and not in a good way. Separately, we are getting reports of riots and other violence within the mountain. Dragons leaving in greater numbers daily. Disappearing. It's not safe."

Meira looked to Samael. She didn't even need to search his expression. Clearly there in the darkness of his eyes lay a hard resolution. They were of one accord when it came to this next step.

Samael took her hand. "The Black Clan needs a leader, or the situation will only continue to degrade. We're going."

Skylar and Ladon exchanged their own glance and silent communication. Then her sister sighed and faced them. "When?"

"Now," Meira said.

Skylar closed her eyes, resignation flitting across her features. But she nodded.

Meira steeled herself for the next part. "If something happens, tell Kasia and Angelika I love them. You too."

Skylar's eyes flashed open. "I wish you were here," she said softly.

Skylar, who was never soft. She was steel. Suddenly Meira was glad she'd left the glass between them solid rather than open a full portal, because if she could feel her sister's emotions in this moment, she might chicken out. "Me too," she whispered.

"Be careful," Skylar urged. "I love you."

"I will." Meira took a deep breath and stepped back. "Good-bye."

With a flick of her will, she changed the view.

Instead of the cavern suite of the King of the Blue Clan, a new caverned room reflected in the mirror before her. The skinniness of the view didn't give her much to go on. All she could see from this vantage point was a basic bathroom. No gilded anything. No marble countertops. A stand-up shower only, blocked by a rock wall that would probably come up to her chin.

She glanced at Samael, who nodded. "That's it."

"Right. Let's go." She held out a hand, but when she went to step into the mirror, he tugged her to a stop.

Flipping her hand over, he placed a kiss in the center of the palm, then closed her fingers over it. "Just in case."

And he meant that. Even through his walls, his fear, mostly for her, was palpable. Hers was, too. Gods help them if this didn't work.

How could she lose him now? Not only because they'd mated, but because they were starting to become a part of each other. Sharing their lives, their worst moments, their fears. Not holding back. To glimpse a life with him as her other half only to have it ripped away would destroy her.

But they had to do this.

Forced single file by the skinny mirror in Kasia's armoire in the cabin, they stepped through. After helping her down from the roughly hewn stone counter, more a part of the cavern wall than anything added after the fact, Samael led her into the suite itself.

He paused in his bedroom and took her face in his hands, kissing her long and soft, lingering over the touch before pulling back to smile down at her. "Welcome home, mate. You look good here. Right."

A sudden lightness coming from Samael, a wellspring of satisfaction, dispelled the weight of worry. Only for a moment, but he was right. Whatever happened next, she had Sam. She would always have him.

"Let me call my men and bring them here. Best if they convene Gorgon's Curia Regis and escort us there. The council are who we must win over first."

Releasing her hand, he disappeared through the large, open doorway that led to the rest of the apartment.

Curious, Meira looked around her at her new mate's home.

The basic bathroom led into a basic bedroom. Single king-size bed. One armoire for clothing and one bedside table also carved from the rock wall, protruding like a hovering ledge. No personal items. No pictures or books or even a small token or memento. As though his life hadn't been worth remembering. A thought that pressed on her heart. Together they'd make memories worthy of keepsakes that they'd both get to enjoy.

The bed was made simply with black sheets and a gray comforter. She smiled at the sight. The colors of his clan, of course.

My clan.

A shout in the hall beyond the suite snapped her out of her wandering, and she swung around to find Samael already crossing a small entryway to a door of solid dragon steel.

"What was that?" she asked.

He held out a hand, telling her to stay there, and she waited quietly as he cracked the door open. She couldn't see, her view blocked by the wall of the bedroom, but she could hear fine. Feet pounded by through the hallway.

Samael closed the door and locked it before moving to the other side of the suite. Meira moved forward, hovering in the doorway that opened into a living/dining/kitchen combo. Like in Ben Nevis, a massive glass door looked out over a stone outcropping. Not a balcony, exactly—more a slab of solid rock, big enough for a dragon to perch, that protruded out over a massive cavern.

Even from her vantage point, she could see dragons flying past, their shadows flashing through the sheer black curtains, though she didn't hear a sound. Silent black dragons. So different from Ben Nevis. The blue dragons created a whirlwind when they flew inside the mountain in any kind of numbers.

Samael turned away from the window, reminding her of a raccoon that used to ransack their trash in Kansas, with black scales surrounding his eyes like a mask. And a look that speared through her heart, pinning it to her spine. "What's happening?" she asked.

"The king!" A shout sounded from the hallway, muffled by the door.

King?

No one had seen them yet. No one knew they were here or that Samael had come to take his throne with his mate at his side. What king were they shouting about?

Realization dawned, and her stomach pitched and rolled as though the solid rock beneath her feet had turned into a sinking ship on roiling ocean waves.

"Sam?"

No emotions filtered to her. Nothing. That invisible wall had slammed up so high around him, she wondered if she'd ever get through again. The nothing from him only fed the fear slithering through her, joining the sensations tossing her around on that violet sea. "Sam. Please. Talk to me."

He slowly raised his gaze, and his eyes... She imagined his eyes might look that way when he died.

"Sam?" she prompted.

"Gorgon isn't dead..." He shook his head, gaze blazing to life even as he took a step away from her. "He is alive, and he has returned."

CHAPTER SIXTEEN

*F*uck.

The king was alive. His king, his friend…was alive. The man who was under the belief that Meira's vows held her to him until he could claim her body…was alive.

And Samael was being torn apart from the inside.

His dragon blasted a roar in his head so loud he shook with it. The sound reverberated with challenge against anyone trying to claim her, but also with terror they'd lose their mate. Especially given where Samael's immediate thoughts were already going. Beneath those first two instinctual, bone-deep emotions lay grief, for the man he'd have to fight was not only his king, whom he'd been loyal to for centuries, but his friend. One of his few true friends.

How could I do this to him? To the clan? How could I have put Meira in this position?

Because his actions would be setting her against her sisters and everything they were trying to achieve, but also against his king and clan—no way would his people ever accept them after this. Not as their king and queen. Not as members of the clan at all.

Not as anything.

Hell wasn't a deep enough pit to hurl him into. As her mate, his job was to *protect* her, make her happy. Fucking impossible now.

He forced himself to look at the woman staring at him with

wide eyes, her face so pale she might as well be translucent. He'd made vows, but so had she. *Sacred* vows in front of the Blue, Gold, and Black Clans. Witnessed. Technically, she belonged to Gorgon.

I have to fix this.

Only one way to do that.

"Stay here," he ordered.

"What?" She started toward him as he unlocked the door and slid it back. "No."

"I'm not asking, Meira. I'm telling you."

She'd lifted an imploring hand toward him as she walked. Now she dropped it to her side, eyes narrowing. "An order?" she asked. "Talk to me, Sam."

"Can't you see my emotions right now?" He snapped the words, feeling like a bigger asshole for turning this on her, but not willing to take it back.

Meira winced. "No. That wall of yours is up."

Good. He didn't want her feeling this. "Stay here. It's for your safety."

"I can use the mirrors to search for him—"

"I know where he is if he's here."

"So I go with you."

"No." His hands curled into fists at his sides. "It's not safe for either of us out there." Not if Gorgon was alive.

"All the more reason to do this together."

"Dammit, Meira." The words came out more dragon than human, the growl snarling out of him. "I can't..."

Fuck. He'd been about to say he couldn't lose her, but if Gorgon was alive, he'd already lost her. She'd never been his.

The mating shouldn't have worked if that was true. He should be a pile of ash.

Except for a phoenix, mating isn't about fate, it's about choice, a voice whispered in his head. Not his dragon, but a voice of doubt. The same voice told him he'd never been worthy. That reaching for her had turned him into Icarus, flying too close to the sun.

A soft hand landed on his arm, yanking him out of his thoughts.

Shock zapped up his spine to find she'd crossed the room to his side without his being aware. "Okay," she said softly. "I'll wait here, but I'll be watching when I can."

A grunt of pain ripped from his throat, and he leaned forward, placing his lips over hers, claiming her, tasting her. The sweetness of jasmine and smoke, and something a little bit him—earthier, like sun-warmed sand—wrapped around him. Not enough for others to notice. Yet. The longer they were mated, the more that would become obvious. Samael pulled her closer with one arm around her waist, lashing her body to his, trying to absorb her softness, her delicate beauty.

Not even Kasia's visions could predict how this was going to end.

He released her abruptly and simply stared. Taking in the sight of her lips, swollen and pink from his kisses, her vibrant curls, the small dip where dimples would show when she smiled.

Meira.

"Sam…" She searched his gaze. "You're starting to scare me."

Again, his dragon unleashed hell inside him, thrashing and demanding release, his roar threatening to blow out Samael's eardrums. Meira's eyes widened slightly. "What was that?" she barely got out through lips gone chalky.

She'd heard? Fuck. This couldn't be happening.

Bottom line. He was scaring the shit out of the woman he loved enough to give his life for, and that went against everything a dragon shifter was wired to do for his mate. "I'm scared."

Panicked. Terrified. Ready to do violence.

Because he knew, without a doubt because they were the same this way, he was going to have to make the hard decisions here. Otherwise, his tenderhearted mate would be torn apart trying to do what was right for everyone. Including him.

"Me too," she whispered.

"I don't know what's going to happen next." He cradled her cheek in one hand, absorbing her warmth, her softness. "But I need you to trust me to do what's right. What's…best for you. Okay?"

Despite the way the spot between her brows gathered in a small frown, Meira leaned into his touch. "I trust you."

"Good." His dragon settled, but only slightly. At least she wasn't watching them as though Samael was a grenade with the pin pulled and tossed away.

That was precisely what he was, but she didn't need to know that. "Give me time, then search for me. Don't come out unless I tell you to."

She nodded, but he didn't believe her eyes, which had turned navy in her distress.

"Promise me, Mir."

Her lips pinched, and she shook her head. "I can't promise that, but I'll try."

The best he was going to get, and he knew it. "Try really, really hard."

That earned him a small smile. Gods, had he lost the right to her smiles?

Samael turned his back on her and forced himself to walk away, every step heavier, harder. He made his way out onto the ledge protruding over a drop that had never scared him, not even when he'd been a boy and couldn't yet access his dragon. His parents would find him out here sitting with his legs dangling over the side and just watching.

But something about staring into a void of blackness—lights glittering from occupied homes around the conical circumference of the hollowed-out atrium, and more lights below, the only indication of a full city at the bottom, swallowed by the size of the cavern, carved out from the center of the mountain ages before—struck him as wrong.

I see my own death in that darkness.

He shook off the thought. He needed to find out if the message traveling through his clan like wildfire was true. Was Gorgon alive? Was the man he'd sworn his life to alive?

Was Meira's true king here?

He hardly had to touch the thought to release his dragon, and the creature was bursting from his skin, faster than might be safe. In shimmering waves of light, he shifted, his new form absorbing everything human about him and swallowing him whole to become the beast, though still entirely Samael. They were one and the same, not separate.

Still…a dangerous move to shift when his animal side was this wild, ready to rip into anything that came between him and his mate. Samael shook with the effort of controlling himself, of keeping from the edge of the abyss where the animal took control and the man vanished, no longer part of the whole. His dragon fought back, desperate to take his mate and fly away from here. Hide out the rest of this war with the gargoyles and guarantee her safety.

Guarantee that he got to keep her.

Samael's control slipped, just a tad, and the dragon slid closer to the doorway, zeroing in on Meira, who stood back, obscured by the curtains, her jasmine and smoke scent drifting out the door he'd left open behind him.

Did she sense his animal's fear?

Fear. They hadn't succumbed to it in centuries. Not since the day he'd forced his way into the still-burning shell of a home to find his sister's form charred in her bed. Not since. Until now.

Fear. The acrid, metallic taste of it filled his mouth.

"It's going to be okay," his mate murmured from inside the room.

His dragon must've believed her, because he breathed, the tension trembling his muscles easing as the animal ceded control to the human side. Except the human side was painfully aware that Meira *couldn't* know that. Not for certain.

Too many variables were in play.

Including a biological, bond-driven need to make sure Meira was safe and happy. No matter the cost to himself. She may have chosen him when she thought Gorgon dead, but if the king wasn't, she would be pulled in a million directions—Samael, Gorgon, her sisters, the clans that depended on the phoenixes to break

Pytheios's hold, the debt he knew she felt she owed her mother, revenge for her father...

As for him, his people were depending on both of them making the right choices. Even if that meant—

Stop. Find out the truth before you make decisions.

Samael jerked his wings out and performed a flipping maneuver off the back of the perch that shot him between two other dragons descending in wide circles, arrowing him straight down.

Ahead of his trajectory, he sent out thoughts to the men he trusted most among the guard. *"Where is he?"*

"Captain?" Bero's voice burst into his mind.

"Are you fucking kidding me?" Guafi's response layered over the other. *"You show your face here? Now?"*

Another three similar responses turned into a shocked jumble of words and sounds in his head.

"Where. Is. He?" Samael cut through the noise to demand. An order. His men would know that.

Silence—way too long given the order—and finally Amun, his lieutenant, responded with the answer Samael was in search of. *"His chambers."*

Samael slammed his trajectory to a halt, flaring his wings in such a way that he changed direction in a sharp arc that bent his back, shooting upward. Toward the perch at the king's residence.

"On my way. If you're not already there, get there." Another order.

He prayed to every god he could think of, even the ones he didn't trust, that his men obeyed. That he still stood as captain in their eyes.

In seconds, Samael reached the outcropping and landed with the silence of his kind. He stalked toward the door, changing back to human as he did. Finding the door locked, he rapped his knuckles—still covered in black scales as he completed his shift—against glass tempered to block out even dragon fire. A new feature installed in the last few decades.

The curtain drew back to show the pale-skinned face of one

of the newer guards among his men. Shock and fear lit the fire in the man's eyes, a pale gray that glittered almost like silver.

"Let me in," Samael commanded, using both his voice and the telepathic link he had access to even as the scales faded from his skin.

"Sir. I don't know—"

The sound of a barked order came from inside the chamber. The guard's face disappeared, only to be replaced by the harsh visage of Amun.

Only he didn't unlock the door. "Where the hell have you been?"

Samael scowled. "You know where. Keeping our queen safe until we could find the king. We knew the man she killed was not him, as we said when she spoke to the clan days ago."

Through the glass, Amun searched his face, no give in the man. The lack of trust in those eyes struck deep. Samael had fought beside these men for ages. Watched them become who they were. Hell, he'd helped most of them become who they were, training them himself.

And now they didn't trust him? He'd expect that from the king's council and the people, but from his own men? Fuck them, then.

Amun gave a sharp nod, and the click of the lock sliding back sounded a heartbeat before the door opened.

"Where is he?" Samael demanded as he stepped inside and strode past.

Silence greeted the question, and he swung around to find Amun staring at him with narrowed eyes. "Why are you missing your king's mark, Captain?"

Fuck. The brand on his hand was still gone.

"Yours isn't? Mine disappeared when I was told the king was dead." He glanced at Amun's hand. Sure enough, the symbol of Gorgon's house stood out in stark prominence.

"Ours returned when he showed back up."

Enhanced senses combined with years of honing his skills as a fighter gave Samael a split-second warning before two bodies flew at him from either side. Twisting down and under, Samael took a punch to the kidney as he spun, but his movement sent one of his attackers flying by. Hands up, feet spread and moving, he made sure to keep Amun's body between him and Bero and the newer guard, so he only fought one man at a time.

At the same time, he kept his senses tuned around him. More than these two had to be on the way.

"You don't want to do this," he warned them. "I am not your enemy."

"Come to the dungeons peacefully," Amun answered. "And we'll sort this out properly."

No. This could be a trap.

Every protective mating instinct inside him went into hyperalert. What if Amun and his men had somehow known he and Meira had arrived, and they had been the ones to send up a false report of Gorgon's return to lure him out? Separate him from her.

Meira.

I never should have left her alone.

• • •

Horror gripped her in icy claws as Meira watched from the mirror in Sam's bathroom. No way was she leaving him out there on his own without backup.

Why were his men attacking him? With Gorgon home, wasn't that proof that she hadn't been lying? That the man she'd killed had been a plant?

"No way. Trust has to go both ways, Amun," Sam snarled.

Those words acted like fire in an oilfield, and all three men moved at once. In a frenzy of punches, kicks, and grappling, at speeds she could hardly comprehend, the men went at each other. As best she could tell, Sam was holding his own. The shorter one with the man-bun, not the one Sam had called Amun, went flying backward thanks to a kick to his chest, knocking into the third younger guy, allowing her mate to face off against Amun, taller than him but lankier. In a swift maneuver that involved a grunt of what sounded like pain, Sam had him in a headlock.

Man-Bun and Youngster jumped back up, rushing them, but Sam swung Amun around, using his body as a blockade even as he rammed his knee into Amun's face over and over. He appeared to be gaining the upper hand, except two things happened at once.

Amun broke his grip, and a shadow from outside her field of view rushed him.

"No!" Meira yelled. Only she wasn't affecting the mirror in a way that he'd hear her warning.

Sam managed to jump back just in time, and the fight continued.

Needing to be closer, she scrambled up on the countertop to put her hands to the mirror and pressed her face in to watch the action, with her heart trying to fly out of her throat and jump into the fray.

Trust me, he'd said.

To what? Get himself killed? She knew why he hadn't gone with his men to the dungeons to sort things out. She'd seen the dawning suspicion in his eyes. That Gorgon's supposed return might be a trap to lure them out of hiding.

If that was the case, it had worked.

Samael's face, covered in blood from his nose, which she hoped wasn't broken, gave him a gruesome appearance. But he kept swinging, his back to the glass door leading outside as he fended off the three men, moving and maneuvering so that he only took on one at a time as much as possible.

If she hadn't been so damn terrified, Meira might've appreciated the skill her mate displayed. No wonder they'd made him captain. She'd heard of his skill in the air as a dragon, but he was damn impressive in human form, too.

Another two shadows flickered at the edge of her view, and two more men joined the fray. No way could he stand up against five. In less than a minute, he went down as the three men coordinated their attack like hyenas taking down a lion so they could steal the kill.

Fear pumped adrenaline through her like a giant needle had been plunged into her heart. Only one thought got through the noise. She *had* to help him. Desperate, Meira let the image go for a second and shifted it to Kasia's mountain, searching as fast as she could.

"Come on," she gritted through clenched teeth. "Where are you?"

The one creature whom she'd trust to send into that room had to be with Kasia. He hardly left her sister's side. Flying through image after image, room after room, getting dizzy with the speed of the blurring outlook before her, Meira didn't stop searching until she found him.

There. A flash of black with glowing red eyes. The image stopped and held.

"Maul," she yelled. "I need you."

The hellhound, who'd been lying in a boulder-size lump at Kasia's feet in a conference room, didn't hesitate, jumping to his feet and bolting for what she guessed on his side of the connection had to be a monitor used for teleconferencing.

"What the hell—" Brand and her sister jumped up.

Meira ignored them. Maul disappeared and then reappeared in the room beside her on a wave of smoke and stench. Immediately, she cut the connection, blanking out her sister's concerned face.

There was not enough room, and the dog was scrunched like packing peanuts into the bathroom that was not designed to hold a hellhound. His thoughts pierced her mind through that physical contact. Images of Meira hurt or bleeding.

"I'm okay. I'm fine. It's Sam. He's in trouble."

Slapping the mirror with her palm, she showed him the room.

Sam had managed to get to his feet, only now he was moving funny. Like one side of his body wasn't working properly. One eye was shut entirely by swelling, and he was clearly protecting his right side.

He backed away from the men, a few of whom had clearly come off worse in the encounter. Slowly, he moved closer to the glass door again.

"Don't let him get into the atrium and shift," one of the men, Amun maybe, said. "We'll never pin him down if he goes dragon."

Sam's lips tipped in a smile that was full-on arrogance, made more sinister by the black flames consuming his one open eye.

"Help him," she begged Maul.

The hellhound, using his own form of teleportation again, disappeared in silence and appeared in the room with Sam a heartbeat later with a snarl that poured shivers down even her spine, and she'd been expecting it.

All five men spun to face the new threat, several backing up rapidly. In the same instant, using their distraction to his advantage, Sam lunged for the window, in what appeared to Meira to be an attempt to jump over the edge and plummet to his death rather than be taken. Four of the men remained facing Maul, but one went after Sam. Amun.

Meira went to change the image and try to catch him through a window as he fell, but she paused when all motion in the room jammed to a stop. Amun's legs braced against the glass door while the top half of him was blocked from view.

"Got you, you son of a bitch," Amun shouted.

Then Sam's obviously limp body was hurled with superhuman strength back into the room. He hit the wall with a crack, then dropped to the floor in a heap. From where she stood, Meira could only see his legs, but he wasn't getting up.

Maul jumped in front of him, and all five men froze, their faces a comical mix of horror and awe. Mostly horror.

She knew it well. The hellhound, with his massive size, glowing red eyes, and putrid scent of death had struck her dumb with fear regularly when they'd first found him, and he'd been nothing but gentle with her and her sisters. Kasia in particular, but Skylar, too, had played with him, while Meira tended to keep her distance. Angelika had been a bit of a mix.

Now Meira was grateful for him as he held the men off.

"He'll take the captain away. We can't let him," Amun said and took a step forward.

Maul pulled his lips back, baring his teeth, and none of them dared come any closer. Not even their leader.

Amun's frustration showed in the way he twitched his shoulders. "If we rush him—"

"Stop!" Meira commanded and stepped through the mirror herself. She didn't shake or hesitate or even think of herself at all, because Samael's life depended on her.

"Fuck me," one of the men muttered under his breath.

"We should have known by the hellhound that *you* were close by," Amun spat.

She ignored the venom in his voice, because she could feel them. These men were confused, and deep down they were scared, looking for someone to blame. That made them lash out, because apparently dragon shifters could be emotionally stunted. She couldn't read minds, too, but Meira was fairly certain these men didn't truly want to hurt their captain. They were doing their job to protect the king.

Which would mean Samael's suspicions were baseless. She had two options. If one didn't work, she'd try the other and have Maul get them out of here.

"We are not your enemies," she said softly, calmly. The way she'd speak to a cornered or abused animal.

She placed her hand on Maul's side, his fur prickling against her palm. With a confused whine, he sat, tongue lolling out of his mouth. Which would be adorable if he wasn't so freaking scary.

The emotions swirling around them only eased a fraction.

"If we surrender, will you promise that no harm will come to us?" she asked.

The men in front of her glanced at one another, confusion almost a color around them, anger still ebbing and flowing.

Sam was going to kill her for this when he woke up. Especially if she was wrong to put her trust in these people. But she had no choice. These men were their clan. Like with Rune and his men, like with Gorgon allying with Brand and Ladon, like she and her sisters were putting their lives in the hands of the creatures they'd run from, trust needed to start somewhere.

Amun eased his stance, and the others followed suit. "We have to put you in the dungeon."

Maul snorted, a sound that came across like a sarcastic laugh, and Amun eyed him warily.

"Is Gorgon truly alive?" she asked.

If not, she'd have Maul teleport the three of them away from here now.

Amun's eyes narrowed. She didn't even need her abilities to read the suspicion. "Yes. He showed up in the hangar, severely beaten but alive. The timing of your arrival can't be a coincidence."

"And yet it is." Crappy timing had become the theme of her life these days. "We'll come with you peacefully. Samael told you... we are not the enemy here."

"That remains to be seen." Amun nodded at his men, two of whom, with visible reluctance, skirted her and Maul to haul Sam up by the arms. His head drooped forward as he dangled between them, dead weight.

"Does he need medical attention?" she asked, trying hard not to show how desperately she wanted to run to him and try phoenix tears to heal him right then and there.

"He'll be fine, but we'll call the healer to the cell we put him in." Amun stepped past her to move to a door leading out into the human-size hallways beyond. "Follow me."

CHAPTER SEVENTEEN

Consciousness returned not softly. More like with a jolt and a big fucking headache. Through the pain, eyes still closed, Samael processed everything his senses were telling him. Cool yet damp air that wasn't moving more than it had to. Thin mattress with no sheets or pillows. The constant sound of dripping.

The dungeons in Ararat sat under a massive underground lake. Damn.

Hand to his head, Samael sat up in the bed he'd been put on and took inventory. They'd broken three of his ribs in the fight, one he was pretty sure had punctured his lung. His nose and possibly his eye socket had also been fractured. He still couldn't see out of his left eye, but he could breathe okay. A good sign. They must've brought the healer in.

"Took you long enough, Captain."

No mistaking Amun's voice coming out of the dark beyond the bars.

That's right. The last thing Samael remembered was Maul jumping into the room and his own last-ditch attempt to shift midair, which meant throwing himself out the window. Only the asshole standing in front of him had snagged him by the foot, and the force of the stop slammed his head against the wall. Everything went black after that.

Except…

In the vague recesses of his memory of those last moments, he'd swear he'd heard Meira gasp. She had to have been close by, now that his brain was engaging, or the hellhound wouldn't have been involved.

"Meira." He jumped up, ignoring the ringing pain in his head, and grasped the dragon-steel bars to peer into the darkness. "Where the hell is she?"

A flicker of dark flame and Amun stepped forward, his eyes alight. "Safe enough. She and the hellhound are in a different area of the dungeons. They came willingly. We didn't have to beat the shit out of them like we did you."

Relief punched the breath from his lungs. "Thank the gods."

Amun said nothing, but no burning questions was a positive sign.

Samael turned serious. "Given the way Gorgon disappeared, someone got to him. I don't know who I can trust. Clearly, I'm not the only one worried about that."

Amun sighed. "Protecting the king is my first priority. *You* taught us that."

"You will never have to protect him from me," Samael ground through clenched teeth. Except for claiming his mate while the king was supposedly dead.

"I hope that is true. But with what's been going on these days since the mating ceremony, we operate now on a policy of ask questions first and trust later."

Another quote Samael had been known to toss at his men. A reluctant smile raised one corner of his mouth. "I'm glad to hear you were listening to at least some of what I said."

Amun smiled back, though the expression remained guarded.

"I assume the fact that I'm *not* dead is a good thing. Please tell me Gorgon is actually here, and that his being alive wasn't part of a trap."

"A trap? Is that what you thought?" Amun crossed his arms. "Makes sense, I guess. Your timing couldn't have been worse."

The implication being pretty damn obvious. "So, he *is* alive."

"Yes."

"I need to see him."

"Why do you think I'm here?"

They stared at each other for a long beat as Amun made no move, then Samael raised his eyebrows. "Are you going to open the door?"

"I need you to give me your word that you're not going to go crazy again."

"I didn't go crazy. I just wasn't going to that dungeon."

Amun shook his head, gaze turning wary. "You didn't see you from my point of view. I've never seen you like that. You fought like a man possessed."

Or like a desperate mate.

"I had reason. I'm protecting the queen."

"That doesn't make me feel any better," Amun said in the lazily sarcastic way that had used to make Samael laugh. "We still have her locked up."

Samael scoffed. "Not if her hellhound is with her, you don't. He teleports. If Meira is still in her cell, it's because she wants to be there."

Amun's eyes widened, the humor disappearing from his eyes. "Fuck me. We thought she sent him through the mirror she stepped through."

"Doubtful. You would have been fucked if she wanted to turn him loose on you. There's little more deadly than a hellhound, brother."

Amun shook his head, but he also keyed in the code, and the lock sprang back with a *clank*. "Let's take you to the king. Dealing with you is hurting my head."

Outside the dungeon, Samael turned right to head up three more levels to the atrium, where they could shift and fly the rest of the way.

Amun grabbed his arm and jerked him the other direction. "If you think I'm letting you loose in dragon form, you've lost your mind. I'm a damn good fighter, but I'm not stupid."

"Right," Samael muttered. Confirm and trust later.

They took the long path through the winding human tunnels of the mountain. Though the tunnels were often fairly empty, they didn't pass a single soul. As though the mountain itself was as empty as Samael's heart.

"What'd you do?" Samael asked. "Clear the tunnels so no one had to lay eyes on me?"

Amun's lips flattened. "Half the clan is gone."

Samael stopped in his tracks to eye the other man. "Gone where?"

But Amun only shook his head. "You should discuss all this with the king."

They made the rest of the journey in silence. At Amun's knock a guard let them into the king's suite. The damage from the fight had been cleaned up. A glance at Bero revealed an equally black eye, and Samael sent the man a smirk, earning a glare in return.

The sound of a voice, soft and broken, sounded from farther inside the chamber, pulling his attention from the room, and Samael turned slightly to find Amun watching him closely, as though he'd turn feral any second and start removing heads.

"Where is he?" Samael asked.

"His bed. He's in bad shape. The healer, other than pausing to work on your ass, has been with him constantly."

That did not help Samael's guilt any.

Each step felt an eternity as Samael crossed through room after room of the king's larger chamber, down a dome-topped hallway—a natural formation of the mountain caves—past an office and several other bedrooms to a doorway left wide open. Inside, he found several of the advisers who made up the king's Curia Regis, along with more of the guard, surrounding the bed, obscuring Samael's vision of the man lying there. Only Gorgon's feet under the blankets showed through gaps in the crowd.

But the scent was undeniable. Familiar. Rain and smoke.

Gorgon.

The men turned and formed a wall. Against their own.

Regardless of the hundreds of years he'd led them, fought at their sides.

"Let him through."

Seven hells. Was that his king's voice? Gorgon sounded as though a razor blade had been taken to his vocal cords.

The men parted, and Samael, ignoring the suspicion ripe in the room, got his first clear look at the king. Gorgon was black and blue from head to toe, bruising gone deep and much of it in various stages of healing. Which meant whoever had taken him had beaten him, let him heal partially, and then done it again. Over and over. The man had also lost weight, his face dramatically thinner, cheekbones protruding.

"Samael." Gorgon reached out a hand, and he crossed to the man who had been like a second father to him. "Why do they protect me from you?"

Instant burning lanced through the skin on his hand. He didn't need to look to know that Gorgon's mark had returned. What did that mean? "They don't know what to believe."

"Why?"

Quickly he filled his leader in on what had happened in the days—had it only been days?—since the mating ceremony. Not everything. He left out his mating the woman who was meant to be Gorgon's queen. Telling him now wouldn't be right. Not while the king was in this condition.

"When *were* you taken, my lord?" Samael asked.

Gorgon's eyebrows raised, probably at the "my lord," then he winced and consciously relaxed his face. "After the ceremony when I talked to Brand and Ladon privately—they left me in the chamber, I don't remember why. All it took was a minute. Someone hit me from behind. I have no idea how they got in or out. My guess is Pytheios's witch."

Fuck. Could that explain how Brock had been tracking them, too? If she could do that inside Ben Nevis, after expending the energy to do that flame thing, nothing could stop the false High King.

"Where is Meira now?" Gorgon asked.

"She's here. Safe." He left out the bit about Maul and the dungeon.

"I want to see her."

Samael searched for the nearest mirror and, finding one, gave a nod. The men around him tensed until, from the large, ornate mirror propped against one wall, Meira appeared, stepping out of the glass like Aphrodite must've stepped out of the sea when she was created. He'd had no doubt that she'd have the hellhound transport her to a place from which she could watch when he was removed from the dungeons. Samael spotted Maul behind her waiting in the room beyond. His own room.

The men shifted on their feet, no doubt realizing now that she could have gotten out any time she wanted. Samael shot Amun a look, and the other man crossed his arms with a glare.

For her part, Meira's gaze skittered over the men in the room, pausing on Samael for a heartbeat before she moved to the bedside. With a gentle smile followed by a grimace of pain, Gorgon reached for her hand, and she sat on the edge of the bed to take it. Samael deliberately stepped back. Either that or gnaw his king's hand off for touching her, his dragon going wild in his head at what he was watching and the thoughts now screaming in his mind.

"I need to explain everything," Gorgon said.

She shook her head. "I heard through the mirror."

"I'm sorry—"

"This is not your fault. This is Pytheios." A quick, unreadable glance at Samael, and he took another step back. Meira's eyes turned darker blue than they already were, but she turned away from him in silence, disappointment written into every line of her tense body. But he couldn't help that. Now he had to be strong for both of them.

"We have no time to waste," Gorgon said. "We must complete our mating now."

The seven hells collapsed in on Samael, raining fire and brimstone down on his head, even as he stood in total silence

in a room filled with those loyal to the man on the bed. Himself
included.

He waited for her to reveal their secret. Tell the king she was
taken. But that was dangerous.

"You must rest." She softened the words with a smile.

Gorgon coughed. "Pytheios has successfully mated the woman
named Tisiphone. She appears to be a legitimate phoenix. All the
signs were in place. I witnessed the coupling myself."

The king paled and suddenly spasmed into a fit of coughing
that racked his body, pain evident in every accompanying grimace
and grunt and the way he tried to cushion his body from each blow.
Finally, he settled back on the pillows, breathing hard, skin ashy
beneath the natural hue and beaded with sweat.

Meira gripped his hand tighter. "We can't mate."

Samael straightened. He had to stop her from confessing to
the king. If she told Gorgon here, with the king this vulnerable,
with all these untrusting eyes focused on the two of them, Samael
couldn't guarantee her safety. "Meira—"

She shot him a warning look and continued. "Not when you're
in this condition, or you risk death. I won't see you burn again.
Let's give you more time to rest, then we should talk with the other
kings and my sisters. There is…much you don't know."

The understatement of the fucking millennium.

• • •

Guards walked ahead of and behind her as Meira returned
to Gorgon after meeting with her sisters. The long skirt of
her dress swished against her legs, swirling the cool mountain air
against her skin. Back in her normal clothes. As though she'd hit
a reset button on her life.

She was hiding again, but the part of her she'd discovered while
she was with Sam, the brave part, was just biding time.

Up ahead, the door to the king's chamber opened. "I'll return
in an hour," someone was saying.

It took everything in her not to stumble to a halt at that familiar, darkly smooth voice. Samael.

She couldn't see him thanks to the guard in front of her having wide shoulders and blocking most of her view.

For two days now, as Gorgon recovered, any time she'd entered a room, her mate had exited. No doubt he'd heard her coming just now. Surprise hadn't lit his gaze as it had connected with hers.

Which meant he was actively avoiding her.

The wall was still up, blocking his emotions from her so completely, he was a void to her. Possibly, now that he knew of her ability, he could actively will that to happen. Either way, she had no idea what to do about it. Except bleed internally and wait.

By unspoken agreement, they had yet to inform Gorgon of their mating. The king was healing, but still weak, calling the healer to provide blood less often now, but still needed. That alone was a strong sign that he wasn't ready to hear the truth.

Samael stayed in his personal rooms while Gorgon had her staying in one of the extra bedrooms in his own suite. When she'd gone to protest, Samael had been the one to override her.

What was he thinking?

As they drew up to the door, Samael turned to leave. Their gazes connected and she waited, heart slowing in each pump of her life's blood through her body.

Time didn't stop. Because he didn't stop, and his walls were solid, keeping her out.

"My queen." He nodded and walked briskly by.

Damn the man.

"Samael." Deliberately, she avoided his nickname.

With visible reluctance, he turned to face her, eyebrows raised.

"I'm not giving up," she said, willing him to understand. Unable to say more because of their audience.

But her lover's walls were sky-high by now. "Of course, my queen."

"Don't," she choked, then sucked in a breath.

Pain, a wasteland of it, lashed out at her, only to be reined in so fast, she almost questioned what she'd felt.

"I must go." Without waiting for her response, Sam turned and walked away.

Time might not have stopped, but her heart came to a screeching halt before plummeting to her feet, where it got trampled to a gory pulp. Her heart crawled, bloody and bruised, in the opposite direction, wanting to go with the man walking away from her.

She had a horrible, piercing dread about what was going on in his head. The fact that his king's brand had returned was a bad sign as far as their mating was concerned. But to acknowledge the terrible possibility of what Sam could be contemplating might kill her, whether or not their bond had solidified.

She wouldn't let him, dammit. But until she could figure out how to convince him, she'd wait. So, for now, she focused on helping the king get better, helping the king bring his lost sheep back into the fold, and discussing next steps with the Blue and Gold Clans. Because Gorgon might be back, but the news he'd brought, about a successfully mated Pytheios, changed everything.

If the woman he'd taken as his mate was truly a phoenix, what the hell did that mean for all of them? What did it mean for this war? Legitimized High King or not, he'd proven himself a corrupt leader. No way could they follow him. He'd kill them all eventually anyway, even if they did pay public tribute.

"Meira?" Gorgon's voice came not from the bedrooms down the hall, but off to her right.

Leaving her guards at the door, she followed the sound to find him in an office—all smoothly carved-out rock walls, built-in bookshelves she could lose herself in, mahogany wood furniture throughout, and one wall of state-of-the-art computing systems. An entire freaking wall.

She tried not to let her gaze linger or run over and touch. It had been too long since her fingers had caressed a keyboard or a touchscreen. Days.

Deliberately, she turned her back on temptation. The back

wall, facing the atrium, was entirely made of glass, the window giving this room an almost normal feel. After five hundred years not living in caves and mountains, the change had been rough. For Angelika, too, she'd bet. Her sister had always preferred to be outdoors and in the sun.

Gorgon, sitting behind his desk, had remained quiet while she'd looked her fill, muted emotions coming from him, as usual, but nothing to cause alarm. She turned her gaze to him with a smile, and suddenly a pulse of elusive emotions ran over her skin. That had been happening with him since he'd returned. She still couldn't put her finger on what, but he didn't *feel* the same as before. Not suspicious or angry. No blame. But something...

She managed to hold her smile as it disappeared, whispered away. "I like this room. It might be my favorite place in Ararat."

He returned the smile—without an accompanying grimace of pain for the first time since he'd returned.

Gorgon got to his feet, the tremors gripping his body the last few days finally gone. "I thought you might. You're excellent with computers, I understand."

Totally geeked out was more like it, though she doubted he'd understand the slang. However, they'd talked about this before the mating ceremony. He'd been courting her—or that's how he'd put it, at least—and the old-fashioned notion had made her warm to him. That and many other things had made it easier to choose him as a mate.

But that was before Samael Veles had finally let her in...

"In fact," Gorgon continued, "I ordered these before we made our vows, so they'd be waiting for you when we returned."

Taking her hand, he led her to the wall of technology. This time she let her gaze devour each detail—a custom-built set of rack-mounted systems. She spotted three Supermicro 2U Barebones with AMD Rome 64 Cores with PNY Technologies Quadro RTX 8000-48 GB. GPUs as opposed to CPUs. They'd handle the cryptographic workload better. Meira hummed as she ran her fingers over the shiny new objects.

She turned back to the man at her side with a grin. "How did you know what to get? I'm pretty sure I didn't tell you specifications."

The king chuckled, obviously pleased with her reaction to his gift. "I may have asked your sisters for advice on a mating gift you would enjoy and talked to the computer system experts in all three clans as well as having my people here research human hackers. I wanted it to be a surprise."

Mating gift.

Trying to keep her smile in place, Meira turned her face away, back to the console he'd built for her. "I can hardly wait to dig in."

If I ever get to.

Gorgon picked up a tablet similar to the one she'd drowned—rice had not helped—and handed to her. "I rarely saw you without your tablet thing before," he said.

She unfolded the device and passed her hand over the smooth glass surface, immediately feeling slightly more grounded than she had a second ago. It would be so easy to sit down at this console and lose herself in her quiet, dependable, predictable digital world again. But the part of her awakened since the ceremony couldn't do that anymore. Couldn't stick her head in the sand and hide.

"I already have a job for you to apply your skills to."

That pulled her gaze back around.

"I received information while in Pytheios's...care." He sneered at the word. "Over the centuries, he's taken a good deal of wealth from the other clans, not to mention other paranormal creatures. Rather than keep it in physical gold or jewels, staying apart from human systems of currency as shifters normally do, he has hidden much of it in human banks and investments."

Meira stared at Gorgon for a second, hardly noticing the yellowing bruises on his face as her mind clicked over on what he'd told her. "We can trust this account?"

He grimaced. "I wasn't sure at first, but the evidence provided to me was enough to make me think it's worth checking into."

She trailed a hand over the keys. "You want me to track the money?"

He cocked his head. "Hit him where it hurts. If what you've told us about the colonies and mates is true, I think cutting off his supplies in many forms would be a..."

"Worthy endeavor?" she supplied.

"Indeed."

She stared at the blank monitors, fingers itching to get started, already bending her mind to where she would start. Getting into Pytheios's network within Everest jumped out as the best bet, but then what?

"I plan to check the veracity of my source with your brother-in-law."

She swung back to him. "Brand?" After all, Kasia's mate had been a rogue and a mercenary, bent on revenge for the murder of his family, before he'd taken the throne. It stood to reason he'd have spies and contacts within each of the clans.

"Ladon."

Ladon? How in the name of all the heavens had the King of the Blue Clan—who'd been the first to take his throne from one of Pytheios's puppet kings in a bloody coup—managed to establish a trusted contact within Pytheios's own mountain? "You're sure we can trust this informant? That he has access to this kind of information?"

"He's one of Pytheios's most trusted advisers."

Her shock must've shown on her face, because Gorgon coughed a chuckle. "My reaction exactly. We'll discuss with Ladon tomorrow on a secure line."

Meira nodded.

"Until then, I have one more day to recover, then we have other things to discuss. Agreed?"

That elusive pulse skated over her again. What was going on in his head? Meira swallowed as she considered the man in front of her. Perhaps the king was ready to hear her news. He appeared a hundred times better today than he had yesterday. The fact that he was out of bed was an encouraging sign.

Meira opened her mouth to say the words, get this over with now. The truth had been eating at her. An acid inside her mind and heart. She *should* tell him before he talked to the other kings. Instead, what came out was, "It's nice to see you on your feet, my lord. We had been told you were dead."

Gorgon's lips twitched. "This is a marked improvement, then."

Guilt surged inside her, but telling Gorgon without Samael at her side, without having discussed it with him at all, wasn't right, either.

Would Sam go for the plan she'd been formulating these last days? Obviously, the two of them ruling the Black Clan was no longer a viable option. Given the glares she received from the few she passed any time she left the king's chambers—hell, her guards would probably have killed her themselves if they weren't under strict orders to keep her alive—told her being accepted as queen would be like pushing a square boulder uphill only to have a giant kick it back down again.

Had this been the Meira pre–Samael Veles, she would have been tempted to think she wasn't built for that kind of challenge. She'd always thought of herself more of a behind-the-scenes girl, anyway.

But now she'd had a taste—a fantasy—of what she could have been to these people...at Sam's side...

In her head, she and Samael would tell Gorgon together, then, most likely depending on the king's response, make it easy on everyone involved and disappear, to the gargoyles maybe, or go to Rune and help him with the problems in the Americas. Help her sisters whenever they needed transportation by mirror or someone to hack a computer system.

If she could get Sam on his own and talk to him, dammit.

"Anyway, I'm glad you like the computers," Gorgon said.

"I do. Do dragon shifters have a native tongue?" she asked, well aware he probably thought this was a random segue. "Mother said they speak most of the contemporary human languages after thousands of years living around them, but…"

"We do. It is a guttural language. Harsh. We call it Vritranvhis. Only older dragon shifters know it any longer. A dying language, I'm afraid."

"How do you say 'thank you' in Vritranvhis?" She stumbled over the word, unfamiliar on her tongue.

He tipped his head, expression apologetic. "No word for thank you exists in my people's language."

That told her a lot.

Gorgon took her hand and escorted her to a small leather sofa set against a wall, seating her first before he dropped heavily into the seat beside her. His legs were obviously still not entirely stable, but she refrained from commenting.

"Did you know the ancient Vritranvhis have a story of how the world ends?" Gorgon paused and ran a hand over his face, which had gone pale, obviously feeling the effects of being up and about.

"Should you lie down?" she asked.

He shook his head. "I am sick to death of that bed." He dropped his hand. "Though perhaps that is an ill choice of phrases."

"Mmm…" Meira patted his hand. "We were immune to human diseases, but Skylar broke her leg once and had to stay in bed for a month. She was a terror to be around the entire time."

"I can imagine."

Meira relaxed, the butter-soft leather making no noise at her movement. "So…how does the world end?" Her curiosity had got the better of her. "In fire?"

He shook his head. "In ice and water."

What dragons feared most.

"Before our kind knew of the Americas, it was said that beyond the great waters were untamed lands. From these lands a terrible war would arise, setting a blaze even we could not calm, scorching all the earth. Every tree, every creature, gone. Leaving nothing in its wake except ash and dragons who are immune to fire. The heat caused by this fire would melt massive sheets of ice at the ends of the world, flooding everything with freezing water and consuming the last of us in the end."

"Sounds like most end-of-the-world stories from culture to culture," Meira murmured. "I wonder that they were wise enough to guess at more land, or even the polar caps, at a time when they couldn't have known."

Gorgon considered that but shook his head. "I think maybe they did know."

She tipped her head in question.

"Humans aren't the only breed with a few adventurous spirits. Even if that wasn't the case, I think your ancestors might have helped?"

"Mine?" Meira raised her eyebrows.

"According to my father's father, who I knew as a boy, a phoenix has ruled beside a dragon since the beginning. If you can walk through mirrors, and Kasia can have visions, I imagine those phoenixes must've seen something."

"Something terrifying." Meira grimaced. "Do you believe in the legend?"

"I believe that the legend is a warning. Your sister has changed a few of the outcomes she's seen, simply by seeing them and telling others. What if one of your early ancestors did the same? Told others to keep it from happening."

"Wouldn't that have been passed down through my kind?" Meira asked. "My mother told us many stories that a phoenix only passes on to her child." Or children, but Serefina Amon had been the first to have more than one.

"I don't know. But I have found, the longer I live, the more wisdom is to be gleaned from ancient beliefs and words. At the very least, they should not be dismissed out of hand."

Meira let her gaze wander away, not really seeing. Had one of the women in her line left a hidden message in an old prophecy? A message meant for her? Or was it simply a story, reflecting the fear of people facing mortality, no matter how long their lives?

That same elusive surge of emotions from the king eddied and then disappeared.

"I never wanted to be king," Gorgon said, his voice lighter suddenly. "In fact, I was never meant to be king."

She turned her head to find him watching her. "But you rule so well."

He huffed a small laugh. "After this many years, I've learned my way around the throne. However, I was a third son, with two brothers ahead of me, never meant to rule. I preferred to operate behind the scenes, as an adviser to my father, particularly in matters of politics, though never officially. My gift is reading people, knowing what they want or need, sometimes before they know themselves."

"A handy talent."

Could he see what she wanted now? Because it no longer included Gorgon. Not as her mate, at least. Only, he didn't know about Sam, and the guilt was pressing on her like stones piling upon her chest poised to crush her.

"My father and I spent many late nights talking," Gorgon said. "Some of my fondest memories. I loved him and miss him to this day." He searched her gaze. "You know the kind of missing I speak of. Your mother—"

"Yes." Pain hurried her to cut him off, and they sat in silence for a long beat. She got the impression Gorgon understood exactly. "What happened to make you king?" she asked.

He cleared his throat. "My father died of old age, taking my mother with him to the grave."

"And your brothers?"

"Both killed in the same fight not a year later. A dispute with the Blue Clan over territory, actually. Before Ladon's time. Before the king before him, even. Suddenly I found myself leading a people who didn't know me. Who wanted anyone but me, to be honest. While I would have preferred to put another man on the throne and be a council to him. But by blood, I could not turn my back on my birthright."

Meira cast her gaze over Gorgon, trying her best to picture him young, inexperienced, and unwilling. Trying to picture the clan unwilling to be led by this man whom they now so obviously revered. "How did you gain their trust?"

"Patience. Time. The latter of which you don't have."

She hummed a dry amusement. "Gee, thanks."

"I will offer this advice..." He paused, as though ensuring she listened. "That which you cannot avoid, welcome."

Meira tried not to frown as she searched the expression of the man in front of her for any clue as to his real thoughts. His emotions remained steady, as usual a barely there thread, like a spider's web brushing against her skin. Was this kindly advice meant to help? Or had he guessed what had happened between her and Sam?

Meira dropped her gaze to her lap. "My mother used to say that if you must play, decide upon three things at the start: the rules of the game, the stakes, and when to quit."

"Wise words, though I'm afraid they don't help me."

She lifted her gaze, raising her brows in question.

"A king doesn't have the luxury of quitting."

What about a queen? What about a phoenix? What about...?

Gorgon leaned toward her, slowly, but with intent clear in his eyes, offering her a kiss.

With a gasp, Meira jerked back slightly, and he froze, his brows lowering at the telling action.

Thinking fast, she licked her lips and hoped the lie didn't sound like a lie. "The last time I kissed you, you died."

A flicker of something in his eyes and a shiver of...questioning?... told her he wasn't buying that. "The last time wasn't me."

Heat rose in her cheeks. "It's stupid, I know."

Gorgon lifted a hand to cup her face, only kindness in his expression now. "You've been through a lot. We all have. Perhaps—"

"My king, we are ready."

Meira flinched at the sound of Sam's voice and jerked her head to find him standing at the entrance to the room, gaze narrowed on her and the king, but no expression. Not a single emotion. A man carved from iron.

Gorgon turned his head more slowly to address his captain. "Excellent."

The king got to his feet, and Meira stood with him. "Ready for what?"

CHAPTER EIGHTEEN

Samael walked ahead of the woman he'd mated not that long ago...and the king she was supposed to belong to.

Every step drove a dagger of ice deeper into his soul.

He hadn't dared go back to his own rooms since they'd found the king alive and returned to the clan. He didn't dare, because Meira might try her mirror trick to corner him there.

And what he planned to do...to set her free so she and her sisters could help set his people free...

He'd seen her face when she'd heard Gorgon was alive. Shock. Guilt. Panic.

Because of him. Because he'd confused her, telling her they were mates, and went along with her when she'd offered herself to him. Because all he'd seen was his need to claim the woman he believed to be his. Selfish. Stupid. He'd put her in this untenable position.

For claiming her, now he would burn.

To fix it. For her. For his clan. He couldn't do that if she touched him again. If she begged him with her lips, with her eyes, and that voice. If her jasmine scent got too heavily into his lungs.

He wasn't as strong as he'd once thought.

His weakness had led them to this place, but he *could* fix it. His brand had yet to appear on her neck. If he could keep apart from her long enough, it would never show. Because he'd be gone.

He would erase himself from the equation in order for the sides to balance. His death wouldn't drag her into the grave, not without the bonding mark. She'd be free to do what she'd vowed before the gods and all their people to do and mate the king.

At least I won't have to watch.

No doubt a fight was headed his way—the war raging around them guaranteed that. He'd go quietly, but damned if he wouldn't go down fighting.

They passed by one of his guards stationed along various vulnerable spots in the hallways, and the man shot him a frown. One Samael ignored even as he flayed himself mentally.

Do your job, Veles.

As they approached the banquet room, Samael slowed. Something wasn't right here. The two guards he'd sent ahead weren't there, and the massive, intricately decorated metal doors remained shut.

He stopped walking, and everyone behind him came to a halt.

"Samael?" Gorgon asked. He never had called him *Captain*, even when he'd been new to the post.

Samael held up a hand, shifting the skin of his hands to scales and sending out a thought to his guards. *"Report."*

Within minutes each of his squad leaders checked in.

Samael relaxed. The guards had been posted inside the room rather than outside. He didn't bother to explain to the others. "All clear."

He walked them to the doors and opened them himself into one of the largest internal rooms in the mountain, meant to accommodate every dragon in the clan—in human size, at least—for important occasions. Like every other part of the mountain, the room had been carved from the stone, but his ancestors had designed a spectacle of grandeur for the entire clan to share. Carved sections with intricate details bracketed the room, like ribs, every fifty feet or so, reminding him of flying buttresses on human Gothic architecture.

Come to think of it, the design reminded him of the communal hall in the gargoyles' castle. Except for the backlit dome the cavern rose to at the center, which was all Ottoman in design. The cavern itself was long, extending back into the heart of the mountain with a wall at the end that could be slid away, leading to the throne room itself. When he was a child, this room had intimidated him. Right now, filled with what remained of their clan, he couldn't shake a similar sensation.

Stepping to the side, he lowered his gaze.

"Where are we going?" Meira asked Gorgon as she approached the doorway. The king hadn't told her?

Gorgon patted her hand. "To introduce you to your clan."

Meira balked, pulling up short, and Samael lifted his gaze long enough to catch the look of panic she flashed his way, questions and worries swirling blue into her pale eyes, her pupils enlarging to consume much of the iris. "What? No—"

"Is there a problem?" Gorgon asked.

Samael turned his head and refused to look at her, pretending to focus outward, scanning the room. Most of those gathered were the upper class. She needed their support, which meant she needed to do this. Meira *could* do this. She had more strength than she realized.

"Are you sure they are ready for me?" she asked. Samael could almost hear the gears clanking over in her mind, searching for a way to stop the inevitable. "Perhaps you should meet with them by yourself first. Let them see you."

"We don't have time to wait. They need to see you and accept you as their queen now."

"But—"

Gorgon took her arm and whisked her away, and Samael had to hold himself still. He may as well have been petrified. Either that or snatch her from the king and fly away.

"I'll take this position." Amun clapped him on the shoulder.

Immediately, Samael snarled, and Amun yanked his hand back with an answering snarl of his own. Before he took his own man's throat out, Samael spun on his heel, leaving the room. "I'll monitor from the war room."

Better if Meira faced the clan without his presence there to muddy things—for her or those who still watched him with suspicion. Dragons didn't let go of their grievances easily. Regardless of obvious proof. Exacerbating their doubts was the connection they no doubt sensed, at least subconsciously, between himself and Meira.

He made it to the next level before a runner caught up with him. "Captain, your presence has been requested by the king."

Dammit.

Keeping his thoughts to himself, Samael turned back to cover the steps he'd just traversed. The closer he got to the now-open doors, the lower his brows dropped over his eyes. Silence. Heavy, pregnant silence.

He walked into the room with a nod at Amun, who didn't bother to nod back. As he moved toward where he could see Meira's bright curls surrounded by others, the king at her side, he realized Gorgon must've already introduced his queen to the general assemblage. Now he and Meira walked from group to group as the king personally introduced her to each person. The soft murmur of her voice and occasional rumble of the king's were the only sounds in the room as the clan looked on in judgmental quiet.

Meira glanced up, directly at him, though he knew for damn sure he hadn't made a sound or movement to attract her attention. Eyes dark-blue pools of apprehension implored him from across the room in a way no mate could have ignored. Samael sped his steps toward her, unable to stop himself. Because, while her forced smile probably appeared pleasant to those watching, her rigid body telegraphed her alarm to him.

Because of what he'd done, because he'd claimed her, she had to be hating this deception. Gorgon was introducing her as his queen when she wasn't. Not to mention the raw emotions no doubt beating at her from every person in the room, even if she was shielding herself from them.

With each step he took toward her, Meira didn't look away.

Don't focus on me, he willed her. Others would notice.

At the same time, however, he couldn't force himself to stop moving or look away himself. Mere feet away, her jasmine scent hit him with the force of a wrecking ball. Sam lifted a hand to reach for her…to do what, he wasn't sure. Tuck her into his side? Place a hand at her back in a show of support? Lean down and kiss her until she relaxed into him and lost that tension?

Except he didn't get a chance, because Gorgon stepped directly into his path.

"Ah, Samael," his king boomed, overjovial. "I was just telling the clan of the service you provided in protecting our queen when I was taken."

Forced to halt his headlong rush to Meira's side, Samael blinked, absorbing Gorgon's words. "I only did what I promised you, my lord. You said to keep her safe if something ever happened to you."

He could have sworn Meira gasped. Except, visible over Gorgon's shoulder, she didn't make a move or a sound. At the same instant, pain cracked through his heart because the words were only a tiny part of the truth. The real truth was he would give his life for Meira Amon. Hell, he'd sell his soul for her.

"Yes, I did give you that order," Gorgon confirmed, his voice filling the room to the domed rafters. "Because this phoenix and her sisters will be the saviors of our people."

A murmur passed through the massive hall.

Gorgon continued as though no sound had been uttered. "I made you the Viceroy of Defense for similar reasons, my most loyal of guards and advisers."

Another soft murmur. Samael's face, meanwhile, was doing a damn good impression of a stone gargoyle as he tried not to let the guilt visibly show.

Gorgon turned, raising his voice even louder to address the entire room. "Those qualities, the same reason why I now name Samael Veles my beta."

The king might as well have beaten him over the head with the spiked end of a dragon's tail. Shock was an electric current rooting his feet to the floor, buzzing in his ears.

Gorgon did not just do that. How was he supposed to do what he intended to do with the title of beta hanging over him?

The murmur turned into more of a low rumble. One of protest. Damn if he'd allow that to pass, though Gorgon made no move to put a stop to it. Pure instinct drove the growl that spilled from Samael, and silence scattered through the room.

They might not approve of him, but he would not allow them to question their king. Stepping forward, shoulders drawn back, he raised his voice. "You may not like a commoner for your beta, but you *will* respect the king who put me in it."

Another beat of silence that turned into more of a stretch. And no wonder. Samael rarely spoke when on duty and was rarely seen outside his rooms when off duty. In his opinion, his role was to stand behind the king and protect. The clan didn't need to hear from him. Perhaps a mistake on his part.

"Spoken like a true alpha, Veles." Jorsha Sachmis, Gorgon's Viceroy of the Reserve, in charge of the wealth of the clan and the biggest kiss-ass on the Curia Regis, clapped Samael on the back. No doubt, Samael would receive an invitation to dine with the man. Networking—a facet of the position of beta he could do without. Good thing he wouldn't be around long to deal with it.

He didn't dare look at Meira, who stood silently beside Gorgon, her arm linked with his. He didn't need to. Her worries were his own.

I can't keep this up for much longer.

Lying to the king, avoiding his mate so that he could let her go, pretending he could still lead these men. Samael sent up prayers that the gods would strike him down here and now.

Gorgon moved to the next group of black dragon shifters standing loosely together. Pulled along by the king, Meira glanced back at Samael, who followed with reluctance dragging at each step.

What are you doing?

Though her lips didn't move, her voice floated through his head in the softest of whispers and Samael almost tripped over his own feet, lungs cinching tight. He could hardly discern that the thought was hers rather than his own, but his dragon rumbled in his head, enjoying the sound of her voice.

Shit. Being able to hear each other's thoughts was one of the signs that their bond was solidifying. How was that possible given the ocean that separated them, that he'd put between them himself? Unfortunately, her hair was down, so he couldn't check her neck to see if his brand had appeared. Because if it had, he couldn't go forward with the plans he'd formulated.

They moved onto the next group. This time, Meira didn't look back. In fact, now she seemed to be avoiding glancing his direction at all. Samael tried to convince himself that was what he wanted.

Sam...why won't you talk to me?

The next flitter of a thought in her voice about took him to his knees, but Meira didn't pause, and the path he'd set for himself wasn't going to change.

A step at a time, he forced himself to keep going.

For the next two hours, Gorgon continued on, introducing not only Meira to each group, but also mentioning Samael's role in her safety and his new role as beta for the clan. Each time they did, the same questions were asked. Where had they been? What had the plan been? The sign that they should move on came when a person in the group they talked to brought up a petty complaint—their trash hadn't been collected in days, or the pipes broke in their bathroom and no one had come to fix them.

By the time they finished, Samael's hand ached from shaking, and every muscle in his neck and shoulders screamed with tension. At least the silence had disappeared in favor of a neutral buzz of voices. By this point, he was numb from forcing his true emotions to a dark corner of his mind, and he wasn't sure if the buzz was positive or negative or if the guarded smiles directed his way were sincere.

How much worse for Meira as an empath.

Gorgon turned to Samael. "I'm ready to return to my rooms."

"My king," Samael acknowledged.

Shifting the smallest part of him, he sent thoughts ahead to his team to clear the path. The king had yet to try to shift since his return to the clan, which meant sticking to the human-size walkways. Leading the small band, Samael escorted Gorgon and Meira through the halls and back spaces of the mountain. The deeper they moved, the more instinct told him something was wrong. Not dangerous. Not a threat. Just wrong.

He almost turned to Meira to ask if she had any insights, could feel emotions ahead of her maybe, even had his mouth open, but realized in time that their relationship wasn't casual like that anymore and snapped it shut with a *clack* of teeth.

About halfway there, Meira's gasp had Samael jerking around, already assuming a defensive position, only to find Gorgon slumped against the wall, Meira trying to hold him up.

"What happened?" he demanded as he rushed to his king, looping Gorgon's arm over his shoulders and hefting him to standing.

"A little dizzy," the king slurred.

Dammit. They shouldn't have held the clan meeting today. Gorgon hadn't been ready.

"We need to get him back to the room quickly," Meira said. "Is there a mirror anywhere close by?"

Samael considered where they'd stopped. The buzzing sound of the massive generators that powered the entire mountain surrounded him. He'd taken them the back way near the inner mechanisms of the mountain—an area he knew from childhood, when his father had worked down here keeping the plumbing functioning, such as it was in that era. "This way."

Hauling Gorgon, who could hardly lift his feet, Samael made his way to a room that didn't have a mirror but did have a full wall of glass that was a one-way mirror. His dad's bosses had sat behind it, watching every single move the men down here made. Judging. Meting out punishment. Adjusting shifts based on production and favoritism.

Sam remembered that part well despite his young age and the centuries since.

Meira glanced his way once she spotted it, questions in her eyes, but said nothing. She lit her fire with ease and, hand on his shoulder burning through his clothes to his skin, though he was certain she didn't let the flames touch him, walked all three of them through the mirror into Gorgon's room. Samael laid the king down on the bed, and she sat at the foot to remove his shoes.

Samael stepped back and, in a moment of pure weakness, watched her. The graceful moves of her hands, slender fingers working to untie the knots on Gorgon's fancy leather shoes. The way she tucked her hair behind one ear to get it out of her face. The glow of her skin, even in the pale light coming from the daylight mimicking strips along the ceiling. It must be cloudy outside today, because the strips only cast a dim light in the room.

Gods above, I need her.

"I'll inform the men." Samael stalked from the room before he could do something stupid like confess his plans or beg her to choose him despite the way such an act would rend her loyalty, pulling her in too many directions.

He couldn't do that to her, force her to make that terrible choice between him and her sisters.

"Samael," Meira called.

He ignored her and kept walking.

"Samael, stop." She was closer now, the patter of her feet in the hallway.

Not pausing, he shook his head. "I need to make sure—"

"Sam, *stop*. Dammit." Her voice broke on the last word, and he couldn't keep going. He stopped and closed his eyes, head bowed.

"Don't do this," she begged, closer still.

Which meant she had a pretty accurate idea of what he was planning. Confirming it would only mean arguing about it.

"Sam." A touch, soft as a kiss, landed on his shoulder, then traveled down his arm until she threaded their fingers together.

Gods help him, he let her.

"Don't do this," she said again. Still quiet.

"Do what? I'm organizing my men. You should be helping the king."

She tugged on that hand in a move that communicated her feelings sharply. "I'm far from stupid."

"Don't I know it," he muttered.

Then he disconnected their fingers and turned to face her, arms crossed so he didn't reach out for her. Deliberately, he assumed the same hard-ass expression he used with new recruits he was training and tried to stuff his emotions as deep as he could. Deep enough that they wouldn't touch her. "I have a job to do. So do you."

Meira's eyes widened, then narrowed. "That's how it's going to be, huh?"

"How it has to be, and you know it."

Rather than disagree, Meira tipped her head, irises the closest to white he'd seen before. Why did he get the gut-sinking feeling she was about to try to rescue him from himself?

"Fine."

Fine? That was it?

Without another word, she turned away, heading back to the king.

Unbidden, possessiveness rose up inside him and short-circuited any intelligent decision making. "Fine?" He stalked after her. "None of this is fine."

He reached for her, but Meira spun to face him, plowed into him, driving him back. "At least you got that part right."

Then she kissed him, soft and sweet. Fuck, he was so screwed.

Surrounded by the taste of her, the scent of her, the softness of her body against his, Samael went wild. With a grunt of pain-edged pleasure, not taking his mouth from hers, he swung them around to pin her body against the smooth rock wall of the hallway, devouring her with kisses that swallowed each moan, each gasp she gifted him with.

Desperation and heartbreak fueled every needy, beautiful, possessive kiss that drugged his mind and sent his dragon soaring, even as his heart plummeted.

He should end this. Gods, he had to end this.

Smoothing his hands up her thighs, he tucked his fingers into the creases of her ass and lifted. In one smooth movement, she responded by wrapping her long legs around his waist, and he pressed his rock-hard cock against the heated core of her.

He broke the kiss to groan against her neck.

Meira shuddered against him. "Please, Sam."

The whispered words were hoarse and as desperate as the sensations buffeting him. His dragon whined in his head, a sound his creature side had never made before. Those two words also dropped him into reality with all the subtlety of a nose-breaking punch to the face.

He was hers. Always. Her Sam. And the most important thing he would ever do with his life was protect this woman.

Even from himself.

Slowly, he pulled his head back, resisting her even as her hands grasped at him, trying to keep him against her. Carefully, he lowered her feet to the ground, then stepped away. Only she stepped with him, arms still around his neck.

"Sam?" The question wobbled, and he thought he might throw up.

Gently, he grasped her wrists and forced her hands down, then stepped back, cutting all physical contact. "I can't do this."

"Captain?" The question preceded Amun into the hallway by only half a second.

Holy hell.

A half second longer touching Meira, kissing her, marking her as his when he couldn't, and they would've had witnesses. He hadn't even heard the door to the chamber open, let alone the approach of his men either down the hall or on the perch from the atrium.

Sucking in a silent breath, Samael hid every terrible emotion behind a blank expression, shutting himself down and ignoring the woman beside him. The only way he'd get through this. "The king is in his room, resting."

Amun nodded, which should've been it. Instead, he stepped closer, gaze serious. "We have a…situation."

CHAPTER NINETEEN

It seemed her life was turning into a coiled mess of bad ideas, thanks to a never-ending stream of worse situations.

"Take my arm, my lord," she said to Gorgon.

She tried not to grunt when the king leaned heavily against her. He was barely keeping his feet already. Meira had to brace her own feet to keep them both from swaying while at the same time trying to appear as though they waited patiently.

They stood inside the massive cavern, not unlike the one at Ben Nevis, that connected to the landing platform outside. A space used not only for training, but apparently for meeting with large numbers of dragon shifters.

Again.

The meeting with the clan previously had been trial enough. She'd had to secretly hold fire in her fist to turn off the emotions screaming at her. Mostly distrust and resentment.

They needed to tell Gorgon. Now. Before Samael had a chance to do something worse than push her away. But now wasn't the best time. Because now they were meeting with the part of the clan that had abandoned their people.

Rather than wait for night, a storm had allowed the deserters to return during the day. Ominous dark-gray thunderheads built like towering cathedrals over the rolling brown lands around the mountain and swirled up and around Ararat's peaks, obscuring the dragons from view of any humans nearby. Outside, a swarm of black almost obliterated the cloudy sky as a torrent of swirling dragons in varying shades of black, gray, and silver swirled down from the high altitudes at which they'd been hovering. In groups of roughly ten, they would land, shift to human, and step out of the way for the next group.

She'd directed Maul, who'd refused to leave her and return to Kasia, to stay in Gorgon's chambers. No need to add to the tension in the room with a hellhound. At the king's orders, Samael, along with the rest of the viceroys of the Curia Regis and soldiers of the King's Guard, stood in a line at her back. Behind them, the rest of the clan had gathered to welcome their brethren home.

In theory.

The twisting of her insides told Meira that maybe this wasn't going to go the way Gorgon hoped. Or it could have something to do with her chosen mate. The man who was abandoning her because he thought it the right thing to do—his emotions a black swirl of pain and determination behind her.

The pain was the only thing keeping her remotely calm. He didn't want to leave her. As if she'd let him. As if she didn't have a voice in what happened to them.

Except every second they stayed, without revealing what they'd done, only dragged them further into an abyss of deceit. Samael was beta now and back to leading the guard...and she, in the eyes of the clan, was queen. She'd have to claw her way out of the grave she'd dug with her silence eventually. Now was not that time.

Finally, the dragons flying home assembled outside on the landing pad and walked toward where she and the king waited inside the massive training chamber.

One man walked ahead of the others.

Their elected speaker, most likely. The one who'd contacted Amun to tell the clan that many of those who'd left when they'd thought Gorgon dead wanted to return to the fold. That they wished to beg mercy from the king himself.

Gorgon remained where he was, and Meira continued to prop

him up, her muscles starting to shake.

As the leader of the group neared, she studied him. But he was just a man. As tall as the other black dragon shifters with the same midnight-colored hair and eyes the color of mercury.

At an unseen signal, he stopped at least fifty feet from where she and the king stood, and those behind him shuffled to a halt as well. The way his gaze darted over her left shoulder, she guessed Samael must've made some sign that they'd come close enough. Meira's gaze skated over the hands she could see. Each blank, missing the king's brand.

According to dragon law, that marked these people as traitors and rogues, to be shunned or even executed on sight.

The pulse of sensations swirling around those wishing to return would have taken her to her knees if she hadn't muted the effect, once again holding a flame in one fist. Still, the emotions reached for her with grasping fingers. The pressure of anxiety. Dizziness that she associated with respect but also a fear of losing control. Either could apply. The itching of blame or jealousy. A heaviness of fear. And a hollowed-out sensation she couldn't put her finger on overlaid everything. Closed mindedness would be a bad sign. Negativity was better, but not by much.

"My name is Haikaf Nar. I own a small produce stand in the city."

Gorgon nodded.

The man named Haikaf continued. "We came to ask our king, face-to-face, to readmit us to the clan."

With a deep breath that likely only she caught because the action pushed against her, Gorgon straightened, taking all his weight. "Why did you leave?" The words were a growl, the king's opinion of his deserters made clear in his tone.

To give him credit, Haikaf paled, and that dizziness of fear of losing control spiked around her. Meira blinked through it. Haikaf stood his ground in the face of his king's disapproval. "We were afraid, my king."

"Afraid? Of what?"

"You were gone, dead, we heard. Your beta dead. Your queen, who many rumored had killed you, disappeared. Even more confusing, the Captain of the Guard gone with her. Then we hear from the same woman that you are not dead. That another man has died in your place. A doppelgänger who posed as you with no one close to you noticing."

"And you didn't believe her? The woman I'd made vows to?" Gorgon's lips pulled back, baring his teeth.

"No." Haikaf shook his head. "We did believe her. Because Samael Veles stood at her side, we believed her."

Meira tried not to show how that one sentence caught her attention, but she allowed her gaze to skate over the men gathered behind Haikaf. These weren't like the people whom the king had introduced her to earlier.

Those men and women had dressed in fine clothes, business suits, some more casual than others, but still in quality with hair perfectly coiffed. Which meant that Gorgon had met primarily with the elite today, the power brokers of the mountain, the politicos who could make or break the support he received from the clan.

But could they?

The people in front of her reminded her more of the humans her family had lived around in Kansas when they'd worked at the diner. Hardworking, hard living. Less educated primarily, and poorer, which often went hand in hand, at least in the human world. Also, at least to Meira's way of thinking, kinder and more grounded. Willing to give their last dime if it helped out someone they felt needed that dime more.

Sam's people.

Gorgon apparently came to the same conclusion. "You've come back because Samael Veles has returned."

Not a question, a statement.

Haikaf shifted on his feet and said nothing, and that hollowness of insecurity thickened in the room.

Samael's walls were mostly up, but a small feathering of surprise slipped through.

Meira had to keep from glancing at Samael, pride in the man she'd chosen for her mate threatening to burst from her, drowning out the emotions coming at her from the gathering. She'd bet if she allowed herself to look it would be to find Sam completely shut down, as stone-faced as Carrick and the other gargoyles. The upper class of the Black Clan may not entirely trust him—yet— but the commoners sure as hell did. Realization whispered in her ear—based on the numbers in front of and behind her, they outnumbered the upper class, at least two to one if not three to one.

Not to mention the services they provided ran the mountain, true in every society she'd experienced. And yet the upper class never clued in to the fact that if the lower-middle and working classes stopped supporting the system, it would crumble beneath their privileged feet.

Samael, look at your people, she silently willed him. Power was found in numbers, power in giving the voiceless a platform, a common element to unite them.

How could he think to walk away from them? From her?

"I will allow your return on one condition," Gorgon said.

Haikaf glanced at the men standing closest to him, as though not quite believing it could be that easy. "What condition, my king?"

"A vow, here and now, that no matter what happens in the days to come, you will not abandon your king, whoever he may be, and clan again."

Haikaf stared at Gorgon for a long beat, then turned his back, a dangerous move a warrior would never have made, to confer with those around him.

Meira watched Gorgon's face, as the king no doubt could hear much of the discussion. She also watched for when he might need to lean on her again. From this angle, she could see how he swayed slightly, like a skyscraper in harsh winds.

"We will," Haikaf snapped at the other men on a burst of prickles over her skin.

She shifted her gaze to the prodigal shifters across the way.

The debate across the room had clearly heated, with Haikaf shaking his head vigorously.

"*I* will," he finally snarled at a man taller than himself by a head, large for a black dragon, more a gold dragon's size with muscles layered over muscles. "Do what you fucking want."

Haikaf stepped back, still facing his people. "If you are unable to make this vow, leave now."

"We will be killed if we try," someone from the back shouted.

"Samael." Gorgon waved his beta forward. Meira couldn't help but turn her gaze to the man who'd stolen her heart—back stiff, head held high, jaw tight, black eyes blazing with fire that set shadows dancing over the planes of his face. Except for an errant lock of hair that refused to stay put, he was about the most intimidating thing she'd ever seen. Sexy as hell.

"I guarantee your safety to get away from the mountain, but not after that," Samael said. "Make your choice."

Damned. I'm damned for loving him even more for that. Everything inside her hurt. Ached in a way that she knew came from holding the truth inside. From Gorgon, but from Sam, too. Her love for him needed to be in the open for all to see and know.

Love. The first time she'd seen him in that mirror, she'd given up her heart to this man, only she hadn't been able to admit it to herself. Promising herself to Gorgon had been the biggest mistake of her life. Why Kasia had seen nothing in her visions, Meira would have to ask her sister later.

She pulled her own shoulders back.

No matter what had brought them here to this moment, she'd be damned if Sam was going to kill them both by sacrificing himself.

Almost as though he'd taken that as a signal, Haikaf turned and went to one knee, his right hand in a fist over his heart. "I vow to never abandon king or clan again."

One by one, each man and woman behind him did the same, their vows becoming a jumble of sound in the room.

Not a single dragon shifter left the mountain.

. . .

Samael cast his gaze out over the people on their knees, his soul shredding with each repeated vow. These were *his* people, those he'd known as both boy and man. Many faces were familiar to him. Haikaf had once worked with his father, though he'd been a younger man at the time.

Vows they made *because* of him.

What would they do when he died, when he no longer remained to hold their trust to keep them safe, to do the right thing by them?

They'll have the king. And Meira.

Meira had not been raised in royalty as she might have been had Pytheios not killed her father and sent her mother into hiding. She'd been raised among everyday humans. A simple life.

He'd leave the clan in her capable hands. With Gorgon, who had the faith of the upper classes, at her side, she'd be unstoppable.

A shout rose up from those behind him who had remained. "Traitors!"

Then another. And another.

One by one those before him rose to their feet, shifting uneasily, every gaze not on the king, but on Samael.

He didn't need Meira's abilities to see the desperation, the fear, and a slowly rising tide of answering anger that visibly rippled through them, evidenced in the tense jaws, slowly clenching fists, and glittering eyes. The people before him and behind him reminded Samael of a haboob sandstorm whipped to a frenzy by powerful winds. Evil winds. Until the skies turned blood orange, leaving behind a frosted coating of sand on everything in its wake. Only, if the violence about to blast through the Black Clan was allowed to happen, blood would be the coating left behind.

The pitch of the shouts gathered and rose, like a tidal wave of sound and fury behind him. The way those before him leaned forward, as though preparing to stand against the blast, the place had turned to a powder keg.

One kiss of fire, and the whole place would burn.

Three things occurred to him all at once. One, he had two jobs—protect his mate and protect the king. Two, Meira stood at Gorgon's side, vulnerable in a way no one else in the room would be. Three, the commoners were *his* people. He would never stand against them.

"Stop," he thundered, his dragon adding to the shout of his voice.

The cacophony of sound ebbed, only to surge back with renewed strength. Pure instinct driving his actions, Samael stepped into the gulf between the factions of his clan and shifted. His dragon's only focus was their mate, and his transformation to creature rode that edge of pain, threatening to tip him over into the abyss where he became only beast, no more humanity within him.

But Samael held the edge.

In a shimmering burst and with a roar that shook the rock mountain, he whipped around to face those behind. Face down the dissenters.

He opened the channel in his mind to communicate to the horde gathered behind and before. "*Abide by your king's decision or leave now, cast out as rogues.*"

The shouts, already dimmed by his sudden transformation, cut off, and silence slipped into the void.

Samael stood before them, the only motion the slashing of his tail behind him as he stared down the riot still trembling at a precipice.

"Of course he would back the traitors. He's one of them." A shout rose up from the back.

"*Are you really that blind?*" Samael didn't bother to tone down his snide voice. "*Other than the guard, most selected and trained from childhood, few of you are fighters. Meanwhile, the shifters behind me exist in a harder reality. My own fighting skills were cut among them. Do you seriously want to risk your lives against them?*"

While some continued to glare at him, trembling with impotent rage, the smarter ones stilled, glancing around, a question clear in their eyes.

"Your lives are possible because of these people. I've listened to your pathetic grumblings. No one to clear your trash or clean your shit, make your plumbing work, cook your food. Even if you survived a fight, could you function without them?"

Even more paused to consider, though the sneers curling their lips said some wanted to argue, prove him wrong. But Samael had lived on both sides now.

"They need us as much as we need them." A new voice rose.

An answering rumble at his back had those in front of him tensing.

"You're not wrong." Samael silenced both sides with the words, though he could feel the heat of anger behind him now redirected to a target on his back.

"They need your leadership, the peace you can create with the other clans, and yes, your money and need for their services to support their livelihoods. No society can exist with only one status. Nor can it function with any one group ostracized, oppressed, or shoved aside. Humans have proven that. Let us learn from their mistakes, and ours. Let us do better."

"Captain." A sharp voice came over the loudspeaker system.

Samael jerked his head to the side, eyeballing the two men manning the security booth. *"What?"*

"Dragons have been sighted to the northwest."

"Ours?"

Bero shook his head. "Green and white. They appeared out of nowhere, sir."

"The traitors were a distraction," several voices called out. Immediately, those behind him started protesting their innocence loudly.

"Silence," Samael boomed.

And the clan obeyed.

He turned his head to his king, who had stood quietly by. *"Your orders?"*

"Take our forces and prepare the mountain for a fight. The rest of us will batten down inside Ararat."

Samael didn't miss the "us," and neither did the others around them. "Us, my lord?" Amun questioned.

Gorgon shrugged, speculative gaze remaining on Samael. "I am too weak to battle and will only be in the way."

For the king to admit his weakness so publicly was tantamount to giving up the throne. Ambitious dragons who thought they were stronger would rise to challenge the king as soon as this fight was over.

At least I won't be here as witness.

"Samael is my beta. You will follow him without question." The king issued the order.

Samael acted.

"*Call the men to assemble,*" he commanded. "*On me.*"

CHAPTER TWENTY

The next five minutes turned into organized chaos nearing panic, but not quite tipping over.

The blare of an alarm pierced the air, blasting throughout the mountain. At the sound, every dragon shifter in the place, all gathered there, jumped into action. Those who couldn't fight, or who would stay behind as a last line of defense, ran into the mountain proper, the cold shards of fear going with them.

From within the city at the base of the atrium, visible through the large doorway connecting the rooms, shadows and flashes indicated most headed inside while others shifted and flew to wherever they stayed when the mountain locked down.

At the same time, warriors poured forward, the pulse of their purpose and courage a tattoo against her skin. One by one, each found space to shift as more bodies vacated the massive room. The entire room appeared to shimmer and writhe like a pit of snakes as more and more dragons replaced the smaller forms of the men they had been.

A horrible, beautiful sight—all glittering scales in hues ranging from the deepest of blacks, like Samael, to silver so pale they could pass as white.

"Help me to my chambers?" Gorgon gripped her arm in order to be able to walk.

Meira wanted to protest. Wanted to shake off the unsteady

king to go to her mate. Samael was flying out, likely to battle alongside forces not entirely under his control, against two clans, and she was certain he had every intention of dying out there. With so many in the room and emotions high she was fully blocking her empathic ability now or she'd drown in it. That meant she couldn't feel him, even if he didn't have his walls up.

"Samael."

She turned her head, even as Gorgon stepped away, taking her with him.

The obsidian dragon, in full command at the front of the room, didn't so much as cant his head in her direction.

"Samael." She had no idea if he could hear her, but she had to tell him. *"Don't do this. Don't do what I can see is in your head."*

Another glance back, and she blinked at how swiftly the dragons had organized. They shifted in waves before they'd leap into the sky, clearing space for the next wave. All the while, Samael stood to the side. Probably directing and giving orders.

"Sam." No visible response. *"Fight for your people, fight for your king. But I need you to fight for me, too. For us."*

Gorgon's weight on her tugged her back around toward the smaller human-size tunnels, and she pulled up. "Let's take the faster way."

She directed them both toward the glassed-in room on the opposite side of the chamber from where her mate prepared to go to war. With each plodding step, she continued to talk to Sam in her head, though hope that he heard suffocated more with each unanswered sentence. As though the words were using up all the air that light needed to stay aflame.

"If you think I could go on without you, even if I survive, you're wrong."

The guards operating the room watched her with wary curiosity as she and Gorgon faced them. With a whisper of her will, she redirected the magic of the flame already cupped in her hand. The guards' eyes went wide a split second before she changed the reflection, Gorgon's chambers reflecting back at her. With Maul, his back to them, sitting at the massive window, no doubt roused by the flurry of dragons and the blasting of the alarm.

"*I chose you.*" She kept talking to Samael as they passed through the reflection. Desperation lashed chains around her, squeezing her while at the same time dragging her down. "*I will always choose you. Even if you leave me. So I am begging you, don't leave me.*"

If only he would talk to her, she could make him see—

"*I love you, Meira.*" With a gasp she whirled, seeing him now framed by the gilded mirror she'd walked the king through.

Sam stood, the only dragon remaining in the chamber, his head turned, watching her. Only she couldn't access his emotions through the mirror.

She stepped toward him, hand raised. "Sam—"

He drew out his wings and dropped off the edge of the platform, like a high-dive platform, then, a second later, shot straight up.

Was that good-bye?

Meira closed her hand into a fist and dropped it to her side. At the same time, she doused her fire. The reflection in the mirror showed a wan woman with flyaway curls and dead eyes. And a king behind her, speculation in his gaze. She didn't care anymore.

Gorgon said nothing.

Don't give up. Meira sucked in as her mother's voice—a memory from childhood and even when she'd been a young woman—sounded clearly in her mind, the image equally as clear.

Meira spun to face Maul, finding the hellhound watching her. He was showing her a real memory. A moment. Telling her to keep going.

Right. Her mate was out there fighting—for his clan and king. "My lord." She turned to Gorgon. "Your forces are going to need help."

Speculation disappeared behind the snap of purpose, his shoulders drawing back. More like the Gorgon she'd known before Pytheios got his rotting hands on him. "Your sisters?"

Meira nodded.

"Do it."

She spun back to the mirror and immediately called up Skylar's mountain in the image. Luck was with her. Her sister's routine of training with the men meant she was easily found in the massive chamber not unlike the one Meira had just been in.

In seconds, the King and Queen of the Blue Clan were summoned across the room to stand in front of Meira and Gorgon. Quickly, Gorgon explained the situation to Ladon and Skylar.

"They're up against twice as many, based on the readings my men are seeing," Gorgon added. "Possibly more."

Meira glanced at the king, only to pause as she realized his eyes were full dragon, narrowed slits for pupils, the black consuming the full orb. He must be communicating with his men telepathically.

"Did they send the full armies of both clans?" Ladon demanded.

Gorgon cocked his head as though listening to an unheard conversation. "No. They've reached our farther scouts. Apparently, their ranks are bolstered with some of our own."

Ladon released a snarl. "Traitors."

For his part, Gorgon remained calm. "Or misguided."

"What do you need from me?" Ladon asked.

Meira shared a glance with the king at her side. "We need Skylar to send as many of your men as she can. Now."

Ladon, eyes already blazing with blue flame, nodded. "Done."

"Come in on the eastern side of the mountain," Gorgon said. "They won't be expecting anyone to approach from behind."

"Understood."

Meira sought first Ladon's gaze, then her sister's. "Thank you."

Skylar reached out and flattened her palm against the mirror, and Meira met the touch. "Stay safe," Skylar commanded.

Meira wouldn't make promises like that. Instead she smiled. "I love you."

Then she doused the flame.

Gorgon took her by the hand. "I need you to take me back to the landing."

Meira frowned and shook her head. "You can't."

"If my people are fighting against their own, it's for a reason. They need to see me."

She knew he was right, knew this was his decision and his alone. Still, no matter what it meant to her and Samael, she wouldn't see Gorgon dead.

"Take me there. Please."

She inhaled, long and slow, reaching for the sense of calm he possessed, a peaceful warmth emanating from the king and settling over her skin. "Are you sure?"

In answer, he stepped forward and, hand cupping her elbow, turned them both to face the mirror.

"Maul," she called. The hellhound lumbered over to stand on Meira's other side. "Protect the king."

He flashed her an image of her own face, and she patted his shoulder. "I can take care of myself."

Maul huffed a sound that might've been agreement or a scoff.

Ignoring him, she put a hand on the king and walked him back into the hangar through the guards' window. Maul popped up beside them in the same instant. The massive dragon-steel door remained open, though the one shutting the hangar off from the rest of the mountain was down. Outside, the storm had rolled in, thick clouds making it almost impossible to see.

Gorgon left her inside the chamber and walked haltingly to the center of the room. There he shifted, mirage-like waves swallowing the man whole and shimmering over the slowly growing form of a dragon, the process taking longer than she'd seen others. But he completed the change and flared his wings wide, trumpeting a blast that sounded almost like triumph.

He dropped to all fours with incredible stealth, almost as though she'd been watching a movie on mute. Then he swung his spiked head around to stare at her. Meira tried not to step back, fear suddenly taking hold of her with scalding claws at the fury in his eyes and the anger radiating from him like sound waves, beating against her.

Bloodlust. Was this that elusive emotion that had been pulsing from him? She wasn't sure.

Had the dragon taken over from the man, or was she seeing the true Gorgon for perhaps the first time?

"*You mated Samael.*" A hushed growl in her head.

The searing fear dug deeper, and she curled her hand into Maul's fur but refused to step back.

"He's my fated mate," she said simply.

The King of the Black Clan said nothing. Instead, he flared his wings wide, took two running steps, and launched himself into the air, disappearing into the fog-filled air beyond.

• • •

Smart of the Green and White Clans to attack during the day, hindering the Black Clan's greatest weapon—their stealth.

The storm, however, while hiding the coming battle from human eyes, would hinder them all. Lightning illuminated the skies in bright flashes, showing the clouds around and above him in stark relief and outlining the bodies of the dragons taking up their positions on the crags and peaks of the mountain.

A dragon in the air was dangerous. One defending a peak more so. Coming at him from above exposed the attacker's belly to slashing claws and fire. Coming at him from below put the attacker in range of that spiked tail, even more deadly when used like a club.

They were still far enough away from night that Samael directed his warriors to man the mountain, keeping a handful flying around it at different levels.

A flash of lightning revealed one of his men to his left. As soon as the light dissipated, he went back to seeing nothing through the dense air. At least the green dragons would have no camouflage among them. The white dragons might have more opportunity to hide at altitude where the clouds remained more their color before topping out in blue skies. Which put them at an advantage, able to dive-bomb his men with little to no warning.

"Amun. Take a squad up top. Above the clouds."

"They'll be able to see us."

Samael's muscles unclenched a millimeter. This was how he and Amun had always communicated—only the two of them where the others couldn't hear the argument so that they presented a united front to the men.

"Not if you see them first. I need someone hitting the fuckers before they can drop on us."

"Sir."

In the flash of illumination from a lightning bolt, the shadows of several dragons angled upward, wings beating to carry them aloft, told him he'd been obeyed.

Next, he sent his thoughts out to his scouts. The men on duty who'd caught the incoming forces in the first place, watchers constantly rotating duty to protect their mountain from all comers. *"Report."*

Silence greeted his command. Not a good sign.

"Japeth?"

Nothing.

"Amun, do you see anything up top?"

"Not a damn thing. This has to be the worst storm we've seen in—"

Only the crackling roar of sound warned Samael that the burst of gray coming at him from the right was flame and not cloud.

Gray. One of his own. Dammit.

"Evasive maneuvers," he shouted as he flipped up and over the column of flame, coming at his attacker from the side.

He barreled into a smoky-colored dragon that blended perfectly with the clouds. Immediately, he recognized Padram. One of *his* men. No satisfaction hit him as the thing's ribs crunched under the impact. Rather than risk the trained fighter's talons and teeth, Samael flared his wings wide, letting the other dragon's momentum carry it into the side of the mountain where two of his faithful dragons waited, ready to beat at whatever came at them. Samael couldn't see what happened, but the sounds of Padram's screeches and the thuds of tails slamming into scales and bones reached him all the same. Followed by the tumble of a body against rock, sliding down the mountainside.

One of his dragon's voices sounded in his mind. *"Was that—"*

"Padram. Yes," Samael answered, voice grim. *"We're fighting some of our own today, brothers. If you can't face them, get the fuck off the mountain."*

A cry went up around him. A roar of fury and grief. No one wanted to fight men they'd lived with, joked with, eaten dinner with, fought beside.

They had no choice.

Use your words. Meira's teasing voice haunted him. Could words help them now?

Samael pulled his wings in against his body, dropping him like cannon shot.

Around him, the sky lit up, not with lightning, but with flame as his outlying forces engaged the larger one coming at them. Only white and black flame.

Where are the green dragons?

Their cunning and extraordinary agility made them the hardest dragon shifters to capture or kill. Which was why few had remained in the blue mountain of Ben Nevis even after the attack that had almost lost Ladon his clan's home.

Coming out underneath the storm in clearer skies, the clouds churning slowly above him, changing shape and color, Samael leveled out.

"Brothers and sisters of the Black Clan." He sent the thought to every dragon in and around Ararat, particularly aiming his message at those black dragons fighting against their people. *"My name is Samael Veles and I am the captain of King Gorgon's guard."*

Immediately protests of *"traitor"* came from a small number of voices. Hopefully not those on the mountain to his left.

"Your king lives."

Another garbled mess of answers, but with less conviction.

"Taken by Pytheios, Gorgon has returned to Ararat and leads us once more. Leave the fight now, and we will welcome you home with open arms after the battle is won."

"How can we trust the word of a commoner who didn't protect his king when it mattered most?"

The single thought penetrated his mind through the noise.

"Because your king commands your trust." Gorgon's voice thundered through Samael's mind, so loud it reverberated against the inside of his skull, and he wobbled in the air.

As soon as he regained control, he swiveled his head to search for the main entrance, the door still wide-open. No black dragon stood in its gaping maw. Only a woman and a hellhound.

Meira.

Where was Gorgon? He'd left for his chambers. Too exhausted to fight. He couldn't be out here.

Silence followed the king's statement.

Why silence?

The blast of dragon roar followed the electric crack of lightning close by. The sky flashed, showing him the clash of titans happening in the raging sky. He couldn't spend any more time appealing to those who fought against their own kind.

"Make your choice," Samael commanded.

He waited for another flash to show him where dragons lurked, then shot straight up, coming at them hard.

In the dense clouds, only the sound of hissing and spitting dragons gave him an idea of what direction to head. That and the sound of the bellows that marked a dragon stoking its fire, told him where to go. He flew through a small pocket without clouds and twisted to avoid hitting the pewter-colored dragon from his own clan who faced off against two white dragons.

Except silver-tipped fire followed Samael as he shot past. Another traitor. Avoiding the flames, he flipped backward then came up under all three. At the last second, he reoriented his body again, coming at them talons first, which he sank into one of the white dragon's belly.

The thing gave a terrible screech as his claws managed to rend their way past dragon scale and the metallic scent of blood filled the air. It thrashed in his grip and would have used its long tail to skewer him, but Samael had struck at such an angle that he'd wrapped his own tail around the white dragon's, immobilizing it.

Sucking in, stoking his own fire, he aimed the black torrent directly at the holes he'd gouged, letting go to drop away as his fire melted the dragon from the inside out, its screams and writhing so violent it hurt him to watch.

It started to spin with one wing out and the other pulled in to cradle its gut, which was spewing a streamer of red blood into the sky. The scent of charred flesh on the air was nauseating.

Samael kept his head angled to watch his back as he dropped away. The dying dragon's partner roared and followed him. A glittering stream of incandescent white flame reached with fiery claws for Samael, but he was falling too fast, and white dragons, while built for distance, were not built for speed.

Confident he wouldn't be caught, Samael turned and finished his dive below the clouds. Then back up, except this time as he arrowed back into the clouds, twice he had to jerk out of the way of falling bodies. Bodies of black dragons. Dragons aflame, like firebombs thrown from a volcano.

The clouds flashed violently now—with lightning, dragon fire, and those plummeting forms flaming out and disintegrating to ash. Each flash illuminated the numbers they were up against. All Samael could see were his people facing two or three and sometimes more. He pulled closer to the mountain, only to find its icy crags teeming with green dragons.

They'd come up at his men from the bottom, climbing up from under the clouds where he'd just been. How had he missed them?

We're losing this battle.

Rage—over everything, his mate, his people, this war—shook up inside him, building like the pressure of a volcano about to erupt. Samael channeled that rage into his dragon.

Forget himself. To give Meira a chance at what she needed to do, to be, he had to die anyway. Right? *"For my king. For my clan. For my mate."*

Shooting like a comet, inevitable and unstoppable, he flew straight at the mountain. Focusing in, the world narrowed to his view of the rocks in front of him and the dragons in his immediate path. At the last minute, he tipped his wings. Flying sideways, belly to the mountain, he hugged the jutting stone peaks and crevices. Sliding to the side, he blasted flame at a pale-green fucker, distracting him long enough for the silver dragon above to clobber him with his tail.

Then he maneuvered up the mountain in time to slam into a buttery-white dragon with his talons, pick him up, and drop him between two of his own. Another white dragon came at him out of the fog. Without missing a beat, Samael flipped up and over the longer creature. Unable to turn in time, it ran into the mountain, a thunder of boulders raining down from its impact.

Samael kept going. Skirting dangerously close to the rock face, avoiding his own dragons and the outcropping of jagged rock alike, he took out four more.

"On your tail, Captain," one of his men warned.

A quick glance showed two green dragons, both the color of new spring leaves, behind him and closing in fast. Time for a maneuver he usually didn't dare use so close to solid ground. If he timed it wrong, he'd slam into the mountain. But he knew this mountain, had grown up on it, had fought on it and trained on it. Which gave him an advantage.

Slowing just enough that they'd think they were gaining, Samael drew the other dragons in closer. On purpose, he dropped nearer to the mountainside at the same time.

Then, swirling clouds still obscuring much of his view—nothing he could do about that—he shot a ball of fire from his maw into the air directly in front of him, then pulled his wings in and slung his tail to one side, which whipped his body around, sliding backward through the black flames. Then flared his wings wide.

Unable to see him through the blast of his flame, both green dragons flew through at full speed. One struck first, right into Samael's talons, which he sank deep into his chest. The momentum gave his razor-sharp claws extra impact, and the thing went limp in his grasp, long neck dangling.

The other dragon had managed to scoot out of his way, right into the vicious outcropping where one of Samael's men lurked, waiting like a spider for its prey. With a roar that sent smaller rocks cascading down the mountain, Samael tossed the dead dragon away.

Then he paused and took stock of his people. Hard to see through the clouds, but what he could see along the mountain was a fucking mess. They continued to fight a losing battle. One after another he watched as his men went down under a swarm of claws and flame and fury. More than came out on top of any encounter. His run had done fuck all to carve a swath through their enemies.

No matter what he did, or how his men fought, they were outnumbered.

They couldn't let their enemies take the mountain. No matter what. *"Close the hangar—"*

A voice cut off his order, cutting through his thoughts.

"We're here." Ladon Ormarr's dark growl reverberated in his head. *"Sitting at altitude above the clouds, coming from the west. What do you need?"*

Thank the gods.

Meira must've contacted her sister. Having experienced Skylar's own particular brand of teleportation, he knew exactly how Ladon and his people had arrived. Via the strangest mode of long-distance teleportation he'd ever experienced.

Samael held his position, despite a wish to join the blue king. He'd have time for relief later.

"Come to us," he relayed back. Then sent the thought out to his people. *"Regroup on the mountain. We have reinforcements."*

A crack of lightning splintered the rock in front of him, close enough that electricity hit his body, shocking his system into paralysis, sending debris straight at him and drowning out any shouts of triumph his men might have sounded. Or perhaps he'd lost his hearing altogether, thanks to the deafening, sizzling boom of immediate thunder.

All Samael knew was the mountain was coming up at him fast, and he couldn't make his body move.

CHAPTER TWENTY-ONE

Rocks tumbled down over the lip of the mountain above to scatter like roaches on the floor of the hangar.

When none struck her, Meira slowly lowered her arms to find Maul suddenly standing over her, protecting her from the fall of rock. From underneath his big head, her gaze zeroed in on the black dragon that plummeted through the air, passing through dense patches of cloud before reappearing, a limp heap of wings and tail.

Samael. She knew it. That lightning strike had come down on top of him.

"He's not stopping himself." Even dragons couldn't withstand the effects of impact with the ground from a great height. "Maul!"

Immediately, the hellhound disappeared, and she watched as, in slow motion the mountain rushed up at Sam's body, still limp as he plummeted.

She couldn't track Maul's progress as he made his short teleportation hops closer and closer to Sam. What the hound could do against a dragon's bulk and momentum, she had no idea. But they had to try.

"Where are you, Maul?" she whispered to herself, trying not to give in to terror for her mate.

In that instant, the form of a dark-gray dragon, wings tucked in close to his body, shot through the clouds above Samael, as though trying to get to him.

The king.

Was he trying to save Samael...or kill him? She couldn't forget that bloodlust she'd felt from the king before he'd taken off.

"Please," she whispered, urging Maul to hurry.

Suddenly, too fast for her to see what happened, especially through the thick clouds, Samael's body disappeared. One second there, the next gone.

The gray dragon pulled up, flapping its wings to hover and craning its neck to search.

With no sound or warning, Maul appeared beside her with Samael. Sides heaving, the black dragon stood on all fours at least, but his head hung between his shoulders, the spikes on his back arching out like a rainbow of death, glittering columns of obsidian glass.

Samael gave his head a shake, then another. Then lifted his head and shot a stream of black flame straight up until it reached the high ceiling, curling back in on itself as it hit rock. Then, just as quickly, he cut the flame off, leaving jarring silence in his wake.

Another shake of his head, and he looked at Meira. *"Say something out loud."*

"Were you struck by the lightning?"

He shook his head again. *"Fuck. I can't hear a damn thing."*

Before she could respond, a cry rose up from the dragons all over the mountain. A funnel of blue dragons pierced the clouds, swirling them out of their way as they descended in a whirling vortex of death and fire. White and green dragons scattered in their wake—not fleeing, being pushed back.

Samael spread his wings, obviously deciding he needed to meet his allies, hearing gone or not. Without a damn word to her.

"Samael—"

His muscles bunched, scales rippling, but he paused, though he didn't turn.

"Gorgon knows."

That got him to swing his slender, spiked head in her direction, blinking at her. Had he heard the words? She repeated them, making the motion of her mouth succinct. Another blink and he nodded and took off, quickly growing smaller as he flew out from the mountain to meet Ladon and his people.

Numbers evened out, the white and green dragons should be retreating, but she didn't see that happening. If anything, they were doubling their efforts, turning into a frenzy of desperation.

Why? Their behavior didn't make any sense—

"No!" Meira shouted as motion caught her attention.

A wave of red rose out of the clouds cresting up and over the blue dragons as they descended to the mountain and a rallying cry rose from White and Green Clans. Only the red dragons suddenly halted midair. A silent, hovering threat.

What were they waiting for?

"Dragon shifters of the Blue, Black, White, and Green Clans, hear me." A voiced boomed through her mind even though she wasn't a shifter.

"I am Pytheios Chandali, the one and true High King of all dragon clans. Witness my phoenix mate."

A massive red dragon dropped slowly through a gap in the clouds, the slow beats of his wings holding him aloft. The Rotting Red King was rotting no longer.

Small holes still pierced the membranes of his wings, allowing pinpoints of light through, and his scales appeared dull, as though coated in dust, but otherwise, this dragon was in excellent health. All reports of ragged, moth-eaten wings, stooped bones, and withered scales that didn't fully cover his hide were either wrong or he had mated successfully, phoenix or not, and was healing rapidly.

Holy hellfires.

Pytheios crumbling and decrepit was one thing. But fully healed…

Pure fear ran through the ranks of her people so sharply, she couldn't block it all, and Meira jerked with the physical pain of it.

How many would fall to his side now? How many would think she and her sisters were lying about who they were?

On his back, a woman stood. She actually stood, rather than riding astride. No fear. Her long, white hair whipped in the wind behind her. Her skin glowed with red flame, a dance of light that brought out a design on her skin.

A design Meira knew only too well. Phoenix.

Could it be true?

It had to be. She was witnessing with her very eyes, and Gorgon had shared his own experience with the woman.

"*Cease your fighting and bow to your true leader...*" Pytheios let the sentence hang. "*Or die.*"

Hatred and determination overrode the wave of fear like a riptide, dragging at her. Not only her emotions, but those of every dragon shifter opposing the monster who killed her parents.

No.

Even with a phoenix at Pytheios's side, no way in hell were she or her sisters, nor their mates, submitting to Pytheios. Ever.

"*We will never accept you.*"

Gods above, that was Sam. He rose in the air to face off against the red king. Defiant. A fighter. A *true* leader.

"*Then you die.*" Pytheios looked to his right, and a massive copper-colored dragon dropped into place beside him.

Brock Hagan.

"*Go get her,*" Pytheios ordered.

Dread cascaded through her in a fall of ice along her nerve endings. Meira had no doubt whom the red king had sent Brock for.

He's coming for me.

With a blast of golden fire, Brock blinked out of sight. He couldn't teleport, so how the hell was he doing that, and where was he?

In the same horrible instant, every red dragon sent up a roar of challenge, plunging into the fray. In one gigantic, enveloping move, dragons from the Red Clan overwhelmed Ladon's forces and Sam with them, vanishing from her sight.

"*There you are.*" An almost cheerful voice slid through her mind.

Meira gasped as a massive gold dragon materialized out of nowhere, the ozone stink of magic all over him as he hovered inside the hangar, then landed with surprising lightness of foot not a hundred feet from her.

Brock.

"Just as Pytheios predicted," he said. Had he been in human form, he'd probably be examining his nails, suiting action to the boredom in his tone, only his emotions were a riot inside him. All that hatred stored up now aimed at her was like poison in the air. *"Your sisters won't stay away long. They'll find some way to try to save you. Then I'll take all four of you to him."*

Meira glanced around, but she was nowhere near a reflection and she was backed against the stone of the mountain. No place to run and hide. Only the edge and the ravine below. Certain death.

As the gold dragon slithered toward her, Meira reached for her fire anyway, but none came. As though her soul had gone coldly empty. Like a switch had been turned off.

Samael—

Her mate's name screamed through her mind a heartbeat before the gold dragon lunged for her and she threw herself from the precipice. Only instead of plummeting off the side, an arm emerged from the mountain itself, wrapped around her waist, and dragged her into the rock.

• • •

Samael had always known the secret to his ability to fight—a lack of fear.

Even as a boy, he'd been able to shut off emotion and focus only on what had to be done. It meant he took risks. Pushed his body and his abilities to the limit and didn't give a damn if the result was his death.

With no family to mourn him, he had little to live for. So he'd lived for his king, his people. What death could be more honorable than sacrifice?

He'd been all set to end his life for Meira. For his mate. Until he'd seen Brock appear out of thin air behind her in the hangar. No doubt sent by Pytheios, who seemed to have disappeared the second his forces engaged.

Smart. Instill doubts and then let the cards fall while he remained in safety, no doubt watching.

But the red king didn't matter. All that mattered was Meira. Facing down Brock, who'd somehow gotten to her. Samael couldn't get to her fast enough. He tasted terror for the first time, acrid and sharp against his tongue, pumping adrenaline through his veins hard. His gut flipped over with the impact.

What was I thinking?

He'd been as bad as Meira when they'd first met, following others almost blindly, letting loyalty and duty drive his actions and his choices, even when he knew those choices were wrong.

The truth slammed through him with more force than that damn lightning bolt. His *mate*, the woman the fates had set on a collision course with him before their birth, the woman they'd gifted him with, was in danger.

He'd thought he could leave her. Gods in hell, he'd never been so wrong.

Samael pelted through the sky, willing his body faster. Wishing for once he was a blue dragon, with their incredible speeds. Another dragon joined him, off to this right, on the same trajectory.

Gorgon.

Brock lunged for his mate.

"*Meira—*" He'd shouted as she turned, her intention to jump to her death obvious in her pale, determined face. A heartbeat before two arms emerged from the rock wall and the mountain swallowed her whole.

What the fuck?

Samael paused, for a half second unsure. Terror had him wanting to go after her. Though how, he had no idea.

A singeing pain suddenly lanced through his neck, and for a terrible second, he thought an enemy had gotten to him and this was the end.

Except no blackness followed, and the pain disappeared as fast as it had come.

Seven hells...the mating bond. Instead of shock, rightness settled through him, followed by a surge of protective terror the likes he'd never known before. Only his mate was gone.

His dragon, however, jerked his focus back to the biggest immediate threat. Brock.

He'd been coming for them since day one. Now they knew, sent by Pytheios himself.

Samael tried to slam into the bastard from the side, but that beat of hesitation combined with the way the previous gold prince moved—there one minute, then gone the next, popping up into the air like a damned kangaroo—and Samael flew by like an asshole.

Gorgon, however, hit Brock dead-on. So close to the ground, the two dragons dropped back to the surface with such force the chamber seemed to shake around him. Meanwhile, Samael executed a pinhead turn and launched himself at the two dragons grappling on the floor.

He tried to come in from Brock's blind side as the gold dragon had Gorgon by the front leg. Except Brock dropped Gorgon and spun to face Samael, who had to jerk out of the way of snapping jaws. He didn't see the spiked tail coming as it struck true in his back hindquarter, puncturing deep, pain ripping up his leg and spine.

With a snarl, Samael did the only thing he could and twisted to land his front claws on Brock's twitching tail. With a twist of his leg, he snapped the spike still embedded in his flesh off, and Brock grunted, the only sign he'd felt that break.

The giant gold dragon spun away, throwing Samael off balance. As he slashed his tail, blood sprayed the stone floor in streaks. Seeming to settle into himself, Brock faced down king and captain together.

Working in tandem, Samael and Gorgon moved in only to hop back, each trying to distract the monster they were up against.

Waiting for the opportunity. The right moment.

Suddenly, out of nowhere, Maul appeared on Brock's head. Crazed snarls ripped from his throat as he sank his teeth down into the gold dragon's face. With a howl of anguish, Brock flailed, and, before he could be thrown off, the hellhound disappeared as suddenly as he'd appeared.

Taking advantage of Brock's distraction, in an instant, they were on him, both going for his back, using their weight to pin his bucking form to the floor. Gold dragons were strong, and Brock, with all he'd lost, was motivated by bloodlust. Maul appeared again, taking a hunk out of his leg before popping away.

In a bucking move, before the hound could rematerialize, Brock tossed Samael from his back. With his hearing out of whack, Samael didn't know he needed to twist away from the stalactite hanging from the ceiling near the closed passage to the rest of the mountain. He rammed into it, full force, headfirst, and dropped to the ground, stunned.

"*Get up.*" A voice sounded in his head. Only he wasn't sure if he was hearing Gorgon, or Meira, or his own voice.

"*Samael!*"

Meira. That was his mate's sweet voice laced with terror. For him.

Where was she?

Only he couldn't think of that now. Instinct spun him to find Brock bearing down on him, mouth wide, ready to snap his neck or rip out his jugular.

Samael, back to the wall, didn't have time to do more than duck, offering his spiked back as a less palatable option. Teeth and claws sank into the side of the spikes, rending scales and flesh from bone. In a small recess of his mind, the sound of Maul's crazed snarls told him the hellhound was helping him, but the gold dragon was relentless, and Samael was pinned.

Every second, every lance of pain, and all he could think was that if he died, he'd kill Meira, too. The need to protect his mate surged, firing his muscles and his own rage. Samael thrashed and squirmed until he finally managed to slam the gold dragon against the wall.

The maneuver only stunned the other dragon. Long enough for Samael to get out from under him, but not far enough away. Brock whipped around, his barbed tail a weapon coming straight for Samael's head with a momentum that made it a deadly weapon.

"*No!*" Gorgon's yell resonated inside his head, penetrated everything else happening around him.

The dark-gray form of his king lunged in front of Samael, taking the blow to the head.

In slow motion, scrambling to stop Gorgon, Samael watched as one long spike penetrated, slipping in and out of the king's skull like an assassin's insidious blade, with amazing precision, striking one of the few weak points, the small hole that made a dragon's ear. Gorgon fell to the ground, his face turned to Samael already slack, eyes going blank in an instant. Dead likely before he knew what hit him.

. . .

Everything had gone black and soundless, pressure and stillness consuming her flesh, encasing her in the very rock of the mountain.

"Let me go. Please let me go." Meira's mouth moved, but no sound had escaped. How her mouth had formed words inside this rock, as she was part of the rock, captured by it, she had no idea.

But she'd known exactly who held her there. The gargoyles.

What little oxygen had been in her lungs was gone, and though sightless, she could feel herself losing consciousness, like falling. She wanted to struggle, to thrash through the rock holding her, only she couldn't move.

Then suddenly, the impenetrable hardness holding her opened around her, the sound of stone grinding on stone painful in her ears, until she emerged in her room in the gargoyle mountain, feet encased in rock. Carrick stood in full gargoyle form, grotesque face and body carved from solid stone, wings flared wide as though he might wrap them around her any second.

In the same instant, a lancing burn at the back of her neck had her clawing at the skin there for a second before realization struck.

Our mating bond.

Sam. *Oh gods.* Had he seen her be swallowed by stone? Did he feel her dread for his life? Whatever had changed for him, it had sealed their connection. Forever. Only death would part them.

Meira lit her fire, relief pouring through her that she could reach it again, that off switch no longer a problem. Only she couldn't reach her mirror.

"Send me back," she begged and demanded at the same time.

With that same grinding noise, Carrick pulled his lips back, baring his teeth. "No."

The old Meira would've stepped back, but her mate was out there, fighting for his life and the lives of every single one of their people.

Meira reached for calm, reached for that place that Samael had shown her, then laid a hand on Carrick's arm. "You have to, my friend. This is *my* fight."

"I swore an oath to protect Serefina's daughter." His carved stone eyes had shifted to her sisters.

Meira swallowed, wishing for once that she could feel the gargoyle's emotions. "My mate is out there."

Carrick nodded, the motion setting off that grinding sound again, sending a shudder down her spine. "I know. I see him."

She sucked in a sharp breath. Then looked to the mirror. She might not be able to get to it to go through, but she could see. In an instant, the mirror changed reflections, showing her the inside of Ararat's hangar and beyond.

Horror stole every gasp, every whimper of fear as she watched the fight between Gorgon, Samael, and Brock.

"No!" Meira screamed as Gorgon went down. At all the images before her. Sam, injured and weak facing off against Brock over his king's body, and their people dying outside as the combined forces of the Red, Green, and White Clans picked them off. Outnumbering them almost two to one.

No longer part of herself, her entire soul with her mate on the other side of the reflection, Meira clawed at the rock that encased her feet, as if she could dig herself out of it. "Let me go. I have to go to him."

"Stop," Carrick ordered in his gravelly voice.

"Let me out!" She pounded a fist against it, the pain jarring up her arm. Then again, ignoring that pain, and again, only vaguely aware of the gargoyle's stone hands trying to pull her back, digging into her skin.

"Carrick, please." Her voice shattered on the shoals of the words. She sucked in a breath as a compromise struck. "I'll go to Kasia and bring more dragons. Please let me do that, at least."

He searched her eyes, stone face unforgiving, and despair threatened to drag her into a pit of darkness. Then a grinding sounded, and the rock around her feet peeled back, parting like a curtain drawn back. As soon as the hole grew big enough, Meira sprinted to the mirror, turning the reflection to a room in Ben Nevis where she knew Skylar waited.

She needed both her sisters for this.

"Fuck me." Skylar spun from her pacing in the war room. On the multiple monitors, one of which Meira had just jumped through, faces reflected back. A dragon from the Black Clan, based on his dark eyes, no doubt in communication about what was happening at Ararat. On the other screen, Kasia and Brand stood in silence, dead serious, worry pinching her sister's lips.

"I need you to—"

"We know," Skylar cut her off. "Kasia saw it in a vision."

"My forces are ready to go," Brand, an image on the screens, said. "We'll meet you in our training room."

No waiting or explaining. Thank the gods for Kasia's visions.

"Let's go." Grabbing Skylar by the hand, she had them both through to the same chamber used for training and to launch dragons out of the hangar in the Gold Clan's mountain. Only here, the skies were clear, pale blue. And quiet. They stepped through the same glassed-in control room to face a legion of gold dragon shifters, still in their human forms, at attention in orderly lines.

Meira studied Skylar. "You already sent Ladon's forces. Can you—"

Skylar strode away, face as white as Meira had ever seen. "My mate is being overwhelmed as we speak, and my people are dying. I'll do what has to be done."

They met Brand in the center of the room, Kasia's hand in his. He didn't bother with small talk. "Do them in batches, Skylar. You've used a lot of your energy already. We can't have my people trapped in that fucking sightless, soundless in-between place."

The blackness Skylar and Kasia both dealt with when they teleported. Meira knew it existed for her, too, but the portal she opened held it at bay. At least, she assumed that was how it worked. No one else did what she did, so who the hell knew?

"Where do you want me to put them?" Skylar asked.

"The hangar in Ararat," Brand said. He leaned down and planted a hard kiss on Kasia's lips, then put his forehead against hers in a silent exchange almost painful to witness.

"I know," Kasia choked and smiled.

Jaw hard, Brand released her to step into line with his men.

Skylar nodded a half second before blue flames licked over her body, her black hair floating away from her body in the fire. Each group of fighters was instructed to hold hands. None balked. Most had seen or at least heard of what the Amon sisters were capable of by now. With a hard shove, the first group of twenty disappeared.

Then another.

And another.

If anything, rather than flagging, Skylar sped up, and Meira lost track of how many had been sent.

Sweat beaded Skylar's brow, and her hands visibly trembled, but she pushed through, continuing on. Until she pitched forward, hands on her knees, chest heaving as she sucked oxygen into lungs as though she'd sprinted a marathon.

"Are you okay?" Meira asked.

Skylar shook her head. "I need to send more. Ladon needs... *more*."

Meira put a hand on the back of her sister's head. "You've done enough. Let me finish."

Before anyone could ask more, she fired her own flames and set the reflection in the glass to that of the Ararat room. Through the portal, they could see Brand's forces. As Samael's had earlier, they shifted in waves, launching into the air with a roar of challenge.

"Go!" she yelled at the remaining fighters. "Fast. I don't know how long I can hold this for so many."

Taking her at her word, the shifters sprinted through. Until, finally, the chamber was empty except for her and her sisters. Kasia supported Skylar with an arm around her waist. Meira, hand still on the mirror, held her other one to her sisters, and together they stepped through into chaos.

Blue, gold, white, green, black, and red dragons—all six clans pitted against each other for the first time in millennia—swarmed the mountain in a mass of color and fire. The scents of sulfur and blood permeated the air. There was no making sense of it.

. . .

A cry rose up from outside, and both Samael and Brock looked up to find gold dragons materializing in waves, each launching itself from the training chamber into the skies, pounding into the fight with their size and strength.

Brand had come with his men. *Thank the gods.*

Five of the gold fighters turned and came after the dragon who'd once been their prince. Shooting Samael a snarling glare, Brock, no fool and obviously realizing the odds had just been evened, took to the air, flying away. Samael stumbled as he went to follow, but as quickly as Brock and all the red dragon shifters had appeared in the fight, they disappeared again.

Black fucking magic.

Gold, blue, and black warriors pulled up. The thundering cry of battle cut off in a beat of confusion before they all realized that the red dragons were gone. The white and green forces remained, it seemed. Still obscured by the clouds, some launched away from the mountain in obvious retreat, while others stayed to give their brethren time to get away.

Samael, adrenaline leaving his body in a whoosh, swayed and fell to the ground, his injuries enough to leave him stunned.

Gorgon was dead.

He knew that, and yet he still managed to lumber to his feet, nosing at his friend, his mentor, his ultimate supporter. Gorgon lay in a limp, unmoving pile, his spirit gone to the underworld, where his deeds and decisions would be weighed.

"*Dragons of the Black Clan...*" He paused to swallow down a grief so stark he slowly turned numb from the inside out. "*Our king is dead.*" He sent the thought to the entire clan.

Tipping his face to the heavens, shrouded by the rock of the mountain above him, Samael roared his grief, a stream of fire blasting from his maw. All around him, inside and outside the mountain, a terrible thunder of roars and wails from his people shook the very stone foundations of Ararat to the core.

Samael didn't stop, not until his belly emptied of the flame, leaving him vulnerable to the remaining forces of white and green dragons in retreat.

The king was dead. The man who'd given him everything had been killed by Brock.

Killed protecting me.

Heavy guilt weighed down the grief, but, in the same instant, the severity of Samael's own wounds penetrated. His legs trembled hard, rattling his entire body. Spots consumed his vision as Samael collapsed beside the man who'd been a father to him. The man he'd repaid with betrayal.

Meira.

On the heels of the guilt and grief came a terror the like he'd never before experienced. Terror for his mate.

Fuck. Was she still embedded in rock? Sounds of continued fighting of those closest to the mountain while their comrades escaped, muffled by his location so deep into the hangar, cracked and roared outside. The storm still thundered away. More danger.

Only he couldn't force his body to move. Not like before, when the lightning paralyzed him. This time, his dragon refused to leave the body of his slain king. That acrid coating of fear washed over his tongue, and the human side of him beat against the dragon from the inside.

Mate.

The dragon side of him, fully in control for the moment, didn't budge.

CHAPTER TWENTY-TWO

M eira left her sisters where they stood at the edge of the cliff and sprinted for Samael. Checking as she went, the cavern appeared wide open. Beyond, from what she could see through the storm, only a dwindling remnant of white and green dragons remained, though not for long. In one glance, she witnessed a green dragon screaming as a gold dragon gutted it. Midscream, it disappeared.

She didn't care.

All she cared about was getting to the black dragon on the other side of the chamber. Her legs burned with the effort, lungs heaving, as she sprinted across the room. A flicker of movement caught the corner of her eye, and she yanked up sharply only to have a white dragon land in front of her.

Meira held up both hands. "As a daughter of Zilant Amon, I have no wish to harm you."

As if she could.

"*I'm coming.*" A dark voice filled her mind. Behind him, Samael suddenly rose from where he'd been lying on the ground. "*Hold on.*"

"*You are a false phoenix,*" the white dragon sneered, though its mouth didn't move. "*An abomination, created by these traitorous kings with dark magic to cause confusion.*"

Samael was still too far away. Trying to distract the creature before her, Meira drew herself up to her full height. "I am the daughter of Serefina Hanyu and Zilant Amon. A phoenix. And rightful heir to the—"

The white dragon snapped its head around, got one look at Samael bearing down, and, in an instant that didn't slow but seemed more to speed up, slashed its tail at her.

Wicked spikes that appeared more like icicles came at her so fast, Meira didn't even have time to lift up her hands in defense.

Except Maul suddenly appeared at her side and, in an instant, they blinked away, but not before he yelped in pain.

The sound cut off in the silence of the in-between. Usually Maul moved so quickly through that plane, you didn't feel the nothingness with him. But that beat of silence told Meira all she needed to know. Before she'd processed everything, they reappeared in Samael's room. A pathetic whine coming from his throat, Maul swayed and dropped to his side. Sticking out from his broad chest, the spike from the white dragon's tail jutted into the air.

"No," Meira whimpered.

She shuffled around to the big dog's head and dropped to her knees. Already his labored breathing sounded squishy, gurgling rushes of air in his lungs.

"No, no, no. Not for me. Not like this."

Glowing red eyes met hers, and a picture flickered in her mind, not steady, but jerking in and out of her consciousness. A picture of her as a child laughing as she threw a ball for a puppy the size of a doghouse. And…happiness that she could feel from him, even in this moment.

"*Maul.*" His name tumbled from her lips.

Working his head up, she managed to lay part of it in her lap, uncaring of the drool and the blood and the stench. "You can't go. You're too strong."

Another image flashed, for less time even than the first. Samael watching her, the longing in his gaze, even in that jerky image, so acute it made her ache. "What are you telling me? That Samael will watch over me now?"

An image of stone men, and a growing sense of cold.

"The gargoyles?" She shook her head. "But *you're* supposed to take care of us." She could hardly get the words out now.

He'd always watched out for them. Even when she didn't want him to. Even when he'd scared her, and she'd stayed away. Why had she stayed away? He never, never would have hurt her.

Maul let out a rattling wheeze, as though he was telling her it would be okay, even as the red glow in his eyes flickered and dimmed.

"No." She shook her head, her curls falling in her face. Tears soaked her cheeks and into her clothes. "I won't let you."

Leaning over him, she blinked the tears onto the hellhound. Then waited. Kasia had healed Brand this way once. She'd said it had taken time.

Please, please, please.

But his breathing slowed, each inhale and exhale more painfully labored than the next.

"Please don't die." She gently moved his head and tried again, letting her sorrow drop onto the wound directly. Then went back to cradling that massive head. She watched and waited, smoothing his big ear with her hand. A faint emotion reached her through his fading…comfort. For her.

But nothing happened.

What if only Kasia could do this?

"It's going to be okay," she assured him.

She needed to get him to her sister. Only she couldn't teleport without a mirror, and no way could she heave his massive body through one. But…Maul could teleport if he could see. "I'm going to get help, boy."

Lighting her fire, what little she had left, she looked toward the glass door leading to the atrium, changing the reflection to the hangar, zooming in on her sister's dark-red hair. Skylar at her side. "Do you see her? Do you see Kasia?"

Her sister was there, at the edge of the landing, out in the open, in view of the entire mountain. Maul whimpered, then wheezed. She was losing him.

"Can you get us to her?"

She'd hardly gotten the words out and they blinked, paused in the black, cold abyss of the in-between, then appeared at Kasia's feet.

"Maul!" her sister screamed.

Meira lifted her tearstained face to them. "I can't fix him. It's not working. It worked for Kasia."

"Oh gods. Please not him." Kasia's voice broke.

Her sister stumbled over his legs, trying to get to him, then placed her hands on the hellhound and did the same thing Meira had, feeding phoenix tears directly to his wound. Tears that should have healing properties.

Maul struggled to lift his head, his body shaking, and gave Kasia the tiniest lick a creature that huge could manage, then dropped back into Meira's lap with a whimper.

He heaved one last breath, the air shuddering from him. The red glow in his eyes went out.

Meira dropped her head so they lay cheek to cheek, softly petting his spiked fur, and cried quietly, her tears soaking his fur, her own emotions blocking everything else out. Kasia's sobs and Skylar's soft murmurs to her sister the only sounds in a world gone utterly silent.

. . .

Samael shifted to human form as fast as his injuries and exhaustion would allow, which was not fucking fast enough.

Stumbling, one leg trying to buckle under his weight, he made his way to where Meira lay with the hellhound. Her emotions were so broken inside him though the channels, barely formed, now binding them together, he had no idea how she could bear them. How had she borne the empathic ability she carried without going mad?

Rather than try to take her away, Samael dropped to the ground behind her and wrapped his arms around her.

She took a deep breath, the only acknowledgment he was there.

But the rawness of the feelings battering him from that link eased slightly, and he knew she took some comfort from his presence.

"I'm sorry," he said. For Maul. For Gorgon. For pushing her away. All of it. "I'm so sorry."

"You were going to leave me." Her accusation was raw.

He squeezed his eyes shut tight. No use denying it. "I'm sorry."

"It's okay," she whispered. "You changed your mind."

The relief and joy she felt, even through her own grief, penetrated the darkness inside him like a sunbeam, warmth spreading throughout him.

A sucked-in breath had them both lifting their heads. Everything stilled inside him, inside her.

Maul was glowing. Not a bright, heavenly light, but red, like his eyes, eerie. His body pulsed with the color that lifted from him like an aura, before solidifying into streamers of flowing red, casting its light over everyone gathered around the hellhound.

The streamers slipped and swirled and coalesced, forming an image. Murky at first, then clearer, each feature of a man becoming more defined with every passing moment until he stood, hovering above the hellhound's body.

Skylar jerked forward, though Ladon, now beside her, tried to stop her. "Father?" she asked.

In his arms, Meira gasped and struggled to her feet. Samael helped her, staying close to her at the same time. He studied the man's face, which was vaguely familiar.

Tyrek Amon's brother. The resemblance *was* there.

Could it be? Legend held that hellhounds were warriors with unfinished business, returned in the form of death incarnate to complete it.

"*Zilant Amon*." The name flew on hushed tones through the chamber and around the mountain. Turning his head, Samael discovered every single white dragon remaining had stopped fighting and hovered, wings beating slowly, staring at the figure of the man.

"The king," those voices said in hushed tones, now in his mind as much as spoken.

The figure of the man looked at each phoenix in turn and smiled.

"Dark magic." A voice boomed through his internal thoughts. Everyone else's, too, if the way the white dragons flinched was any indication. *"Lies."*

A single white dragon dropped lower in the sky, the only one to move. Not King Volos, whom Samael had met in both dragon and human form before. That white dragon's opalescent scales were hard to miss. This one was more the color of curdled milk.

"They killed our king."

Volos was dead? When? Today?

"They go against the true High King," the white dragon continued. *"They feed us lies about more than one phoenix when there has only ever been one. That one has been mated. You've seen with your own eyes the change in our king, no long rotting from old age—"*

He cut off as the figure of Zilant Amon burst into a column of flame that reached a hundred feet into the sky.

The tips turned white, then consumed the red before the flames suddenly disappeared, leaving the spectral figure a pure glowing white. Another smile at his daughters and he held out a hand, as though beckoning them.

Meira stepped forward, but Samael shot out a hand, stopping her. She turned to face him, gaze earnest and untroubled, despite the tears staining her cheeks. "He would never hurt me. He's my father."

Skylar and Kasia also calmed their mates before all three women stepped forward. Zilant Amon's figure turned back into the glowing, twisting ropes that writhed and slithered around them, lifting their hair and setting them awash in ethereal white light.

The ribbons linked the sisters' hands.

Suddenly, Meira's eyes turned bright white, glowing in her face as though she were possessed. Kasia's and Skylar's, too. Almost as though in a trance, they spoke.

"We are the daughters of Zilant Amon and Serefina Hanyu," they said. Samael shivered at the power emanating from the three. It crackled around him like electricity, raising the hairs on his arms. *"Let us show you."*

Suddenly Samael's vision changed, as though someone had taken over his mind. He watched as though a movie played out against his eyelids. Memories, perhaps, or the way Kasia saw visions. Was the ghost of Zilant Amon using his daughters' powers to protect them now?

Images, clips of memories flooded his mind. Zilant Amon, speared on Pytheios's shifted tail and Serefina's scream before she disappeared from the room. Serefina pregnant and alone. Then with four babies.

He's showing them Angelika. No more secrets now.

Four little girls learning and loving at their mother's feet. Four young women, playing with a hellhound puppy in the snow, laughing as he melted it around them, forming puddles to splash in. Four fully grown women, each as beautiful and unique as the other. Each so clearly a reflection of their white dragon shifter father and phoenix mother, the resemblance could no longer be denied. Then Serefina's last moments as she sent her daughters away to safety before turning to ash. The last act of a desperate mother.

A bright flash of light blinded Samael, followed by the electric crack of lightning sizzling the air around it. The blast knocked Samael off his feet. His vision cleared to find everyone on the ground around him, including Meira and her sisters, who looked around, dazed and confused. Zilant Amon's presence was gone.

Samael jerked his head around to see the white dragons disappearing one by one. All the green dragons were already gone.

The lone leader hung in the air the longest, staring at the three phoenixes slowly getting to their feet.

"*Lies*," he hissed before he too disappeared.

Several gasps, Meira's striking him hardest, brought him back around to find Maul's body burning away, tiny flames creeping across his black fur in a steady line of fire, bright-red embers lifting into the sky in their wake, eating at his body until nothing remained.

"Sam," Meira called, her voice broken and small.

She swayed on her feet. Ignoring his own pain, and willing his leg to hold him, he jumped closer and caught her as her eyes rolled back in her head, her body going limp in his arms.

CHAPTER TWENTY-THREE

M eira slowly drifted her way out of sleep, trying hard to stay under, not wanting to let go of the dream that had been so real to her, she had a vague idea she'd cried out her protest at leaving it.

Blinking away the last vestiges of the dream, she couldn't shake the pressing certainty that it had been more than that. A vision.

"Meira? Are you okay?" Warm hands enveloped one of hers where it lay on the bed.

Samael.

Memories rushed in on a swell of heartbreak, and she sucked in a sharp breath, but at the same time, the vision she'd had cocooned the pain, making it more...bearable. She turned her head to find her mate watching her with shadowed eyes. He looked as though he'd aged a decade or two, face pinched and haggard. But the emotions radiating at her reflected her own. Grief cushioned by sheer relief and...happiness.

"Sam," she croaked, throat dry and sore.

"I'm here."

"I just saw—" She paused and shook her head. How could she explain it? He'd think it was a reaction to the trauma she'd been through.

But she knew, that knowledge settling into her heart like a

balm and yet pinning her with an urgency that was undeniable.

He lifted a hand, tracing a finger over her cheek, gaze so tender it made her ache. "What did you see?"

Rather than answer, she leaned over in the bed and placed her lips on his. The need inside her clamored, the ache growing to need at the simple touch, at the sand and fire scent of him in her lungs. The mark on the back of her neck heated and burned, but in a good way.

Samael groaned against her lips, but he took her face in his hands, pulling back gently. "Do you remember anything?"

He thought she'd had the pain of those memories knocked from her? "I remember." The tidal wave threatened to rush back in. "Make me forget, Sam. Just for a little while."

She moved to kiss him again, but he held back, though he swallowed hard. "I want to, Mir. You have no idea how much. But..."

"But?" She searched his face, waited for emotions to pelt her.

Except that wall was up. "We have too much to discuss."

She knew he was right, could feel his need to unburden himself of the emotions he'd been struggling with while she slept. He'd lost a man who'd been as close to him as a father, watched her lose hers all over again, and so much more.

Meira licked her lips. "Tell me."

"The Black Clan has voted to accept me as king and you as queen. They are aware of our mating."

She couldn't get a reading on how he felt about that. "Were they angry?"

"After seeing us both fight and sacrifice for them?" He shook his head. "Most are...welcoming." At that she did sense a sarcastic edge to his thoughts.

"And those who aren't?"

He shrugged. "Some will leave, if they haven't already. Most will stay and wait."

"I see." She blew out, long and low. "I'm so sorry. About Gorgon."

Only a small shaft of blackness pierced the emotions inside him. Guilt and grief all fused together.

She took his face in her hands. "He sacrificed himself for you. Knowing that we'd mated. He forgave you, if he ever harbored any ill will. I'm sure of it."

Samael nodded again. "I'm sorry about Maul."

Meira closed her eyes against the slivers of reaction threatening to set in. "My father." She'd take ages to sort through all that. Right now, all she knew was that underneath her own sorrow and shock was…a grateful heart. "He was with us all that time. Protecting us." She opened her eyes, tears stinging but not falling, and smiled. "I wish I'd known."

Sam nodded. He took a few breaths, as though getting ready to speak but not sure what to say. "And us?"

As if she could leave him? As if she ever would. "We're mates."

"I left you—"

Didn't he understand? She lifted her hair from the back of her neck and turned so he could see the mark there. "You figured it out in the end."

He brushed a finger over the brand, sending shivers of gorgeous sensation skating over every nerve ending.

Then he dropped his hands from her, fisting them on the bed beside her, leather gauntlets, for once, not worn. "You say that, but how can you forgive me? I was going to leave you, die so that you could be another man's. I—"

She picked up one of his scarred hands and pressed a kiss to the puckered skin. "You were acting like a mate. Protecting me the only way you could see. I understand."

"You're amazing," he murmured.

"Not really. I figured something out through all this…"

Her mate both frowned and smiled at the same time, as though the emotions themselves were battling to take over his face even as the struggle in his heart pressed against her. "What's that?"

"That the fates seem to know what they're doing."

"I thought you don't believe in the fates?"

Meira shrugged. "I've seen too much proof lately to not believe. Two things have convinced me the most. One"—she held up a finger—"in the middle of when you were trying your hardest to sacrifice your life in that idiotic plan, our bond solidified, saving us both. Because I would have died without you, bond or no."

The strongest man she knew trembled against her. "Hell, Meira...I don't deserve you."

"And yet I love you anyway—"

She gasped as Samael surged forward, taking her lips in a kiss that was both wild and tender, lips seeking lips, tongue seeking tongue, speaking of forgiveness and love, faith and trust, and a need too long denied. His emotions buffeted her both through her gift and through the unique link that connected them now. Relief and grief and elation and forgiveness all swirling together. Underneath that intensity, a surging need to claim, to bask in the fact that they were mates, now and always. No matter what came next.

Gods, she loved this protective, self-sacrificing man with emotions that ran deeply inside him, an underground river that only she knew.

Shoving aside the blankets, he joined her in the bed, his weight pressing into her in the most delicious way, the hard length of his cock jutting into the soft skin of her belly. Hands turned frantic, and for a second, she hoped... But then, on a long groan, he pulled away, burying his face in her neck and breathing hard.

"Don't stop," she begged.

He groaned again. "I don't want to, but we're not done talking." He lifted his head, and finally...finally she could see hope surging through the depths of grief and self-blame in his eyes.

"You said two?" he pressed.

She smiled, that urgency from her dream surging forward. "I think I've had a vision."

Samael blinked, and she chuckled. He probably wasn't expecting that. "A vision?" he asked slowly.

She nodded. Then, unable to contain herself, she pushed forward to kiss him again. "I've seen our child, Sam," she whispered against his lips. "A son."

Her mate went rigid with shock against her. "I didn't know you had visions."

She tipped her forehead against his. "I didn't, either, but I saw him. He has your hair and beautiful coloring, but my eyes. He's tall and strong and smart, and he'll sit on the throne of the Black Clan one day."

"Gods above," he choked, then gathered her closer in his arms. "When?"

Her body lit up from within, and she smiled. "Put a baby inside me tonight, Samael Veles. My heart chose you the first time I saw you in that mirror. You looked through my magic and saw me when no one else did. But I wouldn't let myself believe."

His erection swelled and pressed against her, but still he shook his head. "To bring a child into this world...now..."

They both had to choose this. One of the few fair things about dragon shifters—both partners had to choose to create a child as they made love.

Meira lifted a hand and gently traced her lover's lips, his eyes. "I don't know how we get there. I don't even know if you and I survive his war, but our child *will* rule this clan. But only if we choose him now."

Samael searched her face. Almost unconsciously, his hips started to pump, and she opened her legs wider, pressing into the slow, driving pressure.

"You want this?" he asked, voice shaking, dropping low.

"I want this." She'd seen her child's face. Had given him the part of her heart a mother reserved for her children.

"Gods forgive me, I want it, too. To see your belly swell with my child. To start a new life with you. A new future for our people."

An incandescent happiness swirled through their bond, coming from both of them, to twine and merge, followed by a rush of superheated need that sensitized every part of her.

Samael took her lips, no hesitation in him this time, no need to back away.

...

My mate.

After everything he'd done to fuck it up, he could hardly believe the woman in his arms was giving herself to him so beautifully.

She moaned against his lips, tasting of Meira and smelling of jasmine and flame.

How on earth was he going to survive this woman, who'd made her his with a single look in a mirror? Whose quiet intelligence and gentle patience won over a lowborn boy from a rough life who'd grown into an agent of death and destruction.

"I'll keep you safe, Meira. Always." Protect this precious gift the fates had graced him with. He whispered the promise even as he tugged her clothes off her body with anxious hands.

She was soft and silky, her breasts made for his hands as he cupped her. She arched into him with a sexy shudder as he tweaked her nipples.

Wanting to make her shudder more, he lowered his head, feasting on her, sucking those sensitive points until she writhed beneath him, bombarding him with whimpers that surged through his body to his heavy, aching cock.

Samael pulled back to look at her, at his mate. Naked beneath him, all long legs and curves, her strawberry-blond curls a riot against the white pillow. In his bed and watching him with eyes gone dark blue and alight. For him.

Samael grinned, and Meira laughed, the sound shooting to his heart.

"You look like a pirate all of a sudden. Ready to take what's yours."

"Damn straight," he growled.

Only he didn't immediately take. Instead, he made his way down her abdomen, pausing to kiss each swath of skin, nipping at her hips, to settle between her thighs. The scent of her arousal only fed his more.

Mine. My mate. My love.

Keeping his eyes on her face, he watched as he stroked his tongue against her flesh, merciless. She gasped then bit into her lip with each lash of his tongue against her clit. He wanted to watch her come apart, then watch as he fed his cock to that lush mouth. He needed her. Not only for the pleasure she could bring. He needed her steadiness. Her faith in him. Her inner core of strength, iron forged in fire and tempered by her heart.

And tonight...tonight was about more.

So he devoured his mate's body until she was begging for release, determined to bring her the greatest possible pleasure, making tonight about her. About them.

Lifting his head, he smiled at her loud moan of protest.

"I'm so close," she complained.

"Me too, love." Fuck, was he.

Her eyes went wide. "But I haven't done much yet. It's all been you."

"It's all been us. Together."

He raised up, snagging her legs under the knees and parting her wider, wrapping those long legs around him as he positioned himself at her core.

His erection was hard as the mountain, pulsing with the need to lay his seed inside her. To claim her once more as his own. Deep in his belly, fire bloomed, adding to the heat raging through him.

"I need you inside me," she demanded, gaze locked to his.

On one long stroke, Samael entered her, sheathed himself in her tight, wet heat, stretching her until he settled deep. And never took his eyes from hers. Watching the pleasure tauten the skin over her cheekbones as he slowly pulled out, then surged back in.

He wanted to lose himself in her, lose the man who only knew blood and fighting to find the man she made him into. A man who would rise to the challenge of leading his people through the worst era in their long history.

Because he could only do that with her.

"I'm yours," he said, thrusting harder.

Meira nodded, panting as he claimed her body.

"Meira…" He dropped to his elbows, his hips still moving. "I'm *yours*."

She lifted her hands between them to cup his face and kissed him, slowly, her tongue tangling with his in an imitation of what his cock was doing to her. Then pulled back and smiled. "I know."

Samael thrust harder, and she took it with a moan. "No, love. I don't think you do." Another hard push. "I was yours when the heavens formed us, I am yours now, and I will be yours forever, even into the afterlife."

With each word he pushed into her. Her body was starting to ripple around his cock, her orgasm close.

With each word, her eyes grew wider, and she searched his expression.

He stopped his thrusting, their pleasure on the tipping point hanging between them, and smoothed her hair from her forehead. "Do you understand?"

No alpha dragon shifter ceded control to anyone. Ever. Not even to a mate, to a certain extent. But he'd learned the hard way what forcing that control over his mate could do. Putting them both in danger. For this woman, he would lay bare everything, give her everything he was. Hers to command. Hers to control.

His dragon, quiet in his head, hummed his own agreement.

"I adore you, Samael Veles." Somewhere in those words, he heard her understanding. And her acceptance.

She would never make him regret giving her that control.

Even more, releasing himself from that control lifted a weight from him that he'd hardly known was there. Together, he and his dragon let go and truly gave themselves to their mate.

Samael growled and slammed into her.

"Yes," Meira cried out.

Setting a punishing pace, he pumped into his mate in hard, brutal pulses that only drove both of their pleasure to a higher precipice.

Then she screamed, clamping down on him hard as her orgasm slammed through her, dragging his own pleasure from his body as his balls drew up and he filled his mate with his essence, willing a child into being. Sensation so vicious he roared his own release, his fire joining them together yet again, not stopping until he'd milked every last ounce of pleasure from her.

As the slowing came over him, Samael collapsed over his mate, breathing hard, and suddenly, in his mind's eye, a child appeared to him. Black hair and his mother's white-blue eyes, stark against dark skin.

Their son.

Wonder flowed through him, like a river through a forest. Pure and true. Until the vision faded.

As the rush slowed and his breathing returned to normal, Meira snuggled into his arms, giving a sigh of contentment. Samael echoed that sigh. At least until the outside world intruded. And it would. But for now, they were safe and loved, and his child grew inside her.

Samael shifted to the side and curved a protective hand over her belly, the image in his mind still startlingly clear.

"I saw him," he whispered. "He's beautiful, Mir. Amazing."

She dropped a kiss on the underside of his jaw and smiled. "I told you."

"I didn't think a phoenix could have a boy," he said.

Meira shook her head, her curls tickling his chin. "Before me and my sisters, there was only ever one. Always a girl. It's a new and changing world, my love."

He wondered if they'd ever discover why. "What's his name?" Samael asked softly.

"Zilant Gorgon Veles," she whispered.

His arms tightened around her convulsively as her words soothed the most painful, jagged edges of his grief. Samael closed his eyes and held his mate and their unborn child in his arms and counted himself lucky to have this one, incandescently perfect moment.

The world they lived in was cruel and deadly, and they'd face that soon enough. Together. Good luck to anyone who tried to take this away—especially the Rotting Red King. They could try, but they'd fucking wish they hadn't.

EPILOGUE

Angelika stood to the side of the hangar in the mountain stronghold of Ararat. The room had been transformed into a banquet hall, glorious with twinkle lights, elegant place settings, and jasmine everywhere, the scent of it filling the air. One of many rooms transformed for Meira's second mating ceremony. This one to Samael Veles, the onetime captain of the guard for the man Meira had originally made vows to.

Rather than wait months, they'd rushed the ceremony forward while all their allies were gathered together in the mountain. This time, Angelika got to stand at the front with her sisters. Her secret was out now, thanks to her father. Holding the ceremony might seem a bit backward to others, given that Meira already bore an intricately knotted mark, the design both her mate's family and elements from the Zilant and Hanyu crests of their parents. Samael's own brand had changed...to match Meira's. But Angelika understood it. Her sister and her mate were making a statement, but also giving their people something to celebrate after a long patch of trouble.

Smart and also full of heart. Just like Meira.

At least they appeared to be supremely happy. Meira deserved that. Angelika had never seen her sister light up like she did around her mate. She practically glowed without the need for her fire to make her.

Just like Kasia. Just like Skylar.

Now it's my turn.

Angelika played with the glass of wine she'd been nursing. Without Jedd and the wolf shifters here—now that her secret was out, they'd gone to seek safety among the Federation of Wolves— she might have felt at loose ends, but she'd never been one to be shy with strangers.

Her sisters were occupied elsewhere, so she'd been enjoying herself, getting to know new people. Not that the dragon shifters had all been welcoming, but they'd come around.

But now she stood by herself, finding herself alone for a moment. Something that gave her—sometimes unfortunately— active imagination a chance to kick in.

She gazed around the chamber and tried to picture it before. Picture where Maul had died. Picture the scene of her own father's second death—a moment she had not been here to witness.

Pain speared her through the heart, and she gasped silently, breathing through it. Something that had happened out of the blue several times since she'd learned of it.

She should have been here. She should have had a chance to say good-bye to him. Taking a deep breath, she focused on the promise she'd made herself. She might have no fire, no power, but she was going to make a difference. She wouldn't sit to the side anymore.

A man walked away from the tables. Here, with the Black, Gold, and Blue Clans together, along with a handful of dragons from the White Clan who'd chosen to leave and pledge themselves to the cause, he didn't stick out as much. His short white hair and broad shoulders on a frame still too slender after his captivity, however, stood out as a beacon to her.

Airk.

Without making the conscious decision to do so, she started moving on a course to intercept, already able to see that he was leaving. He didn't like being around so many at once. She knew that from the way he only stayed as long as he had to.

In the hallway leading behind the city at the base of the atrium to the human tunnels that would take him up to his chambers, she caught up to him.

"Airk."

As he turned, his expression gave nothing away, as usual.

"Angelika," he acknowledged.

She licked her lips, suddenly nervous. "I have an...offer to make you."

Hands clasped behind his back, he faced her more fully, gaze taking in her serious expression, not a single emotion in his eyes. Not even a flicker of curiosity. "Yes?"

"Have you decided what's next yet?"

He cocked his head, but no confusion lit his eyes. He remembered their conversation. "It seems to me," he said in his slow, even tones, "my clan needs help determining what is and is not true about the High King they currently serve."

"They need a new king."

He said nothing, but he didn't deny it.

"I think I'd like to help you with that." She pulled her shoulders back. "For my father."

"And how do you propose offering this help?" Airk asked.

Damn, she wished she could read him better. "Well...I am the daughter of the previous king, and a phoenix."

"With no powers."

She crossed her arms and offered him a chipper smile.

He frowned slightly at her reaction. "Am I wrong?"

"No." She glanced over her shoulder. "Though only a few are aware. We want to keep that a secret as long as possible. But I'm smiling because you're wrong."

"Wrong?"

"Yes. You seem to think powerless means I don't have the ability to make a difference. Such a dragon shifter way of thinking."

He glanced down between their feet, thinking, then raised his glacial eyes to her. "I still don't see how that helps me."

"If we were to mate..."

Airk's eyes narrowed. The biggest show of emotion she'd seen from the man. "I see."

But did he? "It could work—"

"No." One word. That was it. A harsh rejection in a shotgun of a word.

In a jerking motion, Airk spun away from her, striding down the hall. Angelika, shock rooting her feet to the ground, let him go.

But she wasn't giving up. That wasn't in her blood. Even without powers, she knew she *could* matter in this war.

EXCLUSIVE

BONUS CONTENT

Meira

M eira Amon stared at the bedroom door in front of her and braced herself for what was about to come.

Her future stood on the other side of that door, though he didn't know it yet.

She waited in Skylar's bedroom along with Angelika. More specifically, in the royal suite of the King of the Blue Clan in the mountain stronghold of Ben Nevis in Scotland. Today they would reveal their existence to, hopefully, new allies.

Her surroundings barely registered, though, drowned out by a more pressing situation. Unconsciously she reached up to check her hair, glancing in the mirror set to the side. Only instead of herself in that reflection, for a heartbeat she honestly expected to see...him.

A memory she should do her best to forget.

She looked deeper into the reflection just the same. Doing so was becoming a habit. That day when someone had seen through her magic—had seen her on the other side—had happened so fast, and yet it had been gnawing at her ever since. Mirrors and reflections were her gift, her tool of power. Months ago, Meira had secretly looked on as Kasia and Brand had confronted the king's council of the Gold Clan in order to finalize Brand's claim to the throne. Other dragon shifters had stood with Brand and Kasia, stood for them. From the safety of her mirrors, Meira had witnessed the entire thing, with no one the wiser to her presence.

When it had been all over, and Kasia and Brand had led their supporters away. Meira had been about to put a stop to her own voyeurism when one the men supporting her sister's new mate had stepped in front of her.

She'd frozen at first, but then had remembered she was safe behind her reflections. This man was only seeing himself.

For a small, self-indulgent moment, she'd allowed her gaze to travel over him, taking in his appearance. Even now the impression he'd left on her was indelibly deep. He was almost painfully handsome with a strong jaw covered by dark scruff. But it had been the way he carried himself that struck her most—the set military stance, a body honed for battle, and a hard light in eyes as black as night that never stopped checking the corners of the room.

A warrior, the words whispered through her mind.

Then, a kick of unaccustomed awareness had shuddered through her only to be replaced by a cold, stark fear as her gaze had connected with his fathomless eyes.

He was staring *directly* at her.

Meira had held still, not even daring to breathe. He couldn't see her. No one ever saw her.

Only...

"Who are you?" he had demanded.

With a gasp, she'd doused her flames in an instant, cut off the reflection, but even now the shock of his seeing through her magical abilities still rattled her. No one had done that before.

Ever since then, when she looked into mirrors, a small part of her expected to see him standing there, demanding, hard and suspicious.

Stop it, she told herself now. Then frowned at herself.

Why was she remembering him at all?

What was important was what happened next. Right now. Taking a deep breath, she forced her mind and her gaze to the present, and her own reflection.

Do I look pale?

Meira pinched her cheeks and patted her strawberry-blond curls, which she'd twisted into a chignon at the base of her neck and dropped her hand uselessly back to her side.

She'd made her decisions, ones that set her future in stone.

"I didn't know you'd arrived," an unfamiliar voice reached her through the cracked open door. Caution laced the low tones. Was that him? Was that the king?

The dragon shifter she'd promised to mate?

A man she'd never seen, never met. A good man, she'd been assured. A path she'd chosen for herself—after all, what was about to happen next had been her idea. What she was about to offer was too important for her to turn back now.

As one of four phoenix sisters, she had a duty to do everything she could to put a stop to the plague infecting the dragon shifters.

Pytheios.

Meira had a hard time hating anything or anyone. But her hate for that man threatened to consume her, the raw emotion a physical flaying of her heart. Every single day.

Hate for the man who'd murdered and hunted her family, all in pathological pursuit of a crown and power.

She'd learned more recently other proofs of his stomping all over anything or anyone that got in his way. Dead and missing mates, sacrificed to his political ambitions. More rogues than ever. The clans that stood against him sucked dry of their wealth. Now, Kasia and Skylar were irrevocably bound to Brand and Ladon, the two dragon shifter kings who opposed the rotting king.

For Meira...this was what she could do to stop him.

She smoothed trembling hands over the slim skirt of her dress. Essentially her version of a little black dress but in deep purple with a lower cut square neckline and a belt at her waist, paired with black heels. She'd gotten ready today with the intent to impress a king, and maybe bolster her own confidence.

Would he like what he saw?

It's all going to work out the way it's supposed to. Words she'd clung to in all those centuries of running had turned into a mantra of sorts.

"Are you sure about that?"

The question had her blinking open eyes she hadn't even realized she'd shut. Had she said that out loud?

At her side, Angelika gave her hand a squeeze. "You don't have to do this."

Meira mentally grimaced both at the question and the now-daily struggle of holding others' emotions at bay. Sometimes being an empath really sucked. Drawing back her shoulders, she offered Angelika a calm smile. "It's the right step to take."

If I say it enough times, it'll be true.

"For everyone else involved, yes. But—"

Kasia's clear voice reached them. "Skylar and I are not the only ones."

Meira and Angelika both straightened, attention snagged by the signal being voiced on the other side of the door.

"Not the only phoenixes?" a deep voice asked slowly, the same one from a second ago.

"Our mother gave birth to quadruplets," Kasia answered. "Conceived with Zilant Amon, previous King of the White Clan, before his death, and all four of us survived."

"That's our cue," Angelika whispered.

Here goes…everything.

Gods above.

Together they stepped out from the bedroom into a space that served as a living area, formed out of the natural curves and lines of a cavern deep within the mountain. In the back corner, Maul watched from the shadows, eyes glowing red, ever their protector. Across from her other two sisters and their mates stood two men.

Two?

She should've immediately focused on the one standing slightly forward from the other. Obviously, he was Gorgon Ejderha, King of the Black Clan.

But against her will, her gaze was drawn to the other man, and she hesitated a fraction of a beat as recognition struck like a clanging gong.

Samael Veles.

The man from her mirror.

The one who'd seen her. Who'd demanded who she was.

Only the fact that Angelika kept walking moved Meira's feet along too, struggling to hide the shock reverberating through her. Even as she took in the recognition that flashed in his otherwise stony face.

Heavens above. He remembers that day, too.

He looked the same. Onyx eyes and black hair worn slightly shaggy, thick brows, commanding nose and jaw. Smooth skin a sun-brushed oak, that both contrasted with and complimented his hair and eyes.

The captain of the guard for the King of the Black Clan. She'd expected to see him, just not here. Not right now.

The king. Oh gods.

Meira jerked her gaze away, focusing on the man she was here for.

Unaware of Meira's noisy, chaotic thoughts, Kasia waved a hand. "I'd like to introduce you to our sisters—Meira and Angelika Amon."

With a deep breath she hoped no one else saw, Meira stepped forward and addressed Gorgon directly. "As the only other king allied with my sisters and their mates…" She paused to swallow, horribly conscious of Samael's critical gaze on her, then tipped up her chin the way Skylar often did, gaining strength from the small motion. "I would like to…offer myself to you as a mate."

Immediately, emotions reached across the room from the man at the king's side. As though a wall had collapsed under the onslaught. Samael's emotions slammed into her like a hurricane that had once beat down on a tiny island where her family had lived for a short time when she was a child, whipping at her, threatening to peel away every layer of protection to expose her, raw and vulnerable, to the elements.

A cacophony of confusion, rejection, and...protectiveness battered her.

A combination that didn't make a bit of sense. But that last one sent a terrifying answering fire flaring inside her licking over her skin, lighting every nerve in its wake.

She dared to flick him a single swift glance to find neither his expression nor the set of his body showed an iota of what was going on inside him. Totally blank. Before she could shut out the emotions pummeling at her, just as fast as his wall had crumbled, he shored it back up, bricking himself off from her so completely that all she felt now was the echo of her own reaction.

Holy hell fires. How could he stand the cauldron of biting emotion that boiled within him under the surface where none could see?

In desperation, Meira focused on Gorgon. On his steady presence and his more muted emotions, hardly a whisper reaching out to her. Surprise and...maybe...satisfaction.

He stepped forward to take one of her hands between his, searching her gaze. "You *are* a revelation."

Meira studied him back, liking what she saw behind eyes more gunmetal grey than black. Kindness. She hadn't expected that. "A good one I hope?"

They all needed this union to work.

Gorgon smiled, eyes crinkling at the corners naturally, as though the action wasn't foreign to him. "Indeed." He paused as though considering his next words. "Before I accept, I have to ask... Are you sure?"

Unknowingly, he echoed Angelika's question from only moments ago. Meira didn't dare glance at the man with him, shoring up her own mental blocks against the emotions swirling throughout the room, including her own, and smiled back at the king, trying her best to make her stiff lips appear confident. "I'm sure."

"In that case, I accept."

An odd combination of relief and shock shot through her, almost sending her dizzy.

There. It was done.

ACKNOWLEDGMENTS

No matter what is going on in my life, I get to do what I love surrounded by the people I love—a blessing that I thank God for every single day. Writing and publishing a book doesn't happen without the support and help from a host of incredible people.

To my fantastic, equally dragon-obsessed readers (especially my Awesome Nerds Facebook fan group!), thanks for going on these journeys with me, for your kindness, your support, and generally being awesome. Meira and Samael's story was one of heart and learning to believe in yourself, no matter your background or ability or, especially, what other people think. I stopped writing in my teens/twenties because other people thought it was weird, and I wish so hard that I hadn't listened. That experience came out in this story. I hope you fell in love with these characters and their story as much as I did. If you have a free sec, please think about leaving a review. Also, I love to connect with my readers, so I hope you'll drop a line and say "Howdy" on any of my social media accounts!

To my editor, Heather Howland...four years ago I said I wanted to write paranormal romance with you, and I couldn't be prouder of what we've accomplished together!

To my Entangled family...everything you do is awesome!

To my agent, Evan Marshall...thank you for the ride!

To my author sisters/brothers and friends...you inspire me every day!

To my support team of beta readers, critique partners, writing buddies, reviewers, friends, and family (you know who you are), as always, a thousand thanks!

Finally, to my own partner in life and our beautiful kids...I don't know how it's possible, but I love you more every day.

talk about it

Let's talk about books.

Join the conversation:

[f] @harlequinaustralia

[♪] @hqanz

[◉] @harlequinaus

harpercollins.com.au/hq

If you love reading and want to know about our
authors and titles, then let's talk about it.